To understand the nature of t
reading two books: Foxe's Book of Martyrs and the book of Revelation.

Dedication

This book is dedicated to the persecuted Church of this and every age. To these men and women and yes sometimes children who suffer and die for the glory of God, and who, by their sufferings, have brought multitudes to Christ.

Seven Towers

Seven towers of light
Seven cities of might
In the land of was
And will be

One that was great
That loves no more
One that loves still
And serves her Lord

One that is dying
And one that is dead
One that is poor
With crowned head

Two that hold on
When hope is thrust through
The enemies within
Have done it to you

When darkness o'er
The land has sway
Seven great cities
Will stand in its way

The evil that reigns
As some of them fall
Will tremble in terror
Of the Kings call

Then rising those cities
Will stand strong, and free
Evil is vanquished
And all men will see

Seven cities of might
Seven towers of light
In the land of was
And will be

Table of Content

Dedication iii

Seven Towers iv

Preface 2

Tis His Fire 3

Prologue 4

Chapter 1 Andre 7

Chapter 2 The Chuchoteur 15

Chapter 3 Shamgar 23

Chapter 4 Attack on the Dome of Meeting 36

Chapter 5 The Woman 46

Chapter 6 The Boy 54

Chapter 7 Asher Kenspeckle 62

Chapter 8 Know Your Enemy 71

Chapter 9 Concealment and Pain 83

Chapter 10 Black Powder 95

Chapter 11 Foolishness and Flight 106

Chapter 12 Pursuit 120

Chapter 13 Chara 129

Chapter 14 Explosion! 137

Chapter 15 Surveillance 148

Chapter 16 Death 158

Chapter 17 Dark Waters 167

Chapter 18 Photaskia 177

Chapter 19 Snake Pit 193

Chapter 20 Angus 206
Chapter 21 The Pit 215
Chapter 22 Mephosphilis 225
Chapter 23 The Seventh Fall 235
Chapter 24 Cold Fear 248
Chapter 25 Refugees 258
Chapter 26 Confronting Evil Men 269
Chapter 27 Battle for The Tower 279
Chapter 28 Projects for Kesniel 290
Chapter 29 The King-steward 299
Chapter 30 A Feast and Farewells 308
Maps 316
Names 318
Flowers and Their Meanings 322

Preface

What makes a hero? It isn't strength or courage, wisdom or power. Heroes are not paragons. They are people. Heroes aren't made in the moment of crisis. They are made in the fires of adversity that strips them of everything they think they are. Humility makes heroes. No one rises to true greatness without being stripped of everything they think makes them strong. The fires that strip away pride and leave only a molten pool of personality reduce a person to his essence. Then, when all strength is gone and the hero to be knows how small and frail he is, *that* is when he begins to rise, for that is when he not only sees the needs of others but when he begins to feel compassion for them. The King uses such circumstances to forge His greatest weapons – people who rely wholly on Him.

Tis His Fire

'Tis His fire that melteth thee.
For thou must learn what not to be
Fired silver doth shine so bright
For no dross doth block its light
As with it so thou must be
'Tis His fire that melteth thee.

May't be Thy fire melteth me
Filled with wrong I must not be
Thou must burn away my night
Leaving only Thy true light
For like Thou I long to be
May't be Thy fire melteth me

Thou like I wilt surely be
For 'tis My fire refineth thee
No dross shall escape My sight
Thou wilt be forever bright
O so pure thou wilt be
For 'tis My fire refineth thee

Conformed to My likeness be
That thou shalt abide with Me
Truly thou must evil fight
Standing by My holy might
So others in thou wilt see
How thou dost abide with Me

Prologue

Valisa awoke in the dim light of a cell.

"Where's my stone," she said speaking her thoughts aloud.

She swung her feet to the floor and rubbed her eyes as she stood up. The stone floor was slick and cold.

Where am I? Why am I here?

She touched the bump on her head. Thoughts and memories slowly coalesced in her mind.

The Basaners captured us.

As her mind cleared, she realized the light came from beneath the bed. She fell to her knees and groped under the bed for her stone. Her hand closed on it. Pulling it out, she held it aloft. Its light revealed the dingy, dank cell to her unbelieving eyes.

Where is that smell coming from? That large pot in the corner. Aw, that's putrid. Don't they ever empty it? Whoever made this bed was trying to make it uncomfortable. They didn't waste money on it either. Not even enough straw to cover the bottom. This wood is smooth. The work of many hands. They sure didn't sand it and polish it like this. It's stained.

She shuddered.

Red! So is the straw.

She let out a whimper. A sudden noise turned her from the horror that drew her gaze and thoughts. She jumped onto the bed and shrieked as a rat scurried along the wall. The faint glint of metal came from the wall. She held the stone higher.

Chains for a prisoner's hands and feet. A prisoner? They're for my hands and feet!

The wall on her right was blank stone, the same as the floor and the wall on her left except for the iron door. The door had one portal at the base. It was square, obviously for meals but taller than necessary. She pondered a moment.

The opening is big enough for my stone to go through. They want me to give it up, to renounce my allegiance to the King.

She sat back, nibbled at her stone, and waited.

A pair of rough hands shook her awake. Another pair grabbed her stone and cast it into a corner. She was dragged out of bed. When she didn't get immediately to her feet, a huge fist crashed into her jaw. The pain was overwhelming, but she didn't pass out. She got to her feet as quickly as she could, spitting out two teeth as she rose. Her head spun. Her knees buckled as she heard a voice say, "Get her moving. The Fragel doesn't like to be kept waiting."

As her vision faded, two men grabbed her by the arms and dragged her out of the cell.

She awoke suspended from her wrists by iron manacles, her feet just off the ground. At her feet lay her stone.

"I wish we could do something about those stones," said a guard by the stairs.

"What's the matter? You squeamish? Can't stand the sight of blood?" the Fragel said wrapping the cat o nine tails about his wrist.

"No, I just don't like the light. Makes me feel…naked." the guard replied.

"I'm with you." A large man pumped the bellows across the room. "I hate those things."

"It's been tried," the Fragel said. "Whatever you do they disappear and reappear before the prisoner." He looked over at Valisa. "Ah, she's awake. Time to begin." He swung his arm back and let the lash roll out to its full length.

Valisa screamed as the cords cut her flesh. "May the King forgive you," she managed to gasp before the second stroke fell.

Her stone brightened visibly. Angered, the Fragel swung harder and faster. With each stroke the light grew more intense. With lungs heaving, the Fragel paused after several minutes. Valisa raised her head. Her face glowed.

"It isn't too late to seek the King," she said. "The Bridge is never too far away." Then she cried out, "My King, do not hold this against them! They do not understand what they've done!"

The stone gave a tremendous burst of light. Her head slumped forward as the glow surrounding her faded. The men screamed in mental anguish and gnawed their tongues as the stone dissolved and the darkness engulfed them. But the image of what had once been a beautiful woman was seared upon their eyes and memories. They would never be the same.

Chapter 1

Andre

Felansville lay hundreds of miles west of the Great City Agapay. During Andre's long journey he had done much to subvert the work of the Ebenchaim. Less than two miles from Agapay he turned north at the crossroads. Puddles dotted the road before him, shining in the light of the city. To his right, lay a hill surrounded by a field of brilliant white flowers. Oddly, they were a troubling sight.

I don't like those. There's something about them.

His brow furrowed, and he tried to turn his attention away from the sight, but the wind brought a strange voice to his ear.

"You shouldn't do this. Turn back while you can."

Andre cracked the whip. The horse snorted and began to canter. He cracked the whip again and the buggy rattled as the horse put on more speed. The clatter of the wheels crashing through the water dispelled the whispers. Andre relaxed until he crossed a ridge into a steeper descent toward the river and the buggy began swerving back and forth across the road. He gritted his teeth and reined in the horse. Their speed waned and the horse's gait returned to a canter, Andre breathed a sigh of relief. He looked back over his shoulder.

That was too close. Settle down or you won't be the one to stop the spread of the cursed light. Bad enough to fail and be punished, but to die...

He was nearing the river and a wide swath of saplings extended to the cliffs on his right and to the forest on his left. Before him, across the river, the towering, white walls of the city rose before him and the golden gates blazed in the light from the walls. The road curved to the left before crossing the bridge further on.

He slowed the horse to a walk. As they approached the river, he could hear an unintelligible shout from a man on the wall. The gates opened revealing a portcullis forcing him to a halt. A man with a halberd approached him from the right while the man on the left fitted an arrow to his bowstring.

"State your business."

"I'm travelling to each of the Great Cities. I'm searching for jewelry I can sell and for new designs for clothing."

The man with the halberd scrutinized both Andre and the carriage. He circled it, inspecting everything. The guard's face was slack jawed and his eyes were wide. The shiny black coach exuded wealth, and the horse was an exotic black Karabair. Andre smiled.

He's never seen the like.

The guard switched the halberd to his left hand and stroked the horse's flank with his right. He smiled. "Open the gate." He crossed the road as the portcullis rose and resumed his position to the right of the gate.

As the gate reached the top, Andre shook the reins and nodded to the man as the buggy moved through the gate. Driving soon grew difficult as the streets were made for foot traffic, horses, and small carts, but certainly not for the ostentatious carriage he drove. There were many pedestrians as well as a few horses and his way was frequently blocked.

He had driven no more than a hundred yards when he decided to go back to the stable he had seen near the gate. This was not easy as the street barely had room for him to turn his rig around. He blocked the path for the better part of five minutes as he maneuvered to find an opening in the traffic and labored to get the buggy turned.

The task accomplished, he made his way back and soon pulled up at the entrance to Wainwright's Livery, an establishment that drew a lot of business though its appearance indicated it handled little more than horses and the transport of common folk. The ebony carriage and the handsome beast pulling it were out of place and drew the attention of the grooms and stable boys who, though very curious, remained at their work. Mr. Wainwright was quickly informed and soon appeared in the doorway.

"Aye, that's a beautiful rig ya've got there."

"Yes. Can you accommodate it? I don't want it scratched or handled by every attendant you employ."

"Aye, we'll take good care of it and that gem of a horse ya' got pullin' 'er."

"How much my good man?"

"Three karpas a day for the horse and 'nother for the rig."

"Seems a bit high, but done. I expect the best of care for both horse and carriage for that price, mind."

Mr. Wainwright, who had a smile under his thick, gray mustache, looked up at Andre as his smile faded.

He sighed. "Aye, sir."

A sly smile crossed Andre's face as he saw the change in the man's countenance.

"I'll be dropping by from time to time. I may even want to take a ride in the countryside. By the way, the left front wheel is squeaking. Put some grease on it."

The man turned and called for a stable boy and groomsman. He grumbled as he headed back to his office. Andre watched the workers as they led the horse inside. They unhitched the horse and stored the carriage in an empty stall. Satisfied they would be in adequate if not expert hands, Andre left to survey the markets and stores of the city, all the while looking for future opportunities to disrupt and snarl its commerce and industry.

The markets were crowded. He looked over the produce and nonchalantly grabbed an apple when the farmer was looking the other way. Leaving the market he began devouring the apple as he scrutinized the shops for his next stop. There were a couple of clothiers and a dress shop nearby that would help him to establish his cover story.

He entered the dress shop and perused the merchandise. He spent the next hour mired in conversation with a little man with bright red hair and a receding hairline, When he came out of the shop, it was late afternoon, and he decided to forgo the clothiers and moved to the next street. There he spied something of interest – an open stall with a jeweler as its resident. He watched with fascination as the man worked with gold and silver to make a brooch. It would indeed be a thing of beauty.

"Excuse me," came a booming voice from above his head.

Andre, who was half a head taller than the other men in the crowd, turned and looked the giant of a guard square in the belly. His gaze began to slowly traverse upwards to the man's face. He took in the sights along the way – two huge hands placed on the hips, a massive red uniform that he knew must hide muscles that could break him in half as easily as he would snap a twig, and a black beard and curly hair.

He must be eight feet tall!
"Y...Ye...Yes?" Andre stammered.
"You're a stranger here." It was a statement with a menacing edge in it.
"Yes." Andre swallowed hard."Yes sir."

The Guard was examining him closely. His frilly white shirt and tight black pants must have been strange to this man as the citizen's clothes he had seen were unpretentious. His shiny black boots and black cane with the silver knob handle were also objects of interest.

"My name is Max. I'm Sergeant Major of the King's guard. What's your business here?"

The tone was lighter but did nothing to alleviate Andre's nervousness in the presence of the giant.

"I'm...I'm traveling to the Great Cities. I've inherited some money and I wanted to see more of the world?" He hadn't intended the last statement to come out as a question, but he had no idea of this giant guard's intentions.

"What's your name, little man?"
"An..." Andre cleared his throat. "Andre, sir."
"You expect to be here long?" Max asked in a more genial tone.
"Several weeks. Perhaps longer."
"You have a place to stay?"
"No sir."
"Well you do now."
"Ex...excuse me?"
"You can stay with me. It'll save you some of that inherited money."

Andre smoothed his black hair back nervously with his left hand and shifted from one foot to the other and back again.

"I couldn't impose on you like that."
Max raised an eyebrow. "Oh, I insist. We couldn't have a stranger to our city who didn't taste our hospitality, especially one of such importance."

I wish I could get out of this, but best to not make him suspicious. "Since you insist."

The tone of Max's voice was more relaxed. "You have more shopping to do? Our supper will be waiting."

Andre looked around sheepishly. "Lead on my good man," he said trying to slip back into his gallant facade.

They walked in silence, side by side for some time. Andre's thoughts were awhirl.

How can I sabotage this city when this gargantuan guard is watching my every move? I'll have to get into his good graces; win his trust. This is more trouble than I bargained for.

He followed Max up the steps of a house made for a giant. They passed beneath an iron sign above even Max's head and entered through a door that made Andre feel like a child. The living room held a couch and a couple of chairs on one side that were quite normal, but one chair reminded Andre of the one his grandpa used to sit in. He could see himself climbing into his grandpa's lap. The memory faded as the sound of Max's voice intruded.

"Your room is upstairs. I think you'll find it comfortable. The stairs you probably won't. They were a compromise between being for someone my size and someone yours. Bad idea. They're not comfortable for anyone."

Andre wasn't being taken in by this friendly tone, though he tried to act like he was.

What is he up to? Does he suspect me? I certainly don't like all this attention. Watch your step boy. Watch Your Step!

Max turned, "I should have asked, do you have baggage or a pack?"

"Yes, I have a carriage at the stable near the city gate. I left my luggage in it until I could find accommodations."

"I'll have Bercan fetch it. It'll be here by the time we're done with dinner." He turned and yelled up the stairs. "Bercan! Yo! Bercan, boy!"

A young teen, nearly as tall as Andre, came running into the room. He had a lanky form as though he had been stretched on the rack throughout his growing years. His olive skin went perfectly with his wavy black hair and dark brown eyes.

"Yes sir?" Bercan said respectfully.

Max slapped Bercan on the shoulder as he looked at Andre. "This is Bercan. If you need anything, just call for him. He has the room next to yours. Bercan this is Andre, our guest. His baggage is at Wainwright's stable. Bring it here and see that Mr. Wainwright's men have done right by the horse."

"What about dinner?" Bercan said in a downcast tone.

"You can eat when you return. If I know you, you had a meal less than an hour ago. Now off with you." Max swatted the Bercan lightly on the rear as he exited the house.

"The boy's at that age, growing and constantly eating."

A voice called from the doorway of the next room. "Dinner sir."

A matronly woman with a flushed face and a bedraggled wisp of brown hair on her forehead stood in the door of the dining room.

"Thank you Mrs. Hughes. After you, Andre," Max said motioning to the doorway.

Andre stepped into a sizeable room with a table and a large chair at one end and nine others of normal size down the sides and at the other end. A roast and two chickens sat on platters in the middle of the table surrounded by bowls of vegetables, and fruit. All the places were set with knife, fork, spoon, a glass, and a napkin. He was taken aback. He had seen and eaten at such tables before, but he never expected them in the house of a soldier.

"I must say, your table is quite elegant."

"Thank you." Max said nonchalantly. "A privilege of my rank along with the servants and the house. I often entertain and have guests of lesser rank here. It's expected of the Captain of the Guard. One of my duties. Of course the King-steward of the city has a much finer table and entertains many nobler guests. Except for my rank, I am but a common soldier and my guests are much too grand for my company."

"If you, sir, are a common soldier, this city need never fear attack."

"Gracious words. Won't you sit here beside me while we eat? Much easier to converse that way."

As Andre took a seat, thoughts buzzed through his head like gnats on a spring evening.

How did I get into this? This isn't going to be as easy as last time. These are no country bumpkins. Their clothes aside, these people are refined and no doubt well educated. With the Captain of the Guard looking over my shoulder, my work will be risky to say the least. This will require thought, but for now, it's enough just to keep my wits about me. I mustn't make a slip. He'll be dismembering every word I say for the thoughts hidden beneath.

Andre smiled at his host. "Do you often have guests for every seat?" he asked motioning to the empty chairs.

"No, mostly the men of the tower guard dine with me. They'll be coming and going throughout the evening. Sometimes we have a guest or two. I've never had a table set only for guests."

I may have misjudged, but then again there isn't a lot of coming and going in this region. Not at all like the lands of the west.

"What did you do before the inheritance?"

Andre smiled inwardly.

I'm glad they thought to give me a good story to tell.

"Mostly schooling. My family owns most of Felansville and it wasn't so long ago that I looked like Bercan. People take me for older than I am. I should actually still be in college for another two years, but my father's death caused the family responsibilities to fall on me."

"What's this 'college'?"

"A school for older youth that teaches advanced courses. I wish I could have finished but the responsibilities of being the eldest son. You see, this trip isn't for pleasure, but business. I can't say it isn't pleasurable as well. I've had enough of Felansville for a while."

"I understand. I lost my father not long ago and the familiar places still bring pain. A trip would be a fine thing for any reason."

Andre smiled.

He's looking for common ground. Good. The more alike he thinks we are the less I have to worry about.

"Yes, grief is a painful thing. I've never known pain like this."

"I'm sorry. Perhaps we should change the subject."

"Thank you. You're a very kind host."

"Tell me, what kind of business is your family in? Perhaps I know someone you could do business with."

"We're couturiers."

Max's look changed to one of befuddlement. "Come again?"

"You might call us tailors. We also sell jewelry. I'm actually looking for both; jewelry we can sell and new ideas in fashion."

"Ho, ho, ho! So that explains your strange dress. I must tell, you we are rather plain folk here. Your strange garb had me wondering about you."

Got him!

"I see. So that's why you played host."

"No, no, no. You misunderstand. You are quite right about my suspicions. That is why I singled you out, but I would have been glad to give any stranger to our city a place to stay. You're welcome here as long as you like."

"Thank you." Andre pondered for a moment.

Perhaps I should. He'll be less suspicious if I do.

"I think I'll take you up on your generous offer. Your hospitality is certainly flawless."

Just then, the front door opened and Aurora entered the living room. Andre caught sight of her and his fork clattered to his plate. She was a tall woman in her mid to late twenties. Her blonde hair shone like it was made of light. Her slender face and arms and her pale skin also looked like there was a light within. But her sapphire blue eyes are what took him captive.

"Come in Aurora. What brings you here?" Max rumbled.

"It's the second Thursday of the month, Max, or did you forget?"

"I did indeed. You know I love our dinners, but I've been entertaining a guest to our city. This is Andre."

Andre rose and pushed back his chair. "Of Felansville," he added with a bow.

"Pleased to meet you, sir." Aurora curtsied.

"This is my sister, Aurora." Max smiled.

Andre took her hand and kissed it. Aurora blushed.

"I am humbled to be in the presence of one so beautiful, miss."

Chapter 2
The Chuchoteur

Aurora opened her door to find a beautiful golden hibiscus cutting lying on her doorstep, its blossom in the early stages of opening and laced with dew drops.

April 10th

Dearest Lachlaniel,
    I hope everything is going well with you. Everything here is back to dull normal. That is, it was until yesterday. A new man came to town. He's staying with Max. He's very different. He dresses in very tight pants and frilly shirts. The colors of his clothes are frequently striking and ostentatious, though he seems to like black and white best. He's very polite and quite charming. He and Max hit it off well. They will probably be good friends before long.
    It's been a week since you left and I miss you so. How far have you traveled? I long for you to get there as much as, I am sure, you do yourself. I talk to the King about you often and ask for Him to speed your journey and your return, and to keep you safe. I love you. Be safe.

With all my heart,

Aurora

April 17th

Aurora, my Love,

    Sorry I couldn't be with you for Passage day. I hope I'll be back for the feast next year. I've traveled three hundred miles so far. I hope to reach the Great City by the end of June or at least the early part of July. How long the King's task will take only the King knows.

    I came to a little town called Anoigo Thuran today and caused quite a stir with my light. They were all amazed. It's so gratifying that I can bring my light to these peasants who live in darkness. I told them of the Bridge, and nearly the whole town crossed. It was magnificent.

    Not all is going well, however. I'm not perceiving things as clearly as I have. There is no clear trail to follow at times. Thankfully, if I let Aman carry me where he will, we seem to move in the right direction. He's a good horse and I love him like a brother. I do wish these petty annoyances would end. There's some desperate need at the Great City and I begrudge any delay, especially as it keeps me longer from you.

I hope everything is alright there and that you're well. I long to see you and hold you again.

LA

All my love,

Lachalniel

Lachlaniel led the last of the townspeople back to their cheering throngs of neighbors, but unseen, a shadow moved among the people and sidled up to Lachlaniel.

"Friends, I am glad to have been welcomed here and to be cheered by your reception of the King's gift of light. Now, however, I must move on. The King has an urgent task for me in one of the Great Cities far from here. Thank you all for your hospitality."

As he was leaving town, a bedraggled old woman came running as best she could from behind her hut waving her arms frantically as she approached the road in front of him.

"My grandson! My grandson! Please help me sir!" She fell to her knees and broke into sobs.

The shadow, an evil creature of the darkness known as the Chuchoteur, implanted a thought in Lachlaniel's mind. *Why is this woman wasting your time?*

"The King's business is urgent," Lachlaniel said with an edge in his voice. He tried to move the horse around her.

"Oh, please sir! I beg you, come quickly. My grandson's fallen in the well," she said breathlessly.

Lachlaniel responded with aggravation. "Very well."

I must help her, but all these delays when there's urgent business to attend to. The Great City must be in terrible need or the King wouldn't be sending me there. I wish Aurora was here.

"Thank you, sir." The woman wiped her tears. She grabbed his arm and almost pulling him off the horse as he dismounted.

"Hurry sir. Oh please hurry."

She yanked his arm as she attempted to run to the back of the tiny house. Lachlaniel followed, frustrated with her pawing.

"Hurry sir or he'll drown." She yanked at his sleeve.

She reached the well breathing too hard to speak. Lachlaniel peered into the well. Its black depths revealed nothing to his sightless eyes, but in his mind he saw a boy flailing in the dark, cold waters.

"Quickly woman, bring my horse."

The woman waddled as fast as she could back to the front of the house. Her tousled gray hair waved back and forth like a broken spider web in the light breeze. In short order, Aman appeared leading the woman who was hanging on to the reins. She let go and collapsed on the ground trying to breathe. As Lachlaniel leaned his sword against the well, Aman pushed his nose into Lachlaniel's side and gave a worried snort.

Lachlaniel got the rope from the pack on his saddle. He tied one end to the saddle horn and threw the other in the well. He began his descent muttering as he went.

The Chuchoteur whispered to Lachlaniel again.

Children don't think.

Mindless infant. He should know better than to play around a well. Look at all the time this is costing me.

The water came up to Lachlaniel's neck. He grabbed the flailing lad and waited for the boy to get his wits.

"Alright boy, put your arms around my neck."

The boy grasped Lachlaniel with all his might. Lachlaniel could hardly speak.

"It's alright. You're safe now"

Gradually, the child relaxed enough for Lachlaniel to get the rope secured around the boy's chest. Lachlaniel tugged on the rope and Aman backed up until the rope was taut. He pulled the child from his neck.

"Don't let go! Don't let go!" the boy cried in terror.

"It's okay. Grab the rope. My horse won't let you drop into the water. I'm going to climb the rope, and then, we'll pull you out."

The child continued to cling to him.

Children don't listen either.
Why can't he just do what he's told?
"I'm afraid!"
What a waste of time!
Children.

"There's nothing to worry about. I'm going to let go, but I'm right here."

The child whimpered but clutched the rope. Lachlaniel let go and the boy let out a yelp as he began to sway back and forth. Terror filled his eyes for an instant, but then, a slight smile spread across his face.

"Thank you, sir."

Lachlaniel grabbed the rope above the child's head and began his ascent. He crawled over the lip of the well and collapsed on his hands and knees.

"What a climb." He shook himself as he shivered from the cold. "That's cold water," he said to the woman as he urged the horse backward. "You must enjoy it. I must say I'd rather drink it than swim in it."

The woman didn't respond, but stood biting her lip, her hands clasped in front of her.

Emotional foolishness. You have better things to do!
Peasants.

The boy tumbled over the side. His grandmother ran to him. Kneeling down she cradled him in her arms and began brushing his hair out of his eyes while Lachlaniel loosed the rope first from the horse and the boy. She rocked him gently.

"I can't thank you enough." Her tears had changed to joy and gratitude.

Lachlaniel paid her no mind.

Maybe now I can cover some ground.

The Chuchoteur smiled.

Why is it so black? There's nothing to mark my path. Why do I perceive nothing?

Lachlaniel mounted the saddle, and Aman walked back to the road without any prodding....

Max had learned of a mysterious fire in the night at Wainwright's. There seemed to be no cause but the damage was extensive. Most of the animals were saved but the building was a total loss. Several wagons were also lost, including Andre's carriage as well as his horse.

Max paced back and forth waiting for Andre. Andre came down to breakfast whistling a merry tune. Mrs. Hughes had his breakfast ready and waiting. Max sat down in the living room uncomfortable at the conversation that must follow.

I'll let him enjoy his breakfast before I ruin his day.

The minutes passed liked drops of dew from the edge of a leaf with the occasional clatter of a utensil laid on the china, the gurgle of water being poured into a glass, or the sound of knife and fork scraping each other. Max fidgeted.

I wonder how he'll take it. The loss of the carriage would be bad enough. They said it was beautiful; the loss of the horse though... How attached was he to it? This could be very bad.

The sound of the chair being pushed back broke his reverie. He stood up and moved to the dining room doorway as Andre wiped his mouth lightly with the napkin and dropped it on the empty plate. Andre turned to the frowning Max.

"What is it my friend? You look like you've come from a funeral."

"I have bad news. There was a fire last night at Wainwright's."

Andre's smile dissipated like the morning dew.

"How bad?"

"The place is a total loss, your carriage as well."

"Oh no!" His eyes widened. "My horse! My horse! What about Ranger!"

Max looked down. "I'm sorry."

A look of horror and grief erupted on Andre's face. "No! No! No!"

He turned away and pounded the door jamb with his fist. He leaned against the wall and his shoulders slumped.

"No, not Ranger!" His shoulders heaved as tears began to dot the floor between him and the wall.

"I'm sorry." Max put his hand on Andre's shoulder. "I wish there were something I could do or say."

"I had him since he was a colt. He's the last link to the life I knew. First my dad and now Ranger. Only the business remains."

"I am truly sorry."

Andre looked up with tear filled eyes. "Thank you. Excuse me." He headed for the door. Max watched him go, his mouth half open, unable to think of anything else to say.

Aurora walked in the park near her home. She was wandering aimlessly, more or less in the direction of her favorite place, taking in the beautiful late spring morning. The air was crisp and cool though the dew had vanished earlier. Bees buzzed greedily around the honeysuckle while hummingbirds darted back and forth around the bleeding hearts. The early blossoms of the hydrangeas were beautiful, portending a spectacular show in another week or two. Everywhere life and beauty abounded. She knew the secluded bench beneath the red horse-chestnut would be a place of beauty and solitude. Its blossoms were early this year and were already striking. The adjacent red buds and cherry trees lent to the atmosphere. It was a marvelous place to sit and reflect, or to dream.

She rounded the rhododendron only to find her bench occupied by Andre. His hands were on his head and his elbows on his knees while his face was turned to the ground as though he were scrutinizing each pebble. She took two more steps before she could hear him weeping. She started to turn and leave him alone when he looked up. Seeing her, he pulled his handkerchief and dried his eyes and blew his nose.

"What's wrong Andre?"

He gulped as though to choke back tears. "There was a fire at the stable. My horse... my horse was killed."

"Oh! I'm so sorry." She took the seat beside him. "He must have been very special."

"I raised him from a colt. He was a gift from my father. The last thing I had that he gave me. Now, not only is father gone, but Ranger too. I'm alone in the world. There's no one left."

"Oh, Andre!" She put her hand on his arm as tears filled her eyes. "You're not alone. You've already started making friends here. We can't do anything about your loss, but we grieve with you."

"Thank you. This is too much. Losing my father and now Ranger, I feel so small and alone. I thought I was a man. I guess I'm still just a kid."

"You *are* a man. Even Max cried when we lost our father."

The sudden recollection of that loss, only a few weeks ago, hit her hard and her stomach churned as though it had just happened. Her hand trembled and she couldn't hold back the tears. She turned away, put her hands over her face, and sucked in a breath. She let out a whimper.

Andre turned.

"Aurora?" He sniffed. "What's wrong?"

"My father... oh...." Her voice trailed into tears and sobs.

Andre grasped her hand. "It's okay." His voice carried concern.

A shoulder to cry on – any shoulder.

She leaned against Andre. He smoothed her hair and they cried together as the morning passed.

Chapter 3
Shamgar

It was a beautiful morning. Aurora opened her door and found two oak leaved geraniums lying at her feet.

Lachlaniel entered the Dispatch Office. The dispatch manager smiled.
"May I help you sir?"
My name is Lachlaniel. Do you have any letters for me from the Great City Agapay?"
"Why yes sir, I do."
"Could you read it? I'm blind."
"Surely."
The Chuchoteur listened with interest.

April 25th

Dearest Lachlaniel,
　Oh how I miss you too. My love and longing for you grow day by day. Please finish your work for the King as soon as you can. If I knew how long, I would be counting the days. My heart beat faster when I received your letter. Come quickly my darling, my love.
　Kesniel and Max send their greetings, but Ewald is always concerned for you. He says a young blind boy must be careful, even if he is a great general. He petitions the King often on your behalf. He loves you almost as much as I.

Andre, the man I told you about, is the highlight of society now. He comes from Felansville, a town quite some distance to the west. His elegance and his winsome nature have the girls all fluttering around him when he appears, though he doesn't seem interested in them. He's even had dinner with Kesniel. He's very polite. He says hello when he sees me, and on occasion we've passed the time of day.

Yesterday, there was a stable that burned down. They didn't know the cause at first, but it turns out that it was deliberately set. Andre lost a beloved horse and his very fine carriage. He was so upset I spent most of the day with him to cheer him up.

I've told him about you. He's very interested in you, where you are, and what you're doing. I think he would help you if he could.

Well, that's about all. I haven't heard from Farrah in some time, so I'll close for now.

Enclosed with all my heart,

Lachlaniel frowned.
He's after your girl.
I don't like it. Spending the day with some lout. I know she means well but he shouldn't be trusted. She's too innocent. Somebody needs to keep an eye on this snake in the grass. Max.
The Chuchoteur smiled.
"I'd like to dictate a couple of letters if you wouldn't mind."

"Not at all. Glad to help."

May 2nd

Max,

Watch out for your sister, Aurora. I hear there's a new visitor in the city. He seems to be interested in her. I don't like it. With so little to do, my mind runs constantly to Aurora (and the churl). I can see this serpent trying to steal my fiancée. Take care of her for me.

How are your new duties? Is Ewald doing his job and living up to your expectations? Not much happening here, just many miles. Not even anybody on the trip with me to talk to. Aurora may have told you, I've lost my ability to perceive things. Since then, the trip seems interminable. Except for the occasional stranger on the road or people in the towns (which are rare along this stretch), there is only the sound of wildlife and weather.

I hope everything goes well with you and the city.

Your friend,

Lachalniel

The manager looked up. "And the second one?" he said grabbing a new sheet of paper.

May 2nd

Aurora, love of my life,

I'm glad you have a new friend, but be careful of strange men. I worry about you. You can't be so open. You become friends with someone you don't know too easily. Guard your heart. You have mine. Don't let me lose yours.

Nothing has happened in the past week (Has it only been a week?), just riding. I did stop in a little town the day before yesterday. I hardly wanted to stay there. It smelled like a pig farm. But I haven't slept in a bed in over a week, so I stayed the night at a little inn. It was atrocious. Nothing was clean. The food tasted of whatever had been served on that plate the day before, maybe longer (Couldn't even tell what that was, but it was foul). The innkeeper hadn't had a bath in who knows how long, and his wife's breath reeked of ale. All in all an experience I DO NOT wish to repeat.

There must be a lot of Ebenchaim traveling this road. The people of the town took no notice of me. Of course, some of them could be Ebenchaim. I can't even perceive that anymore. I hope things are going better for you. Do stay away from that Felansville guy, Angus.

LA

With all my Love,

Lachlaniel

The Chuchoteur snickered.
This is almost too easy.

It had been a long, tiring day. Both Lachlaniel and Aman were weary and in need of rest, but there had been no place to stop and dismount for many miles.

Is this the main road? The trees have been brushing my sides for hours. Still, without sight and the ability I had to perceive even though I'm blind, I have to trust Aman to follow the right road.

He pulled back on the reins.

What is that foul smell?

He urged the horse forward again only to find that the road widened. Sounds played on his ears. They were indistinct at first, but they began to resolve into voices and the sound of animals. Now the smell became clear to him.

Pig farm. First place I come to in miles is a pig farm? Maybe there's something besides this worthless dung heap a little further on.

The Chuchoteur smiled. His work was progressing nicely.

Lachlaniel hadn't eaten in hours, and as the stench grew, his stomach heaved at its emptiness. The road continued past several farms. He scowled and let out a sigh.

Nothing but these wretched pigsties.

He listened, his ears reaching for the sound of anyone nearby. The horse trudged forward without rest. At last, he heard the sound of someone slopping hogs near the road. He summoned his remaining strength and held the seething anger of his offended stomach in check.

"Excuse me is there some place nearby where we can spend the night? An inn with a stable perhaps."

The farmer continued to slop the hogs unaffected by the sudden presence of light. He replied without looking up.

"A mile straight on. It's on your left."

"Thank you."

Another five hundred yards and the road became crowded with small houses and an occasional business. Even so, the stench persisted. The buildings gave way to an open space and the sound of carts on cobble stones both ahead and to the sides.

Town square. How do they stand the smell?

Maybe they like the stench of manure.

Perhaps. The dairy farmers around Fairvale never seemed to mind the smell from the cattle. It wasn't like this though.

The smell faded but did not cease. For a time his stomach settled, and though he was bone weary, the ride became bearable once more. But just as he thought they were leaving it behind, the smell grew again. They were nearing the inn when on the right the sounds of pigs began to predominate.

Not across from the inn!
You expected something else from these oafs?
Do I have to put up with this? Isn't there some place better?
More suitable for a man of your position?
Exactly. This is intolerable!

The sound of the horse's hooves echoed off a building to the left. Lachlaniel turned Aman to the edge of the road and dismounted. New smells assaulted him as he entered. The man behind the desk reeked of sweat, and grime, and ale. Lachlaniel blanched and backed up a couple of steps. This man too displayed no recognition of the change from darkness to light.

"Can I help you?"

"I'd like a room *(I think)* and can you stable my horse?"

"Sure. You're late for dinner, but if you want to eat, we can find something."

"That would be good. You wouldn't have a bath?"

The man stared blankly and silent seconds slowly ticked by.

He doesn't know what you're talking about.
Wonderful!

"Never mind."

"Mama! We have a customer!"

A woman set the bare wooden table without a word. Lachlaniel crossed the room and felt for a chair. She smelled like her husband with the added smell of rancid bacon, and the acrid smell of burned food.

This will be a meal you will long remember.

Lachlaniel sat down and picked up a fork. It was slimy and slipped through his fingers.

"Just some bread thank you."

Surely that can't be too bad.

He used the stale bread as a spoon for the food on his plate, but only for one bite. He spit the mouthful onto the plate and wiped his mouth on his sleeve when he found no napkin.

No wonder there are so many pig farms. That's all this slop is good for.

He continued to eat the stale bread until he felt something crawling on his lip. His face contorted with revulsion and disgust. He picked it off.

A weevil!

He dropped the bread, flipped his plate, stood up and asked with seething anger, "Which way to my room?"

"Top of the stairs second room on the right." the woman said in a husky voice that held a tinge of fright.

The man behind the desk jumped to his feet, his hands balled into fists. He relaxed and sat back down when the stranger, showing no further sign of hostility, headed for the stairs.

Lachlaniel entered his room, and having gotten a whiff of the bed long before he got near it, decided to sleep on the floor.

How can people live like this?

It suits them.

Perhaps, but I certainly don't understand it. I'll get some sleep and get out of here.

There was the scent of a strange fruit blossom and soft words floated in the air.

"They need to cross the Bridge," Leofwine said softly.

Lachlaniel grunted. Leofwine frowned and a tear formed on His unseen cheek. Lachlaniel rolled to his side, and quickly fell asleep as the stench once again permeated the room.

Leofwine whispered, "Oh, Lachlaniel. Pride goes before destruction and haughtiness before a fall."

Lachlaniel felt his way down the stairs to the tiny 'great room' of the inn. The smell of the man from last night wasn't present but the new smells were no better. Lachlaniel followed the snoring to the desk clerk's counter.

"Excuse me."

There were abrupt choking sounds as the clerk switched from snoring to breathing. The front legs of the chair banged the floor as the man came to his feet.

An ancient voice said, "What can I do for ye? Would ye like breakfast?"

That thought turned Lachlaniel's stomach.

"No," Lachlaniel said emphatically. "I would like to pay my bill."

"Right you are sir. Two karpas."

Lachlaniel dropped two coins on the counter and turned for the door.

"No sir, over this way. Let me help you."

The man grabbed Lachlaniel's arm. The smell was suddenly overwhelming and Lachlaniel's stomach heaved. Two steps and he was in the 'fresh' air of the nearby pigsty as the man returned to his desk.

The voice of a young teen came from the corner. "I'll get your horse sir."

Lachlaniel breathed easier with only the smell of the pigs to contend with.

Filthy vermin!

The Chuchoteur's thought did not have the desired effect, perhaps because in spite of a restless night, Lachlaniel felt somewhat refreshed.

No, I feel sorry for them. No one should have to live like this.

All the same, it'll be nice to get on the road and away from these people.

Lachlaniel nodded affirmatively to the Chuchoteur's implanted thought.

I'm glad I'm not like them. I'm a general of the King. I shouldn't even have to go through a place like this much less stay here.

The morning wore on as Lachlaniel and Aman ambled wearily forward. A voice from his left broke the silence of the forest.

"Hello friend!"

"Who's there?"

Lachlaniel reined the horse in, which was hardly necessary at their pace.

"My name is Casimir. I'm a servant of the King the same as you."

Lachlaniel was having trouble locating the voice among the trees. He looked from one side of the road to the other. Casimir, who was in plain sight in the middle of the road, moved closer.

"What's wrong? Can't you see?"

"No. I'm blind."

Casimir stroked the horse's jaw, and Aman nuzzled his side.

"You smell the sugar in my pocket don't you boy. Is it alright if I give him some? I keep some on me for my own horse."

"Sugar? What's that?"

Casimir mused. "It's a kind food. It makes things sweet like honey does."

"I'm Lachlaniel. I'm sure he could use some food. For that matter so could I."

"Then, you must come to my home. It's not far and you both look spent. Why didn't you stop at Shamgar, the town up the road?"

"The one with the pigs? We did but the smell was too much. We left after a miserable night's rest."

"Come with me. My home's not far." Casimir reiterated.

"Thank you for your hospitality. Lead the way. Aman will follow."

"Smart fellow." Casimir said stroking the horse's neck.

They walked down the road a short distance before there was a clearing in the trees. Casimir's house sat a hundred yards beyond the garden that was his front yard. There was a rhythmic thump, thump, thump of his wife hoeing furiously at a stubborn weed in the row of radishes. Hearing them approach, she looked up.

"Who've you brought back?" she asked in a cheerful tone.

"This is Lachlaniel. And this is my wife Arla."

"Pleased to meet you," Lachlaniel said to the general direction of the voice he had heard.

"I'm honored," Arla said dropping the hoe and curtseying. "Won't you join us for lunch?"

"That's what I brought him for. He and his poor horse spent the night in Shamgar. They're both apt to be ravenous."

"Thank you for your kindness." Lachlaniel dismounted.

I hope it's a good meal.

You deserve one, especially after dealing with those sloppy pig farmers. Detestable louts.

Unknowingly, Lachlaniel nodded in agreement. He dismounted. Following the sound of Casimir's footsteps, he led Aman towards the house.

Andre saw Aurora coming from the direction of the shops. The sun set her golden hair ablaze as it cascaded down her shoulders. This and the brilliance of her white dress were offset by her iridescent blue eyes.

Magnificent! No wonder Lachlaniel is so taken by her.

She was carrying two large baskets of fruit and vegetables with meat wrapped in butcher paper sticking out of one. A loaf of bread with two raisins for eyes flanked by the silk of two corn husks gave the appearance of a small animal peeking over the edge of the other basket. Andre laughed.

"Who's your friend?"

Aurora cocked her head to one side, her face wrinkled with concentration.

"Your friend. Here look."

Andre took the basket and turned it around. Aurora put her hand over her mouth, the laughter oozing between her fingers.

"Oh my goodness! I couldn't imagine what you talking about. That is so funny!"

They laughed together as Andre took the other basket.

"I'll carry them for you," he managed between chuckles.

They walked for a moment still tittering, and then, Aurora grew somber. Andre's smile faded.

"What's wrong?"

"I was thinking about last night."

"Last night?"

"You haven't heard? There was another fire."

Andre's jaw dropped and so did one of the baskets.

"What happened?"

"It was at the stable of the horse guards. The two soldiers who were on guard were killed, the stable was burned down, and many of the city's finest horses died in the blaze."

Andre's knees appeared to buckle and he sat down hard on the pavement. One of the baskets tumped over and fruit and vegetables rolled out. He bent his knees toward his chest, wrapped his arms around them, and put his head on his knees.

"Andre!" Aurora said as she turned. She bent down and took his hand.

He clenched his teeth.

"They have to catch that madman," he growled.

Aurora brushed his hair back.

"They will. The King's guards are looking for him, and Max has been put in charge.

"That's good to hear, but I won't have a moment's peace until he pays for what he did to Ranger."

Andre stood back up and dusted himself off. His face was filled with fury as he jerked the baskets off the ground and began picking up the scattered fruit. Aurora flinched.

"I hope they execute that miserable, murderous..." His voice trailed off.

"Are you thinking of the men that died or Ranger?"

Andre's face softened. "Ranger I suppose. It should be the men, but..." His voice trailed off again. He started down the street again at a quick pace.

Aurora almost had to run to stay up with him. "Andre. Slow down."

"I'm sorry. I forget about my long strides, but this just has my blood boiling."

"Let's not talk about it anymore." Aurora took his arm.

They walked in silence for some time. Aurora watched as his countenance changed and the tension in his muscles relaxed. She finally ventured into a new subject.

"I heard from my sister today."

"The one that married the Einar?"

"Yes."

"I'm sorry. I've forgotten her name."

"Farrah. She gave me some wonderful news."

"Oh?"

"She thinks she's with child."

"That makes you an aunt."

"Only for the fourth time, but it's her first child. I hope Max is home when we get there. It will make him so happy. Jocelyn got a letter from her too, so everyone will know, but I hope I get to break the news to Max."

"Is that where we're headed? I thought I was going to see where you live."

"Perhaps later. It will be dark when I leave for home and with things..." She stopped herself. "I mean I'd feel safer if you'd see me home."

"I'd love to." There was a smugness in Andre's smile as they turned the corner onto Max's street,

Max joined Andre and Aurora on their way out the door.
I like Andre, but I'm not going to let Aurora be escorted by him alone. She's far too trusting. Even if his intentions are good, many is the relationship broken by a friend. Lachlaniel deserves better than that. Hmph. So does Aurora.

He closed the door behind them.

"There's really no need for you to come, Max."

"Perhaps not, but with the things happening in the city I prefer to. Safety in numbers you know. This madman killed two armed guards at the stables before setting it on fire. I'm not about to let something happen to you two."

"Maybe you're right." Andre looked around warily. "You don't know what lies in the shadows."

At that moment there was a clatter from a shed to their left.

"Ah!" Aurora screamed.

A mule stuck his head out of the shed's window and brayed. They all three laughed in relief.

"You're so right, Andre. You never know what lurks in the shadows." Max said as his hand slipped from the hilt of his sword back to his side.

They continued their trek but their gait was faster than it had been. Max' senses were on alert listening to every noise and scanning darkened doorways and alleys.

It's difficult to follow their conversation and watch our surroundings too.

There was movement to his right and Max stopped and peered into a dark alley. Nothing stirred. He walked in a few steps and examined the various objects at length. A cat sprang from behind a box level with his chest. It hissed and screeched, clawing at him to try and get away. In the confusion, a shade slipped silently out of the ally to the far street. Ridding himself of the cat at last, Max drew his sword.

That cat didn't jump out for no reason.

But his scrutiny of the ally revealed nothing.

I'd best get back. If there is someone prowling around, I shouldn't leave them alone.

His size and long strides brought him up with them in a trice. Andre had his arm around Aurora. Max frowned at them as they stopped and turned toward him.

Andre's arm dropped to his side. "Aurora had chills after you left. My hair is standing on end too."

Max raised an eyebrow and said in a disapproving tone, "Well."

"Did you find anything?" Aurora asked.

"A cat."

Don't want to let on that there might be more."

Max smiled. "I think we should be getting you home. Our imaginations are playing tricks on us."

"Sounds good to me." Aurora shivered. "Imagination or not, I don't like it."

"I agree. I'll feel better when Aurora is safe inside her house," Andre added with a note of anxiety in his voice.

They continued, but there was a lingering smirk on Andre's face.

Chapter 4
Attack on the Dome of Meeting

On Aurora's doorstep lay a small bouquet of lilacs.

May 4th

Dearest one,

    His name is Andre, silly. Do not fear, and do not worry. I am yours as you are mine. I don't even see him every day. I don't know what he does, but it certainly isn't pursuing me. My sisters and Max watch out for me. If he does have any wrong intentions, they'll show him the road out of the city quick enough.

    I am, however, concerned about you. I don't like the fact that you no longer see things in your mind. That was a great comfort to me, to know that in battle you could see your opponent and his intentions, sometimes even before he started to move. Now, how will you fight? It must be hard even to do the things daily life requires. I talk to the King about you often. There are times I even find it hard to get my chores done because I'm spending so much of my time in my closet. Take care of yourself, and don't spend any more nights in terrible inns like that one. Wait for a nice town with a good inn. Take care of yourself. Oh, I already wrote that. Now you know how much I worry. I want you back quickly and whole, so do be careful. I love you.

Tears till you return my Love,

Aurora

Lachlaniel and Casimir sat by the empty fireplace after a fine meal. The sound of Arla washing the dishes floated in from the kitchen along with her voice in sweet song.

"You have a fine wife."

Casimir smiled. "The best. Her cooking is fit for a king, she works hard, she petitions the King on my behalf, and she encourages me no end. I don't know what I would do without her. And you Lachlaniel, do you have a wife?"

Not yet. I'm engaged to a wonderful woman named Aurora. She has brought light to my darkness." Lachlaniel frowned as he thought of her most recent letter and Andre.

"What's wrong my friend?"

Not willing to tell his troubles to a stranger, Lachlaniel replied, "I miss her greatly and my darkness has grown as this trip has progressed."

"How so?"

"When I was in battle before the gates of Agapay, I could perceive the things around me even though I couldn't see them with my eyes. Now, not only can I no longer perceive things around me, but my blindness grows blacker by the day. I can't understand it." Lachlaniel leaned back in his chair and clasped his hands in front of him. His brow furrowed with intense thought as he leaned forward again putting his face to his hands.

Why is this so?

"Have you talked to the King about this?" Casimir leaned forward, concern taut on his face.

Lachlaniel sat up. "No. No doubt He is allowing it for a reason. He'll reveal it to me in due time...but it is so aggravating!"

"You should talk to the King, my friend."

Lachlaniel shook his head. "No. I won't bother Him with my trivial problems."

"But..."

Lachlaniel cut him off. "I'm very tired. Perhaps you could show me to my room."

Casimir sighed. Standing up he replied, "This way."

Lachlaniel followed him to a room on the west side of the house. It was small but comfortable. Through the open window he could hear Aman in the barn a few yards away.

"The bed is to the left and there is a table with a wash basin below the window. I hope you're comfortable. Sleep well."

"Thank you. I will."

The door closed behind Casimir and Lachlaniel began readying himself for bed.

The morning brought a refreshing breeze through the window. Lachlaniel stretched and rose.

I haven't had a sleep that good in many days. I hope Aman had a good rest as well. We need to cover some distance today.

He washed his face and dressed. He could smell the aroma of bacon and coffee wafting through the doorway every so often when the breeze reversed directions. His stomach rumbled.

Okay. Okay. I'm hurrying.

He pulled on his boots and headed down the hall. Arla's singing and the rattle of pots and plates was a delightful sound.

Not like the inn, eh? The Chuchoteur whispered to his mind.

No not at all. Lachlaniel smiled.

Casimir looked up from the tool he was mending.

"Good morning, Lachlaniel. Ready for breakfast?"

"Indeed I am. That smell is enough to make a sated man hungry and I'm famished!"

"Let me get cleaned up and we can begin."

Arla, having heard, began setting the table with plates of food. They gathered around the table.

"May the King be praised both for the cook and her repast," Casimir said as they seated themselves. The food was good and the fellowship better. They talked of their pasts and how they came to cross the Bridge. At last they came to the present.

"So you're traveling to the Great City?" Casimir sat back and folded his hands across his middle.

"Yes, Chara. I'm needed there."

"There's a need here too. You know the conditions in Shamgar. There are some Ebenchaim there, but most haven't crossed the Bridge."

Back there?! You don't want to go back there! The stench. The filth. You need to move on.

"No. I won't go back there. The King will have to send someone else. The people of Chara wait for me. I won't delay."

Casimir shifted uneasily in his chair. "These people need help too. Ask the King. I've been petitioning Him for help, and He said He was sending me someone. Are you sure you're not the one?"

"I have more important business to attend to," Lachlaniel said flatly.

"What can be more important than freeing someone from the clutches of Kieran, more important than spreading the light?" Casimir frowned.

Don't listen to him. Tell him you have to leave now.

Lachlaniel's jaw tightened as he gritted his teeth. "I must be going." Lachlaniel pushed his chair back and knocked it over as he rose to his feet. Casimir started to rise, but Lachlaniel was already at the door and headed outside. His hand trembled as he reached for the door knob.

Asking me to go back there for the sake of those...

Hicks!

Yeah, hicks. Asking me to go back to those hicks!

He stepped outside and slammed the door.

The Chuchoteur smiled. *Ridiculous! 'What can be more important?' Indeed!*

Lachlaniel entered the barn intent on leaving as fast as he could, but Aman shied away every time Lachlaniel tried to touch him.

"What's wrong, boy?"

The horse's ears flicked back and forth and his eyes rolled as he nickered.

"Easy! It's okay." Lachlaniel said reassuringly, but Aman refused to let Lachlaniel touch him.

Casimir entered sheepishly. "I'm sorry if I offended you. It's just that the task is too big for me."

"I'm sure someone else will come along." He tried once again to touch Aman but in vain.

"Let me give you a hand."

"I don't understand it. He's never been like this before."

Casimir threw on the blanket and saddle and cinched it down. Aman stood calmly making no sound. Casimir stroked the horse's flanks and scratched behind his ears.

"He seems calm enough now."

Lachlaniel stretched out his hand and Aman once again shied away. He seemed a bit calmer but still unwilling to accept Lachlaniel's touch. Lachlaniel's anger gave way to concern.

"What's wrong boy?"

Casimir placed a sugar cube in Lachlaniel's hand. "Try this."

Lachlaniel moved to Aman's head. The horse's ears moved forward and he took the tidbit. Lachlaniel stroked his forehead and neck and moved cautiously to the horse's side.

Casimir grabbed the bridle just in case. "He seems more at ease now."

Lachlaniel nodded his head in agreement, but concern still covered his face. "I hope so."

He put his foot in the stirrup and eased into the saddle. Casimir let go and Aman shook his head but stood still.

Lachlaniel patted his neck. "I think he'll be okay."

"Safe travels then."

"Goodbye and thanks for the hospitality. We certainly needed the rest and your wife's food was excellent."

"May the King guide you in your journey."

"Thank you. May He prosper your efforts as well."

Lachlaniel turned Aman and headed for the road.

I wish I hadn't gotten so angry.

What do you care?

Why shouldn't I? It never hurts to be polite and pleasant. I should've had more self control.

The Chuchoteur remained silent sensing that this was not a good line of thought to push.

The morning was warm, and it was sultry and still beneath the trees lining the road. Lachlaniel traversed the silent countryside with nothing to disturb his thoughts.

Max hurried to the early morning meeting with the Army Commander. The streets were empty but there were signs of activity in a few houses as the inhabitants began readying themselves for the day.

I hope the commander has come up with a plan to catch this maniac. I'm stumped.

He reached the doorway of city guard headquarters. The two guards snapped to attention. Max looked up at the roof of the inn across the street. He could vaguely see the ends of two crossbows protruding from the edge of the roof. One had been pointed at him, but returned to a neutral position. The guards there could not be seen.

Commendable, but they've got to do more to conceal the weapons as well.

He opened the door and bent low to squeeze his bulk through.

I hate this door. Of all the doors in the city to make lower than the rest!

He breathed a sigh of relief as he entered. Inside it was spacious and had a high ceiling and he relaxed. The commander stood at the conference table pouring over a map. Ewald, Dan, and four other guards looked on.

The commander looked up. "Good we can begin. We've examined where the saboteur has hit. Up to now he hasn't even been seen by anyone who remained alive. He's grown very bold. The Dome of Meeting was attacked last night and three guards were killed. You already know he's expert in stealth. What we have withheld up to now, except from the sergeant major here, is that he's an expert assassin as well. The two guards at the entrance were killed with poison darts; the one inside had his throat slit before he knew there was a danger. We know because he still had a look of surprise on his face. We've determined that there are two places he's more likely to strike. Our focus is on the tower."

"What about the other?" Dan asked.

"It's being taken care of. Now to the plan. Most of you know the layout. For those who don't, we have the Merchants Warehouse to the north but there are no doors to the Tower on that side. To the west is the Tower Inn." He began tapping the map in the appropriate places. "To the south there's The Merchant's League. To the east we have the threshing floor. The four corner buildings are the Mason's Guild, the Carpenter's Guild, the granary, and the Merchant's Livery. We have access to the guilds and the granary, and we've arranged for the stable, the threshing floor, and the inn to be shut down while we conduct operations. We've tripled the guard at each entrance, four inside and two outside. There will also be three crossbowmen at each corner of the tower complex on the roofs." He nodded to Max to take over. "Max."

Max looked at the commander. "Right. Dan, you'll take charge of the guards at the east entrance. The threshing floor doesn't have many places to hide so at least some of your men will have to take up residence in the livery. Ewald, you'll have the west. The inn gives you the most comfortable position. Make sure your men don't get too comfortable. I'll take the south. That's where we think the attack will come, but we can't count on that." He looked at the other men. "You four will oversee the guards in the corner buildings. You'll get your instructions from me. You and your men are to report to the Tower at the first watch. Once there, no one will be allowed to leave until we finish. We're taking no chances with this." He looked back to the commander. "You have anything else?"

"No, but you remain and we'll go over the details. The rest of you are dismissed."

Aurora awoke to a beautiful late spring day. The temperature was mild and the breeze refreshing. The red glow of the Great Stone graced her window with its beauty. She rose and set to work doing her chores for her sister, but the beauty of the morning was soon marred by disturbing news. Jocelyn came into the kitchen breathless.

"Have you heard?"

"Heard what?" Aurora said with a smile that faded as she looked up from her task.

Tears filled Jocelyn's eyes. "Three guards were killed overnight at the Dome of Meeting. The Great Hall was set ablaze, and the memorial of the Bridge was desecrated."

"No!" Pain stabbed Aurora's heart. "How can anyone be so evil?"

"That's not all! I've heard talk against Kesniel and they even say someone else should take over the investigation from Max!"

"Oh! Poor Max! Is there anything we can do?"

"I'm afraid not."

"You can petition the King." Ewald said as he entered the room. "It isn't as bad as it sounds – yet. I'm afraid this is only the beginning. The investigation is not going well. Whoever is behind all this is clever and furtive."

"Yes of course. The King. He'll help." Aurora's face lit up the room. "Let's ask Him."

"Before we do, what brings you here this morning, Ewald?"

"I wanted to ask Miss Aurora if should would mend this jacket," Ewald said handing over a large parcel that was in his arms.

"Max's?"

"How'd you guess?" Ewald said with a smile. "I won't keep you. You have much to do and so do I."

"May the King bless your efforts." Aurora said as she hefted the package.

"Let me be a little more direct," Jocelyn said with a glare. "Catch this madman!"

"Yes ma'am!" Ewald said with a smile as he turned to leave. Then, he added over his shoulder, "Don't worry. We're setting a trap for him."

Aurora and Jocelyn looked at each other with surprise and said in unison, "Let's go talk to the King!"

As Aurora and Jocelyn left the house they almost stepped on the flowers at their feet. They were asters, half a dozen of them.

The Plaza in front of the Dome of Meeting was filled with people. Aurora and Jocelyn had joined a large portion of the city. Anyone who wasn't at work and many who would be but had carved out this time to join with others, met together to petition the King. Kesniel, in his official garb as King-Steward, stood on a hastily erected platform. His voice rang out.

"Friends! My brothers and sisters!" He waited for the noise of the crowd to die down. He pointed to the desecrated statue and the dome "We meet today because of this tragedy. The perpetrator must be found, but I remind you that our King has also said to petition Him on behalf of those who work for Kieran – who work for darkness. No life is so vile that He cannot change it. No heart is so dark that light cannot penetrate it. Let us, therefore, seek our King's favor on behalf of this poor, wretched miscreant. Let us remember too, the families of the fallen. Join me in your closets as we stand united before our King."

As one, the entire group opened their closets and entered the presence of the King.

May 10th

Lachlaniel, my love,

The city is in an uproar. There is a saboteur. Last night he struck at the Dome of Meeting. He desecrated the Bridge monument and set fire to the Great Hall, but worst of all, he killed three guards. Where will he strike next? The Tower? The Residence?

Max is working hard to catch him, but all efforts have been in vain so far. The Army Commander has been asked to help. I do so hope they can come up with a way to catch him.

You needn't worry about me. With Max, Ewald, and Andre watching out for me I'm quite safe, but I would feel better with you here. Petition the King for us. This man must be caught. Come home quickly.

My love to you always,

Aurora

Chapter 5
The Woman

May 13th

Aurora, Heart of My own heart,
 How can I describe the events of the last few days? What I witnessed filled me with anger, bitterness, and a desire for revenge. Tears fill my eyes at the thoughts, and I am overwhelmed with sadness and grief. I want to cry, scream, and draw sword, but there's nothing to fight. It started while I was riding through this forest. I suddenly saw a girl on the road walking towards me. Yes! I saw her! She was not unlike Diaphanous. Brilliant light came from her, though I don't think she was transparent as he is. That part is difficult because I'm still blind, and though I truly saw her there were parts of what happened that I couldn't see clearly. She was dim and far away to start with, but it startled me to actually be seeing something. Men came out of the woods and beat her to death. The details are too horrible to relate...

 As Lachlaniel crested a hill, Aman pulled up short and reared neighing. Light filtered through leaves filling Lachlaniel's sightless eyes.
 "I can see! What's happening?"
 He pulled the stone from his cape but saw nothing. He knew the stone was emitting light but his eyes only saw darkness. He put it back in his cape perplexed and looked up. He saw silhouettes of things between him and the light but nothing more.

He continued looking at the point in the road where the light shone most brightly. A figure emerged from beneath the overhanging trees. Lachlaniel shielded his eyes from the intense light. Aman reared again, and Lachlaniel fell to the ground. As he rose, he knew it wasn't in his mind that he saw the light, for he had to continue to shield his eyes to keep the intense light at bay.

Is the blindness gone? If it is, then why is my stone dark? Why can't I see anything but this new light and the shadows it casts?

His eyes adjusted to the brilliance. As he lowered his arm, he could see the figure of a woman that emitted the light. She was at the base of the hill walking towards him. None of her features was discernible. She was an outline of brighter light amidst the lesser radiance surrounding her.

Is this one of the Uset? I've perceived them before and she's similar. Yet there's something different about her. What is it? I can't quite put my finger on it.

"Lachlaniel, the King sent me with a message."

"Who are you? Are you one of the Uset?"

"No. I'm just like you."

"I beg to differ. The light you emit is visible to me even in my blindness."

She looked down at herself.

"I don't see any light, but it doesn't matter. You must move to the bottom of the hill. From there you will be able to see everything. I too am on a mission for the King." She paused; then, her voice took on an ominous tone, "Now that I've delivered the message I must see my mission to the end,"

She turned and started walking away. Lachlaniel mounted Aman and followed her to the foot of the hill.

She's so sad, as though she doesn't want to do what the King has asked. It must be incredibly difficult. There's a reluctance even in her walk.

Lachlaniel nudged Aman to follow her, but he stood frozen in place. No amount of coaxing would get him to move. Lachlaniel started dismounting when he felt huge hands on his shoulders. He turned first one way and then slowly to the other as he eyed two immense men flanking him. They were over twice as tall as he even mounted as he was.

"Uset," Lachlaniel whispered.

The woman was still walking, and though she was over a quarter of a mile away, he could see her as though she was no more than fifteen feet in front of him. When she was more than half a mile away, six men sprang from the forest and grabbed her. Lachlaniel was aghast not only at what was happening but at the fact that he could see and hear everything as though they were only feet away. The men tied her hands. They hoisted her by them with her face towards a tree. The biggest one took out a whip and began to lash her. With each stroke the light grew brighter.

Lachlaniel could hear her screams both near at hand and echoing in the distance. He tried to move, but the huge hands of the Uset held him firmly in place. Aman pawed the ground. He too wanted to move but could not. Lachlaniel watched as her hair became wet with sweat that ran down and mingled with the blood flowing from the wounds on her back. She was hanging from her wrists now, so exhausted she could no longer stand. His face twisted in agony, he looked into the misty eyes of the Uset.

"Why?"

The Uset's voice quavered, "Because these people need freed from the darkness." He looked up to the sky. "And because her death will prevent many others from dying at these men's hands."

They both looked back to the unfolding horror. The woman was approaching her end, her strength gone. The man with the lash paused, sweat dripping from his brow.

In a whisper barely audible to Lachlaniel, the woman said, "Oh, my King, do not hold this against them, but bring them to truly see the light."

The men stood in stunned silence. She collapsed and was no more. In that moment, there was a burst of light that was indescribably intense. The Uset vanished. Lachlaniel, once again blind, screamed at the top of his lungs. The last thing he had seen was a short bald man stumbling away from the road; his hands waving in front of him. Lachlaniel tried to spur Aman forward, but the good horse had been blinded for the moment by the burst of light. At Lachlaniel's urging, he moved haltingly forward. As his sight returned, he picked up speed. He stopped by the limp form still tied to the tree.

Lachlaniel cried and yelled, swinging his sword, hacking at invisible foes in his anger and his helplessness. He turned his steed off the road. Aman picked his way through the thick woods until a low branch knocked Lachlaniel from the saddle. He landed hard, saved by his armor from serious injury. He got up stunned and trying to breathe again.

"Which way? Which way?" He yelled again and again. He turned this way and that in dazed confusion. "I'll stop them! They'll never harm anyone again!"

He fell to the ground and wept uncontrollably. He rose to his hands and knees. His sides heaved amidst the sobs. He tried but couldn't get up. Aman walked over to his master and putting his nose under his master's chest tried to lift him to a sitting position. Lachlaniel grabbed the horse's bridle, and with his help, he reached his feet.

With tears still streaming down his face, he whispered, "Come on boy. Let's get back to the road."

> ...I must catch them and prevent this from happening ever again. Nothing must stand in my way. I will find them and kill them. They can't be allowed to do this to anyone, but especially to our people.
>
> There are days of hard riding ahead of me. Think of me, and when you think of me, petition the King for me. I love you.
>
> *Lachalniel*

Ignatius regained his sight as he continued to grope through the woods. It was of no use to him though since he had left the blinding brilliance of the dying woman far behind. He sat down in the darkness to rest and take stock, leaning his bald head back on the tree.

Why do these people insist on spreading their disgusting light? Why do so many of them have no fear of what the other Basaners and I do to them? And what happened when this one died? The light became so bright. I still haven't recovered. At least it's dark here. Now, how do I get back to familiar territory?

He got back up, turned carefully to the northwest, and picked his way through the woods on a course that would put him on the road well west of where the woman had been killed.

Lachlaniel and Aman arrived back on the road where the woman hung from the tree by the leather strap that still bound her lifeless hands. That spot in the road had been transformed when she died. There was light for fifty yards in every direction, even among the trees away from the road. It was not caused by her stone which lay below her knees at the base of the tree. This light was different. It gave a strange, unearthly beauty reminiscent of the wonders that lay beyond the Bridge. Everything on which the light fell was vibrant, vivid, and alive. Aman shook his head and snorted from time to time as though his eyes couldn't believe what they were seeing, but to Lachlaniel everything was black. The blindness had returned with her death. A shiver ran through his heart as though the cold wind of death had not only taken her life but had stripped the vitality from his own.

"Why did You let this happen? Why her? Why not me? You've abandoned me. I walk in darkness now. How long is it since I've heard Leofwine's sweet voice and smelled the blossoms of His presence?" Turning his face skyward he yelled. "Is there no end to my agony?"

He led Aman westward, down the road. Leofwine stood alone next to the girl. The scent of a strange fruit blossom filled the air.

"No Lachlaniel, I haven't abandoned you. I've never left your side any more than I ever left hers. Precious in the eyes of the King are the deaths of His Ebenchaim." He looked around satisfied at the light of this place that would never fade away. The woman disappeared from the tree and a fresh grave appeared nearby. He looked down the road. "I'll be watching you." He followed behind Lachlaniel at a distance.

It was a bright and beautiful morning. Aurora wanted to get to the Dispatch Office. Her letter to Lachlaniel was foremost in her mind and she almost ran past the dining room as she intended to skip breakfast. She was brought to a halt by a single yellow iris lying at her place at the table. She started to call up to Jocelyn to ask about it.

No. I don't want anyone to know about the flowers. It might get back to Lachlaniel. Jocelyn knows about the ones the other day. Maybe I should ask her. No. She may not know about the other times and think the ones at the door were a mistake. I'll leave it as is for now, but how did they get into the house?

May 17th

Lachlaniel my love,

Don't worry about the men that killed the woman. The King will take care of them. You focus on what you need to do. Don't let the anger eat at you. Be assured of my petitions on your behalf. I think of you always and talk of you to the King often.

Do be careful. I have a sense of foreboding about this. Let the King take care of it. Find a place where you can rest and take a few days off from your travels. I would rather have you home and in my arms than not home at all.

I wish Max or Ewald had more time. I could use someone to talk to. Their duties keep them quite busy. Farrah would be best of course, but like you she's hundreds of miles from here. Jocey, Cora, and Tova have their own families. Andre tries to cheer me up whenever he sees me, but it's you I want.

It's so hard being apart from you. Don't take chances. Bring me home the man I love.

𝓛𝓐

                                  Your loving,

                                  Aurora

    Aurora wandered in the park in the late morning. She was moody and deep in thought. The news of the destruction at the Dome of Meeting and more especially the deaths of the guards disturbed her.

    Her hair became tangled in some branches and brought her out of her reverie. She found that she had unwittingly wandered into the thicket at the middle of the park. With some difficulty, she freed her golden tresses from the small branches of a young sumac.

    What a mess. Which way leads out of here?

    The light filtered through the trees to her right. She picked her way among the saplings with care and soon was back into the open only to find Andre standing a short distance away. The leaves of a shrub rustled as she brushed past, and he looked in her direction.

    "Are you trying to blend in to the forest?"

    Aurora gave Andre a puzzled expression. He reached up and took two leafy twigs from her hair. She reddened and clapping her hand over her mouth she giggled.

    "Camouflage?" Andre asked with a laugh.

    "No." She recovered her composure. "I thought they would make a great tiara if you must know."

    Now it was Andre's turn to laugh. "Well, in that case, I'm sorry I removed them."

    He handed her the twigs which she promptly slid into her hair.

    "Very becoming." Andre smiled and raised an eyebrow.

    She laughed and they began walking through the park together.

    "What's the word from Lachlaniel? Will he start home soon?"

"My, no. He's only just begun the trip to the Great City. It will be months yet." she frowned.

Andre raised her chin. "Hey now. None of that. It's a beautiful spring day, and you're a pretty girl, so smile. The best way to brighten your day is to brighten someone else's. I'm sure there are dozens of people who would be cheered just by your smile."

A tear came to her eye.

Oh how I miss him!

He brushed away her tear, took her hand and kissed it.

"Don't be sad. What can I do to lift your spirits?"

"You're such a good friend. There's nothing. I just miss him so."

"You need something to take your mind off things. How about some lunch? I know a little inn that has a minstrel. We'll grab one of your sisters and put that smile back on your face."

Chapter 6
The Boy

May 23rd

Aurora,
    I cannot describe my feelings. I have never felt this way before. They've killed again. This time a young boy....

    Lachlaniel had driven Aman and himself hard for the past few days. There was still no sign of the men he sought. He brought Aman to a halt when the horse turned off the main road onto a deer path. He tried to steer the stallion back onto the road, but Aman insisted.
    "Okay boy, you've never led me wrong. You know who we're after. Take me to them."
    The trail seemed to continue on without end. As they went forward, the leaves began to brush Lachlaniel's face and sides.
    Perhaps we should turn around while we can. This trail's getting very narrow.
    No sooner had the thought crossed his mind than the trail widened again. Aman halted abruptly. He and Aman stood on a high ledge overlooking a clearing below. Lachlaniel was astonished as his sightless eyes again beheld a scene unfolding before him. The light of a stone illuminated the clearing and a small boy at play. Eight men entered the clearing.
    "Hey, boy. What are you doin' out here? And who gave you that stone?" the large man, who appeared to be the leader growled.
    Lachlaniel could hear every word distinctly. He watched from his perch as the boy bent down, picked up his stone, and backed away.
    "You can get one too. You just need to cross the Brid..."

He was cut short as the man grabbed the stone from his hands and flung it into the forest. There was a flash of light and the stone reappeared in the boy's hands.

"Huh? Give me that!"

The big man stepped forward and jerked the stone from the boy's hands again. He started to throw it harder into the forest. Then, an evil smile crossed his face.

"So, you like your precious stone, eh?"

The man started to throw the stone at the boy.

"You hurt that boy and I'll hunt you down and kill every one of you."

The man looked up at the ledge.

"How are you going to do that? There's no way down for miles," the man sneered.

Lachlaniel turned Aman away and headed back up the trail. Soon Aman found a trail to the right. In short order, they were descending steeply.

The man watched Lachlaniel turn, and then, threw the stone at the boy. The boy caught it as though he were playing toss with his dad. The man grew red in the face and looked around. He spied the abundance of rocks in the clearing and once again smiled.

"Everyone grab a rock! You like them so much, well, you're gonna have your fill."

"No!" Ignatius screamed. "He's only a child!"

"What? Are you squeamish? Maybe when we get through with the kid we'll start on you!"

Ignatius picked up a rock. The big man threw one at the boy. The boy yelled and fell on his side, but got up. The others followed the leader's example. The boy cried out as he fell and lay whimpering on the ground as the other rocks continued to pummel him. Ignatius looked at the rock and then the boy.

"You gonna throw that or is my next one gonna be aimed for your head?"

The other men paused looking at Ignatius. Ignatius threw the rock half heartedly at the small bleeding form. His head reeled and his stomach heaved. He turned and headed for the woods as the big man's laughter filled his ears. The screams of the child echoed in his mind. He thought of the helpless form lying on the ground. He fell on his knees, and retched.

Lachlaniel reached level ground after half an hour of following the ups and downs of the trail. Aman turned for the clearing without any prodding. There was no one there, only a heap of rocks. The light glowed as it had at the scene of the woman's death, but this time Lachlaniel could see. He dismounted and bent over the heap. Gently, he began removing the rocks revealing the boy's broken form. The boy coughed spitting blood.

"Alive! He's alive!"

Lachlaniel started lifting him, but stopped when the boy winced at the movement of his broken arms. Lachlaniel brushed the boy's hair back out of his eyes.

"Why do they hate the light?" the boy said weakly.

"I don't know, son."

"What happened to my stone? It's dark."

"Your stone is here. You just can't see it right now."

"That's good. I wouldn't want to lose my stone. Why am I so cold?"

"You'll be warm in a few minutes," Lachlaniel choked back tears. Those men, who were they?" Lachlaniel asked softly.

"Why?" the boy whispered.

"Because, I'm going to stop them from doing this to anyone else."

"No. You mustn't." The boy coughed again. "Eleutherias wanted me to come here. He cares for those m...."

Silence filled Lachlaniel's ears as a brilliant light filled the forest. His sight dimmed, but before it was gone he saw a short bald haired man at the edge of the forest.

"You! You were one of the ones that killed the woman."

The man said nothing. He began backing away into the forest without making a sound.

Lachlaniel rose with clenched fists as the sight vanished and the blackness of his visionless night returned.

"I'm going to kill you. Did You Hear Me! **I'M GOING TO KILL YOU!**"

He ran to the spot where the man had been, drawing his sword as he went. He swung viciously for several minutes leaving big gashes in trees and slicing through saplings, but the man was long gone.

...It was a long time before I settled back down enough to even think about going on. I don't understand these people, but I'm going to put an end to these atrocities. I can't get the death of the boy and woman out of my mind. It's all I think about. I haven't eaten in days, and I've barely slept. I wish I had never left your side. All I have here is blackness. The blackness before my eyes and the blackness of my thoughts. I long to be with you.

Yours always,

Lachalniel

Ignatius ran through the woods blindly. When it was totally dark once more, he sat down, breathing heavily.

"Why did they have to kill the boy? He's only a child, or he was." He hung his head and cried. Through his tears he said, "I hate the light and the people that carry the stones as much as anyone, but children? They don't know any better. Why kill them?"

The images of the child as the rocks ripped his body and broke his bones were too much. Ignatius fell to his hands and knees and retched. His stomach continued to heave for some minutes even though it was empty.

"I'm going home," he said to the empty air. "At least there we don't kill children."

Leofwine watched him go. "It's not much, but it's a start. In due time, Ignatius. In due time, you'll learn to love the light and you'll cross the Bridge. In due time."

Max waited near the Tower's southern entrance. He was tired and some of his men nodded off from time to time. Early on, they had engaged in the small talk common to men in the King's army, but by the beginning of the third watch, quiet settled in, and other than a word spoken now and again, silence dominated. Max now spent his time calling out men as they nodded and keeping them alert.

Looks like nothing's happening tonight. I thought for sure this would get him. Maybe tomorrow night.

He heaved a sigh at the thought.

At least the men can rest during the days now. It was hard for them working double shifts today and tonight as well. I hope it doesn't take long before this works.

The door opened and the commander stepped inside.

"A-ten-tion!" Max growled.

The men scrambled to their feet and stood stiff and unblinking.

"At ease. We're done for tonight. He struck at the King-steward's residence."

"Did we catch him?" one of the men asked.

"No. He's extremely good at what he does. With all our precautions, he still killed three men and injured a fourth."

"How? Max asked.

"Like at the Dome, he used darts. Whatever he's using to fire them has a tremendous range for such a weapon. One of the crossbowmen saw him on a roof over 200 feet from the men that were hit. He fired at the man, but it was at the limit of his crossbow's range. He just hit his left arm. We don't know how badly he was hit, but be on the lookout for a man with an injured left arm. It could be slight and look like simple soreness or it could have made it immobile or even broken it."

One of the guards shifted his weight to his other foot and looked expectantly at the commander. "So we're not staying here?"

"No. We don't expect him to attack for at least a day. Whatever state the arm is in he'll need treatment. We intend to watch anyone that has experience in healing or in treating wounds. Hopefully he'll be caught before the end of the day."

Max's jaw tightened and his brow furrowed. "What about our man that survived? How serious is his wound?"

"He was using poison darts."

The men grumbled and anger filled every face.

The commander continued, "Sergeant Will was the last man hit. If he hadn't been diving for cover the dart would have killed him too. As it is, it only broke the skin on his upper arm and he still may not survive. It's almost the end of the fourth watch. Let the other men know and you can all go home and get some sleep at the changing of the guard."

"We'll maintain triple the guards on the tower entrances," Max said flatly.

A couple of men headed for the inn and the threshing floor, and the two guards for the south door returned to their posts. Max shook his head.

"We must catch him," he said half to himself.

The commander looked over his shoulder as he stood in the door.

"We will, Max. We will."

Max watched Andre carefully as he went about the house getting ready to leave for the day. He showed no sign of difficulty with his shoulder. Max requested steak for breakfast, but even while cutting it Andre used his left hand normally and there was no sign of pain crossing his face.

Perhaps my efforts would best be directed elsewhere. Surely an injury to that arm would be giving him significant pain with all he's done this morning. I think I'll have someone follow him anyway. Better to be safe than sorry.

"Excuse me." Max rose from his seat.

"Where are you going Max?" Andre smiled.

"Something I just remembered that needs tending to." He stepped into the living room and called out in his booming voice, "Bercan! Ho, Bercan me lad!"

Bercan raced down the stairs. "Yes sir?"

"Come with me." Max led him out the door so that they wouldn't be heard. "Go to the barracks and get someone who isn't going on duty this morning. Bring him back here double quick. When you get back, make sure he's well hidden; then, come in by yourself."

"Yes sir!" He ran off down the street, his gangly form taking great strides. He rounded a corner and was lost to view.

Good lad. Hurry. I don't know how long before Andre will try to leave.

He returned to the table and resumed the meal. He looked at Andre's plate.

He'll be done in a few moments.

"Would you care for more Andre?"

"No. I think this will be sufficient."

"What are your plans for the day?"

Andre leaned back and smiled. He chewed the steak in his mouth hurriedly so as to be able to answer, dabbing his mouth with his napkin. "I had intended to work more on the dress I had started, but I don't quite like how it's going. I think I'll visit the cloth shops and maybe the jeweler. It'll give me time to think and work out the design problems in my head."

"Is this the dress you're giving Aurora for her birthday?"

"Yes. I want it to be right for her and it feels off somehow. For any other woman it would be fine, but you know Aurora. The clothes she chooses light up a room when she enters."

"That's just her. She has a luminescent personality."

"That's only part of it. She has a knack for wearing clothes that accentuate her luminescence. I want this present to crown her beauty with a *savoir fare,* a... Oh, what is the word? An elegance. Yes that's it. An elegance that will grab people's attention."

"I don't think little sis needs anything to grab people's attention. She does that quite nicely on her own."

"Yes, she does at that. But I want it to... Aw, I don't know. Perhaps my inability to articulate what I want is linked to the failure of my present design. Maybe the walk and the thinking will clear my thoughts."

"It does sound that way. I can't really say I see what you mean. It's very abstract at this point."

Andre frowned. "Yes. It is, isn't it?" He laid his fork and knife by his plate and pushed his seat back. "I should get started. I'm not going to get it right sitting here gabbing."

I've got to stall him.

"Have another cup of coffee. Maybe that will clear away the cobwebs."

"No. I want to get going."

"You won't make any progress without a clear head. Sit back down and have another cup."

Andre hesitated. "Maybe you're right." He sat back down. "But only half a cup."

"Mrs. Hughes! More coffee for Andre if you please."

At that moment, a breathless Bercan entered the living room.

"Sir. I must see you."

Good boy.

Max's brow furrowed. "I wonder what that's about."

He excused himself again and followed Bercan outside leaving Andre to finish his coffee by himself.

"Just in time, lad. Who'd you bring?"

"Asher Kenspeckle."

"Asher!? He's the most arrant, boisterous man in the whole of the city guards. Wasn't there *anyone* else? His presence will be glaring."

"Sorry sir. He was the only one. Everyone else had left already."

"I guess he'll have to do. If we catch him with Asher on his tail, it'll be a miracle. Where is he?"

A loud, obnoxious voice resounded in song from across the street. A look of extreme pain crossed Max's face as he shook his head.

"Go on about your duties Bercan boy. I'll try and convince our 'spy' to stop squawking like a couple of courting geese."

Chapter 7
Asher Kenspeckle

Aurora finished her breakfast and stepped into the living room. She stopped abruptly. There, in her favorite chair lay a perfect, fresh gardenia.

May 25th

Lachlaniel my love,

    I can't imagine what you're going through. Don't let it eat at you like this. The King will take care of those men like I said before. I hurt for the boy and the woman too, but you can't do anything for them now. Lay it aside, beloved, or it will destroy you. Oh, lay it aside Lachlaniel! I can't bear the thought of losing you! Lay it aside for my sake and for yours.

LA

                                        Your own,

                                        Aurora

It was early morning. The wind was hot and dry as it swept into the trees from the fields beyond. Lachlaniel was sullen. Aman plodded along. Having lost the trail of the killers, there didn't seem to be any great hurry, nor any particular destination except the eventual one of the Great City. He had made good time, so he was content to make this a day of rest letting Aman dictate the pace. Near mid-morning he approached a river. As the horse placed a hoof on the bridge, he shied, backing suddenly away.

"What is it boy?" Lachlaniel asked.

Aman neighed in reply. He urged the horse forward. As he too came onto the bridge, he felt it. He couldn't put it into words, but he became abruptly uneasy. As they came to solid ground, he drew his sword.

I don't like it. There is something evil about this place. It's like the very air is malevolent.

He clutched his sword and urged Aman forward. They rode on until evening. Nothing else changed, but both he and the horse were restless and uneasy.

Andre left the house and headed toward the market near the gate.

This birthday dress for Aurora is interfering with the sabotage. Or at least it was until last night.

He started to rub his shoulder as he came to the corner, but when he heard someone whistling a tune some distance behind him, he continued the natural swing of his arms. He turned the corner instead of going straight in order to get a view of the people behind him. There were just five people and three were women. Of the two men, one was a stocky fellow with red hair, orange trousers, a green shirt and bright blue boots. The other man was walking the opposite direction. Andre laughed to himself.

That fellow will stand out in a crowd. If he's following me, I'll have no trouble knowing it.

He headed for the next corner and was about to turn back to his right when he heard the tune to "All the King's Men" come floating down the street. He looked back and there was the garish fellow merrily whistling.

At least he whistles well. That's a horrible tune. We'll see soon enough if he's following. There's a jewelry shop ahead.

Andre winced as he turned the handle.

I mustn't do that again even though it's hurting more. No one has noticed yet, but these streets are almost empty. There'll be a lot more people near the gate.

He entered the shop and perused the merchandise near the window. The red haired man turned into a basket weavers across the street. Andre wandered through the store always keeping his eye on the store across the street. After almost half an hour, he headed for the door empty handed. He hadn't taken three steps when he heard a door behind him and a new tune filled the air.

Andre looked toward the sky as if asking for help.

Must I listen to every tune that praises the King today? How can I get rid of this bumpkin?

A sly smile crossed his lips.

Lachlaniel finished his lunch and prepared to resume the day's journey. He continued down the road. It had been following a stream which was a tributary of the river he'd crossed earlier. He hadn't gone far when it entered a forest. A few miles further, a trail emptied onto the road. As he approached it, a man with a light emerged. Lachlaniel drew the horse up having heard the man's boots slapping the road with each stride.

"Hello." he called to the man.

"Hello. And who might you be?" The man's tone had a note of wariness and he eyed Lachlaniel with caution. "There are few travelers on this road these days. At least, few going your direction."

"I'm Lachlaniel. I come from the city of the Great Stone Agapay."

"I'm Elrad. I serve the King. I see you carry a stone. Have you crossed the Bridge, not the one a few miles back, the King's Bridge?"

"Yes."

"Good. Have you ever been to this region before, or are you new here?" Elrad inquired as he looked the stranger over.

"Why?"

Elrad rubbed the bristly whiskers on his chin as he apprized the stranger before him. "You should be prepared for attacks."

"I don't understand."

"Of course you don't. Forgive me. You come from far away. The nearest great city, other than ours, must be hundreds of leagues from here." He paused contemplating how best to make the stranger understand. "The towns from the Skotos River, which you crossed a few miles back, to the Kerry, which is far beyond the great city, are ruled by men who desire to keep their people in darkness. Only around the Great City is it safe for the Ebenchaim. Of course that is a huge area, perhaps two hundred miles across, but it's grown smaller over the years. The rulers of the towns except for the Great City and those towns near it send out men called Basaners to capture and kill the King's servants.

The Basaners! That's who those men were!

Lachlaniel's face flushed and fire filled his eyes.

"Now I know why I've been summoned to the city. I must rouse the Ebenchaim and lead them into battle against the Basaner's."

"You don't understand the situation here. Perhaps we should travel together for a ways. We're going the same direction and I can fill you in, as long as you don't mind a slower pace. I have no horse, you see."

Lachlaniel smiled a wry smile.

No I don't see.

"That's ok. My horse and I are weary with our travels. A slower pace and a friendly voice would be welcome."

They plodded along in the afternoon sun as Elrad continued, "Those captured by the Basaners are put to unspeakable agonies to try to make them renounce their allegiance to the King, or for the depraved enjoyment of seeing them in torment. They used to try taking the stones from them but they found that impossible. Nor can they keep us long from our closets, but those things just enrage them all the more. Only in the Great City is it safe to be known as the King's servant, and even there we are not well liked anymore."

"Safe? Why do you say it's safe?"

"Kieran's governor here is Mephosphilis. He is known to be one who sympathizes with those in darkness, trying to get them to turn to the light, but it's not so. It's a lie of his own contrivance. He's subtle and devious, more so than Kieran's other servants. He would spread a lake of truth to hide one lie if that lie would poison the waters. He has many under his rule believing the light is evil, and in the Great City he's lulled most of the King's people into sleep and apathy. He is hideously evil though his lies about himself have masked his true nature and have given him a fair form. He hasn't moved against Chara yet, but many of us believe he will soon. Until he does, it's safe for us there, more or less."

"Can you lead me to those who live and work for the King in the shadow of this evil?"

"I can, but it isn't yet prudent to do so. I must grow to know you, and I must confer long with the King before taking such a step. The enemy would love to infiltrate our ranks, and he has done so often in the past. As I say, his ways are subtle and devious, but the journey will give us time to get acquainted."

The wind rustled the leaves in the warmth of the late afternoon. They told each other about their lives, and the day passed much more quickly for Lachlaniel than it had in many days. Elrad noticed, after some time, that Lachlaniel permitted the horse to move as it chose.

After watching them closely for most of the afternoon, he said, "You're blind aren't you?"

"Yes," Lachlaniel said.

"I meant neither harm nor offense in the asking, and take none at my next question whether you answer it or no. How did it happen?"

"I was attacked by Solveig before I could reach the Great City and cross the chasm."

"What persuaded you to go on?"

"Leofwine came and urged me not to go home. He directed me to Eleutherias who showed me the chasm and the Bridge. He helped me to cross and gave me a reason to live."

"And what was that?" Elrad asked, his eyes brightening and a smile coming to his face.

"I live to serve the King."

Elrad could see the change in Lachlaniel's countenance as he spoke of Leofwine and Eleutherias. It was clear he loved them deeply. Elrad rubbed the bristle on his chin and smiled a great smile.

"Tell me what happened," Elrad said.

Lachlaniel told Elrad about his experiences from the time he first saw the light until he crossed the Bridge. As he finished, he could feel the chill in the air as night came and brought with it a cool, evening breeze.

"Is it always this cool at night in the summer?"

"It's a little cooler than normal, and the breeze is off the lakes to our south."

"It will be too cold tonight to sleep out," Lachlaniel said thinking aloud. "Is there some place warm where we can bed down?"

"Not too far ahead is a road on the left that leads to an abandoned hut. That should serve our purposes for the evening. The owner was a friend."

"What happened to him?"

"He was taken by the Basaners from a town south of here. I don't know what happened to him. We never heard from him again."

They traveled on in silence. The trees creaked in the rising wind. Distant thunder began to make itself known. The trees on the left thinned revealing the farmland beyond. Shortly, they came to a road on the left. Turning up it, a tiny house on a hill was revealed by the light of their stones. Rain began falling as Lachlaniel dismounted. He led Aman under an awning at the side and tied him there for the night. It wasn't much but at least the horse would be out of the wind and rain.

The house wasn't much either. The awning was low and Lachlaniel bumped his head as he tried to get to the front door. Inside, the shack was a single room without even a fireplace. Bare rafters lay above their heads. The single, small window was broken letting in a draft, but otherwise it was tight and dry. Elrad was right when he called it a hut. If it had been larger with no floor, it could have been a very small barn. But other than the draft from the window, it was reasonably warm. The blankets of their bedding would keep them quite comfortable as they slept. Lachlaniel hung his cape over the window to keep out some of the night air in the hope it would make the room warmer, and they settled in for the night.

The market was crowded as Andre had expected. Each time he bumped into someone or they brushed his shoulder, pain shot down his arm, but he refused to show it.

There's his tune again. Barely audible above the noise of this crowd. My arm's going to be useless for a while after this. Where's that bypath? There it is!

A narrow alley of dealer's booths appeared on the left as he moved through the press. He managed to get over to it. It was hardly wide enough for the people standing at the booths on each side. He pressed through those along its path, which were fewer than might have been considering the crowds that were about this day. The last booths were empty as usual, and he swiftly rounded the corner into the backstreet where dealers brought their merchandise to fill the stores and booths of the market.

At last! Now to lose that bumpkin.

He raced down the alley past the few out going carts of merchants and teamsters that had delivered their loads. Soon he was standing beneath the gates. He made his way north and west into the heart of the city near the Great Dome. The afternoon was spent winding his way back and forth, back tracking, and doing everything he could to make sure he wasn't followed. As evening drew on, he flitted from corner to corner and doorway to doorway until he was in the backstreets of the northwest corner of the city. There he entered a ramshackle edifice.

Max eyed his flamboyant underling. "You did good Asher. Your whistling alerted a quarter of the city guards. I had to send most of them back to their posts. Unfortunately, we lost him in the twilight."

"Then, it was for nothing?"

"No. We know the ward where he went. There are no residences there, and we caught an old man with no stone trying to make his way back into the heart of the city. His accomplice, no doubt. He refuses to talk, but at least that avenue of aid is no longer open to him. I'm certain Andre's our man. But without proof..."

Asher gave a dejected glance at the floor and shuffled his feet. "What do we do now?"

"Wait and watch. Andre will be under constant surveillance from now on. He's as slippery as an eel. Even with half a dozen men watching him I can't help but feel he'll slip the net and do us more harm, but that's as many as we dare put on his trail."

"Time to petition the King for help?" Asher suggested.

They entered their closets for an audience with His Majesty.

Rain cooled air slithered through the window in spite of Lachlaniel's cloak and slid across the floor to the sleeping men. They shifted with the change in temperature, and pulled the covers tightly around themselves. The soothing patter of rain on the roof coaxed them back into sound slumber.

It was late in the fourth watch, and four men crept stealthily up to the hut through the steady rain. Light from the stones issued from the window as the edges of Lachlaniel's cloak fluttered lightly in the rain inspired zephyr. The men circled to make sure there was no other exit. They came round by the awning where Lachlaniel's horse was tied. Surprised by the men, he snorted and tried to pull loose from the tether. The men moved swiftly and almost soundlessly to the front door. They burst through to find Elrad and Lachlaniel had been roused by the noise of the horse. Lachlaniel held his sword in his hand.

They tried to attack even though they only had clubs. Lachlaniel used the flat of his blade and disarmed the first two. The third managed to strike home, but the blow was deflected by Lachlaniel's shield. The fourth, seeing their attack foiled by a determined foe, fled. The first two picked up their clubs and also beat a hasty retreat. The third man held his ground to guard their escape but began backing towards the door. Lachlaniel threatened to strike, and the man turned to head out through the doorway. As he did so, Lachlaniel struck him on the backside with the flat of his blade and he ran off screaming into the night.

Elrad looked at his companion, a twinkle in his eyes. He was impressed by Lachlaniel's restraint. "The rain stopped. Perhaps we should move on before they return with others."

"A prudent suggestion," Lachlaniel replied sheathing his sword.
I wonder who they were?

"Either robbers or Basaners," Elrad said in answer to the unspoken question.

"Basaners! I should have killed them!"

The Chuchoteur responded to the sudden outburst of rage.
Murderers! They deserve to die!

"No!" Elrad protested. "That isn't the way. The King has given orders for those in this region. We must not retaliate."

"*Not retaliate!?* Do you know the sort of things they do?"

Pain crossed Elrad's face and a tear formed in his eye. "Yes I know. I've lost three friends and two family members to their atrocities. The bodies we recovered were mutilated. Yes I know. But I also know that for the deaths of those five people at least three dozen have crossed the Bridge."

That doesn't matter. Retribution. That's what matters. Vengeance! A quick death is too good for them. They must be made to suffer as they have made others suffer!

Lachlaniel's jaw tightened and his face fused into features of stone in the shape of hatred and rage.

Elrad stared at the transformation, appalled at the suddenness and extent of the change.

"The King will deal with them. It's not our place..."

His voice trailed off. Thinking quickly, he changed the subject. "We should check on your horse."

"I'll see to him." Lachlaniel's voice was harsh and abrupt. He left the hut; his boots striking the ground with determination and his hands alternately and involuntarily clenching into fists and relaxing.

It was much longer than it should have been before he returned. They finished packing in silence and were soon back on the road as a warm morning breeze greeted the new day.

Chapter 8
Know Your Enemy

A warm breeze greeted the new day in Agapay as well, but Aurora shuddered. Where would the flowers show up next? She turned toward the window and terror entered the room. She squealed as shivers ran up and down her spine. On the sill lay a red rose.

The air of summer wafted through Aurora's hair and caressed her cheek as though to comfort her while the birds sang "cheer up, cheer up". Her heart still fluttered as she entered the office of the correspondence dispatcher to pick up a letter from Lachlaniel. Fear dogged her steps as she headed for one of her favorite places, a bench in a park near the Dome of Meeting. The scent of honeysuckle and roses filled the air. The tree over the bench had magnificent orange colored blossoms, and the nearby shrubs lent their white, yellow, and deep red flowers to provide dazzling color to the secluded area. Aurora sat down to read. She had just begun the letter when Andre walked up.

"Hello Aurora. Has the light grown dim? No, it's just a sad face on Lachlaniel's girl. Why so sad? Is it bad news from him?"

"Hello, Andre." She put Lachlaniel's letter aside and smiled at her new friend as she mentally shifted from her troubles to the concerns she had for Lachlaniel. "No. Well at least not the way you might think. He's so angry over what's been happening there. And he's lost his ability to perceive things. I know he was used to living in the darkness for years before he crossed the Bridge, but this is different than farming in the dark. There'll be battles and dangers he's never faced before, dangers I can't even imagine. I'm worried." Her head drooped and a tear splashed on the letter she held.

Andre sat down and put his arm around her shoulder. "He's a grown man who's been in battle before. Besides won't the King take care of him?"

She looked him in the eye. The mentioning of the King sent a shaft of light through her gloom, but the clouds remained. She gave a weak smile at the comfort Andre gave.

"Of course that's true, but it's so easy to lose sight of. Doubts and fears assail me often. I miss him so."

Andre smiled, "Come with me."

He took her hand and gently pulled her from her seat. She resisted but only for a moment.

"Where are we going?"

"I have something to show you."

They made their way from the park to a street near Max's house. She followed him inside the shop of a dressmaker.

"Now you stay here. I'll be right back."

Andre stepped through the curtains in the back of the store. In a moment he returned with a dress form on which a magnificent light blue satin dress rested. It had a golden velvet collar and gold buttons down the front to the waist. The shoulders billowed into long, pleated sleeves that ended in frilly gold cuffs. The bottom fell in gathers almost to the floor where gold fringe was attached to the hem.

Aurora gasped. "Oh, Andre! It's beautiful!"

"Then, put it on. It's yours."

"Mine? No. No, I couldn't."

"Nonsense. I was saving it for your birthday. I know that's still a couple of weeks off, but you could use something to lift your spirits and it's at the point where it needs alterations for a proper fit."

"Oh, Andre."

Andre smiled, "Don't just stand there with your hand over your mouth. Go put it on."

"Go on, girl," Emmett, the shopkeeper, chimed in with a smile.

Aurora returned to the bench in the park. The light of the late afternoon sun filtered through the trees, and an occasional cricket could be heard from somewhere in the deep shade. She began reading Lachlaniel's letter again.

June 9th

Dear Aurora,

A couple of days ago I crossed some sort of boundary. I felt a sudden change as though the wind shifted and it became cold. Not that anything outward had changed. It was a beautiful summer day and continued to be, but the nature of the evil in this area was different, though I didn't understand it at the time. This area is ruled by a very different governor of Kieran. He doesn't make outright attacks on the Ebenchaim. Instead, he sends out Basaners, human torturers, who track down the Kings servants. That's what the groups that killed the woman and the boy were, Basaners. They were far from their normal territory from what I understand. I am sure this is why the King sent me here. I must find a way to stop them.

I appreciate your petitions on my behalf. My blindness continues as does my longing for you. I love you more than I can express. I hope all is well with you. I look forward to your next letter. They are precious to me. I miss you terribly.

LA

Love,

Lachlaniel

Aurora's face paled as she finished Lachlaniel's letter.

Torturers? What kind of land is it that my beloved has entered? How can he avoid these Basaners?

Fear gripped her heart.

I'll find Max. He might know something we can do.

Aurora ran through the streets toward the tower. Max and Ewald were just leaving at the end of their duty shifts when Aurora arrived.

Breathless, she managed to blurt out, "Oh, Max! Lachlaniel is in trouble. He's in a land where the King's people are hunted and tortured!"

Max grabbed her hands to steady her and knowingly asked, "Have you talked to the King about it?"

She breathed in deeply and let out a heavy sigh. "No." She paused and looked at the ground avoiding his gaze. "That would have been the first thing Farrah would do. Why can't I be more like my little sister?" Tears of shame came to her eyes. "Is there anything else we can do?"

"Talk to the King while I think about it."

Aurora knelt as a golden glow surrounded her and a door appeared. She entered her closet while Max and Ewald sat down on a bench on the corner near the tower's entrance.

She crossed the Throne room and knelt before the King. "My Lord, I'm worried about Lachlaniel."

"Don't be." The King brushed away her tears. "I know you fear what the Basaners will do if they catch him, but he must see firsthand their methods and atrocities. He has much to learn. I will look after him so don't fear."

"Isn't there anything I or his friends can do to help him?"

"You will. All in due time. Rest easy," He said with a conclusive air.

"Thank you. I'll try."

"All will be well."

Aurora smiled faintly and turned to leave.

Max studied Aurora's expression as she exited her closet. She smiled but her lip quivered. Max knew her thoughts. She had heard the King say what she wanted to hear, or half of what she wanted to hear, but she was still worried whatever she had heard. He put his arm around her.

"We're going to ask Kesniel to send us along with maybe a hundred men to help Lachlaniel."

"Oh, how wonderful!" Aurora said misinterpreting Max's words. "I'll start getting ready"

"No, you must stay here. It's much too dangerous for you."

"But I must go too. I must see him!"

"No. If you think it's dangerous for Lachlaniel, how much more so would it be for you."

Aurora's heart climbed to her throat as tears welled up in her eyes.

"Am I to be left behind with nothing to do but worry?"

"I thought we just covered that. What would Farrah do if it were Velius?"

The tears could no longer be constrained. "She would be in her closet with the King almost constantly. But Lachlaniel isn't Velius. He's much younger and less experienced. And he's blind"

"Have confidence in your man," Max chided. "Lachlaniel is a great warrior in spite of his blindness, and no doubt the King is using this very situation to give him the experience he lacks. He'll be alright. Isn't that what the King said?"

Aurora hesitated.

"Yes." Her voice was tinged with reluctance. "But I want to go," she pleaded.

"Even if I was so foolish as to allow it, do you think Kesniel would? No. If it came to that, Kesniel would keep us all here rather than allow you to go into such danger. Besides, Lachlaniel will do much better if he doesn't have to worry about your safety."

"I know you're right, but I still want to go. I don't think any of your arguments will make me feel better about staying here. I know there's nothing I could do there to help, and I would be in the way, but I can't bear the thought of him in danger and me comfortable here at home."

"You've done what you can. If you hadn't told us, he'd have no help at all. Now, you go home and we'll go talk to Kesniel."

Aurora turned for home, tears welling up in her eyes. Max watched her trudge down the street as though she had a heavy load. Ewald had sat listening through the whole spectacle, thinking.

"Perhaps we should get her sisters to keep her busy so she won't think so much about it."

Max nodded. "It's a good idea. It might not work, but it's worth a try."

They headed to the shops in the hope of catching Jocelyn before she got home and from there they went to the council chambers at the Dome of Meeting."

A wolf howled in the distance. Lachlaniel drew his sword as he listened intently for answering calls. The sound of the sword being drawn from its sheath startled Elrad.

"Why did you draw your sword?" Elrad asked puzzled.

"Didn't you hear the wolf?"

"Yes. What of it?"

"We must be prepared for their attack."

"Wolves won't attack unless they're ravenous. There's too much game here."

"They're agents of the enemy."

"Not here. They may have attacked you when you were trying to reach the chasm and cross the Bridge, but the wolves here are not like your wolves. You can put your sword away."

Lachlaniel sheathed his sword, but he was uneasy in doing so. The bond between the two men had grown, but it wasn't yet strong enough for Lachlaniel to totally trust this new friend. They continued on in silence for some time with Lachlaniel straining to hear every sound near and far. Gradually his tension eased.

Finally, Elrad broke the silence, "If you're willing, I'll introduce you to a friend."

"Certainly, but what convinced you to trust me?"

"Your reaction to the wolf and the way you've acted since. I can tell you've been tensed for action. You've constantly been turning this way and that, listening."

"I've had many battles with the wolves. They run in great numbers most of the time. They are not to be taken lightly. I knew a great warrior who downed fifty as they attacked him. Warriors like him are few and far between."

"As I told you, the wolves here aren't like that. Mephosphilis doesn't use them or the more deadly of our adversaries. I'm sure he has them in reserve if he needs them, but he chooses a deadlier opponent, men. Men who do not serve the King can be blacker at heart than the darkness they live in. I don't think you yet understand the depths of depravity to which the darkness takes them." Then, he added, "But you will."

Lachlaniel fell silent at the ominous tone Elrad had sounded. It rang true with the apprehension he had felt when he crossed the bridge over the Skotos. Someone who had not seen battle might have turned back at the disquieting and overarching fear that made its presence known more and more as they traveled deeper into this land. On the other hand, there weren't many who could sense the presence of evil as keenly as Lachlaniel. He didn't know how greatly the King had blessed him with the ability to perceive his surroundings both physical and non-physical. Lachlaniel tried for a few moments to absorb what he had been told and what he felt.

"I don't understand. It seems as though you're telling me you don't need warriors."

"We don't. At least, not in the sense you mean."

"Then, what *do* you need?"

"Many things. Here the King's servants can neither buy nor sell except from each other. Any other who sells to us is tortured or killed, and we have little to offer each other. We urgently need those of the King's servants who are well off to share with us. We need to know we are not alone. But most importantly, we need men – warriors who can stand up to the punishment the enemy hands out without flinching and without retaliating."

Lachlaniel hung his head.

The King's people forced to do without food and the necessities of life? Hunted like animals and tortured? How can this be?! It must be stopped!

That's right. Revenge! We must avenge them! The Chuchoteur chimed in.

"Something must be done!"

Elrad didn't answer, and Lachlaniel's words hung in the air. The freshness of the morning and prospects of the new day had grown stale. The Chuchoteur was delighted.

"He showed her the dress today." Emmett held his hands behind his back like a school boy as he reported to Max. "He said she had gotten a letter from Lachlaniel that upset her."

"She did. She's very worried about him." Max raised an eyebrow and sighed. "I'm more worried about her. She seems completely taken in by Andre. Innocent soul; she sees good in him. I don't know where, but she sees it."

"And you don't?"

"No." Max paused a moment. "He did take me in the first few days, but I think he's our man. What do you think? You work closely with him."

"He's very personable, charming even."

"But?"

"But he's not a man you want to make mad. We had a cat."

"Had?" Max broke in.

"Yes, had. The cat liked Andre. He kept rubbing his legs and purring while Andre was working. More than once the cat tripped him up. Three days ago the cat died. Poisoned. I can't prove it was him, but I have no doubts. There has to be a way to catch him."

"All we can do is wait and watch. Sooner or later he'll make a mistake. You've done well. Now out the back way and continue to keep an eye on him."

"What will you do?"

"I'm going to assign two men to watch Aurora. He seems to be targeting her as well."

"Will two be enough?"

"Considering that they'll be watching her only when I can't, yes I think two will be enough."

Emmett raised an eyebrow. "You? You're not easy to hide."

Max smiled. "Have you ever seen me trying to hide?"

Emmett's face changed to one of deep thought. "No."

"Then, I must do it well enough."

A late afternoon lunch had not improved Lachlaniel's somber mood, and he continued to brood as the two men continued their journey. They began a descent as the road followed a rill in a deep ravine to lower land. The forest ended before they reached bottom, and they exited onto a broad grassy plain. A short way later they reached a fork in the road. They took the branch that curved sharply southward. Throughout the early evening, they moved between the fields where the grass waved in the light breeze.

The light from their stones illuminated only the horses' hooves and their next few steps, but sounds could be heard at a great distance here. There were cows lowing far away to their right. Birds chirped and sang from some tree or bushes to their left, and more than once or twice, unknown creatures crossed the road in the darkness ahead of them. At the end of an uneventful day, they approached a house among some trees on their right. Lachlaniel could not see it, of course, but Elrad described it to him as they headed toward it. It was a small structure almost obscured by the bushes that surrounded it. It couldn't have contained more than three or four rooms. There was a porch whose roof had collapsed on the far end. The windows were tightly boarded up. On the roof lay several bricks that had been dislodged from the ancient chimney. They moved to the back and across a small empty yard to a dilapidated barn that stood alone, apart from the trees. They stopped and dismounted. The barn door creaked and an elderly man came out and took their horses in silence. His presence seemed to have a calming effect on the already tranquil creatures.

"Who was that?" Lachlaniel whispered.

Elrad smiled and a silent laugh vented through his nose. "I don't even know his name. He's good with animals though. When he's around they never make a sound."

The wind rustled through the trees and danced through their hair while insects buzzed busily about them. The smell of crushed clover made itself known as they crossed the yard to the back of the house.

There was no sound from the house as they climbed onto the back stoop where the steps had once stood. The little ancient landing groaned under their weight.

I hope this doesn't collapse.

Elrad answered Lachlaniel's thought, "Don't worry. We've reinforced it underneath where it can't be seen." Elrad knocked three times, paused, and knocked twice more. A large man opened the door and ushered them inside. They were in a small kitchen with a door on the walls to the left and right. The smell of rust and soot permeated the tiny space emanating from a moribund stove on the far wall. The man opened the door on their left and the light of several stones filled the hallway. They entered to find seven men, three women, and several children filling the room to capacity. They sat in a circle on the floor around the walls leaving just enough space for the two new comers to sit in the middle. There were no furnishings of any kind. The boarded windows reflected every sound as though intent on withholding from the outside world the joy the room contained. Elrad introduced Lachlaniel to the group. They then began softly singing praises to the King.

"Why are they so quiet?" Lachlaniel asked.

"Even here, miles from the nearest town, it isn't completely safe. You never know when a group of the Basaners will come by looking for someone to haul before the magistrates or worse yet, the Fragel."

"What's a Fragel?"

"A man who oversees the torture of prisoners."

Lachlaniel's anger at the mere mention of the Basaners was first soothed and then totally displaced by the blissful effervescence of the rejoicing ringing in his ears.

I don't understand. Forced into hiding without a fight, tortured and brutalized and yet these people...

A tear came to his eye and intense pride filled his chest. He shook his head.

They have such joy. They're so close to Him. How can this be? I have never felt anything like this! My knowledge of Him seems so paltry compared to theirs. Yet I have led an army in His name, defeated enemies, overcome obstacles.

He hung his head in shame. The Chuchoteur squirmed with nothing to rebut the overwhelming argument of joy.

Lachlaniel excused himself. The kitchen was all but silent. Only glimmers of song wafted through the doorway.

What of these people? How can I stop the attacks; free them from the enemy's grip?

He petitioned the King, but got the terse reply, "Learn." He was both amazed and dumbfounded.

Learn? What? And how?

He returned to the group.

After reading and discussing the King's commands and hearing one of the elders expound on them, the group knelt. Doors appeared and they entered their closets together. The meeting then broke up with individuals leaving the house one at a time and families leaving as a group with a good length of time between each departure. Thoronis, a small man with graying hair, stayed behind at Elrad's request.

"Thoronis will take you to town and show you the things you need to know," Elrad said. "I will meet you again sometime later. It may be days or weeks; in this land one never knows."

"Safe Journeys to you, and may the King smile on your labors."

Elrad left hurriedly, and Thoronis and Lachlaniel sat down to wait until it was safe for them to leave. Lachlaniel would have liked a cup of coffee, but no fire had been made lest it give away the meeting. The two men talked in whispers.

"Elrad said you were a warrior from a far country."

"Yes, the King has sent me to the Great City to help in the fight against the enemy."

"You know there are no straight out battles here. According to what Elrad told me about you, the enemy here uses different tactics from what you're used to. We must use different tactics too."

"Are you able to help many people cross the Bridge?"

"Some. It's difficult, and we must be careful. But the ones who do cross are among the most fiercely loyal subjects of the King you'll find anywhere. The King has entrusted us with a great task but a difficult one."

"There must be a way to bring down Mephosphilis."

"Perhaps, but no one has yet figured out what it is." He paused. "It's time for us to leave."

Thoronis headed for the door but returned when he found that Lachlaniel hadn't followed him.

"Why didn't you come?" he asked. Then, he saw that Lachlaniel was groping his way along the wall, feeling for the door. "You're blind aren't you?"

"Yes. Usually the King leaves me a trail to follow, but lately I haven't been able to find it."

"Take my hand."

Lachlaniel felt a hand close on his own. The grip was firm and strong. Thoronis led him to the door; then, to the old man who had brought his horse from the barn. He mounted and they turned right onto the road. It was now late in the second watch, and after a short trek on the road, Thoronis led Lachlaniel across the field to a small thicket where they would camp for the night. They had a brief supper and lay down to rest while the horse grazed freely.

Chapter 9
Concealment and Pain

Aurora awoke with a start. The early dawn had arrived, but it was not yet time to rise for the day. She rolled over to get the last moments of sleep, but sleep fled from her. There next to her head on the pillow was the bloom of a red salvia. She stifled a scream and, sitting up in bed, drew her knees to her chest. She rocked back and forth as though trying to comfort a little child.

I must tell someone, but who? Max would be angry with me for not coming to him before. He'd be right. I should have gone to him days ago. Longer. Jocey would fret and fuss and be forever looking over my shoulder from now on. Kesniel's too busy. Ewald? Yes Ewald.

Max had informed Mrs. Hughes that he would be rising early and would require breakfast. The smell of bacon and coffee greeted him long before he left his room and headed downstairs. Now, he sat at the table alone mulling over his problem. Mrs. Hughes entered, filled his cup, and started to leave, but the expression on his face made her stop.

"Trouble sir?"

Max looked up and turned his head. His eyes met hers, and he smiled. "Yes."

"The city ag'in?"

"No. Is Andre still in his room?"

She shuffled to the doorway and took a few steps up the stairs. She looked towards Andre's door.

She went back to the table and took the seat next to Max.

"I think he's still thar," she whispered. "At least his door is closed and thar's no light under it."

"Well he's probably still asleep, but since he has no stone, we can't tell. This mustn't go any further. I'm worried about Miss Aurora. He's paying an inordinate amount of attention to her."

"Oh my. Is there anythin' I can do sir?"

"You might. You must be discreet. Listen to his conversations. Watch what he does, and when he leaves, let me know at once."

"I shall be the soul of rrreticence."

Max smiled. He knew that part of her quaint accent asserted itself forcefully when she was determined.

"I must be going."

"Home for lunch sir?"

"Probably not," he said pushing back his chair, "but a lot depends on what our guest does." He smiled at her. "Thank you Mrs. Hughes. You're a gem."

She blushed slightly and began clearing the table as he headed out the door.

Lachlaniel was roused by a painful thump to his ribs. He and Thoronis were surrounded by twelve men. The Basaners had found them.

"Get up, you lightmongers," a large man growled. "I'd love to give you a beating here, but you'll have need of your feet – for the moment."

"Shall we take the horse?" a gold tooth man at the back of the group asked.

"Only if you can catch him before we get these two trussed up. We don't have much time for your greed today, Teeth."

Aman eluded Teeth's grasp and was soon beyond any thought of capture. After a short time, Teeth returned. Thoronis and Lachlaniel were driven down the road at the end of a whip that was used both effectively and frequently. Any hint of a slackening of their pace or a stumble of their feet brought retribution to their backs. Thoronis had little trouble as he knew the way well and had the light of the stones to guide his steps over or around any new obstacles, but Lachlaniel stumbled repeatedly over obstacles that he couldn't see. He might have felt his way along without any trouble except for the pace and the distraction of the lash.

The sounds of the fields gave way first to the sound of trees close at hand and then to the echoes of rocks and rough ground. After a quarter of an hour of winding their way among boulders, the echoes became more pronounced and closer at hand as the group moved through a cut in the hillside that allowed the road a more gradual descent to lower ground. The descent at last became steeper as the walls of the cut gave wave to more open spaces that were once again strewn with boulders. As the road took a turn to the left around the final boulders, the walls of the town became visible to the others and the road reached level ground.

As they entered the town, Lachlaniel and Thoronis were pelted with stones, sticks, rotten vegetables, and any unwanted items that were close at hand. This continued for some time as the squad of Basaners took the most convoluted route they could devise to reach their destination, a castle fortress. At their approach, the gates swung open with the sound of metal grating on metal. They entered a large courtyard. Guards escorted them into the castle while the squad exited through the gates calling out amidst laughter various fates awaiting Lachlaniel and Thoronis. The ground level of the prison was clean and tidy, but as they descended, the passages became dank and slimy. They passed through the cells of the first level. Here the rough voices of men of no conscience sounded through bars jeering at the latest prey of the Basaners. They descended the second flight of stairs to the next level. Here rats scurried along the walls, chattering angrily at the humans who were intruding upon their domain. Moans of pain could be heard coming from men and women in various cells. Screams could be heard ascending from the stairs down to the next level. The acrid, putrid smell of burning flesh hung in the air.

Lachlaniel heard the sound of a door opening on his right. Strong hands gripped his arms. He was thrown into a cell where he tumbled to the ground and slid across the stone floor. He lay sprawled, stunned for a moment by the force of the impact. Someone carelessly cut the ropes on his wrists cutting his right arm in the process. Recovering, he rose to his feet as the cell door clanked shut. He could smell the foul odor of excrement coming from his right. He moved forward groping for the wall. Once he had reached it, he moved towards his left. Feeling the blood running down his arm, he ripped off a piece of his shirt and bandaged the cut as best he could. He felt light headed as he continued along the wall. He crossed a set of chains dangling from the wall. His left hand reached the corner and he turned and began crossing the next wall. There he found the door and the shutter at the bottom where food was passed to the prisoner. He continued the circuit and found the bed, and the blank fourth wall. He returned to the bed and lay down.

What are they doing to Thoronis? Have they simply taken him to a cell, or is he on the lower level being tortured? I wish I could see. I wish I couldn't smell. I must escape and put an end to these atrocities. But how?

His thoughts roamed far and wide, but there were no answers. Gradually his deliberations came to an end as drowsiness overtook him.

"Ewald, I must speak to you."

There was a note of both urgency and fear in Aurora's voice. Ewald climbed down the ladder, a look of concern on his face. He put down the hammer and took her hand. She was trembling.

He looked her in the eye. "This is serious."

"Yes. I'm frightened."

"Oh? Of what?"

"Someone has been leaving me flowers."

"Well that in itself isn't good. What would Lachlaniel think? You don't know who it is?"

"No. I have no idea. At first it seemed harmless – even flattering. They were left on my doorstep. Later there was one at my place on the dining table. The next was on my favorite chair in the living room, then on the sill of my bedroom window."

Ewald's brows raised in alarm. "Did you tell Max?"

"No. I was afraid he would be mad. This morning it was on my pillow when I woke up. An anonymous admirer is one thing but this is more than I can take!" She buried her face in her hands and began to wail.

Ewald lifted her head and drew her into his arms. "Alright now, none of that. Everything's going to be alright," He spoke soothing words as though to a little child. "Settle down and let your old friend, Ewald, think." He paused and her cries subsided into sobs. "That's better isn't it. Now let me see." He took her shoulders and lifted her from his chest until he could see her face. "These flowers. What kind were they?"

"What kind? What difference does that make?" She looked at him as though he were patronizing her.

"Quite a lot. I've noticed the people of the city know very little about plants beyond their names. One thing they're unaware of is that different flowers have different meanings. Now, what kind of flowers were they? Tell me in the order you got them."

Her look changed to one of puzzlement. "A golden hibiscus, a geranium, some asters..."

"What kind of geranium?"

"I think it's called an oak leaf geranium."

"Alright, go on."

"Lilacs, a yellow iris, a gardenia, a rose..."

"Red, I'm sure."

"Yes, how did you know...and this morning a red salvia."

"Oh, girl. We've got a problem."

Max had followed Andre most of the day without result. As a boy, he had learned to move soundlessly as he hunted in the nearby forest. He had become so skillful the animals never noticed as he flitted from one tree to another. Now it was more difficult. The city afforded fewer places of obscurity and even less for someone his size, but his size gave him an advantage also. He could hang much further back from his quarry. This was especially true of Andre whose strange garb made him stand out among the other citizens.

Andre had gone to the dress shop for a couple of hours where, presumably, he had worked. Afterward, he had gone to the market. Max almost lost him three times as the crowds blocked the way. Max's unparalleled knowledge of the city gave him another advantage. He used less traveled side streets and alleys and circled to a new vantage point before Andre could be lost in the crowd. If Andre had known he was being followed, he could have disappeared with ease, but he seemed very intent on his shopping.

Max had been intent on Andre's shopping as well.

First it was herbalists. He was definitely looking for something, but he only bought a couple of things, and they weren't out of the ordinary. He didn't seem satisfied with his purchases though. Then, it was the apothecary for sulfur. Sulfur? What for? Then, jewelry and fabrics. Nothing out of the ordinary there. A tulip from a flower lady. Now, the stable. What could he want there, unless it's to buy a horse? Or rent one? What's he up to?

Max watched from a smithy across the street. He could see Andre conversing with a boy who ran out of the back of the stable. Several minutes later the lad came back with a tightly sealed piece of crockery. Andre placed it in his basket with his other things and pulled out an identical jar and handed it to the boy. The lid clattered to the ground, soundless at this distance. Andre looked about as the boy picked it up. He must have said something harsh to the boy for the boy frowned and hung his head. Andre lifted his chin and gave him a gold coin worth five karpas.

"Exorbitant." Max said to the air.

What's so precious and how did the boy get it? I'll have to set someone to watching the boy to see what he does and where he goes. Uh oh! He's coming this way!

Max fled out the back of the smithy and found a new hiding place to observe the reason for Andre's visit to the smith. He didn't have to wait long. Andre greeted the smith and purchased some coal. He turned and left, the transaction taking but moments. Max moved to the next alleyway to keep from attracting undue attention. He moved cautiously and quickly, but when he got back to the street Andre was nowhere to be seen.

Lost him! What's in that pot and why the coal? Nothing left to do now but return home.

A Sergeant and corporal entered Lachlaniel's cell as the sound of the iron cell door creaking on its hinges roused Lachlaniel from fitful slumber.

"Who's there?" Lachlaniel rose to his feet and groped his way forward.

The sergeant, a large muscular man, watched puzzled at first as the prisoner felt his way forward to the far wall. Lachlaniel turned in their direction and again moved clumsily forward.

"Who's there?" Lachlaniel asked again his tone more urgent.

He stopped and stood more erect. The sergeant moved in front of him and waved his hand in front of Lachlaniel's face. He threw a punch that stopped an inch from Lachlaniel's nose. Lachlaniel didn't flinch.

"Will you please answer me?" Lachlaniel said with rising apprehension.

The sergeant swung his arm back and delivered a crushing blow to the side of Lachlaniel's head.

"He's blind," the sergeant yelled as anger contorted his face.

The corporal caught the stunned form of Lachlaniel. The corporal raised him to his feet and struck him in the midsection sending him flying towards the sergeant who landed another blow. Lachlaniel was battered back and forth from one man to the other. He finally landed on the floor where he was kicked on both sides as the men took perverse pleasure in dealing out pain. When he at last no longer flinched at the blows, the two men wrapped his arms around their shoulders and dragged him out of the cell and down the stairs. The Fragel waited at the bottom.

"He's blind." The sergeant spat on the floor in disgust. "What do you want to do with him?"

"Put him on the rack while I talk to the magistrate about this. And heat up the rod."

The man at the furnace put the iron rod beneath the coals and pumped the bellows. The sergeant and the corporal threw Lachlaniel's limp body onto the rack and bound him with cords. They stretched him to his full length but applied no pressure. The Fragel reserved that for himself.

Aurora followed Ewald through the city.

"Where are we going?" She was breathless as she tried to keep up without breaking into a run. "And can't you slow down a little?"

"To the King-steward's Residence, and no, I can't slow down. I don't want to take a chance on him seeing you and I and where we're going. I'd have waited till night except that's when he leaves the flowers. This is less risky, but it isn't without risk."

"Why are we going to see Kesniel? I'd rather everyone didn't know."

"So had I. The fewer people who know the better. 'A falling tree is heard abroad.' As to why. I think the safest place for you is under Kesniel's watchful eye."

Aurora stopped. "What do you mean?"

Ewald turned and put his hands on her shoulder's. "I think whoever is sending you the flowers is also doing the sabotage."

"Who could it be?"

"We suspect Andre. You're going to disappear for a few days."

A burning sensation in his feet brought Lachlaniel swimming to the surface of consciousness. The sergeant passed the heated rod near enough to cause the pain to rouse the prisoner. This was something with which he was quite expert as he had done it many times for the Fragel. As Lachlaniel's senses returned he could hear footsteps coming down the stairs. The Fragel snapped the scourge in the air. Everyone tensed and took an involuntary step backwards.

"Give me that!" He snatched the rod from the sergeant.

"This thing's too cool." He hit Lachlaniel on the side of the head with it and added, "Besides the magistrate says to let him go."

Lachlaniel moaned.

"Let him go!" the corporal exclaimed as Lachlaniel verged on unconsciousness again.

"He says a stone is of no use to a blind man." His expert swing of the cat flayed Lachlaniel's abdomen, shredding the shirt and leaving bloody red welts. "He doesn't know what light is or what it means. Cut him loose."

The new pain in his belly brought Lachlaniel back to the surface of the sea of unconsciousness when he longed for its depths.

"Drag him out of the city beyond the ridge." The Fragel growled. "But give him something to remember us by."

Lachlaniel felt his hands and feet being freed. The two men dragged him up the stairs again as he tried to keep on his feet. In the courtyard outside the castle, they threw him on a cart and drove it through the gates and across the city.

Lachlaniel wasn't sure of where he was until he heard the echoes off the nearby boulders, and then, off the sides of the cut in the hillside. They drove on for quite a while.

Where are they taking me?

I wish I were dead. The Chuchoteur whispered.

Aurora's form and the light she gave him floated through his mind.

No. I must get back to her. Somehow I must get back.

The cart stopped and he heard the men get down. They grabbed his feet and drug him off the cart. His body and head hit the ground hard. He was dazed. They drug him off the road and gave him another beating and left him there to die.

Ewald led Aurora by a circuitous route through the backstreets of Agapay to the back of the Residence. He left her beyond a corner of the walls and moved swiftly to the gates. There he dismissed the guards giving them a short break while he stood watch. Having cleared the area of all eyes but his own, he ushered Aurora to the servant's entrance near the kitchen.

"You must stay here while I clear the way inside. I have to wait until the guards return before I do that. After I enter, wait the tenth part of an hour and follow me in. Move quickly and quietly and don't let the guards see you. I'll meet you on the other side of the kitchen in the waiter's assembly. Remember, let no one see you."

Aurora nodded and hid in the shrubs near the door. The waiting was interminable, but the guards finally returned and Ewald strode by her into the kitchen as though going to another of his duties.

A cold wind moaned through the cut in the hill. Lachlaniel lay shivering in the shreds of his clothes. Breathing was difficult and fire radiated from his chest to his left shoulder with each breath. Minutes passed and grew into hours. He knew neither day nor night. At times, he slept fitfully. His strength was slow to return. The wind turned to the west and grew warm. In the distance, he heard a horse whinny. Soon, he heard the sound of hoof beats followed by the familiar nickering of Aman. The horse's nose nudged him. He could hardly move his left arm but managed to grasp the reigns which hung down from the bridle.

"Help me up boy," he said to the horse in a raspy whisper.

The horse responded by lifting its head slowly as Lachlaniel rose first to his knees, and then, to his feet. Pain shot upward from the calf of his right leg. He almost fell but managed to hold the horse's neck. His head was spinning and he barely had the strength to pull himself up into the saddle. He leaned forward onto the horse's neck and rested his head between Aman's ears. His legs and arms dangled on the horse's sides.

Aman walked gingerly to the road where he headed north. Lachlaniel fell asleep in the saddle. Thus they moved agonizingly forward retracing the steps back to the house where Lachlaniel had met Thoronis and the others. Lachlaniel woke briefly once.

Are you sure you don't want to die?
No, I'm not sure.

A sudden vision filled his mind. He saw a spring day. There were shrubs and flowers and the grass was soft beneath his feet.

I know this place, but I've never seen it before.

Someone took his hand. He turned. It was...

Aurora! How can this be? She's a thousand miles away! And how can I see?

Aurora smiled.

She's so beautiful. More than I ever knew!

"I love you."

Her words fell like beautiful soothing music on his ears. For a moment there was no pain, only the sound of her voice.

"I love you too." He heard himself say, yet he hadn't spoken.

They walked to a bench surrounded by shrubs and flowers and sat upon it.

I remember this place. It's Aurora's favorite spot.

"Do you have to go?" Aurora whispered.

He kissed her hands.

"Would you have me disobey the King?"

"No, of course not. It's just that my heart breaks at the thought of our parting."

"Mine does too. I will miss you so, but there are people in need and I must help them."

I remember this conversation!

They embraced. Aurora's tears fell on his neck as she whispered in his ear, "I love you."

The vision faded.

No! Death isn't what I want. I want her. I want Aurora.

He patted the horse's neck and slumped forward again.

Aurora slipped out of her hiding place and into the empty kitchen when the guards weren't looking. There was no sound except the crackle of the fire and no movement save the steam rising in curls from the kettle hanging on a rod above it. She entered the hallway beyond passing the pantry on her left and the spiral staircase on her right and entered the waiters' assembly hall. There were glass cabinets filled with fine china and others with silver serving pieces and platters. The tables at the end held napkins rolled up and placed in neat piles, silverware, pitchers filled with drink, a single gold tray, and a delicate porcelain vase with a single stem of newly opened blue bells rising from it, but Ewald was nowhere to be seen. She heard someone coming and dashed beneath the right table concealing herself under its tablecloth.

"Aurora?"

Kesniel's voice. It must be safe.

"Aurora, where are you," Ewald whispered. "Perhaps she isn't here yet..."

Aurora emerged from her hiding place, blushing.

"I thought..."

"You did well girl." Ewald took her hand and lifted her to her feet.

Kesniel looked about. "Quickly, the back stairs."

He lead them to the spiral stairway and was about to ascend when voices came from above. They moved without sound into the pantry to hide.

A woman's voice said "What do you mean a guard ordered you out of the kitchen?"

Another woman answered, "A big burly sergeant with short red hair ordered everyone out. He said to come back only when we were called."

"And you left the King-steward's food to burn!"

The voices paused at the bottom of the stairs.

"Indeed! Just who does he think he is! I run this kitchen. No sergeant – no captain is going to order my people around! Where is he?"

"I don't know mum." the cook said with a lilt in her voice.

"You get back to work. And make sure the King-steward's lunch isn't burnt. I'll find that sergeant and give him a piece of my mind!"

The footsteps of the cook gave almost no sound as she treaded lightly into the kitchen. The kitchen matron's footsteps, however, resounded with authority and anger as she moved through the waiter's assembly. Kesniel peaked out. The matron was gone. Looking around the door, he could see the cook busily moving to and fro with much clattering of utensils as she tried for the moment to do the work of five people.

The trio moved surreptitiously across the hall and up the stairs, the sounds of the kitchen fading in their wake. When they reached the top, Kesniel took them down a hallway to their right and entered an ornate door. He locked the door behind them.

Ewald let out a sigh of relief. "I'm glad I didn't run into her. We might still be arguing."

"Yes, the King smiled upon us. Now tell me, why do we need to hide Miss Aurora?"

As Aman turned off the road toward the little house of meeting, Elrad stepped off the porch. Seeing the man slumped in the saddled, he rushed out to meet them and led Aman back to the house. He slid the limp form of Lachlaniel off the horse and brought him into the house.

"Thelma, come quickly!" Elrad cried as he kicked the door closed behind him.

Elrad laid Lachlaniel's broken form on a cot in one of the back rooms. Thelma entered and cringed at the sight of yet another servant of the King who had been in the hands of the Basaners. She began tending his wounds: binding up broken bones, cleaning and bandaging cuts, and pouring oil from her stone on the bruised and broken flesh.

Elrad went back outside to tend the horse. He removed the bridle and saddle and led him to the watering trough at the rear of the house. Aman drank long and deep, but Elrad led him away before he could take too much. They moved into the barn. He put Aman in a loose box, filled the manger with hay, and, stepping out closed the gate behind him. He returned to the house and entered his closet to speak to the King about Lachlaniel.

"My Lord, Lachlaniel needs your help. The Basaners have done their usual work and brought him close to death."

"He will heal. However, his soul will not be as quick to heal as his body. The road to true health lies long before him. You must help him when and where you can."

"Yes, Sire."

Elrad got up and returned to the world of service, the world of pain and darkness where the light of the King must be spread abroad to dispel the woe and despair. Thelma met him in the hallway.

"How's he doing?" he asked concerned.

"He's in a lot of pain, but I'm more concerned with his heart. He's very angry." She paused thoughtfully and continued, "It's not so much what happened to him but what's happening to others. He's come to hate the Basaners. He doesn't see their great need of being rescued from Kieran."

"He sees the pain they cause but not the pain in their own heart." Elrad scratched his head. "It isn't going to be easy to open his eyes. He's used to a traditional fight, not the underhanded ways of our foes."

He left her in the kitchen and went down the hall to Lachlaniel's room. Lachlaniel was awake; a bundle of anger and pain. Elrad watched for a few moments as Lachlaniel tossed and turned seeking relief from the pain. He took his stone and gave Lachlaniel some of its water. Stepping back, he watched as the pain eased and Lachlaniel grew still and fell asleep.

Chapter 10
Black Powder

A shadowy figure moved outside Aurora's bedroom window. It had been several days since Andre had seen her or had been able to place a flower. The tulip he had bought had wilted. He replaced it with a gladiolus. The house was watched almost constantly, but he managed to slip past the guards and leave the gladiolus on the table by her bed. He slipped away in the growing darkness of the early night.

Aurora paced the length of the suite of rooms to which she was confined as she had for the past two weeks. She would stop near the window and stare for a moment before beginning to pace again. She picked up items along her trek – items she'd picked up hundreds of times before – only to put them down and resume pacing. The fact that she agreed she must stay in hiding did not help her restlessness. She spent much time in her closet talking to the King, asking him to help Lachlaniel, imploring that the saboteur and architect of her imprisonment – the one who left the flowers – would be captured, and lastly, that whoever he was he would embrace the light, cross the Bridge and enter the King's service. She worried what effect her 'disappearance' would have on Max, her sisters, and her friends.

Her musings this morning were interrupted by a knock at the door.
Breakfast I suppose. Too early to be Ewald.
She opened the door to find Kesniel, King-steward of the city, standing before her in all his regalia. She stood mouth agape.
"May I come in?"
"Yes please." She opened the door wider.
He entered the anteroom and hung his cloak on the hook near the door.

"Why the dumbfounded look, Miss Aurora?"

"I've never seen you in your finery before, except for speeches or at state functions, certainly never face to face."

"Yes, well, there's a reason for that. One I hope you'll be glad to hear." He began removing his sword and scabbard.

"News?" She straightened his cloak.

Lachlaniel's return? There's been no letter in two weeks. The saboteur. They caught the saboteur. No, those aren't reasons for the state dress.

She looked at Kesniel expectantly. "I can't begin to guess."

"We've been working on a plan to give you more freedom here without your presence becoming known."

Joy crossed her face brightening the room for an instant, but questions quickly followed. "How? I'd love to walk the streets again and visit the shops, but how?"

"Kesniel sighed. "I didn't intend to get your hopes up so much. Let's move into the sitting room."

Aurora sat on the end of the immense divan, a long piece of furniture that could comfortably sit six people. Kesniel seated himself on the ornate, high backed, wing chair next to her and lay his sword on the low mahogany table in front of them.

"It won't be that much freedom, I'm afraid. We've had a grand coach brought in from a small city some distance from here. Everyone saw it come through the gates a little bit ago. Its curtains were drawn. We made a big show of it coming to the residence. Talk is already spreading that a foreign dignitary has come for a visit and has some business with me. That is why I'm roaming the halls in this getup. For your part we'll have to dye your hair and such to alter your appearance. That's for this afternoon..."

"Why? How's all this going to give me any freedom?" Aurora frowned.

"None of the servants here knows you by sight, and though some of the guards do, we'll make sure they are either off duty or they can only see you from a distance, or in the evening, or at night."

She looked doubtful of the prospect. "There's a lot of light even then. The Great Stone is dimmer at night, but you can almost read by its light. And what about my stone won't it give me away? It will be very bright you know."

"The soldiers know how to reduce that so it only shines on your path. We've also asked the King for help. Your light need only show you your next step."

She folded her arms, the excitement on her face retreating into thoughts that were increasingly somber.

"Isn't this a bit much just to get me out of this room? Not that I mind, but..." She let the sentence trail off."

"It's become apparent to us that you may be here for quite some time. We're more convinced than ever that Andre is our man, but we haven't been able to catch him doing anything. The sabotage has stopped. He frequents the markets every few days, usually buying the same items, but we don't know what he uses them for. He has bought some flowers like those that have been showing up at your house, but lately he hasn't even done that. As far as catching him leaving the flowers, he seems able to elude us whenever he wants. He disappears and returns without anyone seeing him come or go. The next day there's a flower."

"That's frightening." She shivered at the thought.

"That's why you must stay here. We want to give you as much freedom of movement as possible within the residence, but venturing outside the walls is out of the question."

Aurora rubbed the goose bumps on her arms. "You make me want to go to bed and hide under the covers."

"It isn't that bad. He did search for you at first, but we have reason to believe his attitude toward you has changed."

She frowned and her brows furrowed.

Kesniel caught the expression and reached over and patted her arm. "Don't trouble yourself child. No one but Jocelyn, Max, Ewald, you, and I know you're in hiding and even Max and Jocelyn don't know where. Once you're ready, we'll move you into the larger accommodations reserved for leaders of other cities."

"Larger quarters? This set of rooms is larger than my sister's entire house."

"None the less, a foreign dignitary would have the larger rooms. You must play the part or you'll arouse suspicion."

Aurora shook her head and stared at the floor. "I just want to go home."

Two weeks of constant care saw Lachlaniel back on his feet. Rage boiled within him and would not let him rest. One morning during breakfast, he could stand it no longer. He rose to his feet flipping the table over scattering dishes and food across the room. He saddled Aman in a fury that knew no bounds, mounted, and headed for the road to the town and castle where the Basaners tortured his fellow Ebenchaim.

An hour saw him approaching the cut in the hillside. As they left the trees, Aman slowed to a walk and refused to go faster despite all of Lachlaniel's efforts. Lachlaniel muttered as he tried to get the horse to move faster. The anger and the blackness of his thoughts blinded his ears as well as his sense of impending danger. He knew nothing of the presence of the Basaners until he found himself on the ground.

Rising to his feet he drew his sword. He flailed blindly as the men sought an opening to pounce upon him. One man ventured to close and the sword hacked off his right arm. It was the only stroke Lachlaniel would land. As Aman ran back up the road a short distance, Lachlaniel was overwhelmed by twelve men. Six pinned him to the ground, one each on his arms and legs and two on his chest. The others began beating him with clubs as he struggled, helpless to free himself. This continued for several minutes until he quit struggling. Those holding him got up. They picked up stones and began flinging them as hard as they could at their helpless victim. This continued until Lachlaniel no longer moved or moaned.

Damon, the leader of the murderous gang of men, walked over to the unmoving form. He kicked him first in the side, then in the head, and then in the side again.

"Alright, back to the rocks. Somebody catch that horse," he growled with authority.

The men scrambled back among the boulders while three of their number went to catch Aman, but he was too quick and wary for them. They returned empty-handed.

"You three will stand double shifts watching the road for the next week," Damon snarled.

The three men along with two others climbed up to their posts. As their comrades moved out of earshot one said, "Damon's on a rampage." all became deathly quiet. The body of Lachlaniel lay motionless on the road.

Aurora looked at herself in the mirror. A strange black-haired woman looked back at her. The hair was long and twirled on top of her head, capped with a silver tiara laced with diamonds. Diamonds and sapphires cascaded from her newly pierced ears, the sapphires setting her blue eyes ablaze. The powder they had brushed over her eyes made them look both larger and a deeper shade of blue. They had also lengthened and curled her lashes which enhanced the effect. In addition, powder was applied to her cheeks and some sticky red stuff was put on her lips that made them look like they were bleeding. The dress had a large circular collar around her neck, hugely puffy sleeves, and not enough room as it narrowed to her waist. There was plenty of room below that as the bottom section blossomed gigantically from her hips and descended to the floor. A tear formed in her eye and she looked down.

I don't know whether to laugh, or be angry, or just cry. How am I supposed to walk around like this? More freedom? This cage is worse than a suite of rooms ever could be! They disguised me alright. I don't think I would know me if I met me!

She stifled a laugh. "How am I supposed to get through doors?"

"In your rooms you can eliminate all this and be yourself, except for the black hair of course." Kesniel's mustache drooped as he saw her eyes in the mirror. "Hrmph. Yes, well, I am sorry my dear. It was the best we could think of."

She turned and looked at him, her eyes welling again with tears. "I know you did the best you could, and perhaps it won't be so bad once I...I get...used to it."

She ran from the room as the tears and sobs burst forth, no longer to be contained. Kesniel stood in the silence of the empty room, unsure of what to do. He looked at the slump shouldered man in the mirror and sighed.

"Bad idea. What should we do now?" he asked the reflection. He stood staring for a moment, turned and walked to the door with his tail between his legs like a whipped puppy.

Two hours passed. To the amazement of the guards, the blind man they had thrown in the field beyond the rocks stirred. One of the guards jumped down from his post and ran to report to Damon. He returned quickly and motioned to the others to hold their positions. The man crawled towards the road. He fell on his face when his strength failed, and he would lay unmoving for several minutes breathing heavily. Rising to his hands and knees, he continued his torturous journey.

The guards watched for more than an hour and a half as the man they thought they had killed moved painfully up the road. They heard the horse they had tried to catch whinny from some distance. It sauntered up to the motionless man who had once again fallen. He was trying to summon more strength for another effort. He grabbed a stirrup, then the saddle horn, and with great effort lay across the saddle of the gentle creature. The horse turned and took his master up the road and out of danger.

Max looked at Asher in the fading light of evening as the others trickled in. "Well?"

"We lost him again, but we're getting closer."

Max eyed Asher with a scrutinizing gaze. "You're lucky you can follow him at all." He lifted Asher's bright red shirt with the tip of his sword; then, with a flick, he knocked the green cap and its purple feather off Asher's head and into his hands. "How many times have I got to tell you, you need to blend into the background?"

"Ever since I saw light, I've loved colors—bright colors. You know that. These are the plainest clothes I've got."

Max reached into his pocket and pulled out a ten karpa gold piece. "Then, buy some new ones." As an afterthought he added, "Brown. I don't want to see anything bright, understand?"

"Don't worry."

"Now how close *did* you get?"

"He's was within a six block area."

"You're sure he's not there now?" Max put his hands on his hips and glowered.

One of the other men spoke up. "I was just about to head for here when I saw him go by. I was in the shadows. He headed towards the center of town empty-handed."

"Then, we've got a chance. I want every building in that area searched. I don't want so much as a mouse hole to go unchecked. Understood?"

Everyone shouted, "Aye sir."

"Dismissed."

Ewald and Aurora walked in the soft evening light in the flower garden of the King-steward's residence. The rosy evening light of the Great Stone mingled with the darkening blue hues of the light of the city and of their smaller stones.

"Oh, Ewald. I feel so ridiculous. I look like a jester."

Ewald looked her up and down. She frowned and turned her face away. Ewald put a finger under her chin and pulled her face back. He looked into her eyes.

"Listen missy. You've got to stop this. Kesniel said you stayed in your room all day crying like a child. Are you trying to make him feel bad?"

"Of course not." Her voice was soft and sad.

"Then, stop this nonsense. You're a beautiful woman. This is what nobility wears in some places. There, you would be considered the belle of the ball."

Her eyebrows drooped and she frowned and looked at the ground in front of her.

Ewald smiled. "I think you look quite fetching."

Something in the tone of his voice must have touched a chord. She raised her head and smiled.

"Do you really think so?"

"I do. The change in hair color is the only thing that throws me. I'm not used to it."

She started pouting before realizing he was needling her. Smiling, she folded her fan and hit him in mock annoyance.

"There now. That's much better." Ewald grinned. "Any word from Lachlaniel?"

"I haven't heard from him in over two weeks. I'm worried."

"Have you written him?"

Her head sank to her chest.

"No. No, I haven't. I've been self absorbed. I'm so childish."

"Hey. Let's not go there again." He paused until she looked at him. "If you've been wrong, change it. Make it right. Write him. I'm sure he's waiting for your letter as much as you're waiting for his."

"I'll go do it now." She turned, but he grabbed her hand.

"Now? How many hours did you spend getting into your dress?"

She turned back to him. "Leaving now would be a waste, wouldn't it?"

"Relax missy. The night is beautiful. The scents of summer are in the air, the nightingale is singing, and you're a young woman in love with your whole life ahead of you. Drink in the cool night air. Enjoy your walk through the garden and be at peace."

"It's been so long since I've felt that way." She took a step, head high, eyes closed. "You've made me feel so much better." She opened her eyes. "How did you become so wise?"

"Brmmm... well... umm... I..." He blushed. "I'm not, you know. If I were, I wouldn't have been taken in by those fellows on the road to Fairvale. Almost missed the battle because of that."

She laughed. "I'm glad I know you. You're a good friend."

Max walked the streets as his men searched the buildings. After each search was completed one of the men would run up and report, but each report was as discouraging as the last.

Nothing new. No sign of where Andre has been or what he's been doing. Are we looking in the right place, or is his hiding place somewhere else?

Asher ran up from the next street, breathless and bare headed. "We've found something. Something strange."

"What?"

"Come and see. Maybe you'll know what it is."

The two men walked back to the next street. Asher stopped and picked up his cap.

Max frowned. "You and that hat."

Asher ignored the comment and took the lead. "Over here."

They were headed to a warehouse, one that had seen better days. The shutters hung crookedly in the windows. A beam that held up the awning above the door sagged. As they opened the door, the rusted hinges screeched like a wraith exposed to the light. Inside, the rafters had the same sag as the beam outside. Shafts of the city's light descended from rifts in the roof like water in a cataract. In a far corner, two guards stood by an open barrel. A pile of flour lay in a heap on top of another barrel. A smaller lid leaned against the barrel. The men smiled at Max and Asher's approach.

"This one had a false bottom, if you could call it that." The taller of the two guards said with a smile.

Max gazed down on the barrel opening. Less than half a foot below the top was a rim to hold the inner lid. Max bent down on one knee and reached deep into the barrel. His huge hand withdrew a fistful of black powder,

He eyed it and asked, "How did you find it?"

The shorter guard beamed. "I thumped the barrels. This one was hollow sounding. I opened it. It appeared to be full of flour, so I figured it had to have a false bottom."

"Clever. Asher, go find a bag. I want to take some of this and have it examined."

"You think it's what we're looking for?" Asher asked.

"I don't know. It could be. I've never seen powder like this. It could be Andre's."

Asher started to say something else, but the scowl on Max's face said "Move!" He ran to the other end of the warehouse and returned with a flour sack.

"Kind of big." Max examined the bag for rips or holes. "It'll do. Put two handfuls in here. We don't want Andre to suspect we found it, so put everything back just as it was. When you're done, come and get me."

Asher put his hands behind his back, smiled, and bounced on his heels, "What are you going to do?"

Max raised an eyebrow and looked at Asher. "Make sure the other men keep looking. This may not be what we're looking for."

Chapter 11

Foolishness and Flight

Elrad and Thelma tended Lachlaniel's wounds. This time, however, he was more thoughtful during his recovery.

I must have help. I can't handle the Basaners alone. The Great City. I'll go there as soon as I can mount a horse. I must rouse the Ebenchaim and rid this country of the Basaners.

Elrad interrupted his thoughts.

"I got a letter from the dispatcher for you. It's from Aurora. It's almost two weeks old. Would you like me to read it to you?"

The black cloud of anger lightened and a faint smile darted across Lachlaniel's lips and was gone.

"Yes please."

June 25th

Dear Lachlaniel,

It is so hard to be without you. I miss you so terribly, and now more than ever. You were right about Andre. We believe he is the saboteur. Ewald and Kesniel are afraid for my safety, so they've hidden me in the King-steward's residence for the past two weeks. We don't know how long I'll be here, so now I must wear a horrid disguise so that I can leave the confines of these rooms. The rooms are quite spacious, but after a time, the walls start closing in, and you long for fresh air and sunshine. It's like being cooped up by a blizzard. Last night I got to walk in the gardens for the first time since I've been here.

The search for evidence against Andre continues without results. He seems to be able to elude our guards at will. There haven't been any acts of sabotage lately, but everyone is on edge. Something big is coming. You can feel it in the air. Tension haunts every brow. I've never seen anything like this.

I long for you like I long for the fresh air, relief from the tension, and a swift conclusion to this awful chapter in the life of our beloved city. Take care of yourself. Write me soon. Your silence only adds to my cares. I love you more each day. The days and hours drag by without you. I want and need you. Come swiftly my love.

Your own,

Aurora

Lachlaniel put his face in his hands as he sat on the bed. He didn't move for a moment. He ran his hands through his hair, and looked at Elrad.

"Thanks."

His jaw set and his face tensed. He swung his feet off the bed and sat up.

"Trying to re-crack those ribs? That'll make them heal faster."

Lachlaniel's twisted as he cringed from the pain and he stifled a moan. "The love of my life is in danger. What do you think I'm doing?"

"The love of your life is *fifteen hundred miles from here*, and this letter is ten days old. Look at the date. Whatever is going to happen will happen long before you can get there."

Lachlaniel took a step and dropped to his knees.

"Which will be never if you don't get back in bed."

He helped Lachlaniel up and eased him onto the bed.

"Trust your friends. They'll take care of Aurora and keep Andre away from her."

"*That guy?*' he sneered. "How? The slippery eel. They can't even keep him from slipping their surveillance."

"Then, trust the King."

Lachlaniel sighed and slid under the covers.

"Get some rest. Your duty to the King lies here and you can't get back to it until you mend."

Max entered the apothecary's shop. The apothecary looked up from his work. The mortar was filled with black powder. A small sample rested on a paper by the pestle.

"Ah, Sergeant Major. I've been expecting you."

"Have you discovered what it is?"

"No. But I have discovered a few things. It's not a poison." He moved a candle closer. "It's practically inert..." A flaming drop of wax fell on the sample he was examining which erupted into a flash of flames with a **'*crack!*'** Max jumped but quickly recovered. The apothecary turned his blackened face to Max.

"Unless touched by flame."

Max chuckled. "So I see."

His face went slack and his skin paled. His eyes grew as big as saucers. Without a word he flew out the door nearly pulling it off its hinges.

Ewald was inspecting the entrances to the Tower which were still under triple guard. The west entrance guards caught his attention.

There's something wrong here. Something out of place.

He eyed the two men. Both were wearing gold rings that neither could afford. He moved closer, and the men, who were already at attention, stiffened. A sweet yet masculine scent hung in the air.

"Present arms."

The men moved their halberds in front of them in unison. As they did so, there was a flash of white at their wrists. Ewald snatched the halberd from the man on the right. He pulled the pole down and examined the blade.

"Sloppy. When was the last time you sharpened this blade?"

"Yesterday."

"Yesterday? Really?"

Ewald slammed the blade into the wooden door by the man's head. The blade bounced off hitting the man's helmet.

"Honestly! I picked it up from the smith this morning!" the man said resuming a position of attention.

Ewald squinted at him. There was fear in his eyes.

"Perhaps you should find another smith" Ewald growled. "Or perhaps you should learn not to lie!"

He shoved the halberd back into the man's hands watching his wrists as he took the weapon.

Frilly sleeves under his coat? Something's up and I've been so busy looking after Aurora I hadn't noticed the change.

"You'll both stand double watches for the next month."

"Why me?" The other guard complained.

"You should have paid more attention to your friend's sloppiness."

The guard started to say something but was stopped by Ewald's next statement.

"Would you like me to do a *close* inspection of you and your equipment so the two of you can do two months?"

The two men stood at stiff attention in utter silence. Ewald turned and headed toward the south entrance.

Those men have come into some money and I don't think it was legitimately.

He eyed the guards at the south entrance and sniffed the air,

Everything seems normal here.

He pulled the weapon from the guard on the left. "Go get Max. I'll take your place. Make sure you bring him in from the east. And make it quick."

Max ran down the street with people screaming as they jumped out of his way. He put on a burst of speed as he neared the warehouse. The door screamed as it splintered into a thousand pieces. Max didn't even slow down. Two guards lay dead in the middle of the floor. His eyes landed on the corner where the barrel once stood and his determination was arrested by what he didn't see. He dropped to his knees.

"**Noooo!!!!**"The rafters shook with the power of his cry and loose shingles fell from their perch by the holes in the roof.

His head hung and his arms drooped as he rose to his feet. His powerful hands rose to his face and ran through his hair as he entered his closet. He fell to his knees in the presence of the King.

"My Lord, I have failed. The city is in peril and it's my fault!"

"Get up Max. You haven't failed. The city is in peril, but it will be safe. Now go. Ewald sent someone to look for you. He has important news."

Max rose with a heart that was somehow lighter and new strength in his limbs.

Andre told the driver of the cart to stop. The alley behind Jocelyn's house was empty. He climbed down and opened the cellar doors. The driver slid a long board off the cart, and together they laid it over the steps of the cellar making a ramp. They rolled the barrel down the ramp and into an empty corner. Returning to the cart the driver slid the board in the back and took his place. Andre took his basket off the seat and paid the driver returning to the cellar as the cart moved off down the alley.

They think they can outsmart me? Mess with me again and Aurora's house and sister will be ashes.

He removed the lid from the barrel and carefully placed a small device containing two carefully balanced vials of liquids on the inner lid. He laid a flower, an oleander, on top of the barrel, climbed the steps to the outside, turned and looked back down towards the barrel.

Try and find the rest if you can!

He closed the doors and slithered down the alley unseen.

Max arrived at the south entrance and the guard that brought him returned to guarding the door. Ewald grabbed Max's arm and led him to the corner. Their two heads peered around the corner, Max's about two feet above Ewald's. They moved away from the corner along the south side of the tower.

Ewald whispered to Max, "What do you think?"

"Frilly shirts huh. I think you're right." He gritted his teeth, the anger coursing through him. "If it were up to me, I'd jerk them up here and now, and they'd wish they'd never been born."

"But?"

"But I conferred with Kesniel. We're to leave them alone. I want six of the most trusted men we have to guard the entrance from the inside when those two are on duty. Another six need to guard the entrance on the outside. Find some good places to hide. I want a couple of them on the roof of the inn across the street and I want you and nine of our guards to take a room at the inn. No one else is to be there but our guards. No one."

"What of Andre and the powder?"

"We've got to find a way to monitor his movements without losing him."

"We haven't been any good at that so far."

"I know, but we've got to find a way. That snake has gone far enough. He's targeting the tower, but we don't know if that's his only target or how much of that powder he has."

"From what you've said he could hit us in a number of places just with the powder in that barrel."

Max winced. "I know, I know." He paused "Let everyone that we can trust know. Cut those two out of the loop of any critical information."

"Shouldn't we cut them out completely?"

"No. That might make them or Andre suspicious. Besides, we might want to give them information that will lead Andre in the wrong direction."

"A trap."

"Yes if we can pull one off."

I can't stand this. Cooped up. Wearing that awful disguise. I miss Lachlaniel. I'm not doing any good here...

She let her hair down and looked at herself in the mirror.

I need to look like a servant. Even my normal clothes won't work for that.

She slipped quietly out of her room and down the deserted hall. Her normal attire made moving a lot easier. She made her way to the lowest floor and slipped through a window. She strode across the lawn as though she owned it.

The servant's quarters should be deserted.

She entered the building and walked boldly through the halls looking in closets until she found what she was looking for. It was a closet full of uniforms, both male and female. She stepped inside and closed the door behind her. She found one uniform close to her size and quickly changed.

I'll need something better than these clothes to travel in but that will have to wait.

Stuffing her clothes under her arm, she made her way out the back and over to a storage building near the stables. Inside was a wide variety of equipment. She walked down the aisles until she came to the packs.

Just what I need.

She stuffed her clothes inside and continued down the aisles picking and choosing the things she would need for a trip. She placed the pack under a bush and headed for the barn, wandering in as though she was a new servant curious about her surroundings. She looked at the animals, petting and stroking them while she waited for someone to become curious about her, which didn't take long.

"What ere ya doin' here?"

"Oh! You startled me." Aurora played coy. "I love animals, but I've never seen horses before. They're so beautiful and powerful. Who are you?"

"I'm Capaleanan. And what'd be your name?"

"I'm Ophelia."

"Well now, miss Ophelia who'd be likin' the horses..." He smiled. "...would ya care to be seein' a little more? I can show you around a bit."

"I'd love to."

They walked through the stables for an hour with Aurora wide eyed and asking questions. By the time she left, her act had filled many gaps in her knowledge of horses, and she had picked one whose temperament and physique should suit her needs. She retrieved the pack and slipped back into the residence and up to her room. She changed clothes, finished filling the pack, and waited patiently for evening.

Elrad looked at Thelma as the rooster crowed. The smell of bacon and coffee made his stomach rumble with anticipation. The cool air of dawn flowed through the open door as the rain pattered on the roof.

He put his hand on her shoulder. "We can't stay here much longer. The Basaners have moved into this area again. How long before he can move?"

She finished turning the bacon. "I've never seen anyone heal this fast. Yesterday morning he couldn't sit up. By the afternoon after you read the letter, he could not only sit up but stand. In the middle of the night, I heard him get up and go to the outhouse."

"What!? Did he show any pain?'

"He didn't make a sound. It gave me the willies."

"It has to be the King's doing. I don't know what's up, but the King has a reason for him being here."

"I wish I knew what it was." She shivered in spite of the heat of the stove. That man should have died. Twice!"

"I know. But back to the question. How soon can we leave?"

"Soon, I think. We'll see what he looks like at breakfast."

"See what who looks like at breakfast?" Lachlaniel stood in the doorway, his hand resting on the top of the frame.

Thelma dropped the spatula in the pan, her mouth agape. "Wha... What are you doing out of bed?" Her hands trembled, and she wiped them on her apron to keep them still.

"I feel fine this morning, so I thought I'd have breakfast in here with you two."

"You really shouldn't be up you know." Elrad looked at Lachlaniel like he was some strange new creature. The vacant stare of the blind man's eyes was unnerving. "You should stay in bed. Rest for another day."

"Nonsense. There's no pain. I admit my strength isn't completely back, but there are things to be done. I must get to the great city."

"You shouldn't ride yet." Thelma's voice quavered. "Bouncing on the back of a horse for hours could crack those ribs. I'm sure they're not completely healed."

She picked up the skillet to serve the eggs. Her hand trembled and she wrapped both hands around the handle. Even so, she barely made it to the table and the skillet came to rest with a clang.

"Perhaps you're right. I'll make it a short day." Lachlaniel took a seat at the table. "I'll start after lunch and I'll walk instead of ride. How's that?"

Elrad sat down across from him. "That might be better. You rest until noon. We've got to make this place look abandoned. After lunch, we'll get started."

Aurora crept down the hall and stairs. Her pack, which was only half full, hung on one shoulder, and she held the strap in her hand. She had yet to get food for the journey. At the bottom of the spiral stairs, she peeked around the corner. The kitchen and waiter's assembly were empty. She stole into the pantry.

I've got to hurry. It won't be long before they close the gates and I want to go out with the last of the crowd.

She filled her pack with well-preserved food that would last many days. Her pack full, she slipped through the empty kitchen. Wisps of smoke ascended the chimney from smoldering embers. Outside the air was moist and dew lay on the grass. Nothing stirred until the calm was disturbed by a single dog barking in the distance. As she approached the barn, the smell of hay and manure assaulted her nose. A cat ran across the opening, and she jumped. Her heart pounded and her legs went weak. The horses shuffled in the darkness within, disturbed by her approach. Entering, the light of her stone filled the stalls and seemed to have a calming effect on the beasts. She found the horse she had picked out, a beautiful black mare named Cinnamon.

She laid her pack at the end of the stall and entered the tack room. Retrieving a saddle and blanket she started back out but caught her leather dress on a nail. She tried to free it but stopped abruptly. A horse nickered. Someone had entered the barn.

"Oy Rusty. And it's only me."

Capaleanan.

"You'll be wantin' a lump o' sugar, I'd be thinking. Now where did I put it? Glory be! And you're a rascally fellow this evenin'."

Aurora's eyes grew wide.

The pack!

She held her breath.

"Now be a good fella 'n' let me see ta the others."

There was silence as minutes passed. Minutes she couldn't afford to lose. She set the saddle down as gingerly as she could but the sound seemed to reverberate in the darkness as though someone had banged a drum. With her hands free, she freed her dress and looked up in time to see Capaleanan open the door.

"Miss Ophelia. And what be ye a doin' skulkin' 'round here? Sure 'n' it's too late ta be goin' for a ride."

"I'm trying to leave."

"And what'd ye be doin' that for? A fine young girl like you oughtn't to be runnin' 'round with that murderer on the loose."

"No. I'm leaving the city. It's an emergency. She paused and bit her lip, unsure what to say next.

"Ener... emert... Nev'r could pronounce that word. And what would that be?"

Best to tell the truth. As much as I can anyway, without letting on.

"My fiancée is in trouble. I have to get to him."

"Trouble eh. Pray be tellin' me – what kind of trouble?"

"He's entered a land of people called Basaners. They're chasing him."

"Basaners is it. Well I doubt that a wee young wisp of a girl will be any help."

"Oh please let me go!" Tears filled her eyes and ran down her cheeks. "I can't stand it. I've got to go to him!"

"Here now! None o' that! I didn't say I wouldn't let ya go. But ya can't go alone."

Aurora wiped her tears. "Not alone? You mean you'll go with me?"

"Me!? I think not. And what'd I be doin' leavin' me fine friends here to the hands of some lout? No, I was thinkin' me son Grady might go."

"Oh thank you!" Aurora said with half a laugh. "Thank you!"

She threw her arms around him in a tight hug.

"Here now! None o' that! None o' that! And what'd me missus say if she saw us?" he said pushing her away. "We've just time to get ye out o' here before they close the gates. There's a pack in the corner. Take it 'n' fill it with food while Grady and I saddle the horses. You'll be wantin' Cinnamon I'm thinkin'"

"Yes. Oh, thank you."

As she grabbed the pack, the bun of hair came loose. She hurried back to the kitchen, her hair flying behind her like a flag in a stiff breeze.

Lachlaniel was tired and sore. The afternoon had been long but the company good. The evening was warm. A fire wasn't necessary, except for cooking, but somehow as he sat near it, even though he couldn't see it, it warmed his heart. Perhaps it was its crackling embers, but whatever it was, it brought to mind old Diaphanous whose words and counsel added light to his path, mighty Max standing unyielding before the Aidan, Velius and Kesniel fighting to bring him to the Bridge, and Ewald and home.

I wish they were here. I wish any one of them was here. In spite of Elrad's and Thelma's company, I feel cold and alone.

A sudden shiver ran up his spine.

"A chill?"

Thelma's voice was musical, but it only served to deepen his sadness.

"No. Homesick I think. I feel cold and alone. Tomorrow we part company. Maybe I'm looking forward as well as back."

Thelma nodded.

"I understand. This country can make you feel alone. Cut off. Sometimes despair crouches at my door."

"I've felt that too," Elrad chimed in. "But Leofwine is always close. There's no need or place for despair. The King has everything in hand and works all for our good even when bad things happen."

Lachlaniel picked up a stick from the pile and snapped it in two. He threw it on the fire.

"If that's so, then why doesn't He do something about the Basaners? If Leofwine is close at hand, why doesn't He speak to me?"

Elrad stared into the fire for a moment. "The King brought you here didn't He? His plan will work out. As for the other... I don't know. There are times in the life of each of us when we look for Him, but He doesn't seem to be there; when we speak to Him, hoping He will answer, but there is only silence."

The fire continued to crackle as gloom seemed to settle on them.

Thelma broke the silence. "What you have to know and remember in those times is that He is still near. Sometimes He tests the faith of our friendship with Him. In those times, we must trust Him. Darkness doesn't last forever. It has no power against the Light."

Lachlaniel remained silent, brooding.

All that doesn't help when you're in the darkness and He's silent.

The Chuchoteur tried to tamp down this ember of hope. *Don't let them fool you. He's deserted you.*

Maybe.

Lachlaniel got up and laid out his bed roll. He tumbled on to it, bone weary in body and soul. Pulling the blanket over him, he slipped into the darkness of sleep.

Aurora and Grady approached the gate with a dozen other travelers who were leaving the city before the closing of the gate. The guards eyed each of the people who were leaving. Security had been tightened since the sabotage began. Before, only the gate keeper would have been present at closing, and the greatest scrutiny he would have given would have been to say 'Goodnight'. Now Aurora pulled her cloak about her.

I wish I could put my hood up, but as warm as it is, it would only make the guards suspicious. Perhaps the dark hair will be enough.

"You there!"

Aurora's heart sank. She pulled her kerchief and sneezed as the guard approached.

"Aren't you Capaleanan's son?"

"Why, yes sir. I'm Grady."

Aurora put her hand down. She looked up and away from the guard.

"Why are you leaving the city?"

"My father asked me to escort this lady on a journey."

"Journey eh? Where to?"

Grady looked over at Aurora. She pulled her kerchief back to her nose and sniffed.

"West." She blew her nose loudly. "I'm not sure how far. At least a couple of days ride." She continued wiping her nose.

"Bad cold?"

"Miserable."

"Summer colds are the worst."

Aurora sneezed again.

"If you don't mind my saying so miss, you ought to be in bed, not on a journey."

"It's an emergency."

"Well, the best of luck to you." Then, the guard shouted, "Let them pass."

Grady and Aurora put their heels to the horses' ribs and moved forward through the gate. She put her kerchief away.

"What was that all about? If you have a cold, then I've got pneumonia."

"I didn't want word to get back that I've left the city. How far do you think we can go before stopping for the night?"

Grady looked at her askance, and scratched his head. The gates clanged shut behind them.

"Three hours since sundown. If you're up to it, we might ride three hours before we make camp."

"Good. The farther down the road the better."

Grady looked at her with unspoken questions in his eyes.

"That much closer to my future husband."

And that much farther from the gates. When they find out I'm gone, they'll search the city, and then... Yes. The farther, the better.

She shook the reins and Cinnamon broke into a trot. Grady was caught unawares and spurred his horse to catch up.

"Are you trying to get away from me too?"

"What makes you say that?"

"That act at the gate. The hurry. And your phony answers. I'm not saying you lied, understand, but you're not telling me the whole truth."

Aurora rode on in silence.

"Alright. Don't answer. But don't try to get away during the night. The road is no place for a lady to be alone. Besides, I think you're going to need my help before we're through."

They rode on in silence. The scent of cut hay carried on the light summer breeze was their only company.

Chapter 12
Pursuit

Lachlaniel parted company with Elrad and Thelma at the main road. They headed east and he went west. The cool of the morning had worn away. By the time of their parting, it was hot. Now under the trees with no wind, it was stifling. The blackness of last night's mood, which had abated somewhat with the morning, now returned. A ferocious gnawing hunger for home and friends clawed his thoughts as he rode beneath the silent trees alone. Noon came and went with only what he could eat as he rode.

*I've come so far. To what purpose? I've failed to do anything about these...***Basaners**. *I haven't stopped them from killing a single person much less their torturing, but I must somehow. I hope the people of Chara will help. Why haven't they done anything about this before? Don't they care, or don't they know anything about it, and how could that be? Their fellow Ebenchaim slaughtered like sheep without their knowing? If they do know, how can they sleep nights? Surely there'll be someone there who will help me. I wonder how much farther.*

The thoughts rolled over and over in his mind as the weary miles passed beneath the horse's hooves. He met no one along the way. The brooding silence matched his mood. It was as though he were the last man alive.

"**WHAT!?** What do you mean she's missing!" Kesniel's bellow rattled the cups on the tray and brought the guards from outside the door.

His outburst frightened the maid so much she began to cry. "I'm sorry! I'm sorry!" the poor girl wailed.

Kesniel clenched his fists. The chair screeched as he pushed himself away from the table. He tried to control himself and martial his thoughts. The girl fell on her knees and continued to sob. He grabbed his old walking staff and stood up.

"No, please, don't."

The girl's pitiful plea fell on Kesniel's shoulders more than his ears. He leaned so on the staff he thought it would break.

"I'm not going to hit you, but you've taken all my strength." He fought hard against the weakness and slowly the strength returned to his legs.

"You must tell me exactly what happened."

The girl continued crying at his feet.

"We haven't time for this," he said gently. "If you want to help her, you must tell me what happened."

His softer tone was enough to slow the flood of tears. She turned her face up to him still crying.

"I went to her room this morning with breakfast, but there was no answer. I left the tray on the table in the antechamber. I returned with lunch a few minutes ago and the tray hadn't been touched. I knocked on her bedroom door, but there was no answer there either. I opened the door a crack. The bed was still made. I called for her and searched the entire suite."

"Was there a flower left anywhere?"

The girl's crying ceased as she closed her eyes trying to picture the scene.

"This is important. You must remember." Kesniel waited only briefly. "Never mind. Show me what you found."

The girl led him to the rooms. The windows were open and the warm breeze danced with the fluttering curtains. The tray lay on the low table by the divan, steam still emerging and immediately dissipating leaving only the aroma of tea. Kesniel left the maid in the parlor. In the bedroom, the dress that was her disguise lay on a chair and her new jewelry lay on the vanity. Kesniel went to her closet. Most of her clothes were still there, but some were obvious ones were missing.

"No flower anywhere. What could have happened? Did he take her or did she leave?" The silent air returned no answer. He returned to the parlor. "Have all the other servants search every inch of the grounds. Quickly now!"

The girl raced towards the door as Kesniel's voice echoed behind her.

"We must find her. She's in grave danger."

The portcullis dropped suddenly and seconds later the great gates closed. Runners reached every barracks and the home of every guard and soldier in the city. Within half an hour, they were searching every house, business, and public building in the city. Indeed, every nook and cranny of every building underwent a thorough search.

The sudden burst of activity was not lost on Andre.

Are they looking for me? No, they're everywhere and I'm in plain sight. They couldn't have missed me. I need to find out what this is all about.

He went into one of the shops after the soldiers had finished searching it. He looked at the owner.

"What's that all about?" he asked with a jerk of his thumb.

"I don't know. They're looking for someone, but they didn't say who. Can I help you with something?"

"Eh, no. No. I came in here to get out of the hubbub going on out there. You mind if I check out your fine establishment until that dies down a little?"

The shopkeeper smiled. "Not at all. Perhaps you'll find something that strikes your fancy."

Andre spent the next hour pretending to look over the shop's wares never straying far from the front window. The soldiers moved methodically from one building to the next. Their search was quick and thorough. When they had finally moved down the street and the traffic returned to something near normal he exited the shop and slipped into the crowds of shoppers.

Kesniel reached Ewald and was giving him the news when Mrs. Hughes entered. She was disheveled and breathless.

"Ewald, you've got to come! Quick, he'll kill him!"

"Who'll kill who?" Ewald and Kesniel said in unison.

"It's Max! He's going after Andrrre. I've never seen him so mad! You've got to stop him!"

Kesniel's face went pale. "Where is he?"

"He went rrround the corner, heading towarrrd the gate."

Kesniel looked at Ewald in alarm. "Go after him and grab as many men as you can along the way! I'll send word to the rest of our men to stop him!"

Ewald flew from the house as though it were on fire. He whistled and waved to every soldier he passed indicating they were to follow, but he never slackened his pace.

Andre might have kidnapped Aurora, and he might deserve everything Max will dish out, but Max will regret it. I've got to find him!

Ewald turned the corner and headed toward the gate, but just ahead the crowd had parted like water in the wake of a boat and at the center was Max. Ewald put on a burst of speed, the other soldiers at his heels. As he came up behind Max, he drew his sword and slapped the flat of the blade behind the big man's knees. Max went down in a heap, momentarily stunned. It was enough for the other soldiers to jump on him. In spite of this, he started to rise. Ewald yelled and another dozen men from the crowd added their weight to the pile. Max struggled, and for a moment the end was in doubt, but he finally succumbed after much effort. The entire pile of men as well as Max were breathless and exhausted, too exhausted to notice a tall figure in a frilly shirt carrying a cane slip out of sight through the crowd.

"We can't keep up this pace. The horses are worn out." Grady looked at Aurora with pleading eyes.

Last night they had covered thirty miles. After a short night's rest, they had covered another forty before noon.

"I'm sure your right, but I begrudge any delay."

"You haven't had much experience at this sort of thing have you?"

"No."

"Then, let me set the pace. I promise I'll get us there as fast as we can. There's a stream just up ahead. The horses need food and water. While they graze, we'll eat too."

They dismounted and walked the horses down to the stream. After making sure they didn't drink too much, they let them graze, tethered in the meadow beyond the trees. That accomplished they prepared to have lunch. Aurora started to get light fare out of the packs, but Grady stopped her.

"No Miss Ophelia. We ought to have a hot lunch. It will be some time before the horses will be ready to travel again."

"It's time I told you. My name isn't Ophelia."

Grady looked at her with pressed lips and a raised eyebrow.

"It's Aurora. I was sequestered in the residence to protect me from a man named Andre. They think he's the one guilty of the murders and mayhem in the city."

Grady threw his hands in the air. "Oh great! You're a fugitive! And not just any fugitive. You've got both a murderer and the King's men after us. I'd get on the horses now, but where to? Back into the arms of the murderer? Forward? To what? The danger your fiancée faces? You do have a fiancée?"

Aurora hung her head at his diatribe. "Yes. Can't we push on towards Lachlaniel?"

Grady sat down, his head in his hands. "How did I get into this mess?" He paused for a long moment. "Yes, we'll press on."

Aurora started towards the horses.

"But not now. Those poor things have to rest and eat. We'll do as I planned. A hot lunch for us, and rest for them."

Aurora started thinking about what she should pull from the packs while Grady rummaged through his saddle bags for his flint.

"When do you think we'll be able to start again?"

"The horses should rest most of the afternoon, but don't worry. We should be able to put some more miles under our feet before we stop for the night. If we can find an inn, that would be best. Both we and the horses would be well rested in the morning, and we should make good time tomorrow."

"How far do you think we can go by day's end?"

"Another fifteen or twenty miles but not much more. Less would be better."

Aurora bit her lip and looked back up the road.

They're sure to be looking for me already. They'll probably start following us soon, if they haven't by now. I hope we have enough of a head start.

"How far ahead do you think you're fiancée is?"

Grady's question broke her from her contemplations. I don't know several days anyway."

Grady's face changed to a look of intense thought. After a moment, he looked at her. "We probably won't catch him for two weeks if he's still on the move. We'll have to keep from pushing at this pace unless we get some true rest, like a night at an inn. Even then, we shouldn't push as hard as we have. And we should think about a day of complete rest every week. I know that's not what you want to hear, but it's the only way to catch up to him."

Aurora frowned. She looked down the road ahead; then, at the road behind and sighed. "Whatever you say. I just wish we could go faster."

She sat by the fire turning the food so it wouldn't burn.

Stay safe Lachlaniel, my love. I'm coming, and I'm sure to have a large group of soldiers right behind me. If they don't catch me first.

Lachlaniel had traveled alone on the road for some time, but as he passed smaller roads that joined the road to the great city, people became more and more frequent. The sounds of wagons, and carts, and people absorbed in conversation filled his ears.

It's like small streams joining a great river. The city must be quite large. With so many people, why haven't they done anything about the Basaners? Don't they care?

The Chuchoteur grew more ill at ease with every step toward the city.

No, they don't. This is all pointless. Give it up.

Lachlaniel gritted his teeth.

No. Not even if no one helps me, and I have to go back and face them alone again.

He passed through several towns. As he neared the crossroads in front of the city, the towns merged into one continuous community. There were merchants and shops of all sorts along the road, and along the various byways that sprang from it every hundred yards or so. There were vast inns that were indeed so large they could hardly be called inns any longer. Eateries also abounded with such an array of delights as to dazzle the senses as well as the palate. None of this mattered to Lachlaniel as a black, menacing cloud hung over his infuriated, gloomy thoughts. He stopped at an inn for the night. In the morning, he would enter the city.

Andre went to meet with the two tower guards he had bribed.
All is set. Tomorrow.
The two guards were waiting for him.
"Good evening gentlemen. I told you that you would be well paid for this mission and that it was of high importance to the commander. The time has come for the next step. Tomorrow during your watch, I will deliver to the tower a barrel for the mission."

The guards fidgeted. It was the taller guard who spoke, first. "You said we would receive another payment."

"You weren't satisfied with the first?"

"Yes. Certainly..." the shorter guard started.

"But?"

"But we didn't know it would be so secret that even our sergeant wouldn't know."

"You said something to him?"

"No. Of course not. The written orders you gave us from the commander were quite specific," the shorter guard answered.

The taller guard interrupted, "Specific about the punishment for saying anything about it to anyone too." He shuddered.

"So what's the problem?"

The shorter man began again. "Our sergeant inspected us and gave us double shifts for a month."

The taller guard glared at him. "I told you we couldn't let anything slip. Why didn't you get that blade sharpened?"

"I did. I picked it up from the smith like I told him," the shorter man shot back.

"So you think you should be paid extra for the extra shifts." Andre sighed.

"Well...yes," the shorter man replied shifting his feet."

Complications. Do they suspect the guards are up to something or is it just an overzealous sergeant trying to keep discipline?

"Alright. Agreed. Extra pay for the extra shifts."

The men smiled.

"But only after the mission is complete. You'll receive it with the final payment."

The two men looked at each other, then back at Andre, and nodded their assent.

"Now, when will you go on duty?"

Max had been escorted by a company of thirty men and half a dozen mounted horse guards to the king-steward's residence. It was late and Max was still stewing when Kesniel entered. He and Ewald rose and reseated themselves. Kesniel sat at the end of a conference table filled with officers and commanders.

"The entire city has been searched. She isn't here." Kesniel frowned.

Max banged his fist on the table in anger making even his two friends jump. "It's Andre's doing. I know it is."

There was a knock at the door and a guard opened it. Capaleanan looked at him sheepishly, his hat in his hand. The guard looked at him sternly and pointed toward the table. Capaleanan looked down. He started toward the table as though it was a gallows on which he was to be hung.

"I take it you have something to tell us." Kesniel scowled at the man.

"I think I know where the lady you're lookin' for has gone."

"Oh?" Kesniel's scowl did not soften.

"Out with it man!" Max bellowed.

The poor man looked as though he had been struck.

"A servant girl was in the barn last night. She said she had to leave the city. She said her fiancée was in trouble, and she had to go to him."

"And you let her go?" Max roared rising to his feet.

Capaleanan cowered in fear below the giant's towering figure.

"I didn't let her go alone. I sent me son Grady with her. They must've made it before the closing of the gates because they didna return."

"What did the girl look like?" Kesniel asked just to be sure.

"A real ailleacht she was. Raven black hair and skin so fair the Uset must've sung at her birth. Tall she was and well spoken for a servin' girl."

"That's Aurora alright." Ewald smiled.

"At least we know Andre hasn't got her." Kesniel said with a sigh of relief. "I'll deal with you later. Get whatever help you need and get the horses ready. All of them. Ewald, get a company of the Horse Guard. Have them ready to travel in half an hour. Max, you come with me."

Max sat on a horse at the gate with Kesniel and half a dozen guards. He made the great Clydesdale beneath him look like a pony. Behind them a group of wranglers surrounded the rest of the horses from the residence. The Horse Guards arrived with their extra mounts. Wrangler's rapidly herded these into their group of horses. The gates opened and the contingent rode forth in silence leaving Ewald to deal with Andre.

Chapter 13
Chara

The Great City Chara was more bustling inside than out, if that was possible. The streets were crowded with people buying and selling, with those going to or coming from a destination, and a few strangers, like Lachlaniel, who were taking in the sights. Lachlaniel was, of course, blind to the sights, and he paid no heed to the people around him. A man on a horse moved easily enough through the streets as the pedestrians moved out of the way lest they be trampled underfoot. This was not an easy task for them, but it was one they managed time and again as Lachlaniel was not the only one on horseback. He sensed this, however, as the horse never slackened his pace for an obstruction.

He found his senses overwhelmed. He was surrounded by the sounds, smells, and even the feel of the city as he sometimes brushed someone who's avoidance of the horseman left them closer than they might have wanted. It all gave him an impression of the city and its inhabitants. He heard the ring of a hammer on iron and turned in to the smithy hoping it might also be a livery. Dismounting, he followed the sound and the smell of hot steel to the anvil. The smith was engaged in shaping a shoe for the hoof of a horse he was shoeing.

"Have you a place for my horse?"

The smith looked up from the anvil to the side of the horse. The stranger was facing away from him.

"Are you blin...." He stopped in mid sentence; then, he continued. "No. No we don't keep horses here. There's a livery down the street about a quarter mile on the left. But if I were you, I would reconsider stabling your animal before you're ready to get off the market streets. Negotiating them will be difficult for a blind man. The horse will make it easier for you."

"I would, but I want to get a feel for the city and its people. It's hard to do that from horseback."

"Perhaps I can offer a solution. My son could act as a guide for some small payment."

How much?" Lachlaniel asked noting how much money played a part in the lives of these people.

"Five karpas a day"

"Done," Lachlaniel said despite the exorbitance of the amount.

"I'll get my son."

Lachlaniel pondered the grip riches had not only on this man but the entire city. He had noticed the prices of meals and lodging steadily increasing the closer he got. Altruism was not unknown here. In fact, he had observed great acts of benevolence, but those same people also seemed to be consumed with gain. He found this perplexing and disturbing.

The smith came back with a lad of about fourteen years.

"This is my son, Wyn. He'll guide you."

"Well Wyn, show me to the stables."

The boy led Lachlaniel back into the streets. Lachlaniel walked by him leading Aman. Lachlaniel heard the sounds of the people as they jostled around him. There were few beggars, but he heard the clink of many coins every time they cried out "Alms! Alms for the poor?" He gave some coins to the two that were near enough to reach. If he hadn't needed to be out in this crowd, he would have avoided it. Many were rude, even obnoxious, while others were indifferent, but a few were gracious, begging peoples pardon if they caused someone else distress of any sort. Some cursed Lachlaniel for bringing a horse into the marketplace even though this was the road that led into the city from the main gate. A few simply stood in the way and forced Lachlaniel and Wyn to find a way around them.

After half an hour of fighting the crowds, they came at last to the livery. Many horses were stabled there.

"I'm not sure they have room," Wyn said looking around for an empty stall.

"I'd like to at least get him off the streets."

"You may wish you had him with you once we venture back into the crowds."

"I hope they take good care of him."

"They will. This is one of the better liveries. My father knows the owner." Wyn looked around again and added, "That is they'll take good care of him if they have any room."

Lachlaniel heard heavy footsteps coming up from behind them. He turned as a crusty voice rang in his ears.

"Can I help you? Oh, it's you Wyn. What can I do for you and this gentlemen?"

"I need to stable my horse," Lachlaniel replied.

"Well you're in luck. We're pretty full even though it's so early, but we should have a couple of stalls left. Follow me."

They passed many stalls, some with the horses tied outside while young men cleaned them out. Others had groomsmen rubbing down and currying their charges. The sweet smell of hay and oats wafted through the air except where the stalls were being cleaned. A couple of the horses they passed smelled of liniment. All the activity eased Lachlaniel's mind as there was no doubt that the steeds were being well cared for. They came to a halt and the man took the reins from Lachlaniel.

"It's a loose box," the man said. "It's a little more, but it's all we have left. Ten karpas a day, the first day in advance."

Lachlaniel stiffened. It was more than he would've had to pay for a room at the best inn in Agapay and far more than any accommodation for man and horse both in Fairvale.

"Done," he said pulling out his purse. "I'll be here a few days: I don't know how many, yet. I may need him from time to time."

"It's five karpas extra to hold the stall for you."

Lachlaniel raised an eyebrow.

"Well, we're very busy as you can tell," the man said trying to justify his blatant greed.

"Very well, but see that you take special care of him for that price."

The man nodded and led Aman into the stall as Lachlaniel and Wyn headed back to the front of the livery. As they entered the street, there seemed to be great confusion a short way up the road. There was a large circle of people that blocked the way. Lachlaniel pushed his way forward when he heard raised voices. Wyn kept close to him as the people closed in behind them. They broke into the clear to find five men making sport of a man past middle age and a young girl.

Lachlaniel heard one man say, "Come on old man let us have her. Your kind doesn't belong here. This is our country. Let us have her, and we'll let you go unharmed."

Lachlaniel couldn't believe his ears, but what was worse, none of the people forming the circle moved in any way to help the beleaguered pair. He stepped forward and drew his sword. Very faintly, he perceived the man and girl. They were a hint of gold in his blackness.

"I think they belong here more than you." Lachlaniel declared, his anger rising.

"Not in our city," the man retorted.

"Your city?" Lachlaniel laughed with sarcasm. "This is the city of the King."

"We know no king, nor do we recognize any authority but our own."

"Of that I have no doubt, but you shall!"

Lachlaniel raised his sword to strike, and the men backed away, cowering in fear, but before he could strike, he felt a gentle touch on his arm.

"Do them no harm," the man said.

"Very well," Lachlaniel replied, his sword dropping to the ready. "If they leave. If not, they will feel my blade and be sorry for it," he said, his voice rising in anger.

The men entered the crowd which began dispersing. The girl put her face in her grandfather's chest and began to cry as fear fled and her pent up emotions were released. Lachlaniel sheathed his sword.

"There now child. It's all over. You're safe," the man said, holding the girl tight.

He held out a hand to Lachlaniel. When it wasn't taken, he looked up.

"You're blind, aren't you?" he asked.

"Yes."

The man took Lachlaniel's hand and shook it.

"I'm glad the King sent you our way. It was a near thing."

Lachlaniel looked towards him, but now saw only blackness.

"Who are you?" he asked as Wyn came forward and joined the three.

"I'm Jason. This is my granddaughter, Viera."

"I'm Lachlaniel and this is Wyn. He's my guide around the city."

"I think my granddaughter has had enough of the streets for now. Won't you come home with us? We would be honored to have you as our guests."

"Thank you. You're most kind."

Jason and Viera turned and headed up the street in the direction Lachlaniel and Wyn had been going. They followed pushing through the crowds as best they could. The four of them turned left at the next street and shortly were moving down a much less crowded avenue.

"What happened to the crowds?" Lachlaniel asked.

"You're not from around here, are you? Most of the shops and inns and such are on the main roads. Once you get off them, the traffic dissipates rapidly. My home isn't far now."

They turned right and went about two hundred yards and turned left again. As they approached the third house on the right, delicious aromas filled the air. Steak was the first scent Lachlaniel detected. It was followed by apples and cinnamon, some mixture of fruit, and finally, subtly mingling with the others, a faint odor he couldn't recognize. They reached the door and once inside were met by a sturdy woman in an apron.

"Dinner's not quite ready, sir. I wasn't expecting you back so soon."

"There was an incident. We were helped by this man. His name is Lachlaniel. This is my housekeeper, Zenia."

"How do you do?" Lachlaniel said as he bowed.

"Quite well I'm sure," Zenia said tittering.

"Zenia, would you set two more places at the table? And Viera, you see that the guest room is ready." Jason said.

"I hadn't intended to stay the night, and I'm sure Wyn's father will be expecting him."

"Nonsense. Where were you going to stay? At an inn? That will never do. We can't have friends staying with strangers. As to the boy, you may be right, but I won't send him home without a meal." Jason said adamantly with a smile.

Lachlaniel yielded to his host's hospitality. Jason showed them to comfortable chairs in the den while Zenia and Viera went to make things ready.

Soon the aroma of two fresh steaks being broiled floated in from the kitchen. This was followed by the clatter of dinnerware and plates being added to the table.

"Where are you from," Jason asked.

"The Great City Agapay, though it seems much smaller now that I've seen this sprawling behemoth and its teeming masses." Catching his host's movements he added, "I mean no detraction; I'm just overawed by its size. My hometown is an anthill in comparison."

"Then, you're not originally from Agapay."

"No, a town to the south called Fairvale. Agapay seemed massive. I had no idea people lived in any place this large though."

"Chara is the largest of the Seven Cities. Its population is many hundreds of thousands of people. It and its surrounding towns have merged into one giant conurbation. As a result, you can find things here that you couldn't find anywhere else in a thousand leagues. Fresh fish from the ocean is one of the few things you won't find, more's the pity."

"Then, you're not originally from here either?" Lachlaniel said inquisitively.

"No, I come from across the sea, but I moved to Egkratia on the coast and later here. This has been my home for many years now. My son married here and my granddaughter was born here."

"I should like to meet your son."

"He and his wife are both dead. They were killed by the Basaners."

"I'm sorry. This is most troubling to me. Perhaps you can answer my question. Why isn't anything done about the Basaners?"

"Most people here don't even know about them, nor would they care."

"Why?"

"Once, this city was filled with Ebenchaim. Now, less than half the population are. The city grew, and as it grew, it became wealthy. Many people immigrated. The desire for gain began to override all else. A sense of benevolence and charity still reside here. They were planted deep at this city's foundation, but such acts have become easy because of the great affluence. The Ebenchaim have become lazy in their service to the King. There are many who still serve Him with a whole heart, but many have been lulled to sleep. Instead of living by the King's commands, of trying to bring people to the Bridge and getting them across the chasm, they enjoy a life of ease and luxury.

There are no Basaners here, mind you, but there are many who do not like us, and their numbers are growing. It is difficult enough to get the Ebenchaim to recognize *that* problem. They are blind and deaf, begging pardon, to the evil in the surrounding countryside. All they see is the need to keep up with the Edoms and maintain their status."

"Dinner is ready," Zenia interrupted.

They adjourned to the dining room. Lachlaniel sensed that this was a nice home but not overly so. He brushed the drapes as he was shown to his place at the table. They were of a light material, not the heavier material that opulence could afford, but they were drapes. The touch of the table said good wood, but there was no carving, ornate or otherwise. He sat in a chair that was sturdy and reasonably comfortable, but not upholstered. Steak for dinner was out of place, but he was soon to find out why.

Viera didn't join them, though Zenia did. She came in and served everyone, and then, she sat at Jason's right.

"Let us praise the King for our bounty."

"Aren't we going to wait for Viera?" Lachlaniel asked puzzled.

"She never eats on her father's birthday anymore, but it is still my habit to celebrate the day," Jason answered.

He thanked the King in song for His protection through Lachlaniel, for the provision of food, and for his son and daughter-in-law. They passed the meal with small talk. At the end of the meal, Wyn who had been silent throughout the afternoon stood and said, "I should get back home."

Lachlaniel gave the boy the agreed amount and asked, "Can you guide me tomorrow also?"

"Sure."

"Meet me here at ten o'clock."

"Yes sir." Wyn said as they left the dining room and moved toward the front door.

He turned as he entered the street and said, "Thank you for the meal." Then, he turned back and headed for home.

"I'd like to go to the Dome of Meeting tomorrow," Lachlaniel said grabbing his cloak.

"Which one? There are several."

"I'll start with yours," Lachlaniel said surprised.

"I can see by your expression you didn't expect there to be more than one. We have one main one that houses the council, but the need was great so lesser ones were built specifically for the Ebenchaim to have more meeting places," Jason explained and smiled. "Well it is a big city."

Lachlaniel shook his head in wonder. "Perhaps you should show me my room. Tomorrow is liable to be a busy day."

Max was still indignant. The poor beast carrying him suffered under his constant shifting. At last, Kesniel could stand to see this no more.

"Get down from that poor creature."

"You would have me walk?"

Kesniel scowled. "No, that would slow us down. I would have you run. If you're not going to settle down, then perhaps we can run off some of your excess energy."

Max was taken aback. No words came to him for a retort, so he dismounted and began running to keep up. His great strides ate up the ground. He found that it wasn't too difficult as the horses were not being pushed hard. After a quarter of an hour, Kesniel called a halt. The men dismounted to walk by their horses. Max stopped, puffing.

"Not you." Kesniel said.

"What?"

"You keep running."

Max looked skyward and took a deep breath. "Is this a joke?"

"No." Kesniel's statement was flat and showed no hint of humor. His face said he was not to be trifled with on this point.

Max made no reply but muttered something unintelligible after his first few strides. Kesniel looked at the Asher and smiled.

"We'll all get new mounts when we catch him. Maybe by that point he'll be too tired to be surly."

The Asher watched the big man run. "I hope so. It isn't good when Max is out of sorts."

If we have to, we'll run him till we make camp. A good night's sleep, and he might see things in a new light."

Chapter 14
Explosion!

The Carpenters Guild was a building that sat catty-corner to the west side of the tower. It was a meeting place for builders and out of work carpenters. It was rarely used anymore and made a perfect hiding place for Andre.

This is the day I have waited for. Today I will be rid of the accursed light in that tower!

Andre sat up. The dingy room with its cobwebs and mouse holes mocked him.

After today, this city will be mine, and I won't have to hide or live in filth like this. My kingdom will expand and my reach will lengthen. Soon, even Meph will bow to me instead of me to him.

His stomach growled. There would be no breakfast today.

When I'm done, I will feast.

He threw on his clothes as fast as he could and headed out for the day's endeavors, but he paused at the door. Looking at the room with contempt he spat on the floor and left.

Ewald greeted the dawn. The half dozen guards that had taken up residence in the second floor room of the inn across from the west entrance to the tower were sleeping soundly. Ewald rubbed his eyes. The two guards below, who were under suspicion, were just being relieved by the next watch.

"Good I can get some rest now."

He stood up and stretched. He watched the two as they moved south down the street. There was rapid movement along the wall of the Carpenter's Guild that disappeared into the doorway.

That'd be Dan. Second best tracker in the guards. I'm glad he's assigned to keep an eye on them today.

He began shaking the sleeping men.

"Rise and shine. 'A sleeping stone shows no light'."

That's a silly saying. The stones always give light.

Men rolled out of their beds rubbing their eyes and stretching. The next man on watch stretched and yawned as he went to the chair before the window.

He seated himself and called without looking back, "Send up some breakfast...and some coffee, will you Ewald."

Ewald grunted as he left the room. The night had been long and he was tired. As he descended the stairs, the aromas of the kitchen rose to greet him. He half-smiled until he smelled the coffee.

Not today! I've got to get some sleep. I have a feeling tonight will be a busy night.

What he didn't know was that Andre had come down from his room in the empty Carpenters Guild and was even now moving a barrel in the basement towards the hoist.

Lachlaniel was up long before nine, which seemed to be the normal time for the people of Chara to rise. At least, that was when he began noticing traffic in the street beneath his window. The sounds of carts and voices reached his ears about the same time as the scent of breakfast reached his nose. Knowing it was safe to descend the stairs without rousing the whole house he repaired to the kitchen. Zenia stirred a pot, turned meat, whipped eggs, and made sure the coffee didn't boil over. The clank of utensils and the breeze from her flurried movements told Lachlaniel she was much too busy to be engaged in conversation, so he seated himself at the table.

"Wise move." Jason said with a smile.

Lachlaniel jumped. "You're as quiet as a cat. Have you been sitting there or did you just come down?"

"I just came down. I used to scout for the army in the days when the city wasn't so large and populous. Now days they have no use for Ebenchaim in the army."

Lachlaniel's expression changed to one of incredulity. "No place? This is the King's city."

"Was," Jason corrected. "Many do not even recognize that much. Those that feel that way do not even believe there is a King."

"But the light?"

"Some are glad for certain aspects of the light and some for others, but very few who aren't Ebenchaim recognize where the light comes from. They all want to change the light and often try. They fail miserably of course. All they do is block the light. Here in this Great City of the King, areas of darkness have formed and have begun to grow. Even many Ebenchaim have fallen into this snare of the enemy."

Lachlaniel shook his head in disbelief.

"Enough of your politics," Zenia said interrupting. "It's time to eat."

She placed the food on the table and called Viera. Viera came and Zenia exited.

Zenia's not eating with us?"

"No she doesn't eat breakfast. She likes to get about her housework."

There was little talk at the meal. The men lapsed into silence and busied themselves with the food before them. Afterwards, Lachlaniel and Jason retired to the living room and got to know each other better. Before they knew it, there was a knock on the door as Wyn showed up punctually at ten. Jason answered the door.

"Come in my boy," he said.

Wyn took off his cap. "Thank you sir,"

I'm glad I told him ten o'clock. We wouldn't have finished breakfast otherwise.

"Now where is your Dome of Meeting," Lachlaniel asked Jason

After a few short directions during which Wyn nodded that he knew the way, Lachlaniel thanked his host, and he and Wyn headed off down the street. Wyn followed the directions meticulously, and they soon arrived at the domed building. It was perhaps half the size of the Dome of Meeting in Agapay. They, along with many citizens, climbed the steps and entered the building.

There was a foyer that had a few doors leading to other rooms but no hallways. The large main doors lead to the auditorium where a few had already gathered. Lachlaniel led the way and chose some seats down front. The lectern was up a short flight of steps to the top of the dais and stood a few feet to their left. They sat back and waited for the Chief Halvord to arrive. Lachlaniel contemplated what he would say when he got the opportunity.

As the last of the people took their seats, the Chief Halvord entered and strode to the lectern. He spoke for some time about the war with Kieran, the chasm, and the Bridge. All the while, Wyn squirmed in his seat. When He finished speaking, Lachlaniel stood and asked to be recognized. After a moment of conferring with all the Halvord that were present, Lachlaniel was shown to the lectern. Wyn, who had been standing on the edge of the group, caught the Chief Halvord as the group dispersed. Lachlaniel addressed the assembly.

"People of Chara, I have been sent to this city by the King. As I traveled, I learned that the areas beyond the influence of this city are controlled by the Basaners. This group of evil men and those that rule them are capturing the King's servants whom they beat, torture, and kill. I myself have been beaten by them twice. I know of your benevolent acts, but now is the time to go beyond benevolence and rise up to free your brothers. Those who are willing, meet me here in front of the lectern."

Lachlaniel walked down the steps and waited. Slowly men began to gather. Twelve men out of the congregation volunteered.

"It will be about five or six days for there and back, and how long we will be there I don't know. But our brothers and sisters need us. Will you go with me and fight until they're free no matter how long it takes?"

There was murmuring as the men discussed the proposal. The murmuring stopped after some minutes. A short man stepped forward. He was slight of build and looked as though a gentle breeze would break him in half, but he had a fiery spirit and a passion for the King that was beyond physical strength.

"We're with you, all of us," he said with a deep voice that was incongruous with his body. "I am Wilmot, the small."

"He may be small but you don't want to fight him!" a hefty voice from the back called out with a laugh. The rest of the men chuckled in agreement.

"What do you want us to do," Wilmot asked.

"Gather what you need for the trip, and meet me here at eight o'clock tomorrow morning." He paused as he suddenly became aware of Wyn's absence. "Have any of you seen the boy who was with me?"

There was a general murmuring again as the men discussed the situation. Abruptly, a man on the left said, "We think he went with Aldhelm, the Chief Halvord. They will probably be back soon."

"Good. If you see them, tell Wyn I'm waiting here."

The men dispersed and Lachlaniel took a seat on the first row in front of the lectern. Twenty minutes went by as he pondered what they must do and how to accomplish the task. Wyn's voice pulled him from his thoughts.

"Lachlaniel? Sir?"

Lachlaniel stirred and sat up.

"I thought you must be asleep. I've called you several times," the boy said anxiously.

"No, just deep in thought," Lachlaniel replied. "Where have you been?"

"I took him to the Bridge," Aldhelm interjected.

"Good for you Wyn!" Lachlaniel exclaimed as he took Wyn's hand and shook it. "You must tell me about it." He turned to Aldhelm and said, "Thank you. I'm afraid I haven't even given a thought to the boy's needs in all this."

"You needn't worry about him now, but from what he tells me, you might help with his father."

"I will." He put his arm about the boy's shoulders, and they walked out of the building with Wyn chattering a mile a minute.

Lachlaniel and Wyn had visited three more meetings before they had started for home. His somber mood matched the dimming light of dusk.

Forty men from four meetings. Less than a dozen each. This in a city of hundreds of thousands!

It isn't worth even trying. Call it off. When they meet in the morning, tell them to go back home.

Maybe I should, but I won't. I'll take whatever help I can get. Forty men. Maybe I should postpone and go to more of the domes.

No! This can't wait. Use the ones you've got!

Yes. It's too important to wait. We'll start with those who come in the morning.

Ewald was awakened by one of the guards.

"It's almost evening sir. Time for your watch."

Ewald rolled to his side and brushed his hair back with his hand. He rubbed his eyes as he sat up.

"That late already?"

"Yes sir. Everyone's in position."

"Good." He said brushing back the hair that had once again fallen in his eyes. "Go down to the kitchen and bring me some food. I'm going to take the chair."

"Do you think he'll try tonight?"

"Can't tell. He might."

The guard exited as Ewald crossed the room to the basin of water on the dresser. He splashed water on his face and rubbed the sleep from his eyes. After dressing, he moved to the next room and took over from the guard in the chair. He looked down on the street. Everything was quiet. The two guards were at their posts. He was about to sit down when he saw something by the corner of the tower. He couldn't make it out in the fading light but there was a small object lying on the ground.

"Wait!" he called to the guard who was about to leave. "Come back over here."

The guard came to the window. "Yes sir?"

"What is that?"

The guard looked at the spot on the street where Ewald was pointing. "I don't know sir."

"Stay here and watch. I'm going to check it out."

Ewald raced down the stairs. He came to a stop at the doorway and peered into the street. There was no one to be seen. He moved as stealthily as possible to get a view of the flower. It was a tansy.

Andre was just starting to roll the barrel up the street from the guild when he a caught a hint of movement by the inn. He pulled the barrel back into the shadows and looked around.

They're on to me. I can't hide it here any longer. Nothing for it now.

He took out a knife, pried the lid open, inserted a fuse, and closed it again. He rolled the barrel into the street and lit the fuse.

I hope it makes it as far as the corner of the tower.

He kicked the barrel with all his might. The barrel began rolling up the street far faster than it should have.

Well! I hope it doesn't go past the doors!

He melded with the shadows and was gone.

Ewald heard something rolling in the street and turned to see flying sparks and a rolling object. He yelled at the guards near the door.

"Get inside!"

He turned and leaped through the inn's doorway as the barrel passed the corner. A brilliant light and tremendous thunder reached his ears at the same instant. Glass from the window blew in striking his back, and the wall crumbled leaving him buried beneath the debris.

His last thought was, *I'll be facing the King soon to tell Him I failed.*

Aurora and Grady crested a hill. It was late afternoon, and the air was still and sultry. Neither leaf nor blade of grass stirred. They led their mounts toward the fork in the road which lay before them.

"I think we should be ready to ride fast and hard. The birds are in their nests and the animals their burrows. The storm will break on us soon, I'm thinkin'."

Aurora looked at him with a wisp of a smile. "Your father's in your voice."

"Aye. It happens when I'm nervous or scared."

"Which are you now?"

He gave a nervous chuckle. "A little of both, I expect. We haven't walked them enough, but we should get mounted. When the storm comes, it'll come suddenly."

When they had mounted, Aurora asked, "Which way? I have a feeling Lachlaniel went south but the other is the main road."

Grady looked up at the clouds. His voice quavered. "The north fork. The clouds are lowering and swirling."

Lightning flashed behind them.

"Ride!"

Grady slapped the rump of her horse as he put the spurs to his own. Before they reached a gallop, thunder boomed and the wind began to rise to a roar. They passed a great oak in the middle of the fork and were just under the trees as the limbs began swaying maniacally. Aurora looked back in time to see the great oak pulled up from the ground by a swirling cloud and thrown over the trees above them.

"Aghhhh!!"

Grady didn't look up as the tree crashed down to their right ripping limbs and splintering wood as it came.

His face was ashen. "RIDE!"

The horses needed no spurring. They too were wild eyed fleeing the destruction at their heels. Aurora fell on her horse's neck and clung for life.

"Run, Cinnamon! RUN!"

The swirling cloud was ripping a swath through the trees not a hundred yards behind them to their left. Hail pelted the road before them. Behind, the swirling wind drew closer as it crossed to the north side of the road. Branches were ripped from trees above their heads as the horse's hooves crunched the fallen hail. The cloud was now snapping tree trunks not fifty yards to their right as the road began curving away from the horrific sight. Aurora could see Grady's mouth moving as he yelled something, whether to the horse or her made no difference as only the deafening roar of the spinning wind could be heard. They rounded the curve and caught sight of a farm house and barn a quarter of a mile further on.

The road had veered from the path of destruction, but the cloud, as though it had a mind of its own, turned and moved toward the road again. The hail let up. It too was being sucked into the malevolent rotating wind. Aurora's hair was whipping to her right and she could feel her body growing light as it lifted in the saddle despite her grip. Grady grabbed her horse's harness and slowed the crazed beast as he turned into the courtyard of the house and barn. The barn door flapped wildly in the tempest's gale. They rode through the gaping hole into the supposed safety of the barn. Grady jumped from his horse and ran to the door to close it, but the funnel of wind was approaching. As he was forced to retreat, he saw the spiraling cloud lift from the ground ripping the roof off the barn as it spun overhead. Aurora was standing frozen in place where she had dismounted. Grady threw himself at her knocking her into a pile of hay and covering her with his body. Then, as quickly as it had come, it was gone leaving silence and a ravaged countryside behind it.

Rain fell through the ruptured roof soaking the body of an unconscious Grady as he lay atop Aurora. He was a lot heavier than she had supposed, and she found it difficult to roll him off of her enough to extract herself. Having managed it, she rose. Part of a beam lay across his leg. She got a rope from his horse. She tied it around the beam and threw the other end over the rafter. Fastening it to the horse's saddle, she urged the beast forward. The beam rose, and she moved the limp form far enough to clear where the beam would come to rest. A shard of the roof had pierced his side breaking ribs in the process. She left the barn hoping there was someone alive in the house who had more skill in healing than she had.

We've made good time since we changed mounts after lunch. We should be catching up to Aurora soon. Even if they're pushing hard, they shouldn't be more than a half a day ahead.

As they were about to crest the next hill, a scout came galloping back to them. He came to a halt in front of Kesniel spattering them with mud.

"There's great devastation ahead."

"The enemy?"

"I don't think so. If it is, it isn't any of his normal troops. Trees and limbs scattered across the road, some torn up by the roots and some snapped in half like twigs."

Kesniel's eyes grew wide and he frowned. He motioned the men forward.

"Draw swords."

They crested the hill. From its bottom forward to beyond where the road forked, tree limbs from small to those of great size were strewn across the road. The north fork was blocked by a massive walnut tree that had been uprooted and cast aside. As they neared the fork, they could see the hole where it had once stood on the south side of the fork. The south fork was not blocked, but the going would be slow and torturous down that road.

Max was incredulous. "What do you think?"

Kesniel looked around. "I don't think it was the enemy or at least not directly. Look here." He pointed. "And there. See the path whatever it was made. It's erratic."

Max followed the track with his eyes. Devastation starting in the tops of the trees at the bottom of the hill where limbs were torn off, moving down to the ground by the time it reached the fork. There it tore the walnut tree out of the ground along with many smaller trees. It moved to the middle of the fork where there was another huge hole. It moved along the road for several hundred yards. Max could see where it crossed the north fork ripping the road and leaving what could only be described as freshly plowed earth. It also grew wider. It followed the north fork west for a hundred more yards before it was lost to his sight among the trees.

He looked down the road from his perch atop the Clydesdale with a more intent gaze. "We can pick our way forward for a while, but we're going to have to dismount and use some axes on the mess up ahead."

"If we're going to have to do that we might as well clear the road for future travelers. Only a few of us can work on what's in front of us. The rest can clear that south fork and clean up the downed branches. It will be a lot of work before we can get moving ahead. How long do you think?"

Max scrunched his mouth and squinted. "About a day unless there's more of this further on."

"That was what I thought too. I wish Ewald were here. The work might go more quickly with his supervision. The path it took is pretty clear of debris on the north side of the road. We can use it for a base. Have the cooks and their helpers set up camp there. Send some scouts down the south fork. The rest of us have a lot to do before night fall."

Chapter 15

Surveillance

The next morning Lachlaniel was awakened by a cock crowing somewhere in the distance. Jason fed him breakfast and saw him off. He arrived at the Dome of Meeting by seven-thirty. The first men started showing up by seven-forty; the stragglers by eight-ten. The last to arrive was Jason.

"I decided to join you."

Lachlaniel's dour expression changed, and the corners of his mouth took a slight upward turn. "I'm glad you're here. We can use every man we can get. Let's be off."

They gathered their things and the few with horses mounted them, and they started at a walk until they noticed Lachlaniel was pulling up the rear.

"Shouldn't the leader be in front?" one man asked.

"I don't know the way," Lachlaniel stated flatly.

"Why, you're blind!" Wilmot exclaimed aghast.

"Yes, I am, but that doesn't stop me. The last battle I was in, I led an army."

"I find that a little hard to believe," came a voice from the back.

"Do any of you want to back out? Now is the time. Think about it, but remember the people we were going to help." Lachlaniel declared hotly.

"Us getting killed won't help them," a man said turning to leave.

He and three others headed for their homes while the rest looked on and Lachlaniel frowned.

"Alright, if the rest of you are with me, let's go. Time is wasting."

"Where to?" Wilmot asked.

"The main road into the city. I need to pick up my horse at the livery and stop at the smithy near the gates."

"The livery nearest the smithy?" Wilmot asked.

"Yes, and let's be quick about it."

"I don't know how quick we'll be. The market will already be crowded, but we'll do our best."

There was hardly a pause before Lachlaniel said, "Those of you with horses ride on our flanks to make a way for us through the crowds."

The men smiled nodding approval. Everyone formed up, and they marched off to a song of the King through the side streets as they made their way toward the main avenue. It was almost nine o'clock before they reached the livery. Lachlaniel told the owner he needed his horse and wouldn't be back for some time. He paid the man, and the group headed back out into the street toward the smithy and the gates. Lachlaniel dismounted and stepped into the smithy. Wyn saw him and took him to his father. Lachlaniel extended his hand and said, "Thank you both. He was a good guide. If I return, I'd like to use his services again."

"You know he entered the King's service," the smith said sternly looking at Lachlaniel's hand.

Lachlaniel dropped his hand. "Yes. I'm sorry he didn't let you know about it first."

"The boy's old enough to make his own decisions, but I don't like people who meddle in others affairs." he snapped.

"I'm sorry. I didn't know anything about it until after."

"Well, I'll overlook it, but I'm not happy about it," he said in a milder though still perturbed tone of voice.

"I would still like to use him as a guide when I return, if that's ok."

"Talk to me when you get back. I'll decide then," the smith said brusquely as he turned back to his work.

Lachlaniel stood there for a moment; then, he returned to the waiting men and his horse. He mounted, and they proceeded to the city gates. As they moved forward through the crowds, he thought about the incident.

The smith will not be an easy one to get across the chasm. It will require delicacy and finesse. I'm glad Wyn crossed though. At least, this wasn't a wasted trip even if I didn't take him to the Bridge myself.

When he turned his attention from the smith and Wyn back to the trip, he found they were making their way through the city gates. The sound of hooves and voices and many other things echoed off the walls, He could sense the protectiveness of the city falling away as they moved out into the avenues beyond the walls. The sounds of commerce filled his ears as they rode on through the day. They didn't stop for the night until late.

Wilmot turned and looked at Lachlaniel. His head was drooped forward. Several of the other men were also asleep in the saddle. The rest were haggard.

He gently roused Lachlaniel. "This is the last of the large inns. From here, we're likely not to find rooms for all of us in one place. Besides the horses are spent and the men are falling asleep while riding."

"Alright. We'll stop here."

"Dismount!" Wilmot called out.

The innkeeper came out in a huff.

"What do you think you're doing? Are you trying to wake everyone in the inn?"

Wilmot looked at the small heavyset man. "We need rooms. We've been riding all day and can't go any further."

The man looked at the crowd and began to smile as he counted heads.

"Yes certainly. You'll have to crowd together. There's only a few rooms, but we can find enough cots for everyone. There's a stable in back. I'll send a couple of boys to help with the horses, but do be quieter. I'm the only one up at this hour."

The weary men turned toward the back of the establishment, and the innkeeper went to wrest two of his attendants from their sleep.

What!?

Ewald's mind rose crazily to the surface of the sea of unconsciousness. Sounds, at first strange, assaulted his ears, and gradually sharpened into the familiar – footsteps, voices, the clanging of bowls and metal. He opened his eyes.

What happened?

He started to sit up, but hands on his shoulders restrained him.

"You just lie still."

The voice was unfamiliar. His eyes began to focus. There was a face staring down at him.

"You're lucky to be alive."

"The explosion. Is the Tower okay!?"

"Slight damage. The doors were blown in. The inn wasn't so lucky. The whole front collapsed. It was hours before we pulled you from the rubble."

Ewald scowled as his head pounded. "What about the men?"

"Those on the second floor were sent crashing into the street when the floor collapsed beneath them. We got to them first. No serious injuries." His face grew grave. "The ones guarding the door to the tower were dismembered. No one else was injured."

Ewald put his hand on his head. "Did we catch him?"

"No, I'm afraid not."

Ewald started to get up again, but the man pinned his shoulders to the mattress. "You're not going anywhere today. I'm a healer. Your healer. If you give me any trouble, you'll be here tomorrow too."

Ewald's muscles relaxed and the man let go and stood up.

"If I can't go anywhere then I must see Dan."

The healer thought for a moment.

"All right, but he can't stay long. You must rest."

"But I feel fine."

"You've quite a lump on the back of your head as well as cuts from the glass. If you try to get up, we'll be picking you up off the floor. You may not feel much now, but when the 'Uset's Touch' begins to wear off..."

"Uset's touch?"

"You haven't been around healers much, have you? 'Uset's Touch' is an aromatic herb. Broken and soaked in water it relieves pain. That's why you feel so good right now. This afternoon we'll stop the treatment and you probably won't feel like moving. At least until tomorrow. After that, you should be able to do anything you feel up to. Dan's trying to organize protection for the Dome, the Residence, and the Tower, but I'll send word to come when he's free."

Ewald closed his eyes. He felt suddenly tired.

The healer stood up. "Sleep, that's best."

"Wake me when he comes. I must talk to him."

Ewald felt himself drifting off and fought to stay awake, but the sea beckoned to him and was too strong to resist.

The warm breeze stirred the tattered curtains of the farm house. The farmer's wife, a strong woman about Aurora's age with brown hair and eyes, entered the bedroom. Aurora sat by the bed, her head slumped forward. The woman crossed the room and checked the bandage on Grady's side. He hadn't been injured nearly as badly as first appeared. Once removed, the wound showed that the shard had not penetrated all the way to the bone though two ribs were broken. The gash was deep but once stitched it would cause fewer problems than the ribs. They had bound the chest tightly and made Grady sleep sitting up. There was no blood on the bandages and the woman turned to Aurora. The raven locks of her dyed hair seemed to pick up the light from the stone at her side reflecting its radiance in strange hues. The woman picked up the stone and looked at the dark world outside her window.

What a marvelous thing this light is. What beauty it brings.

She turned back to Aurora and lightly put her hand on Aurora's shoulder. Aurora jumped and sat straight up.

"The roof! It's falling!"

The woman put the stone in Aurora's hand and spoke soothingly. "No. It was a dream. There's no storm. Everything's alright."

Aurora clasped the woman's hand to the stone and leaned her head on the woman's side.

"It was so horrible."

She looked up. The woman had tears in her eyes.

"I want to cross the Bridge. I want to serve your King as you do."

Aurora smiled and stood. She brushed the tears from the woman's eyes and then from her own.

"Of course." She paused. "I don't even know your name."

"Brigit."

Before they could move, the noise of horses approaching came through the window. Aurora peered out the window. It was a group of soldiers. She recognized several, but she couldn't see any sign of Max or Kesniel from this angle.

"You mustn't let them know we're here."

"I'll not breathe a word."

The Brigit pulled her hand from the stone leaving Aurora's on it. She closed the door behind her.

When she came into the courtyard, she was confronted by a huge horse with an even more enormous man riding it.

"Excuse me ma'am, we're looking for a young man and a beautiful woman who may have come riding through here."

"We've been trying to take care of the damage from the whirling wind," Brigit said truthfully.

"We must find them."

She turned her attention to the regal looking man who was so dwarfed by his companion that she hadn't noticed him.

Kesniel looked at her intently. "Is this the main road?"

"Yes sir."

"What of the other road?"

She didn't like the way his eyes pierced her. There was something disturbing—unsettling in that look.

"It moves southwest from here. It's well traveled."

"If you should see them would you go to the dispatch and send me word?"

"Dispatch?"

"You're not a servant of the king?"

"No sir."

"Very well. If you see them, try to get them to take the main road, but say nothing of us."

"Yes sir, I will."

The men turned. Moving back onto the road the regal man signaled for the group to move forward, and they filed by the courtyard at a walk in twos and threes.

Kesniel called a halt a mile down the road.

Max raised an eyebrow. "What do you think?"

Kesniel pulled at the corner of his mustache. "They could be there. The light we saw from the window could be their stones. On the other hand they may have moved on."

"She said she wasn't a servant of the King."

"That doesn't mean everyone living there is like her. No, I think she's hiding something. The question is, '*What* is she hiding'. I'm going to send two men to watch the house and two to take the other road. If they see anything, one can report back while the other continues to watch."

"Shrewd. I'd like to watch the house."

Kesniel mused for a moment. "No, I think I still want you with me. We need direction from the King, and you should be there."

Max breathed out a slow long sigh. "I'm sure you're right but it's not what I want to do."

"Is following the King ever easy?"

"In twenty-five years, I have never found it easy to do what He wants when what He wants is not what I want."

Kesniel smiled. "It's been a lot longer for me, but submitting to His will is never easy, even now. Thankfully I find that as I've grown older and known Him better, my will lines up with His more." His smile faded. "I wish it always did."

Aurora peeked from the bedroom doorway waiting for Brigit to return. Brigit came back in alone, and Aurora could hear the horses and men moving off down the street.

"It's okay. They've gone."

"What did they want?"

"You."

"And?"

"They think you've gone ahead on the main road apparently."

"You didn't say anything?"

"I said we'd been cleaning up after the whirling wind."

"Who did you talk to? What did they look like?"

"One was a huge man on a big horse. It looked like a pony beneath him. The other was quite regal. I didn't like the way he looked at me though. It was unsettling."

"Max and Kesniel." Aurora frowned and bit her lip. "How soon can we leave?"

"Your friend might move tomorrow, but he won't be able to ride for many days. You could use some rest yourself. You've hardly slept. I didn't want to disturb you but I want to cross the Bridge. My husband, Garth, too. We're ready to serve the King."

"When will he return?"

"He should be back by evening."

"I'll talk to the King and see where we need to go to cross."

"Don't you know?"

"Me? Oh my, no."

"But I thought you crossed."

"I have, but the crossing point is different for each person."

"There's more than one Bridge?"

"No, no, no. The Bridge doesn't change, but where it crosses in your life is not the same as mine. How you get there and what brings you to the Bridge is different for every person, but there is only one Bridge made by Eleutherias. It's narrow. Only one person can cross at a time even if many have come to the same place."

"It's all so very different than anything I've known. Like the Light. I never imagined anything so beautiful."

"Yes it is. I grew up with the Light all around me. I can't imagine what it's like to live in darkness never even knowing the Light existed. My fiancée never saw the Light until shortly before he crossed the Bridge, but before he got to the Bridge, he went blind."

"What happened?"

"He was attacked by the enemy."

"Then, why did he cross the Bridge?"

"It's not just about the Light. It's about living to serve the King. Following His ways. Enjoying His presence." Aurora frowned as if in pain.

"Are you alright?"

"I wish he were here. I haven't heard from him in weeks Oh, I hope he's alright."

"We'll get you back on the road soon."

"How? Even when he can walk, Grady won't be able to ride. It will be months before we can get to Chara."

"Don't worry. My husband will think of something. He's the smartest man I know. Just you wait and see."

"I hope so. We can't stay here. It won't take long for Kesniel to realize he missed us somehow." She frowned. "I've got to get to Lachlaniel."

The woman gave Aurora a hug. "You will. You will."
She left the room. Aurora turned to Grady. Tears came to her eyes.

"It's my fault. If I hadn't left the city, if I had stayed where I was supposed to, none of this would have happened to you."

Ewald awoke to pain in his neck and shoulders. They felt like they were on fire and his head felt much the same as it had after he'd been hit by the poisoned arrow. He looked around. Dan was sitting in a chair in the corner reading.

"Why didn't you wake me?"

"They said you'd be waking up soon. They weren't using the herbs anymore, and they said the pain would bring you around shortly."

"It's bringing me around alright." Ewald winced and moaned. "I'd like to crawl out of my skin and leave it behind. What about Andre?"

"No sign of him. You think he left the city?"

Ewald slowly rolled to a sitting position. "I doubt it. He's intent on destroying the light. He hasn't accomplished his purpose. I doubt we've seen the last of those barrels either. With the doors down on the west side of the tower, he's liable to try to kill the guards and roll one through the doorway, so be prepared. Put every man we've got on rotating twelve-hour shifts. Have them patrol every inch of the city. Have the guards at critical places spelled every hour." He paused and winced, then added, "Change up the pairings. If he could bribe those two at the Tower, he could have bribed others as well. And ask the Army Commander to have some of his troops patrol the city nonchalantly. The healers say I'll be out of here tomorrow. Until then, make sure nothing happens. After that, we can plan what to do about finding him."

Dan had a look of concern. "Get some rest. You'll need it because finding him won't be easy."

"No, but..." He winced again. "...it may be easier than getting any rest will be."

He lay back down hoping to ease the pain. Dan paused at the door and looked back at him. Ewald groaned as he tried to find a comfortable position. He noticed Dan at the door.

"Off with ya! You've got work to do."

Dan closed the door, and Ewald settled his head on the pillow.

"He's a good man, but he shouldn't worry about me so much."

Chapter 16
Death

Lachlaniel and his men filtered out of the inn after breakfast. They had rested well but were still tired and sore from the long day before. The attendants were busy leading the last of the horses to the courtyard. It was midmorning and the road was filled with travelers. The men started out walking as the horses were still not rested enough to be ridden.

The day grew hot and there was no shade until nearly noon when the buildings began to thin and trees lined the road on occasion. They stopped near one of these spots and took an early lunch while the horses grazed. They rounded up the horses and gathered the belongings they had used for lunch. By this time, it was very hot and the men looked forward to the time when the trees would cover the road without break.

Lachlaniel addressed the men before they started. "I would like to ride but the mounts wouldn't be worth anything after a short time in this heat, so we'll walk until the road is shaded. Not long after that, the road will turn south. We should be approaching the city of the Basaners sometime tomorrow. I don't believe there's any danger of attack until we're much closer since there are many of us, and we're armed; however, as we draw closer, we'll need to exercise more caution. We'll also need to use more stealth. Access to the city is through a pass, which is where I've been attacked twice before. We need to see if there is a way around the pass and come at them from the rear."

"I'm somewhat familiar with that region," Wilmot said thoughtfully. "The place you speak of is an escarpment a little ways north of the city. I'm afraid there is no other path unless you're willing to go weeks out of the way. To the west, the ridge gets higher until it joins the mountains. To the east, the ridge continues fifty miles before ending in a swamp. Even at the lowest point the cliff drops fifty feet directly into the swamp."

"It seems the direct approach is all that is left to us," Lachlaniel concluded. "The woods end a little before the cut that leads to lower ground. Beyond that is a plain before the boulders and outcroppings of the cut begin. We'll stop there at the edge of the woods and reconnoiter. Let's get moving. We need to cover many miles before nightfall."

The sounds of the men's voices showed their eagerness to join battle with this depraved aggregation of humanity that was causing so much agony to so many.

What a simple solution.

Aurora watched as Garth filled the cart with hay and hitched the horses to it.

"Can you drive a cart?"

"I never have."

What other problems will I run into?

"Then, it would be best to walk. Your horses should follow you. It will be slow but you'll be making progress." Garth led the horses into the barnyard where chickens clucked and pecked the ground.

"No doubt the boy will want to drive the cart, but you must make him rest for at least the next few days. It will be good for him to walk part of the time, but he shouldn't be jostled. Those ribs need time to start to mend. Avoid the potholes. If you can, have him walk till you're past them. The hay will be cushion enough for the road normally, but bumps and holes are something else again."

Aurora nodded understanding. She reached for the seat where her pack rested.

"No. No need to pay for the cart or anything else. You've brought the Light and shown us to the Bridge. We are forever in your debt."

Aurora gave an awkward smile. "I only did as my King commands."

"True, but now He is our King as well, and we must serve Him too. You'll need your money."

Brigit came out of the house with Grady walking beside her with his arm around her shoulder. He didn't really need the help, but she insisted. They helped him into the back of the cart above his objections.

"Now you just lay there youngster. Do what the lady tells you and don't give her any trouble."

Grady started to object, but one look at the woman's face, and he thought better of it. He'd seen that look on his mother's face, and he knew what followed.

"Yes ma'am."

Brigit scurried off to the house as the man took Aurora's hand and kissed it.

"May the King protect you and speed your journey."

Aurora blushed and curtseyed.

The woman came out of the house carrying a large basket as Aurora grabbed the harness of one of the horses.

"Some food for the trip."

"You shouldn't have."

"Speak for yourself!" Grady interjected as the aroma reached his nostrils. "It smells good enough to stop for lunch right now!"

"Growing boys and food," Brigit said smiling. "Be careful and safe."

"Thank you for all you've done." Aurora whispered in Brigit's ear as she hugged her.

Brigit wiped a tear away and smiled.

Aurora led the horses toward the road as the birds sang sweetly in the trees above them. At the road she stopped, turned, and waved at the couple who waved back before returning to the work of cleaning up and repairing things from the storm.

A short way up the road, there was a cut through to the south road. It was more like a trail, hardly large enough to be passable for the cart, but at this point, Aurora felt it was better to travel the more southern of the two roads.

Not far behind her, the two men Kesniel had watching the house stopped as Aurora took the cart down the path. They discussed the situation briefly and then split up, one going for Kesniel and the other continuing to follow Aurora,

Ewald groaned as he walked. He was stiff and sore, and his head hurt. He had covered his pain while the healers were around, but now, as he

went through the streets of town it was no longer necessary. The tower loomed in front of him.

I hope work takes my mind off the pain.

He turned onto the street that held the west door and the tumbled ruins of the inn. Men were busy filling carts with the rubble and driving them out of the city to the dump. On three rooftops near the doors of the tower, he could see hints of his men. He frowned.

We can't have that. I'll have to check the residence and the dome as well.

"Hey! You!" he yelled at a man he didn't recognize by the Tower's doorway. The man pointed at himself. "Yes, you. Come over here."

The man looked sheepishly at his companion. "What'd I do now?"

He started to walk towards Ewald.

"Get a move on!" Ewald barked.

The man broke into a run and was quickly in front of his superior.

"You see the hats sticking up on the roofs there, there, and there?" Ewald pointed.

"Yes sir."

"You tell those men that if I see any hint of their positions again they'll be standing double guard duty for the next month. You might spread that word around too."

"Yes sir!" the man said snapping to attention. Then, he was off on his errands.

Ewald entered the tower and made sure there was ample protection. He sent a guard to replace the man he had dispatched to correct the others. Finding everything else to his satisfaction he headed for the stairs leading to the turret and the Great Stone. At the top, he found Dan looking out across the city. He joined him at the parapet.

Dan shook his head. "I don't see how he eludes us."

"I know. It's like trying to find Diaphanous. Only I'm sure our 'friend' isn't transparent."

"He must be very well trained."

Ewald nodded. "No doubt. He certainly knows a great deal about how to destroy things and wreak havoc. I doubt he'll try in the daytime. At least he hasn't so far."

They grew silent as they scanned the city.

Jocelyn left the house for the shops. With Aurora gone, there was much more work, and time was precious. She closed the door behind her and hurried down the steps when there was a large clatter from the side of the house. She turned around in time to see a cat spring into the street.

"Featherstep! What have you done? Well, no time to clean up your messes now. I must hurry or the shops will close before I'm finished."

Jocelyn turned back and moved quite rapidly for her matronly size. Andre wiped the sweat from his face.

That was close. How can I be so lithe in the dark and so clumsy when trying to stay hidden during the day? I would have liked to blow the place up with Jocelyn, Aurora, and a house full of guests in it. Now, I hope it's empty. No more mistakes. Good thing the cat was handy.

He placed the flower on the doorstep and slithered to the back of the house where the cellar and his barrel awaited him.

Ewald was about to leave when there was a tremendous explosion. He and Dan threw themselves behind the parapet. When they rose, fragments of roofing tiles rained down on buildings just a few streets away. Black smoke roiled and billowed from the empty place where a house had once stood.

"Jocelyn's house!" Ewald grabbed Dan's arm. "Come on!"

They rushed down the stairs yelling at the men as they went. "Stay at your posts!" "Keep your eyes open!" "This may be a ruse! Stay focused on your job!"

Clearing the doors, they ran through the streets. People were running in every direction. Soldiers were all moving towards the scene of the explosion. Ewald deployed them in an attempt to catch Andre trying to slip away in the crowds.

"Dan, circle around and try to cover the other side."

"Right."

As he ran on, the debris grew from bits of mortar, splinters of wood and pulverized stone to pieces of lumber, bricks from the chimney, a mattress, then beams and larger pieces of the walls and roof. Men were sifting through the wreckage when he arrived. The commander was on the undamaged front steps holding a withered, soot stained oleander.

"Was anyone in..."

"Not that we can tell." The commander looked at the flower in his hand. "I found this on the steps. Any idea what it means?"

"Trouble. He's been leaving flowers in various places. This one means 'beware'." He took the flower from the commander. "Withered. Perhaps it hadn't been discovered."

"I found it on the steps. There's no way it hadn't been seen if it was fresh when he laid it there."

Ewald tried to piece together the events before the explosion. "Perhaps when he placed the barrel, he laid it there and removed it before he set off that powder of his. Then, he laid it on the steps and escaped."

"Perhaps. Any idea why?"

Ewald scowled. "He wants to hurt Aurora."

"I hope she's not buried under the rubble!"

"You needn't concern yourself about her." He looked at the commander. She's safe. I just hope there wasn't anyone else in the house."

The two men let their gaze sweep over the devastation.

In the lowering light of dusk, Andre slipped over the wall of the residence. Hiding in the shrubbery he waited for the light from the stones of the city to reach their lowest ebb. In the middle of the second watch, he moved. He lit the fuse of the barrel he had placed days before beneath the window of Aurora's room. The light from the fuse was well hidden behind the bushes, and the fuse was ample enough to give him time to get out of the city.

He crossed the grounds unseen and entered the stable. He expected no one and had planned on killing a horse, but there was someone there caring for a mare which was foaling. The man was quite busy and knew nothing until the knife slipped between his ribs. He lay convulsing on the ground while Andre slit the throat of the mare. He laid a lobelia between the two and slipped out of the stable and over the wall.

The streets were deserted except for soldiers and guards. A dawn to dusk curfew was being strictly enforced. Still, he had no trouble making his way through the city to the stairs of the south wall. He ascended the stairs swiftly and nimbly, nothing more than a shadow sliding toward the top. His timing was impeccable and his skill with a knife unmatched. The guard never knew what happened as his neck was cut in one swift stroke by the cold steel of the blade. He slumped to the ground.

Andre threw his slender rope over the wall. He laid a black rose by the body. All remained silent as he leaped over the wall and rappelled down its surface. In seconds, he was on the ground. As he loosed the waiting horse, there was a loud explosion in the city. Voices sounded on the wall above him. He mounted and was soon on the road leading south. Horns and shouts erupted from the wall. He could hear arrows hitting the road behind him, but he was on the bridge now, and he and the black stallion provided no target.

Now to get her.

The explosion threw Ewald's bed in the air, and he landed with a thud by the door. Stunned and breathless it would be a moment before he could try to sit up. There was pressure at his back.

Someone's trying to open the door. Got to get up!

In spite of the flames and the urgency, his attempt to rise ended with him hitting the floor with a thud and rolling onto his side.

"Ewald! Ewald! Are you alright?"

It was Dan's voice. Ewald tried again this time rolling to his knees and crawling away from the door before trying to stand. The door opened enough for Dan to slide through. He helped Ewald to his feet, slung his arm over his shoulder and helped him into the hall. Servants had come running from every quarter. They helped Dan get Ewald down the stairs to the front of the residence. On the way down, Ewald finally got his breath back.

"I didn't expect that," Ewald wheezed.

"Why not? He's demonstrated he has plenty of that powder."

Ewald finally drew in a big breath and said in a more normal voice, "I didn't think he could get a barrel of it onto the grounds."

With a raised eyebrow and half a smile, Dan said sarcastically, "Didn't I tell you not to sleep in there?"

"I should have listened. I expected an attack but not this."

"Yes. Well you're lucky to be alive. Are you injured at all?"

"No. Had the wind knocked out of me and my legs had no strength, but it's coming back now."

"Can you walk?"

"I think so. Let's get outside and see what happened."

They left the front entrance and circled to the back. The blast had centered at the ground floor below the bedroom Aurora had used. Most of the suite as well as the rooms beneath it were scattered over the entire compound. What hadn't been destroyed had collapsed on the rooms below except for a small part of the antechamber. The part where Ewald had been sleeping.

"You were fortunate my friend. Be glad the King is watching you."

"Yes. I certainly underestimated Andre, didn't I."

They continued watching as the servants fought the flames from the furnishings and the few bits of lumber used in the construction. After a few moments, there was a great deal of commotion behind them. They turned to see what the yelling was about and were confronted by four men carrying a body from the stable. They rushed over. The sight that met them made them draw in their breath.

"Capaleanan." Ewald shook his head."

"You'll want to look in the barn too," one of the men said.

Dan and Ewald entered the stable. The far stall held the gutted horse and dead foal lying on the blood soaked straw. There was an indentation in the straw where the body of Capaleanan had been found and between the two a single lobelia.

"What does it mean?" Dan asked in a whisper.

"Malevolence." It was a flat emotionless statement that was belied by his balled fists. There was a moment of silence as rage boiled up to his face contorting it in anger and anguish. Then Ewald yelled, "Why?!"

At that moment, a guard rushed in breathless.

"The front wall... He got away... Killed one of the guards... Seen riding across the bridge."

Ewald and Dan bolted from the stable and raced across the grounds and courtyard, through the gates and down the street. They started to climb the stairs to the top of the wall when soldiers coming down with the body of the guard met them. They backed off the stairs to let them pass.

"Dan, get a troop of horse guards and saddle a horse for me. I'm going after him."

"What about the city? He might be trying to get you and more of our men away from here."

"Perhaps. You'll be in charge of the guards. Coordinate with the Army Commander. Do what you have to, but no more incidents."

"Right. What will you do?"

"He's obsessed with Aurora. I think he'll be trying to find her. I must find him *before* he finds her."

Dan turned away and Ewald raced up the stairs. At the top were a group of men. Some stood around an object on the ground while the rest were looking over the wall. Ewald shoved his way between the men. A black rose lay in their midst, an evil omen that no one wanted to touch. Ewald stooped down and picked it up. He studied it for several moments.

One of the guards broke the silence. "What does it mean sir?"

"Death."

Chapter 17
Dark Waters

Aurora's feet drug the ground as she took her steps, her head was slumped forward as she stared at the road immediately in front of her feet, and she grabbed the bridle with all the strength she had left to keep herself steady. She had walked all day and it was now past midnight.

Must keep going.

Her eyes closed for an instant, her head slumped to her chest, and her hand slipped from the harness. She jerked awake as her legs collapsed. She got back to her feet as the horses came to a stop.

"Are we finally stopping for the night?" Grady yelled from the cart.

"No. No."

Grady's voice was full of concern. "You've got to rest sometime and the horses need it as well."

"I've got to keep going. Kesniel and Max won't let up till they've found us."

"Speaking of them, there are lights behind us. Still quite a ways back."

"What will I do? I can't let them catch me!"

Grady rose from the cart, a look of anguish on his face, and drew his knife.

"You've got to get out of here. I'm cutting a horse free from the cart."

He worked swiftly and deftly with a moan here and there as his movements brought pain.

"What about you?" Aurora poured water from the water bag on her head.

"I'll be fine. They'll take care of me." He led the horse away from the cart. "You'll have to ride bareback I'm afraid."

"I don't know about that, and I don't like leaving you."

"There's no time for that. You'll have to try" He took the pouch of coins from around his neck.

"No."

"Take it!" he said thrusting it into her hands. "You'll need all of it, and I won't."

Aurora took it reluctantly, and he helped her mount as best he could.

"Take any side road you can, but make sure you keep heading west. Now get out of here. They'll be here any minute."

She leaned down from the horse and kissed him on the forehead. "Goodbye Grady, and thank you."

"Cover your stone as best you can and don't look back."

He slapped the horse on the rear and it cantered into the darkness ahead. Aurora wrapped the stone in her cloak leaving a slit open to illumine the road ahead.

A trail met the road on her left which would take her well off her route. Hesitating, she reined in the horse. She looked back up the road, down the road, and then at the trail.

If I take this trail I'll be headed south, not west. But if I stay on the road they'll catch me in no time. The horse is so tired. But it doesn't lead west. It's a narrow trail. If they're riding hard they might miss it. But it goes south!

Light glinted on the road behind her. The trail was narrow and twigs tore at her hair allowing no more than a walk, but the horse couldn't have run much further anyway. About a hundred yards down the trail, the thunder of hooves echoed behind her. She stopped, covered her stone, and watched. A glimmer of light reached her for a few moments before it disappeared. Exhaling, she lightened her grip on the reins, lay forward on the neck of the horse to avoid the overhanging branches, uncovered her stone, and began the trek forward into the unknown.

"They're just ahead."

The scout looked to Kesniel for new orders.

"Stay with us. Forward men!"

The troop sprang forward at a gallop. In a few moments, they could see light on the road ahead, a cart, standing still. There was someone lying in the back. Max and Kesniel dismounted. A guard moved to the front of the cart to hold the horses while Max and Kesniel stood at the rear.

"Grady." Kesniel said

"Asleep no less. Up you sluggard!" Max boomed.

Grady rose up to an elbow; the white of his bandages showed beneath his unbuttoned shirt.

"What happened to you, son" Kesniel asked with concern in his voice.

"The whirling wind. I broke some ribs."

"Where's Aurora." Max demanded with a growl.

"Easy Max. Where is she son?"

"She's not here? She was."

The guard came back to Kesniel.

"There's a knife on the ground. She must have seen us coming, cut a horse free from the harnessing, and rode off."

Kesniel dismounted. He picked up the knife and examined it, then returned to his horse. He motioned to the man who had found the knife. "You take the boy back to Agapay."

Kesniel jumped to saddle like a man a quarter his age, and the troop broke into a gallop once more. They rode for thirty minutes, but there was nothing on the road.

"Spread out and search the woods on both sides of the road." The concern in Kesniel's voice was apparent.

"What do you think?" Max asked.

"I think she's getting away and our efforts are being hampered. Time to consult the King."

He dismounted followed by Max. Together they entered their closets.

Lachlaniel reined in his horse. The other men followed suit.

"We don't want to get too near, or they'll see the light from our stones. We'll cover them before going on."

The men watched as Lachlaniel covered his stone with his cloak. They quickly did the same and began crossing the treeless stretch of road that led to the pass. They were almost to the first outcroppings of rock when arrows assailed them in volleys of three dozen or more each. The men were swift to pull their shields, but several horses went down. The fallen riders mounted other horses and rode double in retreat. Lachlaniel, in the lead, pressed on. He pulled his sword and swung it frenetically at his unseen foes. The arrows ceased, and a group formed around the lone figure. Several tried to get close enough to knock Lachlaniel from his horse. The flailing sword of the blind Lachlaniel failed to down any attackers, but the well aimed hooves of Aman had great effect. The men backed up. One picked up a rock. The projectile hit Lachlaniel's helmet. He fell from Aman but the blow didn't even stun him. He was on his feet in an instant with his sword menacing and at the ready. Another rock hit his sword arm and the weapon clattered to the ground. Five men pounced on him and pinned him to the ground. Aman beat a hasty retreat beyond the men's grasp.

"It's the blind guy that we caught twice before!"

"What'll we do with him?"

Damon shoved his way through the men to the fallen figure squirming to be free.

"The pond. Bind him and weight him. He won't get away again."

A lone figure with a bald head and the stump of a right arm sat on the top of a rock watching by the light of Lachlaniel's sword as its owner was dragged away to death by drowning.

The men watched from the trees.

A man from the rear shouted, "What do we do know?"

A large man took charge. "We go home. We'll stop at the house where we left Jason. It shouldn't take long to patch up the few scrapes and bruises."

Wilmot stared in disbelief at the others." We can't leave him behind in their hands."

The men turned and rode off one by one in silence like whipped dogs with their tails between their legs.

One of the men at Wilmot's side looked across the plain and said, "You do what you want. We're going home."

Wilmot stood in silence watching the men ride into the night. He turned and looked across the plain to the rocks. In the dim light, he could see a group of men carrying Lachlaniel to the west while a lone figure watched from the top of a rock.

Ignatius watched as the others took the blind man to the pond. His anger towards the Ebenchaim had been cooled by his rage at the Basaners.

They treat me like the lightmongers. They'd have killed me if they hadn't been interrupted by him and the others.

He watched them row out on the pond.

Hard to see. His stone makes them silhouettes and the light from his sword isn't enough to reach that far. I wish there were more light .Hmph! **I'm** *wishing for more light. That's a thought I never would have entertained before. I certainly think differently about my 'friends' since I lost my arm. I'm an outcast now. Useless.*

The loud plop of the body going into the water made him look up. It was dark on the pond except for an occasional glint of light from the sword reflecting off a wet oar.

Amazing! Maybe I've thought about light all wrong before. Maybe I've thought about the lightmongers wrong as well. He was more upset by the child's death than I was.

Ewald's troop reached the crossroads south of Agapay.

"Who's the best tracker here?" The impatience in Ewald's voice was palpable.

"Theron," came the resounding response of multiple voices.

"Theron! You take the road east. If you find nothing, as is likely, you and your men return to the city for fresh mounts; then, bring me word. Otherwise follow him, but don't try to take him alone. Make sure you get plenty of help." He pointed to two other men. "You two go with him."

Theron headed east at a walk looking for any sign that he was on the right road.

"West men!" Ewald put his heel to his horse and they set out at a canter in order to make the best time without wearing out the horses.

Aurora awoke with her arms around the horse's neck, hands clutching the bridle. The horse was standing still.
How did I keep from falling off?
She looked around. It was a strange half lit village. On one side, lay darkness where the light faded; on the other, were houses, flowers, and animals living in the light. People were at work in gardens, shops, and taverns.
What kind of place is this? I've never seen a place where the light didn't dispel the darkness.
Her head nodded.
I've got to get some rest.
She slid from the horse. Walking to the center of town, she sat on a bench beneath a tree in the middle of the road.
I'll rest a minute before I find an inn, if they have one.
She leaned back against the tree and was instantly asleep.

The men threw Lachlaniel in the bottom of a boat, climbed in and rowed out into the middle of the pond. Others bound his hands in front of him so that he was holding his stone and tied his feet with a line that had a large rock on the end.
They're going to drown me! What can I do?!
His thoughts raced but no viable plan came to mind. The men finished and rolled the rock over the side. The sinking rock jerked the line taut and wrenched his legs against the gunwale.
"Alright, over the side with him."
They lifted him up and over the side. The cool water prickled his skin raising goose bumps. He looked up as he struggled with the ropes.
I hope I've got enough air.
The faces of the men as they watched him descending into the depths faded. He was alone in a dark watery world. The rock hit bottom, and he

floated above it at the end of the rope. In his struggles, air escaped his lungs. He sank and came to rest on his hands and knees.

Give up. How long can you hold your breath? Give up. Accept the inevitable.

A Voice sounded in his ears. "No! Crawl!"

It was a familiar voice like the voice of someone long forgotten. "Crawl!"

His mind reeled but his body obeyed. He inched across the bottom dragging the stone behind him.

Wilmot watched the men rowing to the middle of the pond. A still small Voice whispered in the trees. He smiled. He headed through the woods towards the far side of the lake. Aman was waiting at the edge of the trees. He looked at the pond. It was dark, but he could see the silhouette of the crowded little boat as it came to rest on the far shore. In the distance Lachlaniel's sword stood as a cross rising from the land and casting its tiny light. He grabbed Aman's reins and led him to the pond's shore.

Minutes ticked by. The men retreated to the rocks. One of them grabbed the sword and threw it as hard as he could. The world of the far shore lapsed into darkness. The minutes continued to fly by: five, ten, fifteen.

What am I waiting here for?

He started to leave. The small Voice whispered, "Wait."

He looked at the surface of the pond. There was a glimmer of light. It disappeared. It returned, brighter. He watched it inch closer and grow in brightness. The top of Lachlaniel's head broke the surface not ten feet from shore. Wilmot jumped from his horse and raised Lachlaniel from the water. He dragged him to shore. Lachlaniel was unmoving. Wilmot sighed as grief struck him.

He's dead.

"Yes, but wait," the Voice said.

Lachlaniel breathed in gulps as he coughed and spit water.

How?

The question was unanswered. Wilmot cut the remnants of the rope from his hands and severed the cords that bound his feet to the rock.

We can't stay here. They're probably already trying to encircle us.

"Come on we've got to move," he said trying to help the limp form to his feet. "Come on!"

Lachlaniel rolled to his hands and knees and threw his arms around Wilmot's shoulders. He got to his feet and made it to his horse before he succumbed to the coughing and weakness. Wilmot got him across the saddle on his belly. Mounting his horse, Wilmot grabbed Aman's reins and rode for the woods. Once there he made for the road. Lachlaniel continued spitting water and coughing for a while, but by the time they got to the road he lay very still.

I hope he's not dead. Hmph. Why would Leofwine bring him back to life only to let him die? Dead or not we've got to keep moving.

The night air was cool wafting across the road from beneath the trees. Nightingales sang in the distance while frogs could be heard croaking from many hidden sanctuaries, but from Lachlaniel, there continued to be no sound. Wilmot caught sight of the ruts that led to the house where Jason had left them. His light brought two men from the house to investigate. One helped Wilmot remove Lachlaniel from the horse and carry him toward the house while the other took the horses to the barn.

"We must hurry. It isn't safe to show a light in this country."

Wilmot heard the whisper of singing voices behind the closed door.

"The Basaners force you to meet in secret." It was a statement rather than a question.

"Yes," the man replied as he opened the door.

There was an instant hush as someone must have called a halt to the singing.

"Where did you find him?"

"I didn't. I and men from Chara were following him to put an end to the Basaners." Wilmot helped lower Lachlaniel onto a bed.

"So you know Lachlaniel?"

Wilmot leaned back against the wall. "Yes, but how do you know him?"

"He was here before. Elrad and Thelma tended him a couple of times. They're not here now, but there's a man named Jason who has skill in healing."

"Yes, I know him. He rode with us from the city."

They laid Lachlaniel on a bed. Jason entered the room and looked at Wilmot and Lachlaniel, "It seems that we've been chosen by the King to tend him until he succeeds or dies."

"I don't think killing him will be easy. Leofwine is keeping him alive." Wilmot looked down with concern on the young man he had so briefly known.

"What happened?"

They tried to drown him. Tied him hand and foot with a rock for a weight and threw him into a pond. Leofwine told me to go to the far side and wait. I did, but after fifteen minutes, I decided to leave. There was no hope. Leofwine whispered again 'Wait'. I saw a faint light below the water. Then, his head broke the surface and I pulled him out.

"The King has something for him to do. Until he accomplishes it…" Jason's voice trailed off as the limp body moaned.

Lachlaniel's arms and legs began thrashing about, but before either man could try to restrain him, he sat up straight in the bed and gasped. Jason touched his shoulder and he gulped air and fell back on the pillow. He breathed heavily, his eyes wild with fear.

"Where am I?"

Wilmot grasped his hand and Jason once again touched his shoulder.

"In the house where you were tended twice before."

"What happened?"

"You almost drowned," Wilmot said softly. "The Basaners threw you in the pond."

A pained expression crossed Lachlaniel's face. "The last thing I remember is my lungs feeling like they were on fire."

"You were under the water…" The touch of Jason's hand on his arm brought Wilmot's sentence to a halt.

"You need to rest now. Relax. Sleep."

The words were soothing and melodious. Lachlaniel's eyes closed and though he tried several times to open them he drifted into a deep sleep.

"I've never seen anything like that!"

Jason put a finger to his mouth and ushered Wilmot into the hall.

"A gift from the King. I can help people to heal. Sometimes all they need is sleep."

"How…?"

"Oh, it's not me. The King is the one who does it. Somehow, He communicates what to do, and I simply do what He says."

"Does it happen every time?"

"No. Sometimes the healing is slower, sometimes faster. He needs rest. Lots of it. In time he'll be ready."

"Ready? Ready for what?"

"Only the King can answer that."

They lapsed into silence and peeked through the door at the sleeping man.

Chapter 18
Photaskia

"Wake up deary! Wake up."

Aurora opened bleary eyes. It was almost evening. The lighted side of the road was fast turning to the deep blue the stones gave off at night. Her arms were as heavy as her eyelids. She finally focused on the hunched figure before her. An old woman with gray hair that had turned silver in several streaks was standing over her. She was hardly two-thirds of her erect height, the effects of age having deformed her plump form into a hunchbacked, permanently stooping dwarf of her younger self.

I hope I don't look like that when I get older.

The woman grabbed her hand. "Get up deary! Get up! It isn't safe!"

Aurora pulled away and stifled a yawn. "What isn't safe?"

"You can't stay out here! They might catch you!"

"They? Who are they?"

"No time for talk!" She grabbed Aurora's hand again and pulled. "Hurry! Hurry!"

Aurora rose reluctantly to her feet.

Cinnamon. Where's cinnamon?

"Where's my horse?" Aurora asked pulling back against the old woman's tugs.

"My husband's already putting her away. Please! We must get off the streets. It isn't safe."

Aurora relented, following the woman without further struggle. Her escort's frenzied scrutiny of their surroundings was disturbing though the house wasn't far, and they were soon safely inside. As the door closed behind them, Aurora crossed her arms and frowned at the woman.

"Now, who are 'they' and what makes it so urgent to get off the streets?" Aurora's foot patted impatiently as she awaited an answer.

The woman wrung her hands. "First a cup of coffee." She turned to lock and bar the door.

Aurora grabbed her shoulder and spun her around. The not yet secured bar slid from her hands and clattered to the ground.

That's not like me! Why am I so angry?

The woman winced in pain and Aurora released her grip.

"I'm sorry, but I want an answer."

"Please. I must sit down." The woman placed the bar on the door and crossed the room to a very old but comfortable looking chair wheezing as she went. "Please sit down," the woman said as she plopped into the chair which groaned under her weight.

Aurora, foot tapping again, stared at the woman. "Well?"

The woman looked at the tapping foot. "I'm Leah. There are roaming bands that come through at night." The woman continued gazing at Aurora's foot as she talked. "They grab anyone with a stone who is alone on the streets. They're called Basaners."

Aurora followed the woman's gaze to her patting foot.

What is wrong with me!

She forced her foot to be still and unfolded her crossed arms. "I'm sorry."

The woman looked up frowning. "You reminded me of my mother. She used to cross her arms and pat her foot when she was scolding me."

"I *am* sorry." Aurora sat down next to Leah. Putting her hand on Leah's knee, she continued. "I've heard of the Basaners," she said changing the subject back to her questions.

"Ohhh! They're evil people. Evil. They snatch people up and beat them. Many are never seen again!" Leah shuddered. "I could really use some coffee."

"Let me get it."

"Oh no, I'll do it." Leah rose with effort. "Would you like some?"

"Yes, thank you."

Leah hobbled into the kitchen.

She called from the other room, "Do you like sugar?"

"Yes, please." Aurora forced her thoughts to slow. She breathed deeply and let it out as a sigh.

There was a clatter of cups and saucers and the tinkling of a spoon against the china. In a moment, Leah returned with two steaming cups. As she sat down, her husband entered. Leah looked up with a weak smile.

"You two must have been talking about the Basaners."

Aurora looked up perplexed. "Yes. How did you know?"

"I'm Nestor." He bowed. "She gets upset by talking about them. She invariably drinks coffee when she's upset." He scowled at his wife and she looked at the floor. "She makes more of the situation than it is. Not to say that what she says isn't true. They killed our son."

"You don't kno…"

"You have another explanation for him not returning?" He turned to Aurora. "Two years ago they came through and beat an old couple who were out for an evening stroll. The woman died that night, the man two days later. He recovered just long enough to learn of his wife's death. The next night our son went to check the horses when they were making a racket. He never came back."

"It's as though the earth swallowed him," Leah said through tears.

"It was the Basaners."

Aurora looked puzzled "But you said it wasn't as bad…"

"It isn't. They do beat any Ebenchaim they catch. Many times they kill them. "His look told Aurora not to ask more about how. "But they don't come through often. In fact, their intrusions are quite rare, but further west it's a different story. Still, we make sure that everyone is off the streets before nightfall." His continued gaze said a change of subject was in order.

"Why is the other side of the street dark?"

The Ebenchaim live on this side, and they will not share the light with those still in darkness."

"Is that because…"

"*No!*" His reply was abrupt and was both an answer and a rebuke. He paused. "No. There are many reasons. Excuses really. We all have them. If someone from over there crosses the Bridge, they move to this side of the street."

'Over there.' It's as if they're diseased. Why? Why won't the Ebenchaim here share the light with their neighbors?

She looked at the man. He frowned at her. The wife was trembling and on the verge of tears.

Best to leave it alone.

He forced a smile. "We'll show you to your room."

Lachlaniel awoke to the sound of Wilmot snoring in the corner, "Who's there?"

A few strange noises issued from Wilmot's mouth followed by, "Huh? What?"

"I said who's there?"

The chair rocked forward to sit on all fours as Wilmot rubbed his eyes. When he opened them, Lachlaniel was sitting up in bed with his head cocked to one side.

"It's me, Lachlaniel. Wilmot. I brought you here last night. You had a rough time. It's a good thing Jason is here. He helped you and said you have pneumonia. You're going to be here a couple of weeks."

"No. I'm going back there." Lachlaniel started to get up and began coughing.

"I don't think you're going anywhere for quite a while."

As he continued coughing, the pain in his chest radiated outward throughout his body until his toes tingled. He fell back on the pillow, and the coughing subsided. His blank eyes stared at the ceiling.

"What makes you think you'll fare any better this time?"

Lachlaniel's voice was feeble. "Eleutherias trained me. I've led armies into battle. I've faced foes far worse than this rabble."

"Then, why haven't you beaten them before."

It was Wilmot's voice but the question was Leofwine's. Lachlaniel paused.

The Chuchoteur was frantic. *They're no match for you! You need a different method, that's all.*

Maybe I shouldn't rush back. If I'm to be stuck here, I'll make a plan. This might work out for the best. Think and plan. That's what I need to do. A frontal assault hasn't worked. Subtlety, that's what's needed.

That's the ticket. Now you're thinking. Trick them.

Aurora had been up late contemplating all she had learned. The unnatural divide in the town between the dark and the light, her entry into a land frequented by the Basaners, missing and tortured people, it was all so different from anything she had known.

What must Lachlaniel be facing?

When sleep came, it was fitful and filled with ugly and horrible dreams.

"Lachlaniel! No! Aghhhhhhhhhh!!!!!" It was a blood curdling scream. She sat up crying as sleep fled and reality returned.

Seconds later, Nestor came crashing into the room, sword in hand. He lowered it and called to Leah.

"I need you my dear!"

Leah peeked through the doorway.

"It's okay. She's had a bad dream, I think. You take care of her and I'll get some coffee."

Leah moved to the head of the bed and put her arm around Aurora's shoulders.

"Shhh. Shhh. It was just a dream. It was just a dream," she whispered. "It's alright. Everything is alright." She hugged the shivering woman, pulled a handkerchief from her pocket and handed it to Aurora.

"But it's not! He's in danger! I have to get to him!" She threw the covers off as she ripped herself from Leah's embrace.

"Who?"

"Lachlaniel," Aurora said as she started getting dressed, oblivious to the fact that Nestor could return at any second.

"Who's Lachlaniel?"

"My fiancée. He's in the land of the Basaners"

Leah grew pale.

Aurora finished dressing and almost collided with Nestor as he entered the room, coffee in hand.

"Where are you going?"

Aurora looked at the man who blocked her path. He looked past her to his wife whose face was now ashen.

"You need to sit down and drink this."

"No! I've got to get to him!"

Leah's voice was small and frightened, "He's in the Basaner's realm."

Nestor shoved the coffee cup into Aurora's hands spilling some into the saucer. Aurora took it by reflex. Nestor grabbed her free hand and led her back to the bed with her resisting every step of the way. Coffee splattered on the floor all the way across the room, and the cup and saucer bounced on the rug as Nestor flung Aurora to a seat on the bed. He drew close to her face.

"You can't go there by yourself." He looked at the determination on her face and backed up a little. "I can't say you should go there at all, but if you have to go, then you must have an experienced warrior with you." He paused at his own statement as he realized the implications. He pulled himself from his momentary thoughts and looked her in the eye. "And you must have a plan and the necessary preparations. The King's blessing must be upon you. If we hadn't happened upon you, you assuredly would have met your end."

Leah whimpered at the words.

"There's no time for all that!" Aurora started to rise, but Nestor's hands on her shoulders forced her back down.

"There must be. I'll go with you, but we must prepare, and you must tell me the whole story. I won't go with you blindly, and if I don't go with you, then you won't be going either."

Kesniel's look was one of astonishment.

"A town with one half light and the other half dark? Preposterous. Unbelievable."

The soldier looked at him unflinching. "I saw it with my own eyes."

"Incredible. If we had the time, I'd investigate it, but what did you find of Aurora?"

The man frowned. "Nothing. Not a trace."

Kesniel's brows knit in deep thought as the man awaited further orders.

Max, who had been listening to the conversation, finally said to him, "Get some sleep. You'll have to be back in the saddle soon."

The man looked at Max, snapped to attention, and left the tent. Max watched Kesniel for several minutes before he spoke.

"What are you thinking?"

"It's hard to believe that she is eluding us. There may be more at work here than meets the eye." Kesniel raised an eyebrow.

"The King?"

"Possibly, but more likely the enemy." Kesniel twirled his mustache and stroked his beard. "You know He said she had left the protection He had provided. She's on her own because she walked away from Him. We must redouble our efforts."

"How? We're stretched as thin as we can be."

"Send out my personal guard. Add them to the search."

"I don't like the sound of that."

"My dear friend, with you around, what have I to fear? Besides, there are the soldiers who have come back from patrol. They may be asleep, but you know they'll spring into action at the drop of a hat. After all, you trained them."

Max smiled.

"I'll send them out. I need to stretch my legs." He looked at the roof of the tent.

Kesniel followed his gaze to where Max's head lifted the canvas and smiled

Max looked at him. "Being in this place too long makes me feel cramped."

"Alright. You take a walk. But don't worry about the men. I'll send them out."

Nestor looked at the horses one last time to make sure everything was in order.

Aurora alternated between looking at the house, the road, and the ground. "I hate to take you away from your wife, she was crying so."

183

"The neighbors will take good care of her, besides which I told her I would be looking for our son as we go along."

"But you don't think he's alive."

"There's always the possibility. We should never lose hope, but my wife puts too much into the thought that he'll return. Hope for the best and prepare for the worst."

Aurora smiled, and he stepped forward to help her onto her horse.

"It's good to know you haven't completely given up hope for him. I could never give up on Lachlaniel unless I knew he was…" The thought caught in her throat and a tear came to her eye.

"We'll find your man. Don't you worry." But a worried look crossed his face as he took the lead. The land of the Basaners was not a place where he ever wanted to set foot.

Max walked down the road from the camp, his feet thumping the ground. He broke from his brooding at a flash of movement ahead. He looked up to find three men ahead of him, and hearing movement behind him, he turned to find two more. He chuckled and then roared with a laughter that made the leaves rattle on the trees. The men, who had been bold, quivered.

"So you've surrounded me eh?"

"We mean to kill you." The leader appeared to be as confident as ever.

"Well come ahead, *if you're able*!" The last came out as a growl. Max drew sword and pulled his shield.

The men circled him warily drawing the ring tighter. Max watched them, shifting his gaze from front to rear. Tension filled the air. He stopped his watching and fixed his eyes on the leader. A second later a yell came from behind him. He swung his shield towards his blind side, and the blow of his foe's sword crashed against his shield. The sound resounded through the woods. The attacker's hands trembled from the force of the blow. He dropped his sword and fell to his knees looking at his empty, useless hands and moaned.

Max turned to the left and landed a crashing blow to the head of the man to the leader's right with his sword filled hand. The man crumpled like a discarded letter. Turning back to the front, Max parri leader's stroke and then the man on his right. Both fell back, and he continued to his right delivering a blow with the flat of his sword to the backside of the fifth man who had turned to flee.

Continuing his turn to the right, he roared at the man who had struck first who still groveled on the ground attempting to get up. The man quit trying and crawled away as fast as he could. The next man, who had been downed by the blow to his head, threw a rock as he rose to his feet. Max hit it with the flat of his sword sending the fragments slamming back into the man's chest. He went down again as Max parried another stroke of the leader's sword driving him back several feet. Then, Max parried the stroke of the man on his right knocking the sword from his hand in the process.

As his last move, he slammed his shield with his full weight into the leader's charge. The leader went sprawling twenty yards down the road. He lay limp. With three foes fleeing and two lying in stunned amazement, Max stowed his sword and shield as he grabbed the man on his right by the back of his shirt. He thumped the man's hand with his forefinger. The man cried out and dropped his sword. He hung from Max's left hand, his feet dangling several inches off the ground. Max grabbed the still stunned leader in the same way and carried them back to the camp swinging them like two grocery filled baskets as he walked.

It was nearing noon when Aurora and Nestor reached a crossroads.
"Which way?" Aurora asked.
"The road to the left leads north of course. Not the direction you want to go. The main road, the one in the center, begins to bear right and again runs towards your friends. The one to the left is the one we want. Although it heads south, it eventually turns west through a land that's uninhabited. We should meet neither your friends nor any Basaners. We'll come to a crossroad with this road again after ten days or so. After that we'll hit the main road again."
"What about Max and Kesniel, I mean, my friends?"
"With them searching for you, their progress should be slow, and we should be far ahead of them." He started his horse down the chosen path.

"We'll need to eat soon and the horses must rest. We'll get past the next bend and have lunch. We should be far enough ahead at that point to relax a little."

Beyond the bend, the trees gave way to a grassy meadow. A cow grazed at the far end where the trees started again. Across the road were some deer, and occasionally a rabbit could be seen above the grass as it jumped. They let the horses graze while they ate.

Ewald's efforts had produced nothing. Theron had returned from his trek to the east with nothing to show for it but a tired horse. Ewald pondered what to do next as Theron and his men continued to search westward.

I hope he hasn't slipped back into the city. Every available guard is with me. They have just enough for guard duty at the key points, and the army isn't equipped to handle a saboteur. All I can hope is that we're driving him west, and he'll be caught between us and Kesniel. Woe be to him if Max is the one who finds him. But he's so skilled at stealth, he might slide through Kesniel's searchers too. I hope Kesniel finds Aurora before that happens.

Theron laid his shield by his bedroll, took off his helmet, and eased himself onto the ground. He groaned as he rolled onto his back.

"I'm not as young as I used to be."

Ewald snickered. "Who is? Any news?"

"Nothing, no trace at all. Three days. You'd think he would've left some sign."

A rumbling sound came from Ewald's throat and his brow furrowed.

Theron rolled to his side and propped himself up on an elbow. "What are you thinking?"

"We're not likely to catch him in open country when we couldn't catch him in a walled city."

"Any ideas?"

Ewald shook his head. "I haven't a clue. I'm worried he'll find Aurora before we can find him or Kesniel can find her."

"It's a problem. I have no answer."

"We need help." Ewald opened his closet and stepped in to speak to the King."

Nestor and Aurora made good time throughout the afternoon and evening. The landscape regularly changed from woods to meadows and back to woods. They had seen nothing as they trekked onward.

Nestor sighed. "This used to be farming country. Fields, meadows for cattle, gardens, even towns."

"What happened?"

"The Basaners came. They left nothing behind them."

"You mean this was a land with only Ebenchaim?"

"No. It was actually a mix, a very fertile place for the King's servants to rescue the people from Kieran's grip."

"Did the others leave?"

"No, they were killed too. The Basaners hate the light so much they'll even kill those content to live in the light. Not all Basaners are like that of course, but that's the basis of their thought. They've taken Kieran's way of thinking. He's a liar, a thief, and a murderer."

Aurora shook her head as she looked at the fallow fields. "It must have been long ago,"

"Several lifetimes. People are just now beginning to come back here. My village is a fairly new settlement. So far this area is only settled at the edges. Another generation and it will all be settled. The land is very fertile, but it will only bring the Basaners as it has to Photaskia."

"I don't understand how anyone can be so evil."

They rode on in silence.

Max looked at the two men on the ground before him, then to Kesniel. "What do you think?"

"I doubt they're telling the truth, at least not the whole truth." He gave a cold hard stare at the leader. "This king of yours, what's his name?"

"I don't know." There was defiance in the man's voice.

Kesniel looked at the second man who gave a quick, frightened glance first at Kesniel and then at Max. Max glowered at him with bared teeth. The man looked at the ground in front of him, swallowed hard, and trembling said, "His name is Andre."

The leader blurted out, "He'll kill you for this if I don't first."

Max gave the leader a gentle rap on the head, and he fell forward and lay still.

"You don't have to worry about him."

"But the king is powerful and crafty. He'll find a way to kill me! I know he will!"

"Then join us."

"You? Join you and live in that accursed light?" The man spit.

Max started to slap him, but Kesniel grabbed his arm. "'Do good to those who hate you', remember?"

Max dropped his hand, grabbed the man by the arm and gently raised him to his feet. He raised the man's chin and looked him in the eye. The man tried to avoid Max's gaze.

"How about something to eat?" Max's tone was genial.

The man didn't respond. Max put his arm on the man's shoulder and marched him out of the tent to the cook's tent leaving Kesniel to think and plan.

Ewald's men, having been recalled, rode behind him. They crested a hill and below them the road forked. He slowed his horse to a walk and began to look for a place to make camp. Trees lined the road as far as he could see, but beyond the fork fallen trees had been cut and moved off the road.

"Dismount! I need someone who still has some life in him."

The men looked at each other with expressionless faces.

"I've got just the man…er, boy for you," came a voice from the back.

The men made way and a guard came forward hauling a thin, armor-clad youth by his ear.

Ewald's eyebrows rose in astonishment. "Bercan! What are you doing here?"

"There was nothing to do when Max left, so I…"

"So you thought you'd tag along."

"I want to be a soldier, a member of the City Guards."

"And what were you going to do when Max found out?"

Fear came into Bercan's eyes.

Ewald snorted. "You mean you didn't think about the punishment he'd dish out? A guard has to think ahead, Bercan. Furthermore, you failed to submit to Max's authority. A guard has to know how to take orders."

"But a guard has to know how to take initiative. Max said so." Bercan was still frightened but was trying not to show it.

"Yes, but there's a big difference between initiative and disobedience. You have a lot to learn. Your punishment is to chop wood and haul water for the men for the rest of the trip. What Max will do is up to him."

Bercan's shoulders slumped and he looked at the ground.

"The rest of the men are worn out. You look like you have a little life left in you. Can you go ahead and scout out a place to camp?"

Bercan came to attention and a light came to his eyes. "Yes sir."

"Then you must do exactly as I say, no more and no less. Do you understand me?"

"Yes sir!"

"Alright then, find us a place to camp. No wandering off and no dawdling. Find us a place that's near and make it double quick. I want you back in less than an hour. Do a good job, obey my orders, and get back here on time," he paused and smiled, "and I'll speak to Max about your punishment."

Bercan turned to run for his horse.

Ewald called after him. "Bercan!"

Bercan turned.

"A guard always salutes his superior before leaving."

Bercan smiled, snapped to attention, and saluted then turned and ran like the wind for his horse.

Bercan did good. Not too far off the road, and the clearing is big enough for the men and the horses.

Ewald smiled. "Alright men let's get bedded down. We need to get back on the road as soon as we can."

Men dashed from place to place more quickly than their weary condition would have allowed. The prospect of rest, and more importantly of losing a minute of it, drove them beyond their fatigue. The chores were soon done, and everyone except the two guards was sound asleep.

The watch changed three times without incident. In the fourth watch, the guards were roused from the edge of sleep by the sound of hoof beats and wheels on the road. One guard stepped onto the road while the other remained out of sight. A cart came into view with the driver illuminated by a stone. The guard held up his hand for the driver to stop.

"It's one of our men," he said to the other guard.

The driver looked down. "What are you doing here?"

"Andre blew up several places in the city and escaped. We're on his trail. What about you?"

"We caught up with Grady a couple of days ago. He's in back with broken ribs."

"What happened?"

"Apparently you didn't get a good look at this region. The boy and Aurora were caught in a strange, whirling wind. It devastated this area from a mile back to the fork you just passed."

"What about Aurora? Is she alright?"

"Grady says so. She's still eluding us."

"Then you're heading back to the city. You'll want to talk to Ewald." He began whispering, "The boy's father is dead. Andre."

The driver sucked air through his teeth like he had been hit by an intense pain. "Oh, no."

"Best let Ewald break it to him."

After breakfast Kesniel called a guard. "Get two men mounted and saddle two extra horses. Then bring me the prisoners."

"Yes sir."

Max looked up from his plate of food. "What are you going to do?"

"They can't tell us much more if anything. I'm sending them back to the city."

"But if they can?"

"They'll slow us down. It's not worth it."

"We're moving at a snail's pace anyway."

Yes, but it's will take men away from scouting in order to guard them. Besides, if they were to escape they could make things worse. They know something of our numbers and abilities. They know we're looking for someone, too."

"Umm. You're right."

The prisoners walked up with the mounted guards and the extra horses right behind them.

Kesniel looked at the guards. "You two are going to escort the prisoners back to Agapay."

The leader's eyes grew wide. The guard behind him lowered his halberd and touched the point to his side. The man stood stone still, but terror filled his face.

Kesniel eyed him closely. "You know Andre is in Agapay."

The man's words caught in his throat, and he nodded vigorously.

"Then you'd best help us catch him." Kesniel looked at the other man. "What about you?"

"I want to cross the Bridge."

The leader, rage on his face, squirmed trying to get at the other man. The tip of both the guards' halberds brought his resistance to an end, but not his rage.

"I'll kill you."

"Get him on a horse and set out."

When the leader was out of earshot, Kesniel ordered the other man to be set free.

"Max, show this man to the Bridge. After he crosses, let him go."
The man looked at Kesniel. "Go? Go where?"
"Anywhere you want my friend. Anywhere you want."

Chapter 19
Snake Pit

Kesniel's men had searched far afield as the days dragged on, but there was no sign of Aurora. The scouts had passed a small town of pig farmers called Shamgar four days ago and the farm house and the place they picked up Grady lay two weeks behind them. The most of the men had been switched back to the main road as it was the shortest route to Chara.

Kesniel looked at Max on his Clydesdale. "I'm worried we've made a mistake in coming back to the main road."

Max shifted in his saddle and his horse shook his head. "Eventually, Aurora has to come back to it. We've still got men on the south road and every dog path in between."

"I'm becoming concerned that she's outrun us. She could be in the land of the Basaners now."

Max involuntarily spurred his horse, and Kesniel was obliged to spur his as well to keep up.

That was the wrong thing to say!

"Easy Max. It will do no good to hurry so much we miss her."

"We've got to find her."

They slowed their horses to a walk to allow the men to catch up.

Kesniel looked at the concern on his giant friend's face. "We'll find her. Patience my friend. The King is concerned for her too."

The light of two stones coming from men on horseback was reassuring, but there was a man riding with them who bore no stone. As they came closer, the garb of the King's guards became visible.

"Men from Agapay," the guard on the road said to his companion in hiding. "Some of the King-stewards guards."

The horsemen came to a halt.

"A prisoner?"

"Yes. What are you doing so far from Agapay?"

"Chasing Andre. I fear he's given us the slip."

"Again? That man is like an eel."

"How goes the search for Aurora?"

"Nothing."

"How far ahead?"

"Maybe three days."

"I'll let Ewald know."

"See you back at the city." He snapped the reins, and the other horsemen rode with him into the night."

Their light faded to a glimmer as the guard watched. The other guard had already left his hiding place and moved silently through the camp to Ewald's kip. It took effort to silence the snores and wake the exhausted sergeant.

"We stopped two city guards on the road. They were taking a prisoner back to the city. Kesniel, Aurora, and Max are about a three day's ride ahead."

"That means a week or more to catch up. We still need to search for Andre too. How long till dawn?"

"About an hour."

"Get the men up. Tell them to grab a quick bite and saddle up. You and the other men who stood watch get some rest and follow us."

Bleary-eyed men tied their bedrolls and saddled their horses as they ate. It would be a long day in the saddle again.

The morning was beautiful and the ride was somehow relaxing. Aurora watched as nature moved in a magnificent panoply. She was so intent that Nestor's sudden stop caught her by surprise and she had to turn back a few steps. He stood in his stirrups looking far ahead.

"The crossroads."

Aurora turned and looked back. "Finally."

"From here on, we must be careful. Your friends and the Basaners may be about." He let out a sigh. "I thought we'd be here sooner."

Aurora's eyes grew wide. "You think they'll catch us?"

"I don't know. Let's get across and out of sight before we take lunch. No doubt your friends are watching this road, so hopefully the Basaners won't be a problem."

After crossing, the tress were at times closer to the road and at times further away, but they never covered it. Sometimes, small meadows appeared. They reached an area with a clearing amongst the trees on their left and a small meadow on the right. It had become very humid, and the afternoon threatened to be hot with a threat of thunderstorms. They dismounted and Nestor set the horses free to graze in the meadow while Aurora made lunch. As they ate, the grass across the road began to be whipped by the wind. The horses raised their heads, their eyes wide. There was a clap of thunder, and they came trotting across the road. Nestor put down his sandwich and grabbed their reins while Aurora looked nervously at the sky as she gathered their things in haste and packed them away.

"What'll we do?"

"We must get into the trees. It isn't safe on a bare road with lightning playing about you." He tied the horses to a tree and got out their rain gear. "Help me get them saddled."

Aurora obeyed but her questions wouldn't wait. "Not safe?"

"No. Have you ever seen lightning split an oak?"

"No, I haven't."

"I have."

As if in answer, lightning struck the far side of the field.

"I've seen a tree a hundred and fifty feet high split to its roots. It was the only tree in the field. On the road, you look like that tree to a lightning bolt. We'll make our way through the trees while the storm lasts."

Their gear on and the horses saddled, they waded through the trees. They continued northwest away from the road for some time with rain pattering on the leaves above their heads and muffled thunder sounding all around them. Without warning the trees gave way to a tiny road running east and west. With the storm abating, they turned west and soon crested a small hill. Amazement filled their eyes. A light shone in the distance. It wasn't the light of a stone, and there was no one on the road. They moved cautiously forward on the wet roadway. The air had gotten still and Aurora became anxious.

Has the storm stopped or is there another whirling wind coming?

Just beyond the bottom of the hill, stood a tree beside the road and a grave beneath it from whence the light came. They dismounted.

Aurora felt tears welling up in her eyes. "It's as though the anger of the storm has turned to sadness beside this grave."

Nestor walked to the tree. Above the top of his head there was red on the trunk. He reached up and touched it.

"It looks like blood. The Basaners! This is the work of the Basaners. They tied someone to this tree and tortured them."

"Lachlaniel was here. He told me about this! It must have been horrible." She put her face in her hands and wept uncontrollably.

Nestor stepped to her side and held her close. "It's alright young one. He'll be alright, and we'll find him. What happened here won't be washed away by your tears. What will happen won't be stopped by them either. We must get moving if you want to see your man."

Aurora looked up. She tried to fight back the tears to no avail. Nestor let her go. She mounted her horse, her breath coming in sobs as she went.

They let the horses determine the pace and moved forward as though in time to a dirge.

Ewald and his men were riding hard and walking their mounts when necessary to cover the ground swiftly. The road was open with nothing to impede them.

"I hope we catch them soon, but what if we don't?" Theron's voice was tired and he looked haggard.

Ewald's lips pressed in determination. "We press on as far as we can. The King said it was urgent that we should meet up with them."

He wouldn't admit it, but he was approaching his limits as well. He looked behind him. The men were strung out for half a mile and were no longer organized.

"It looks like we've reached that point."

A scout burst into the tent. "We found a small road south of here in the middle of the woods."

Kesniel looked up annoyed by the breach in protocol until he heard about the road. "And?"

"The place where I came across it is well behind us. There was no one on the road. I've sent men to scout both east and west."

"Good. Well done. I want someone to ride hard and fast and get on that road well ahead of us."

Max's brow furrowed. "You think she's that far ahead?"

"Perhaps. Perhaps not, but I'm hoping we can cut her off. If we can get ahead of her, she may run into us. At any rate, this road is the only new possibility we've encountered in a week."

A ray of hope shone in Max's expression. "Let's hope she's on it, and we can find her."

Kesniel bent over his map and added a small section of road to the south of the main road. "Yes. Let's."

Lachlaniel awoke breathing normally. He smiled and sat up as Wilmot entered.

"Feeling better?"

Lachlaniel threw back the covers and turned to sit on the edge of the bed. The floor was cold to his bare feet even though the air was warm. He shivered.

"Where are my clothes?"

"Draped over the table beside you. Your boots are in front of them."

Lachlaniel got up and started to dress.

"What are you going to do?"

"I'm going back to finish what I started."

"I asked you before. What makes you think you'll fare any better this time?"

Lachlaniel smiled. "I have a plan."

"I'll come with you."

"I don't need you."

Wilmot shrugged his shoulders and sighed in resignation as Lachlaniel stalked out slamming the door behind him.

Aurora and Nestor had followed the road as it wound its way through the woods. Now, the road, having turned right, was descending while on the left side of the road the ground rose. Soon, the road curved left as the roadside became a cliff looming above them. After half an hour, they paused and looked at each other. The road made a sharp right, and beside the road was a child's grave.

"The Basaners?" Nestor shook his head in disgust.

"I'm afraid we're following Lachlaniel's path. He told me after the young woman they flogged to death, they stoned a little boy." She began to weep.

Nestor let out a sigh. "I wish I could find the murderous thugs."

"No! That's what Lachlaniel wanted, and I haven't heard…" An ache welled up in her chest and she buried her face in her hands as the tears flowed from her bloodshot eyes.

"Come on. Let's ask the King's protection for him and for us."

Nestor dismounted, rounded the horses, and helped Aurora down. They opened their closets and entered the magnificent throne room. They knelt before the King.

Aurora sniffed. "My Lord, I ask for Lachlaniel's protection."

"And for our own," Nestor added.

"Limited protection is all I can give Lachlaniel. He is not following Me. He thinks he knows what I would have him do." He paused and looked sternly at Aurora. "You too are not doing My will."

Aurora's eyes widened and filled with tears. "My Lord?"

You should not have left the city. You have removed yourself from My protection by removing yourself from Kesniel's protection."

"I know. What happened to Grady is…"

"The past is past. There is a clearing ahead. Make camp there and wait for Kesniel. Nestor you must stay awhile. I must talk to you."

Aurora left but turned at the door.

I wonder what that's all about.

Stepping out she gathered some flowers, and placing them on the grave she sat down by it to wait for Nestor.

The birds in the trees sang a sad song, and a brief shower ensued.

It's as if all nature wept over the boy. Or is it weeping over me and my failure to follow my King? Oh, Lachlaniel, what have we done?

Tears welled up in her eyes.

I'm so ashamed.

She put her head on her knees and became oblivious to all else.

Kesniel looked at the scout that had come in. "Were you searching the east end of the road or the west?"

"East. End is the right word. It became nothing more than a deer path that ended in a thicket. Before I got that far, I came across something strange."

Max looked up. "Strange?"

"Yes. There was a golden light coming from a tree beside the road. Beside the tree, there was a grave that was maybe a month old."

Max stood up and looked at Kesniel. "Aurora?"

"I doubt it." He looked back to the scout. "What else?"

There were hoofprints of two horses in the dried mud."

Max's eyes brightened and a smile crossed his face. "Aurora!"

The scout continued. "They had to have been made during that storm a few days ago or just after. It's been hot and dry and the mud would've been dry after a day or two at most."

"She can't be far ahead. Break camp. Let's get moving."

Lachlaniel had worked hard all day making various kinds of traps among the trees. Now, he stood at the edge of the woods. His light shone like a beacon across the plain illuminating everything from the trees to the cliff.

I'll walk around so they can see the light. If that doesn't work, I'll make a fire a little way out so that they can see I'm alone.

An hour passed, then two, but there was no sign of them. He brazenly gathered wood and made a fire in the open, but there was still no sign of the Basaners. Without warning, they came yelling from the rocks. Lachlaniel stood up smiling as he drew sword and ran towards the forest. Twigs snapped ahead of him as many feet pounded the forest floor.

Trapped!

He stood his ground, sword at the ready. But these men had seen him before. They stopped twenty yards away rocks in hand. Lachlaniel waited, listening. There was only the faint crackle of his fire behind him muffled by the sound of many bodies. Three rocks hit his back and two his front. He went down losing his grip on his sword. They rushed in before he could recover.

"Damon, now that we have him, *again*, what are we going to do with him?"

Damon mused a moment, stroking his chin. "He's a tough man to kill."

"The governor's snake pit," a third man suggested.

Damon smiled. "Perfect. But we're not gonna just walk away this time. First, we watch the fun, and then I want a dozen men to stay and make sure he's dead."

The men began murmuring. The first man spoke up, "How're we gonna do that?"

Damon's smile widened. "Well, Cashin, you're going to go in and make sure."

"*Me!?*" Cashin cried incredulous at the prospect.

"*You.*"

"Why me?"

Damon's sneer showed a row of chipped and crooked teeth. "You just volunteered."

The other men gave a collected sigh of relief.

"Alright! Bind him."

Lachlaniel winced as they bound his hands. His face flushed with rage as he struggled against their efforts.

Stupid! That was so stupid! I accomplished nothing. Bunch of worthless marauders. I should have killed them all. I will yet!

Twisting violently, he felt a sharp pain on the back of his head and a crack reached his ears. His head was spinning, and he slumped forward. Just before he lost consciousness, hands grabbed him beneath the arms and began dragging him. Then all went black.

Ignatius saw the man with the stone come out of the trees. He stood waiting for something.

What's he doing? Doesn't he know they'll catch him again? This doesn't make sense.

He watched looking from the man to the places where he knew Damon and the Basaners waited. He circled the pond to the edge of the woods. After much time had passed, the man started gathering sticks.

Maybe I should warn him.

Some of his former friends shoved him to the ground as they entered the woods. He hadn't gotten used to his missing right arm, and was slow to rise. When he finally looked back toward the man, a fire was already flickering near him.

Ignatius started to yell a warning, but it was already too late. The Basaners were descending the rocks and crossing the plain yelling as they came. He watched helpless as they surrounded and captured the man. There was some discussion, but the voices were muffled by the crowd. He followed at a distance and then stopped in his tracks.

The snake pit! They're taking him to the snake pit!

It was late in the day and Aurora was still crying when Asher came upon her in the clearing.

"I found you!" He jumped off his horse and ran towards her when Nestor came out of the trees carrying wood for the fire.

"Who is this?" Asher said pulling his sword.

Aurora looked at him through glassy, tear filled eyes. "Put away your sword, Asher. This is Nestor."

Nestor dropped his load of wood by the fire, and Asher slid the sword back into its sheath.

"We've been looking everywhere for you."

Nestor eyed the stranger. His garish yellow boots, green pants, purple shirt, blue cap topped off by an orange feather screamed at his surroundings.

"I don't see how anyone could miss *you*. You look like some birds I've seen in the far south. Are you *trying* to get caught by the Basaners?"

Asher looked at him puzzled. "Trying to get caught? Who are the Basaners?"

"It's a long story." Aurora turned wiping her eyes with her kerchief. "This is Asher one of our more flamboyant guards."

Asher doffed his hat and made a sweeping bow.

"At your service."

"And this is Nestor. Nestor has been kind enough to escort me through this dangerous land."

"The pleasure is mine," Nestor said imitating the bow.

Aurora wiped her nose. "The King said to wait here for Kesniel."

"That's good, but how's he going to find us?" Asher looked about him. "I'm lost."

"You have to go back to him and lead him to us," Aurora said.

"I'm not sure about that. Leave you after you led us on this wild goose chase. How do I know you won't fly away once I'm gone?"

"Didn't I say that the King said to wait for you? I'm not going anywhere."

"And I won't leave her alone in this country. We've seen evidence that the Basaners frequent this road."

Asher threw up his hands. "Fine, but which way?"

Nestor looked at Asher. "How's your sense of direction?"

"I never get lost." Asher looked around. He gave a wide, toothy grin with a furrowed brow. "Well almost never."

Nestor laughed. "Simply head north. You should find the main road in an hour or so." He laughed again.

Lachlaniel awoke beside the pit. He could feel the sharp drop off inches away. From the pit came rattles and hisses. He struggled against the bonds but it was useless.

"He's awake!"

"Good." It was the voice of Damon. "Slice the ropes so he can get free, and shove him in. I want to watch this. It's the only thing their stinking light is good for."

Lachlaniel felt a knife on the ropes and tried to grab the man. It was a futile attempt. A boot kicked his side, and he went rolling over the edge. There was laughter from the crowd above him as he landed on dozens of vipers. A voice above began counting. The impact broke the ropes, but before he could stand, the onslaught began. Fangs ripped the flesh of his arms and legs.

Their venom is like fire. I've got to get out of here.

He struggled to his feet and felt for the wall of the pit as snakes struck repeatedly at his legs. He was already woozy when he found the wall and searched for a hand or foot hold.

You're not going to make it.

The Chuchoteur's implanted thought had little effect.

No I don't suppose I will, but I've got to try.

He continued clawing at the wall while the men above howled with glee. The fire in his legs had climbed to his chest and his heart pounded.

Not much time!

And if you do get out? They'll just throw you back in!

I can't give up. Can't...

The sound of the clamor above faded. His arms fell limp at his sides, and his legs collapsed. The snakes were hitting higher targets now – his arms and back, but he no longer felt them. He fell to his side and was still. The counting stopped and money began to change hands.

The men settled down and watched the motionless body. The vipers continued to strike for several minutes with the strikes becoming more and more random and infrequent. They finally moved to the far side of the pit.

"Looks like that's it," one man said.

"Not yet." Damon stood up. "I'm taking no chances. This guy has slipped through my fingers three times. Cashin and I will stay here. Everybody else back to your positions."

"Why me?"

"I told you, you're going down to make sure he's dead. Now sit down and wait. We'll watch for a couple of hours. When the body's cold, you'll go down and make sure it's cold."

Cashin gulped and sat down. Perspiration beaded up on his forehead. He fidgeted and checked his armor.

"Relax. Enjoy these last few moments of life."

Cashin wrung his hands as he got up and paced. "How can I? Why don't you just let me go down now and get it over with?"

"Because I want the body to be cold before you go in to make sure!" Damon snapped. Then he smiled. "Besides, you might make it out alive if you're quick enough."

Cashin swore and cursed, but his actions only made Damon angry. He sat down again. His every movement enraged Damon more. Only an hour had passed before Damon stood up.

"I've had enough of your whimpering. Get down there and check him!"

Cashin rose to his feet, his hands trembling.

"Go on!" Damon shoved him almost knocking him into the pit.

Cashin rounded the pit to the side where Lachlaniel lay.

"You'll pull me out when I get done?"

"Sure."

The word wasn't reassuring at all. He lowered himself over the side and dropped to the bottom. He eyed the far side of the pit where the snakes were. They weren't moving. He eased himself onto one knee by the lifeless body. The ashen look said death. He placed his hand on the body's chest. Still, lifeless, and cold. He looked up.

"Now his face." Damon stared down at him watching his every move and that of the snakes.

He felt the face. It was as cold as stone. "He's dead. Now get me out of here."

Damon laid on the ground and reached his hand down.

"Oh no – the snakes! The Snakes! Hurry!"

Cashin gripped Damon's hand. His feet struck at the wall trying to get traction. The snakes began striking his legs. He looked up. Damon was smiling as he let go. He could hear Damon laughing. Cashin screamed as serpent after serpent struck home, their bites filling him with venom. Damon watched as Cashin's movements became erratic and finally ceased. He turned to go back to his men.

Unseen Hands lifted Lachlaniel from the pit and laid him gently on the ground. One Hand stroked his hair while another touched his face. His flesh warmed and the color returned to his cheeks. The Hands lifted him to his feet and pointed him towards the trees. He began walking. He was groggy and he stumbled several times. Slowly, his strides became steady and his pace quickened.

Chapter 20
Angus

Kesniel looked up when Asher entered the tent.

"I found her,"

"Then *where* is she?"

"I left her in the woods."

Clouds of anger began to rise in Kesniel's face. "*Alone?*"

"Of course not! There was a man with her, named Nestor."

The clouds of anger erupted into a storm lashing Asher with fierce winds. "Oh. So you left her in the woods with a man named Nestor. *We've been searching the area for days and when you found her you just left her in the woods!* **What's wrong with you! You should've brought her back here!**"

Asher became uneasy and kicked the dirt with his foot. He looked up but didn't meet Kesniel's piercing gaze.

"They're waiting for us."

"Waiting… Get out of here! Find Max! Take him where you found her!"

Asher, like a whipped dog with his tail between his legs, turned slowly.

"**Move!!**"

Kesniel followed him out of the tent. "Bugler!"

A man came running up with a horn in his hand.

"Sound assembly." Kesniel scanned the area. "You there! Take five men and follow Max and Asher. Let us know where they go."

The horn sounded and men began to scurry into formation from everywhere. Before they even finished gathering, Kesniel began to address them.

"We've found Aurora, but we don't know if she is still there. Break camp! Recall the scouts!" He pointed to the first five men in the front row. "You five stay here. Send the scouts after us as they come in. Keep in touch. When the scouts are all in, follow us. I'll be sending back orders for the disbursement of the scouts as we move forward."

The men began to scatter to their tasks. The tents began to come down as Max and Asher left the camp.

The forest resounded with shouts and drunken song. Aurora rolled over and threw off her covers. Nestor was already standing, sword drawn.

Aurora sat up. "What is it?"

"Two drunks. I don't know if they're dangerous, but they have no stones. You'd better get up. Hide as best you can."

Aurora got up and quickly folded up her bedroll and carried it a little further into the woods.

At least they might think he's alone.

Nestor eyed the men as they approached. His hand dropped to the hilt of his sword. He moved onto the road.

"Hey look! It's one of those light people."

"Let's get him."

Nestor drew his sword and took his stand squarely in the center of the road.

"You boys sound like you're up to no good." He pulled his shield from his back. "Take my advice and get rid of the ale. You've had way too much already."

The men looked at one another and smiled. They corked their goatskins and tossed them to the side of the road as they drew their knives and ran toward Nestor. One man stumbled and fell on his face. Nestor merely sidestepped the other whose momentum also made him fall. Aurora watched as Nestor stepped back towards the trees where they made camp to keep the men in front of him and Aurora behind him.

The men were slow to get up and stumbled several times. They looked at the man in front of them. They whispered to each other. It was hard to see and Aurora moved to a different tree to get a better angle. As she did, one of the men stood still looking in her direction.

"Hey. What's that?" He pointed towards Aurora. "Protecting someone? A daughter? A wife?"

They whispered again. The man on the left ran at Nestor. The one on the right ran towards Aurora. She moved back to the next line of trees pulling her sword as she went. Nestor slammed his shield into the head of the man on the left sending him sprawling, then he dashed to cut off the man on the right who was closing the distance on Aurora.

Aurora dived into a thicket of saplings. She couldn't see what happened, but there was the sound of several more shouting voices up the road.

I hope Nestor hears that. I better put on my armor. He'll never be able to keep all of them off me.

A very large hand was suddenly over her mouth.

"Shh… Be quiet sis."

It was Max.

"Asher, stay here and protect her."

Asher nodded.

Max moved forward but stayed in the trees. Asher and Aurora tried to see, but the trees and undergrowth were too thick here. They moved to the right and inched forward. Max was watching the fight between two drunkards and an armored man. The drunkards were losing, but to their right Aurora could hear the other men marching forward and shouting. Max had heard them too. He stepped out from the trees. The drunkards got to their feet and scurried up the road toward the marching men. Nestor turned to attack Max, but seeing the light he turned to stand by Max and face the approaching men. Aurora craned her neck trying to count the men. There were at least eight or ten.

"Basaners," she whispered.

Asher looked at her and then the men. "Max can take that rabble by himself."

The men did not seem to be perturbed. They continued marching.

"Are you so anxious to die?" Max bellowed.

The men hesitated but the leader marched on.

Max drew sword and shield. As he did so, a light appeared behind the group. Four of Kesniel's men on horseback closed their escape route. The men stopped and looked backwards and forwards. They began to yell. The leader stopped when his men began crying out. He turned to see his tight-knit group running for their lives into the woods, and courage left him as well.

"Shall we pursue?" one of the mounted riders asked.

"No." Max answered. He looked at the woods. "No. They know these woods, and pursuit on horseback would be too dangerous. We can't afford to lose one man in this country." He looked at Nestor. "Do you have any idea of their numbers?"

"No. They attack our people at will here, but how many there are; I just don't know."

Asher and Aurora emerged from the woods.

"What do we do now?" Asher asked.

On seeing the gaudy outfit again, Nestor laughed. "Is Asher your jester?"

Max chuckled. "No, just one of our flamboyant guards." He looked at his friend with the eyes of the stranger and chuckled again. "We'll wait here for Kesniel, and since you know the way best, you must bring him back. Watch yourself, Asher. This group is abroad. No doubt they would like to catch one of us to wash away the stench of their mortifying experience."

"They won't catch me!"

"Well it won't be because they didn't see you!" Nestor yelled after him and laughed again.

Lachlaniel awoke again in the bed where Jason had tended him before.

"How long will you insist on fighting them?"

Lachlaniel turned his head with great effort and much pain to face Jason."

"Until they cease killing people or I've killed them."

"Or until they've killed you, which is more likely."

Lachlaniel tried to rise, but the pain made the attempt unbearable.

"Do you know how many times those snakes bit you? We counted *eighty seven* pairs of fang marks. You should be dead already. In fact, any of the wounds you received at their hands should have killed you. Why you're alive, the King only knows." He paused. "Perhaps that's the answer. He has something for you to do and won't let you die until it's accomplished."

"Then, I must try again."

"But perhaps you're trying to do it in the wrong way. Or perhaps this isn't even the task He wants you to do."

"*No!* This *is* the task, and I *will* finish it!"

"Very well. I can see your mind is made up and there's no use talking to you." Jason shook his head and left the room.

His pain might change his mind, but I doubt it.

Wilmot was in the kitchen.

"What do you think?" He took a bite of biscuit.

"I think he's a very stubborn man." Jason scratched his head. "He thinks he's serving the King."

"But?"

"But he's doing this all himself. Pride has him in its grip. I don't know what will break that. As I say, he's very stubborn. You plan on staying?"

Wilmot moved his biscuit into his cheek with his tongue. "The King says to." His words were almost indiscernible. He swallowed and continued. "I think I'm here to catch him when he falls."

"Another fall like this one…" Jason shook his head.

"The King won't let him die. I think He's trying to break his pride. As you say, he's very stubborn." Wilmot picked up another biscuit. "How's he doing physically?"

Jason grabbed a plate. "It should be days before those wounds heal maybe weeks, but I think he'll be at it again tomorrow." He put two biscuits on the plate. He smothered one in gravy and stuffed the other with butter and jam. "He should rest, but knowing him he's already thinking of some other way to get at them which he'll try tomorrow."

"Hmm. Then, I'd better see to the horses and get some rest myself."

Wilmot stuffed the last bite of biscuit in his mouth and went to the door.

"I hope this ends soon. He's aged five years in the couple of weeks I've known him." The door closed behind him.

Jason stared at the table. "I know."

The five guards had waited at the roadside all night. Ewald and his men arrived late in the morning just as the last scout rode up.

"What's the word? Where's Kesniel and Max?" Ewald dismounted.

"They're ahead of us. I can't say how far. They sent word back during the night. We were to meet them when this scout got back."

"Good. We'll follow, but we need to rest."

"We'll leave a man to show you the way."

Ewald tilted his head to one side and his brow furrowed. "They're not on this road?"

"No. There's another road. You have to trek through the forest to get to it."

Ewald nodded his head. "Okay. Good. We'll follow in two hours. The horses couldn't have gone much farther. The men either for that matter."

"I'll let them know."

"Dismount!" Ewald bellowed.

The men sighed as they slid off their horses, and conversations in hushed tones sprang up among them. Ewald looked back as Kesniel's guards mounted.

"Tell them to be ready for us. We'll be in need of food and rest. We'll be there as quick as we can."

"We'll be waiting."

The men rode off and Ewald and his men settled in for an early lunch.

Lachlaniel rose early. Wilmot found him in the barn.

"Do you really intend to try again?"

Lachlaniel gave Wilmot an icy stare. "Are there still Basaners?"

Wilmot shook his head. "Why are you so insistent on doing it this way?"

"Because they should all be killed."

"Why?"

"Ask the woman they beat to death as I was on my way here, or the little boy. Ask those in their dungeons. How many have to die before you people wake up?"

"You're not doing any good. There has to be another way."

Lachlaniel mounted Aman. "When you think of it let me know." He kicked Aman's flank, and they sprang from the barn door at a canter.

Fool! The only thing the Basaners understand is the sword. He is right about one thing; I've got to try a different way. There must be another approach.

He rode in silence letting Aman set the pace as he thought through the problem. When Aman stopped at the edge of the forest, it was several minutes before Lachlaniel realized he wasn't moving. He looked up. The sounds of the plain lying stark and bare before him resounded in his ears. Sounds of bird cries echoing off the rocks mingled with the sound of the wind in the trees behind him, but ahead the wind moved soundlessly over the plain.

They'll know I'm here now. Best to backtrack into the trees and out of sight. Out of sight! That's it! I'll come from behind. I'll lower myself over the cliff **and come from behind**! *They said there was no other way, but for one man there just might be.*

He turned back up the road until he was certain to be out of their sight. Leaving the road, he moved among the trees parallel to the cliff as best he could tell. He traveled for the better part of two hours that way before he turned to his right. It took some time before he reached the edge of the trees again.

I must have veered further north than I thought. I should be far enough east to keep my light from alerting them, but I'll cover it anyway.

He wrapped the stone in his cloak and sighed. He urged Aman forward across the plain and then gave him freedom to go or stop at his own pace.

"You're my eyes boy. Take me to the edge."

The horse moved forward at a slow walk at first, but soon moved with hesitation. Lachlaniel slipped off the saddle and walked beside him, reins in hand.

Surely we aren't close to the cliff already?

Aman stopped and Lachlaniel took one more step. The ground gave way beneath his foot. Pulling on the reins to regain his balance, he jumped away from the edge of the cliff. He lifted himself back to his feet.

Either the trees grow nearer to the cliff here or the cliff took a turn back toward the tree line somewhere.

He took the rope from his pack and tied it to the saddle. He tied the other end around his waist. Lowering himself to the ground, he inched forward feeling his way to the edge. Once there, he tossed the excess over the side of the cliff, grabbed the line coming from the saddle, and lowered himself over the side. He felt the line go taught and Aman start to pull back.

"Easy boy."

Aman stood in place and Lachlaniel slid down the rope toward the ground below.

A hundred feet. I hope it's enough, or it will be a difficult climb back up.

He fended himself off the rocky wall several times with his feet, but other than that, the trip down was uneventful. He reached the end of the rope.

What now?

Try climbing down the face of the rock. It can't be too far to the bottom.

Or it could be hundreds of feet.

What choice do you have? Climb back up? What will you do then?

Lachlaniel let out a long slow sigh.

"Down it is."

He felt the wall with his hands and feet for any kind of a handhold. He found one and removed the rope, but as he let it go, it started sliding upward.

Aman's moving away from the cliff. I hope he'll be alright until I get back to him.

It was a long slow descent and he began to tire. After an hour, he reached a point where the face of the rock became smooth. Hand and footholds became few, and those that existed were barely sufficient to hold on. The face of the rock was also moving away from him so that he found himself hanging by his hands several times. His handhold gave way, and he fell landing on his back. He lay still for a moment and then laughed out loud.

I couldn't have fallen more than four or five feet. I thought I was done for.

He got up and worked his way west along the base of the cliff, scrutinizing every sound. He stopped and sniffed the air. The smells were those of late summer but nothing more. The breeze was from the west.

The ground was uneven and rocky He had to creep forward to keep from tripping.

The wall curved northward. His progress was slow and torturous until he felt the wall of the cliff turn back toward the west. There was a small bush, ragged and bare of leaves that had grown from the wall on his right and a small man sized boulder on his left. His next footfall brought him to a halt. The ground was no longer rough. The biggest rocks he felt were mere pebbles. He took another step.

A path! That isn't good. They may patrol this area.

He drew his sword, and moved forward more cautiously and slowly than ever. He hadn't gone twenty paces more when he was entangled in a net that was thrown over him. His sword sliced through it like air, but a set of strong arms clenched him from behind. He struggled in vain. The man was powerful and large.

"Not as large as Max, but he'll do."

It was a strange voice. It had an oily quality, as though it regularly spit out lies.

"Who are you?"

"Me? Why I'm Angus."

Lachlaniel's face frowned and his forehead lined in deep thought.

Angus. That's familiar.

"Can't remember? Oh, well. It'll come to you. By the way, Aurora says hello."

Lachlaniel's sword fell from limp fingers.

Chapter 21

The Pit

It was early evening when Ewald's men came riding into Kesniel's camp. Max and Nestor were in the tent with Kesniel, but Aurora sat alone by the fire. Ewald gave the reins of his horse to one of the guards and joined her.

"You've caused a lot of trouble young lady."

His stern look almost set her to crying again.

"I know it. The King rebuked me."

Ewald's countenance softened.

I know what that feels like.

"Then I won't add mine." He decided to change the subject. "Andre is loose. He fled the city. We've been trying to trail him."

"Did you have any luck? Where's he headed?"

"This way as far as we can tell. He's eluded us the whole way. We've hardly seen any trace of him, much less sighting him or catching him."

Concern lined her face. "Where do you think he's headed?"

Ewald smiled. "He won't find Lachlaniel even if he's looking for him. Even we don't know where Lachlaniel is."

Aurora began to cry, and Ewald was taken aback.

What did I say? What do I do now? What do you do with a crying woman?

He put his hand on her shoulder. "Don't you worry. That man of yours is quite the warrior for a blind man."

Aurora stood up and ran wailing to her tent. Ewald stood up and scratched his head.

What have I done?

He walked toward Kesniel's tent as Max looked out to see what the commotion was.

"What happened?"

"Must've been something I said."

Max looked hard at him.

"What were you talking about?"

Ewald stooped down, picked up a rock and threw it into the woods. He looked back at Max and was about to say something when the rock hit a tree and a man sprang from behind it and raced into the woods.

"Guards!" Ewald shouted.

"Don't bother," Max said. "We've tried catching them. They know these woods too well."

"Them? More than one? How many?"

"We don't know, but they're watching us pretty closely."

Ewald grit his teeth.

"Basaners," Max continued. "Too few, apparently, to want to do anything, but watch your step and don't wander into the woods. We were just discussing them. You should give your report, and we'll fill you in on what we know."

Max held back the tent flap and the two men entered. Kesniel and another man sat on two freshly cut logs, talking. Ewald sat on one of the other two logs while Max, for whom the log was too small, sat on the ground.

Kesniel motioned to the other man. "This is Nestor. He was escorting Aurora." He motioned toward Ewald. "This is Ewald, a sergeant of our guards. What brought you out of the city?"

Ewald's face turned grim. "Capaleanan's dead."

Max's jaw dropped, "Capaleanan's dead? How?"

"Andre. First he tried to blow up the tower. He only blew in the doors on the west side. We lost the guards watching the door. Several others were hurt. Next it was Jocelyn's house. No one was hurt there. Then, he blew up part of the Residence, knifed Capaleanan, and killed a horse. He killed a guard and got over the wall."

Max clenched his fists and Kesniel banged the log beside him.

"Basaner," Nestor muttered.

The others looked at him and then the attention turned back to Ewald who proceeded with his tale.

"He left another flower atop the wall when he went over the side. A black rose."

Kesniel's face changed at the mention of the flower. He had a faraway look as if his thought were now thousands of miles away.

"We trailed him as best we could. He's headed west, but we don't know where. The trail is long cold whenever we find a trace of him."

Kesniel broke in, "What about these flowers he leaves? You said they have meanings?"

"Yes. They started with meanings of his interest in Aurora. As she didn't respond, they grew stronger in meaning and then changed to threats."

"And the last one? The black rose?"

Ewald's voice became flat and lifeless. "It means death."

Max ground his huge fist into the dirt and stood up to his full height nearly bringing the tent down on them before he remembered to hunch down. "Who do you think the rose was meant for?"

"All of you," Nestor chimed in.

"You know him?" Kesniel asked.

"No. About a year ago a man rode through our village. Someone saw him leave a flower on the bench beneath the town oak. It was a black rose. The Basaners came the next day. We've been in a reign of terror from them ever since."

Kesniel stood, put his hands behind his back, and began to pace. "And you think Andre is the same man?"

Nestor's eyes followed his movements. "It could be. It certainly sounds like the same man."

Max eyed Kesniel. "What do you think?"

"I think it's him. From what Ewald has said, I think he's ahead of us or soon will be. Ewald's men can't go on without rest. Somehow we've got to make better time."

Max sat back down. "What if we send scouts ahead with the extra horses, the ones that are worn out."

Kesniel scratched his chin. "How will they be fresh? They'll still have run the distance the others have."

"They can trade them for fresh mounts that we can use when we arrive."

Ewald smiled at his large friend. "That's a good plan."

"I agree." Kesniel stopped pacing. He went to the door of the tent and threw back the flap. "Asher!" Kesniel ducked back into the tent.

Nestor frowned, tight lipped. "You'd better send a large group to protect the horses. They would make a prime target for the Basaners."

"I intend to."

It took a couple of minutes for Asher to present himself in the tent. Kesniel stood waiting, his hands behind his back.

"Get some men, about thirty. Round up our remuda and take them ahead. Trade them for fresh mounts and wait for us."

Asher ran out of the tent double quick.

"The rest of us must get some rest. The road from here will be hard."

They all frowned.

Max looked at the ground. "We'll all have to trade our own horses too. Who's going to break **that** to Aurora?"

"It's ready."

Andre looked at the man and smiled. "Good."

He left the tent and strode with an air of imperiousness toward his enemy. Lachlaniel sat on a rock waiting.

"I hear you're a hard man to kill. I don't think you'll be walking away from this one." Andre looked at his men. "Get him up."

The men grabbed Lachlaniel's arms and brought him forward.

"Before the main course, I'm personally going to serve the hors d'oeuvres."

Andre punched Lachlaniel in the face, then in the ribs and stomach. This went on for many minutes with Andre's men forcing Lachlaniel to stand whenever he fell. When Lachlaniel could no longer stand even with their help, they let him fall on his face. Andre stepped forward, rolled him over, and stood towering over him.

"I rule here. Soon, I will rule everywhere, and everywhere I rule the light will be extinguished."

"The King rules."

"Then let him show himself. I'll defeat him also and Aurora will be mine."

Lachlaniel spit blood; then he laughed. "You rule? You're a petty dictator with a gang of thugs."

Andre kicked Lachlaniel knocking the wind out of him. "Take him."

The men dragged Lachlaniel up the road, beyond the boulders, and onto the plain. Ahead of them was a ring of wood and thatch with a post in the middle. The men tied Lachlaniel securely to the post. Andre and five men with torches in their hands moved forward. Others finished filling the ring with wood, sticks, and thatch. The five men moved to positions around the ring. Andre stood at the entrance.

"That's good enough."

When the men had exited the ring, Andre called out, "Now we'll see how hard it is to kill you."

With that he plunged his torch into the waiting wood and the five men did likewise. The men returned to their posts. Andre stepped back as the heat rose. Beads of sweat peppered his face, and his shirt became damp. In the middle of the flames, Lachlaniel stood held up only by the ropes. When they burned through, he fell. There was no more movement, so Andre turned back up the road. He had just started to descend towards the city when there was a clatter behind him. When he turned, every man stood frozen, statue-like, their weapons at their feet. He raced back up the path. At the top, he stopped as though he had run into an unseen wall. His jaw went slack and his knees knocked together. There was a Man standing in the fire who reached down and helped Lachlaniel to his feet. He put His arm around him, and they walked through the opening, down the road, and into the woods.

Ignatius watched the man dragged into the ring of firewood. From his hiding place he couldn't see inside the ring, but he knew quite well what was happening.

I didn't see how he could survive the pond or the snakes but this?

There was the scent of a strange fruit blossom and then a Voice. "But he will survive."

Ignatius' hands trembled as he looked about. "Where are you and how did you know what I was thinking?"

"I know everything about you, Ignatius. I know you've turned from the Basaners, and though you haven't yet embraced the light, you're thinking about it."

Ignatius leaned back against a tree grabbing it as best he could with his left hand. His legs felt weak.

"You know about the Bridge and the King. What keeps you from crossing?"

"Fear."

"And what are you afraid of? Andre, your king? He isn't your king anymore, you know. If he caught you, the Fragel would have another person to kill. That's all you are to them now, just another person to kill."

"But all of the King's people I've helped kill…"

"The King loves you Ignatius. He sent the boy to start you on the path to this moment."

"He sent the boy to die?"

"Would anything less have turned you from the Basaners. Your heart wasn't with them long before you lost your arm. That was merely the final straw."

"But the King won't win. We kill His people and He does nothing."

"Do you think He can't? He could have saved the woman and the boy and all that the Basaners seek to kill. They have no power. His is the only real power. Watch."

Ignatius looked at the ring of fire. Two men walked out of the opening – out of the fire. Ignatius' back slid down the tree as his knees buckled.

"How? How…"

"The King has more for Lachlaniel to do. He has things for you to do as well. The Bridge is here."

Ignatius turned his head to the right and saw it. It brought fear into his heart.

"Cross that?"

"Look back to the fire."

Ignatius stood and turned. The man, Lachlaniel, was walking alone now, just entering the woods. Andre, and The Basaners were standing motionless with their weapons lying on the ground.

"That's the power of the King. If He can keep Lachlaniel safe from them, don't you think He can see you safely across the Bridge? Trust Him."

Ignatius turned and walked boldly to the Bridge.

The morning broke hot, but beneath the trees it was cool and humid. The cook had arisen early and had made biscuits and cooked sausage. Out of these he had made a strange sandwich that could be eaten while riding. Kesniel had ordered that Ewald and his men should not be disturbed until the horses were ready and packed. This accomplished they were on the road in less than fifteen minutes. No one looked forward to the day's riding they had ahead.

They pushed the horses hard and reached the guards and their fresh mounts long before noon. As they transferred to the new mounts, the cook came out with his second wonder – a bread nugget made of corn. The men were grateful for this not only because breakfast had been hours ago but the taste was truly a marvel. They were longing for coffee or ale to wash it down, but water had to suffice. They continued eating as they went as they had no time to waste on a more casual meal.

Lachlaniel awoke once again to a breeze wafting over him from the window.

How many times is this? Four? Five? Six?

He threw back the covers and sat up, but when he started to rise, his knees buckled. He caught himself with his hands, his nose inches from the floor. Every move brought agonizing pain, but he managed to crawl back into bed moaning as he went. He took a deep breath and nearly passed out. His head hit the pillow and a wave of pain shot through his face. Jason burst into the room, brought by the sound of his scream. Lachlaniel was lying face up, his fists clenched and his teeth grit.

Jason gave a half grin and raised an eyebrow. "Good morning."

Lachlaniel tried to sit up and then thought better of it. "I'd call it anything but good. What happened?"

"I was being sarcastic. When we found you, it was apparent that you'd been beaten, but we also found this." He put a piece of burned rope in Lachlaniel's hands.

He rubbed the burned cords between his fingers. "I don't know. I don't remember."

Jason folded his arms. "Do you remember leaving here?"

"Yes. I… I… Tell Wilmot I'm sorry."

"I can't. He followed you and brought back your horse. Then he left without a word."

"Where?"

"Back to the city I suppose." Jason leaned against the door jamb and rubbed his whiskers. "Where did you go?"

"Back to the Basaners. I let myself down over the cliff by rope. I remember feeling my way along the wall." Lachlaniel paused.

It's all so hazy.

"And?"

Lachlaniel's unseeing eyes stared at the ceiling. "I don't know."

"Then rest. Try not to think about it. Sleep if you can."

Only Lachlaniel's acute hearing allowed him to sense Jason's exit.

I wish I could remember.

The pace of the afternoon was slower as they tried to keep the mounts fresh as long as they could. This gave the scouting party time to get the weary horses far enough ahead before they tried to trade them for fresh ones again. They met the scouts in the early evening before the stone's light had begun to fade to their overnight hues. The cook pulled off another marvel giving the men bags of strips cut from potatoes, cooked, and salted. These went well with the dried beef which was the only meat they had left.

Lachlaniel rose in the middle of the night. He had remembered enough to make him ignore the pain.

Andre! I'll kill him!

That's the ticket. He stole your girl. He deserves to die.

Lachlaniel hardly heard the tiny voice in his head. He needed no prodding. He saddled his horse by rote as murderous thoughts, both his and the Chuchoteur's, filled his head. He grabbed the reins to lead Aman from the stall, but the horse resisted. This time no soothing words flowed from his lips. He jerked the reins and Aman followed. When they exited the barn, he jumped on without the aid of the stirrups and sunk his spurs hard into Aman's side. The horse was at full stride before they reached the road.

Aman was lathered and breathing hard as they approached the edge of the woods and Lachlaniel finally slowed him to a walk. He was about to dismount when someone jumping from above knocked him off his horse and two others joined in from ground level. He was subdued before he knew there was a fight. Others seemed to be trying to get Aman. He could hear the horse rearing, neighing and kicking. Presently the sound of hooves galloping up the road told him the Basaners were unsuccessful.

Good boy. At least they didn't get you. You've got more sense than I do. They're likely to succeed this time. What kind of death do they have waiting this time?

I wish I could get my hands on Andre! I'd kill him! The Chuchoteur whispered.

I wish I could get my hands on Andre! I'd kill him! Lachlaniel's thoughts echoed. *I wish I could kill them all!*

His hands and feet bound, the Basaners slid a pole between his legs and then his arms. They carried him to the rocks hanging by his ankles and wrists with two men on each end of the pole. There was no way to try to free himself, and anytime his hands managed to grasp the pole, he received a bone cracking rap on the back of his hands with a stick and another across the ribs. He managed to try three times before his hands were not only numb but broken and useless. He hung motionless trying to breathe through the pain of cracked ribs.

A voice rose above the pain. It was Andre's.

"Take him to the pit."

Lachlaniel felt himself sway back and forth in time to the footfalls of his bearers. Every step they took brought pain, and every breath was agony. He was semiconscious when he was unceremoniously dropped to the ground. The intensity of that pain brought him around. His bonds were cut and the pole removed. His arms and legs were limp and useless. Only his hearing still functioned, but it was no help. Instead, it betrayed him, bringing into his mind the sound of Andre's voice.

"Move him to the edge of the pit. Pull his stone and set it by the edge too."

The men moved quickly at his command. Lachlaniel felt someone's presence bending over him and then a voice whispered in his ear.

"It's three hundred feet to the bottom. You won't survive the fall. If whatever has protected you before does manage to keep you alive on the way down, your body will be too broken to do anything before you die of starvation or thirst. Beyond that there's a three hundred foot climb to get out. Three hundred feet of moss slickened rock *if* you can find a hand hold. This is the last I'll see of you. By the way, on the way down you might want to congratulate Aurora on her upcoming wedding to me."

Fiery anger coursed through his broken, useless limbs as he fell bouncing from one wall to the other. The last sound he heard was a cackling laugh in his mind before he lost consciousness. The Chuchoteur had fled.

Chapter 22
Mephosphilis

They trekked on with Kesniel in the lead. They had only gone a little over an hour when they came to a bridge. Kesniel's pace had carried him and his horse across the bridge before the horse could come to a halt. The horse reared and Kesniel landed heavily on his back. The other horses had managed to stop before the bridge and refused to move forward. Max, Ewald, and Theron dismounted and raced across the bridge. As they bent down, Kesniel came around.

"What happened?" the dazed man asked.

"The horses are afraid. They won't cross the bridge. Yours ran back across before we could even dismount."

"I don't blame them."

The men stared at him as if the fall had wrested him from reality.

Kesniel sat up. "Don't you feel it?"

The men stood up. They looked at each other.

"N…" Max stopped with the word half finished. The hair on his neck and arms stood on end. He looked at the other two. The blood had drained from their faces. They drew swords as one man. Max lifted Kesniel to his feet. They looked back to the bridge but could see nothing. A black mist seemed to rise from the ground obscuring their sight. As they watched, it encircled them. Without a word, they moved to stand back-to-back.

A voice came from the mist, its sound coming from every direction. "So you think to invade my realm? Are you that anxious to die?"

Something black came out of the mist and flew between their heads. They ducked as it brushed past. The men's hands trembled. It swooped in again and Theron dropped his sword and fell to his knees. The others were paralyzed. A black figure rose from the ground growing to immense proportions. The men, except for Theron who lay trembling on the ground, stood transfixed. The form was that of a man with the head of a dragon. Its hair was snakes of flame. Its tail swished back and forth with anticipation. It waited as though drawing strength from their fear.

"I am death. Who are you to venture into my kingdom?"

A light burst forth from the men's stones. The demon shielded its eyes. Its tail stopped.

"Someone is petitioning the King!" Kesniel cried raising his sword.

"King!" the creature spat out. "I'll show you who's king!"

The light of flame came to his eyes. Max pulled his shield and moved between the creature and the other men as a flood of fire belched from its mouth. Max was engulfed in flame. The others could hear him cry out in agony.

None of them had ever heard Max give any indication of pain before and it shook their resolve, but only for a moment. They leaped past their friend who was on one knee still clutching shield and sword. The beast was beset by sword strokes from all directions. With each stroke their swords grew brighter. The demon fell to its knees then rose exuding power that blew all four men back. It rose into the air.

"I am Mephistopheles." It began to dissolve into a black mist above their heads. "Death awaits you. Death awaits all of your kind who cross my bridge."

The words echoed in the air as Kesniel rose to his feet. "We have crossed the King's Bridge and have no fear of death or you."

The mist had dissolved and the light of the stones was returning to normal. The men looked back to the bridge and saw Aurora crossing at the head of the troops. She glowed like the light of dawn in Agapay, as though a thousand stones resided within her. The men behind her were glowing as well, though not as brilliantly.

"She's been in the presence of the King," Kesniel said with an air of thankfulness. "You were the one who called for aid and wrought the victory!"

"No. I and the men called on the King. He gave the victory."

Max walked forward wincing from the pain. "We're very glad you did."

Aurora jumped off her horse. "Oh Max! Let me have a look!"

"Cookie!" Kesniel yelled.

The cook sprinted forward.

"Have you got anything for burns?"

"Uset's touch for the pain,."

Kesniel looked at Aurora. She was already anointing the burns with oil from her stone.

"Get it." He looked at the men. "Nobody travels alone or even in small groups from here on. We travel as a group. Be ready at any instant to fight or to petition the King. This enemy isn't just dangerous; he's deadly."

The men looked at Max as he sat head down, his strength spent. They murmured and nodded ascent. If the enemy could best Max, a dozen of the best men in the guards or in the army would be no match for him.

It was midday before they began to move again. With great difficulty they got the horses to cross the bridge. They remained wary and moved at a walk. Max could hardly stay on his horse. Pain wracked him with every step the horse made in spite of the Uset's touch. Evening was still an hour away when Kesniel called a halt.

Ewald looked at Kesniel. "Why are we stopping here?"

Kesniel pointed. "Look at Max. He couldn't go another mile. It's only my concern for being caught with no defendable position as a camp that's allowed this to go on this long. He has to have rest and care."

"What about defense?"

"This will have to do. There's meadow beyond the trees. The first open spot I've seen in miles."

Ewald looked right and left. To the left the trees were no more than three deep with grass beyond.

Kesniel looked at the concern on Ewald's face. "I know. I don't like it either, but it's better than being caught strung out along the road."

"I guess so." Ewald shook his head. "I just hope they don't catch us at all."

"We'll double the guard tonight. It's early and we'll have more time to rest to make up for the extra duty."

"I hope tomorrow will be a better day than today."

Kesniel frowned. "So do I."

Lachlaniel stirred. He could hear the steady drip of water, but it was too indistinct to discern the direction.

What a mess I've made!

He tried to move, but broken limbs failed to respond. He turned his head and screamed in pain.

"Yiiiiiii!"

The sound reverberated off the walls growing fainter, then louder, then fainter again until the echoes ceased. It was only moments before he could think of anything but the pain, but it seemed an eternity.

I'm going to die here!

"No, you won't die."

It was that soft voice like the wind in the trees. The smell of fruit blossoms filled the air.

"Leofwine?" Lachlaniel felt suddenly ashamed. "I failed you."

"You've gone your own way for a long time."

"Why are you so patient? I don't deserve it."

"My child, you have much to learn. Much to learn. You know so little about the King, or Eleutherias, or Me. We will never give up on you."

"How can you stand to be around me? I thought I'd learned so much. Eleutherias tutored me, made me a knight and then a general, I defeated foes. I…"

Lachlaniel could see himself as he left the farm, as he crossed the Bridge, as he fought at Fairvale and Agapay. In each scene, he could see the vague, elusive figure of Leofwine at his side. He was never clearly seen even in these visions, but He was always there.

Tears came to his eyes. "It was never me, was it?"

"You have so much to learn. Of course it was you, but we aided you. Just like right now, you can do nothing, but with Our help you can do anything. Now sit up."

"Sit up?! I can't even turn my head without pain. My arms and legs are useless."

"Yes, I know. Now sit up."

"If you say so, I'll try.'

Lachlaniel bent his neck forward and found no pain. He pushed up onto his elbows and then his hands. He slid back until he rested against the wall.

"How?"

"Do you remember the first time they captured you?"

"Yes, they beat me almost to death."

"Almost? What about the next time? Then the lake, and the snake pit? The fire? Do you really think you could survive a three hundred foot fall and live? You're alive because We didn't let you die."

Lachlaniel began to weep uncontrollably. His sides heaved with the sobs. When he could weep no more, he whimpered like an inconsolable child only to begin crying again.

Oil from his stone for his burns and Uset's touch for the pain had given Max a good night's sleep. Kesniel made him stay in his bedroll while the men broke camp. They set out late in the morning and moved at a snail's pace. Max was alright for a while, but by the time they stopped in the early afternoon, each step of the horse once again brought pain. Lunch and an hour's rest did little to help his weariness, but the Uset's touch brought some relief for the pain.

It was late when they found a road to the left that led out of the trees. Night had long since fallen, and they were looking eagerly for a place to stop for the night. As they broke into the open, they could see a shack in the midst of a field. They dismounted and busied themselves making camp. Kesniel and Ewald entered the shack.

"Not a bad place. Max should have it for a place to rest. Have Aurora stay in here to tend her brother."

Ewald left to get Max and Aurora. He stopped Max from trying to help unload the horses for which Max was grateful. The big man sat by his saddle frowning as he watched the others work. Ewald found Aurora and took her back to Max. When he told Max of the sleeping arrangements, both Max and Aurora laughed.

"Do you think I could squeeze through that tiny door? I'd have to get on my knees just to get under the roof of the porch!"

He laughed again. Aurora, who hadn't stopped laughing, kissed Ewald on the forehead. The kiss, which was filled with her laughter, took him by surprise. He grinned in spite of himself. He looked back at the shack and realized that both he and Kesniel had ducked to keep from hitting their heads on the awning.

"My mistake, my giant-sized friend. I guess Kesniel will have a headquarters. We must be more tired than we thought."

Max frowned. "Oh no! Aurora gets the cabin."

Ewald tried to be forceful. "Kesniel said she's to take care of you."

Max folded his arms. "I'll be fine, but my sister is in need of as good a night's sleep as she can get."

Ewald smiled at his adamant friend. "I'll tell Kesniel."

He went back inside where Kesniel and one of the men were trying to make the room as comfortable as possible.

Ewald tried to look like an important guest addressing an innkeeper. "Accommodations for one please."

He paused to see the expression on Kesniel's face. He wasn't disappointed. "We forgot our friend's large size," he said with a grin.

Kesniel stared at the doorway and smiled. "Max outgrew this place when he was a boy."

"He says to put Aurora in here. She's worn out with worry for both Lachlaniel and Max, and from the long ride."

Kesniel looked at the guard who was helping him. "You finish up. I want this place fit for a queen." He looked around at the ramshackle surroundings. "Well, as fit for a queen as it can be."

Ewald and Kesniel stepped out into the cool night air. There must have been a stream nearby for fog hung in the low spots above the tops of the short grass. The horses were picketed, the guards set, and several fires had been lit. Some men drank coffee as they waited for the cook and his helpers to finish making the meal. The night was peaceful, and quiet reigned supreme other than the occasional clatter of pots or dishes, but toward the road, the trees had eyes.

Lachlaniel woke up aching. He tried to move. His arms and legs responded but the pain was too great. He lay back down.

How could I have been so foolish?

Leofwine's soft voice came in answer to his thoughts. "You're young. We gave you a taste of leadership, but leadership isn't an easy thing. A proud person makes a poor leader. To be a good leader, you have to be humble."

"That's something I'm not."

"Good. That's the first step in becoming humble. Realize you're proud."

Lachlaniel felt something touch his eyes.

What was that?

He blinked. Then he blinked again.

"My perception's returned!"

"Partially. You've begun to perceive because you've begun to see yourself. The more you look at yourself the more you will see yourself as you are and the clearer your perception will become."

"I'm ready," Lachlaniel said with confidence.

"Are you?" It was a rhetorical question.

Lachlaniel's brows knitted and deepened into furrows.

What does He mean by that?

There was silence for several minutes and then the light dawned on Lachlaniel.

"That was pride too, wasn't it? I should have asked 'Am I ready?'"

Now you begin to understand. Taking a long look at yourself isn't easy and it isn't pleasant. Before you can be stripped of your pride, you have to recognize it in your life."

Why is pride so wrong?

"Pride puts you in opposition to the King. Whatever you do becomes about you, about what you have and what you can accomplish instead of a grateful attitude of service to the King."

Lachlaniel rose to his feet ignoring the pain. Tears welled up in his eyes. He looked down and tears dropped on his boots.

How could I have forgotten so soon about the Bridge and the world without light, about the beauty I beheld if only briefly, about the wonders on the far side of the Bridge. How long has it been since I've been in my closet, in the throne room?

"We've missed you. We never left your side, but We longed for the fellowship that's been broken."

Lachlaniel fell to his knees. "I'm sorry. I'm so sorry. Forgive me."

He felt a hand on his right shoulder, then another on his left, and a third on his head. The voices of the King, Eleutherias, and Leofwine echoed in the darkness, and for a moment light rent the darkness and Lachlaniel could see that meadow he had seen so long ago, and joy filled his heart.

Aurora awoke before dawn to shouts in the camp outside. A flaming arrow came flying through the window. The flames licked the aged wood of the wall greedily like a hungry dog with a fresh bone. Aurora jumped up snatching her blanket from the bedroll. She slapped the flames knocking the arrow to the floor. She covered it with the blanket and crushed the life out of devouring incendiary.

Outside, bands of men had attacked the guards. The camp had become a beehive of activity. Men had grabbed weapons and started to pursue the intruders. Basaners and guards lay groaning on the ground. Others lay still, never to move again.

Kesniel was about to have the bugler sound recall, when he heard the horses on the picket line screaming and then the sound of hooves scattering in every direction.

"Rally on the commander!"

He raced toward the empty picket line, sword and shield in hand. Aurora came onto the porch in time to see the dragon-headed foe from the bridge knock Kesniel to the ground. She screamed and entered her closet. Max and five other men arrived at the fallen leader. They sprang over the body yelling like wild men and fell on their foe with the ferocity of a mother lion robbed of her cubs. The foe laughed and swatted at them like flies. Aurora shot from her closet on brilliant white charger. Her hair had lost its black dye. It flew in the wind behind her glowing like brass in the refiner's furnace. Her sword and shield could not be seen for the brilliance of the light they emitted. Her presence on the field of battle caused Mephistopheles to cringe. As her horse raced forward, he shrank back from the luminosity which she radiated. Before the men could rise, she arrived where their enemy had been, but he had fled.

Ewald ran up and Max turned back. They yelled over each other, "The horses!" "Kesniel!"

Max stooped down and scooped up his friend while Ewald and the men ran off trying to round up the scattered steeds. Aurora bent forward from her horse and touched Kesniel. She looked up at Max's tear filled eyes.

"He's not dead. Max!" She touched his arm. "He's not dead. Bring him over to the fire."

Max dutifully marched over to a fire and laid the fallen King-steward on an empty bedroll. Aurora put some of the remaining Uset's touch in water that was to have been coffee. She brought the pot of boiling brew to the prostrate man and wafted the rising steam toward his nose. There was no response.

"Are you sur…" Max started.

Kesniel's eyes twitched stopping him in midsentence. Kesniel raised his hand to his forehead.

"Oh my head!"

Aurora put a hand on his shoulder. "Lie still."

Kesniel opened his eyes. The glow on Aurora was fading.

"You've seen the King again. That's twice your petitions have saved me." He took her hand. "May the King be praised." His eyes closed and his hand slipped from hers as the vapors of the Uset's touch swept him into a healing sleep.

"We need to rethink what we're doing," Max said to no one in particular."

Aurora touched Kesniel's forehead. "It will be some time before he can go anywhere."

"How long?"

"Perhaps tomorrow. I'm not sure."

Max put his hand to his face and rubbed his forefinger across his lips. He dropped his hand and his brow furrowed.

"Then we'll concentrate on rounding up the horses. Once that's done, as many of us as can will petition the King together and see what He says."

He stood up and looked around.

"Boy!" He called to the bugler.

A man in his thirties came running up, bugle in hand.

"Yes sir.'"

"Sound recall."

The sound of the horn filled the meadow and the surrounding woods. It took many minutes for the men to begin showing up and more than half an hour for the stragglers to come in.

"Is this everyone?" Max asked.

"All but those who are on horseback chasing the horses. They're too far afield to hear the call."

"How many horses do we have?"

"I don't know. Less than ten, I should guess. At any rate, only those we could catch on foot."

"Then perhaps we should leave that to them until we get some more mounts. Put men on the mounts we have and send them out to help the others." Max looked around. "In the meantime, we need to dig graves and tend to any wounded."

Chapter 23

The Seventh Fall

Lachlaniel looked up. It was midday. A strange bright light poured down from the top of the pit. It was only his perception, but there was something up there.

"It's good to be able to 'see' things again."

"There are hard tasks in front of you. You have much to learn yet before you can again set foot on solid ground."

"Like what?" It was the question of a little child asking 'why the sky is blue' or 'how do birds fly'.

Leofwine smiled. "You have to learn to see things that are real in the King's presence but not yet real here in the Darkened Land."

"I don't understand."

"These are things that will be. They haven't come to be, but in the King's eyes they are just as real as the ground beneath your feet."

"How can that be?"

"Do you remember crossing the Bridge."

"Yes."

"What did it look like from this side?"

Lachlaniel thought back. He laughed. "Like no one should dare set foot on it."

"And from the other side?"

"There was no way for it to fall."

"You believed the King, so in spite of what you saw you crossed."

"Yes."

"Now you must learn to trust Him when there's nothing in front of you at all. You must learn to see things as though they're real because He says they are, even though everyone and everything tells you they aren't."

"But You said I would see them. How can I see what isn't there."

"You've been given a great gift Lachlaniel."

"What gift?"

"Your blindness. You now see things that others can't. You perceive truth. Truth isn't always seen. Look up."

Lachlaniel tilted his head back.

"What do you see?"

"A ball of light in the sky."

"That's called the sun. No man has truly seen that in thousands of years. The darkness that covers the land has obscured its light, yet you can now perceive its light. As you humble yourself, you will grow in understanding and your perception of the true nature of things will deepen."

Lachlaniel let out a deep sigh. "Am I not yet humble?"

"No, not yet. You have begun to discard the pride, but many of the words of the Chuchoteur still reside in you. Do you remember the grandmother, and the child that fell in the well?"

"Yes."

"Do you still consider him a mindless infant and her a peasant? Do you still think of helping such people as a waste of your time?"

Lachlaniel shook his head and sat down.

"Saving a life, any life isn't a waste of time, particularly *your* time."

My time?

"What do you mean?"

"Is it really your time, Lachlaniel? Isn't it the King's time? You're His servant. Isn't *your* time really *His* time?"

Lachlaniel looked up, his lip trembling. "How could I have been so foolish?" His eyes caught a glint of a metal ladder near the top of the pit. He stood up to see if it extended all the way down. The clank of chains turned his attention downward. He looked at his hands and feet. He felt no shackles, but his perception told him they were there. A wistful look came to his eyes.

"Yes the ladder is there and so are the chains."

"How did I…"

"The chains are of your own making. You fashioned them and put them on by yourself. Your pride has you shackled. The way up is to go down. When you understand this, you will be ready to climb, but not yet ready for the task ahead."

It was late in the day when the horses were finally rounded up though a couple still hadn't been found. The wounded, both Basaners and guards, were being treated. Two of the Basaners had been taken to the Bridge and entered the King's service. Others were likely to follow when they healed. Kesniel had recovered and was holding a council of war with his top men.

"We can't risk campfires tonight, and the stones must give only the most minimal light." Kesniel raised himself to a sitting position. He was about to continue when the cook interrupted.

"But the fires are needed for the wounded."

Kesniel was in no mood for debate. "In what way? Warmth or to help with their treatment?"

"They could use the warmth, but if we can find more Uset's touch, it will need to be steeped in boiling water."

"We'll see they have enough blankets to keep them warm. We'll make a fire behind the shack and make a screen to block its light." Max suggested.

"That's what I need, prudent suggestions. We must be prepared before nightfall. The horses must be in a protected position. We must leave as soon as possible. No one must be on guard alone. They must be in small groups and have a bugler with them."

Ewald stood with his hands behind his back like a schoolboy (This kind of meeting always made him nervous). "I suggest we have a reserve group for attack if the alarm signal is blown."

"Another good suggestion. The wounded will need to be taken out of this area. We can't spare many men. We'll need transport. Send Asher back to the nearest settlement to get help."

Concern grew on Max's face. "Don't you think he would be a bit conspicuous? Why not send Theron?"

"Yes. Theron. My head is pounding and my thoughts are growing fuzzy and confused. Those men must be out of here before nightfall."

The cook's apprehensiveness grew to alarm. "Sir you must rest. We'll get the wounded away from here as fast as we can, but you *must* rest."

"Yes." Kesniel rubbed his face with his hands and lay back on his bedroll. "Yes. You're right. Max, I leave the rest of the details to you. Be wise and wary, my friend."

He closed his eyes. The men left quickly and quietly. Theron took a horse and left to try to find the needed transport. The rest followed Max who was looking for another secluded place to finish the meeting. He eventually found one behind the shack.

He looked at the cook. "Kesniel is right, but we can't get them out of here by nightfall. They must be ready by daybreak. Besides the reserve, we'll need men ready to petition the King. We have no defense against this servant of Kieran. We must all try to get some rest as well. We've got to move a long way tomorrow. We must be in a totally different area before nightfall. I think that covers it unless you have anything else."

The cook spoke up. "Some of the men helping me were wounded. The hunters got us some meat before the attack, but I could use some help cooking, or we're going to be eating only dried beef."

Max looked down on him and pursed his lips. "Aurora will be helping, but we'll get a couple of men as well. Will Kesniel be well enough to go with us tomorrow?"

"Yes. Nothing wrong with him now that a good night's sleep won't cure."

Max shook his head. 'Then we're set. Let's get about our tasks."

The task ahead.

Lachlaniel had been thinking and wondering about the 'task ahead' all afternoon.

"It's no good thinking about it. It could be any one of a million things or it could be none of them," he said to himself. "Besides, there are other things to take care of before I even get that far."

The woman and the child. How could I have been so contemptuous of them?

Then a new thought struck him.

The town with the pigs! If I treated the woman and the child with contempt, then the people of Shamgar were dirt beneath my feet! I never even thought of bringing them to the Bridge!

Tears flooded his eyes.

I don't deserve to be the King's servant! I am so foolish, so lacking in everything that makes a servant a servant much less a good one.

"I'm not worthy to be in your service."

"Now you begin to understand. No one is 'worthy'. It is by the King's grace that you serve Him. It is by His grace you stand in His presence. You can't serve Him on your own. You can't even stand on your own. If you wish to stand in the face of your enemies—His enemies—then you must rely on Him to accomplish it through you."

"I see the ladder now." Lachlaniel put out his hand to touch it. "It isn't there. Why do I see it if it isn't there?"

"It is there, but not yet in this realm. Your perception allows you to see it as the King sees it. When you understand this concept, you will be ready to climb the ladder and complete your task.

Night fell, a dark night, a night where every stone was cloaked and the guards, though posted, did not move. There was no sound but the wind in the trees and the grass. Every ear was strained for the sound of movement, but even the horses made no move or sound.

The first watch passed, then the second and third. The men watched and waited. No one but the wounded slept. Many petitions were laid before the King. Then in the fourth watch, as dawn neared, there was a sound coming across the fields. The horses began to stir. Soon the sound of horses pulling carts across the meadow could be heard. It was Theron followed by several carts. They stopped. Theron dismounted and led them forward in the pitch blackness. Max let a tiny amount of light from his stone shine showing them the path.

Theron moved cautiously and quietly forward. The carts too moved forward but even though the men did their best the sound of the creaking wheels grated on everyone's ears. The guard's muscles tensed for action. The wind continued to stir the leaves of the trees, but that and the noise of the carts were the only sounds. The men who weren't on duty helped to move the wounded onto the carts. As the last of them were loaded, Kesniel sent word from the shack to uncover the stones. The long night was over and a long day lay before them.

Men grabbed a cup of coffee and a quick bite to eat while others saddled the horses, but the guards remained at their posts. The carts set out on their journey home accompanied by the first of the men to take to saddle. The men who had eaten replaced the guards. When the guards had eaten and the last of the equipment was stowed, everyone mounted their horses and headed for the road. They arrived in time to see a dozen men scattering into the woods.

"Let them go!" Kesniel shouted as men started to go after them. "We have no time for that."

The men returned to the formation.

"Let's move out."

The men rode forward cautiously, but nothing out of the ordinary happened. After an hour, the men began to relax.

Max moved up to ride by Kesniel. "Why do you suppose we're not being opposed?"

Kesniel scanned the surrounding forest. "I'm not sure. It could be the King. He certainly has a hand in it. The enemy could be busy elsewhere, in which case we should make haste. Or…"

"Or?"

"Or they could be preparing a surprise for us."

"What should we do?"

"I think our best option is to pick up the pace." Kesniel turned and called out behind him, "At the gallop!"

The men urged their mounts to greater speed. After a mile, they dismounted and walked the horses for a quarter of a mile. They mounted again and galloped another mile before again dismounting for a quarter.

"Hopefully, any plans they had for ambush are behind us and we're clear to proceed at a more suitable pace for man and beast."

Max looked at Kesniel with a dour smile. "Let's hope so."

Kesniel mounted his horse. "Yes, let's."

The riding continued without break other than to walk the horses. The company once again ate in the saddle. By the end of the day, they had covered many miles, more than their mounts could bear. They stopped early, and moved into a meadow on the south side of the road. A line of trees a mile away held the promise of a road going south, but they weren't headed in that direction.

Lachlaniel had thought all day about the ladder being there and yet not being there.

He asked Leofwine, "Is it a matter of timing?"

"Yes. The King's timing is always perfect."

"How do I know when it's time?"

"When events come together that make it necessary, then it's time."

"I think I see."

"You'll understand in the morning. For now get some sleep. Tomorrow will be a long day."

The morning broke fair and very cool. The wind had shifted to the north. The horses had been hobbled instead of picketed. With the increased light of the stones that came with dawn, they could be seen spread over the meadow grazing.

The men were slow to rise. The rigors of yesterday were wearing off…slowly. Kesniel allowed them extra rest. The city still lay some distance to the west, and he didn't know how soon they would be called to battle or even if they would be.

The cook banging a spoon on a plate roused everyone and announced breakfast was ready. As the last man filled his plate with food, two men rode into camp. They were challenged even though they were obviously Ebenchaim. They were taken to Kesniel who was having a breakfast conference with Max, Ewald, and Theron.

"These men asked to see you sir," the guard said.

"And who are you?" Kesniel scrutinized the strangers.

"I'm Jason and this is Wilmot. We've been sent to meet you."

"I see."

Leofwine whispered to Kesniel,

Wilmot spoke up. "We need you at the Great City. We should have no problem getting there, but forces are on the move against the city."

"The forces are small, but they aren't coming as an army. They come to infiltrate and destroy from within," Jason added.

Kesniel looked at the ground squinting. "We need to get there quickly, but the horses and men are almost exhausted."

"The horses shouldn't be a problem. Fresh mounts are being sent from the city."

"How far is it?"

"About a day and a half to two days ride. Maybe longer if your men need rest that badly. But there are inns along the way, so they should get some good food and adequate rest."

"We'll have to try and make it in two. I'd like to rest within the city on the second night. What about provisions."

"There are some coming that should meet us about noon After that, there are plenty of places to eat along the way. We'll save time if we don't have to cook or clean up."

"Hmm." Kesniel gave an affirmative nod. Then we should get moving as soon as we can." Kesniel started to issue orders but Jason cut him off.

"I have a different purpose. I've been sent to get Aurora and two others."

Kesniel became wary and eyed him with suspicion. Max stood up. Leofwine whispered again, this time to both Kesniel and Max.

"Aurora is my sister. She isn't going anywhere alone." Max folded his arms and stared at Jason.

"Then you must be Max. The King said I should bring you and Nestor along with her. Lachlaniel will be there when we arrive."

Max unfolded his arms. "You know Lachlaniel?"

"He's been in my care a few times."

Kesniel and Ewald slipped away to get the men moving, and Theron went to find Nestor as Max continued his conversation with Jason.

"Where is he now?"

"That I don't know. I only know that Aurora will be needed there and that you two are to accompany her."

Max's brow furrowed. He cocked his head to one side. "You said he'd been in your 'care'. What did you mean?"

"He's been fighting the Basaners. He's been wounded several times. He almost died."

Max straightened up and his eyes grew wide. "I wouldn't mention that to Aurora."

"I hadn't intended to. That's best left to Lachlaniel."

"Let's get packed and get moving. Aurora will want to see him as soon as she can. We'll have to slow her down for her own good."

Lachlaniel woke to someone yelling from the top of the pit.

"Yo!" Lachlaniel yelled and stood up. "Who's there?"

Indistinct sounds echoed off the walls.

"What?"

More sounds. He reached out without thinking and took hold of the ladder. It was there, as solid as the rock wall behind it. Lachlaniel grinned.

"You see. When it's needed, it's there. Trust the King. You have nothing to fear and nothing to worry about." Leofwine's soft voice whispered.

"I'm coming up!"

He began the long climb out of the pit where his pride had imprisoned him. When he neared the top, he saw a familiar bald headed face that he didn't quite recognize.

The man extended his left hand to help Lachlaniel up. Lachlaniel reached for the hand and stopped short. The man had no right arm.

"You're the man from the forest. The woman and the boy." There was no animosity in Lachlaniel's voice, only sorrow.

The man dropped his hand and his smile faded. "Yes. I was part of that. I'm Ignatius."

"My name is Lachlaniel. I'm the one who cut off your arm. I'm sorry."

"Don't be. After that, the Basaners had no use for me. That's why I crossed the Bridge."

"You're an Ebenchaim."

The man extended his hand again. "Yes. He pulled and Lachlaniel stepped up onto solid ground.

"How did you know I was here?"

"I watched them throw you into the pit. I thought you were dead, but Leofwine told me you weren't. He said I was to help you."

"Thank you. I don't know the next step. The rocks are close at hand, so we'd better move back to the trees."

They hurried, often looking over their shoulders as they went.

"Your fiancée will be here soon."

Lachlaniel stopped and grabbed Ignatius by the shoulders. "Aurora? Here? How do you know?"

"Leofwine. But He said you mustn't stop what you're doing, whatever it is, because of her. She'll be waiting when you're finished."

Lachlaniel looked back toward the rocks. He could perceive something sticking up from the ground there.

A cross? No. It's a sword stuck in the ground. What is that just beyond it?

He squinted to get a better look. And then his eyes grew wide.

A body. My body! Something yet to be! I must face them again!

"I know what I must do."

He turned at the sound of horses in the trees behind them.

"Tell Aurora I love her." He shook Ignatius' hand and strode onto the plain.

Aurora, Max, Nestor, and Jason dismounted. Aurora ran forward. Ignatius caught her and held her.

"What is he doing!"

Ignatius turned her face toward his while Max gripped her shoulders.

"He's doing what Leofwine and the King told him to do," Ignatius said. "You mustn't interfere. He's done this six times."

Max was incredulous. "Six times?"

"Yes, but I think this time will end differently."

Perhaps this is the price I must pay for my foolishness.
Tears formed in his eyes.

I wish Aurora didn't have to pay for my foolishness as well.

His eyes narrowed as he drew his sword. When he reached the point he had seen in the vision, he stuck his sword in the ground, took off his cape and armor, and placed them together on the ground. He stepped forward bare of any protection.

"Damon! Andre! Here I am. You've tried six times to kill me and I'm still alive. Will you face me again?" He waited. There was no answer, only the north wind which had grown cold. "I've laid aside my armor. How easy do you want me to make it for you? Are you afraid?"

A voice answered from the rocks. "Afraid? Of you?"

There was boisterous laughter as Damon stepped forward. Lachlaniel perceived him as he drew nearer. He held a club in his hand.

I didn't know he was so big.

Damon stopped a few feet away and looked down on Lachlaniel. He was about seven feet tall. He waited as though expecting something.

"Well? Defend yourself!"

Lachlaniel stood as though rooted to the ground. "No."

"You make this too easy."

Lachlaniel made neither move nor sound. In the trees, Aurora squealed and tried to free herself from Max's firm grip.

"If you won't defend yourself then diiiie!"

Damon swung the club with all his strength hitting Lachlaniel on his left arm. Lachlaniel hit the ground hard and rolled several times. Aurora turned and buried her head in Max's chest. The others bowed their heads. Lachlaniel got up and looked at Damon, blood dripping from a cut above his eye, his broken left arm hanging limp at his side.

"Don't you understand? You can't kill me until the King says you can. You brought me to the point of death six times. Go ahead make it seven, but until I fulfill His purpose for me, you can't kill me. I may fall, but I'll get up again. This puny mob," he said with a sweeping motion of his good hand toward the score of men that had come from the rocks. "They can't do the job. A hundred like them can't. The victory lies in the hands of the King, and *you don't know Him*." He paused as a brilliant point of light appeared a hundred yards to his right and grew into a portal to the Bridge. At this, the group in the woods looked up in wonder.

"The King is here," Max whispered.

Aurora stopped crying and smiled.

"There's the way to life," Lachlaniel continued. "Stay here and death awaits you. Kieran is coming to kill you because you can't defeat me. Your hope lies there," He said pointing to the Bridge.

Damon looked at the Bridge and then back to Lachlaniel. He raised his club and struck him to the ground.

Max picked up Aurora and held her like a small child. She hid her face in Max's neck.

"Kill him!" Damon cried.

The men stood frozen in place looking at the fallen man.

"Do what I say!"

The men slowly began moving, one by one. They beat the fallen, limp form until there was no more strength to raise a weapon. They stopped, their chests heaving. A few moments passed as they waited for their strength to return.

Damon pointed at Lachlaniel. "Now shoot him."

"But he's dead!" one man said foolishly.

Damon grabbed him by the throat. "I said fill him with arrows!"

He threw the man to the ground. Those with bows began stringing shafts and pointing them at the lifeless form. They hesitated, but only for an instant. Then a hail of arrows pierced the corpse before them. When they had finished, twenty arrows pinned the body to the ground. The light from the sword lay across the body.

"He won't get up from that," Damon growled.

But just then one of the men gasped. The *broken arm* was moving. It grasped an arrow from the midsection and pulled it out. It dropped to the ground as the hand reached for another. The Basaners stood slack jawed and wide-eyed as the arm which had been broken removed each arrow. It plucked out the last arrow and the lifeless eyes opened.

Max whispered to Aurora, "Look."

She raised her head and saw Lachlaniel rise, the last arrow still in his hand. He moved toward Damon as half the men ran screaming into the darkness. The other half was split between those who had fallen on their faces in terror and those who headed for the portal and the Bridge. Damon stood trembling at the approach of a man he couldn't kill.

Lachlaniel grabbed his hand and placed the arrow in his palm and closed it into a fist around the shaft. "I came for you."

The dumbfounded man dropped to his knees.

"I think you know this is your last chance. Won't you take it?" He lifted the man to his feet. "Come on. Cross the Bridge. You won't regret it."

"I can't! I can't!" There was terror in his voice.

"You think Kieran can defeat the King? The King holds the power of life and death. How can *He* be defeated. Yield to Him and even Kieran can't touch you. The King will determine your fate. Life will be what it should be; what He wants it to be."

Damon looked up, screamed, and ran for the rocks. The light grew in intensity filling every nook and cranny and dispersing every shadow. As Damon ran beyond the rocks and descended out of sight, the ground began to shake, boulders moved, the edge of the cliff fell away. Lachlaniel stood his ground. In both directions, as far as the eye could see, the barrier of the cliff was gone. Two new paths joined the old one down, what was now, a rolling descent to the city of Felansville.

The city could now be seen in the distance; its dark gates destroyed, its towers crumbled. The castle fortress had a great rent from which a brilliant golden light shone forth. Lachlaniel could faintly perceive prisoners issuing from the bowels of its dungeons.

Lachlaniel looked around him. It was as though he were looking from a great height. All across the plain and in the woods, he could perceive many groups of Ebenchaim, hundreds, nay, thousands of them lifting their voices in praise to the King. There were many areas of light, not the light of the stones, but a different light, golden and bright. He knew what these areas of light were. He had seen them before. Like the place where the woman and boy died, these were places where the Basaners had killed Ebenchaim; places made glorious by their deaths. They were lights in the Darkened Land showing those trapped in the darkness that the King yet reigns.

Chapter 24
Cold Fear

Andre rode at the head of his group of men. They were still more than two days from the great city, but here in the twilight land the light revealed many things. His black cape flew behind him. A golden crown rested on his head. His white, frilly shirt bore a crest on the left breast, an image of a fiery dragon. His pants and boots were black and a sword of steel hung from his right hip. He rode a black stallion that pranced at the head of his troops.

Fear crawled up his spine.

Something's wrong.

Without warning, a black mist rose from the ground before him. His men fell on their faces crying as though in great pain. The mist took shape and Andre fell from his horse. His crown fell from his head and rolled to a stop before him.

Meph!

"Mephistopheles to you, imp! The city has fallen!" He picked up the crown. "You are no longer king of anything." He let the statement sink in. "You've managed to lose your kingdom. Fail me in this mission and you'll lose your life."

"I… I… I won't fail. We will destroy the tower and its stone."

"That's what you said about Agapay! Yet it *still* stands. You sniveling coward. You crawl over the wall like an insect and flee for your life to the safety of *your* city. The city was MINE! You brought about its destruction. You caused us the loss of those prisoners. Worst of all we lost men in my service, *king*!" He spit fire as he said king and it scorched the earth near Andre and singed the hair of his head.

Andre cried like a small child that had been whipped. "I will not fail!"

"See that you don't."

The dreaded figure faded into mist and was gone.

It was a long time before Andre could get to his feet. Even then, his legs were weak and he wobbled as he tried to find out if there was solid ground beneath him. The men were unconscious and had to be roused individually. This took some time. Thus they lost the last half of the day and were forced to camp where they were for the night.

Aurora ran from the trees. Lachlaniel turned to a rising light from his back to see the beaming light of dawn he had first beheld at the wedding reception of Velius and Farrah. Aurora fell into his arms, tears in her eyes. They held a long kiss, and clasped each other in an embrace that they wished would never end.

At last, Aurora pulled back. She looked at her man. There were lines in his face that had not been there at their parting. His temples held flecks of gray, and there were gray wisps in his hair. She touched his hands as they held her face, and she felt the scars.

My poor darling!

She wanted to speak to give vent to her sorrow for what he had gone through, but the words would not come and she fell against his neck and cried. He brushed her hair back and held her close.

He whispered in her ear, "It's alright now. We're together. You're safe, and we're together."

"Your hands and face! What horrors have you been through? I want to touch them and heal them. I want to heal you, heart and soul!"

"If the times have been rough, they've been of my own making."

She pushed him away. The blood of his recently healed wounds covered his shirt and her dress.

She sobbed, "Oh Lachlaniel my love!"

The light he perceived coming from her dimmed. He touched her chin and lifted her head.

"I was wrong. So wrong. But because of it, the King has taught me much. Don't cry my darling. I am more fit for His service than before, though I still have much to learn."

"This is so hard. I don't want to lose you!"

"Nor I you. But the King's plans are never wrong. He makes all things beautiful in His time. Wait and see." He kissed her forehead and embraced her, whispering in her ear, "There are wonderful things ahead even if the times are hard and dark. Hold fast. We'll be married yet."

She cried for some time before she took his hand and they walked back to the trees. Max and Jason were talking to Nestor. Jason smiled. What they had witnessed stirred his heart.

He looked at Nestor. "Max, Lachlaniel and Aurora must head to the city. But I think if you go with me, you might find news of your son."

"Go with you where?"

Jason pointed south to the city. "There, in Felansville. There in the chaos you may find hope and joy."

Nestor's hands trembled. "How…"

"You may never know. What you'll find, only the King can say, but if I were you I wouldn't hesitate."

"I… I'm not. It's just… I'm afraid of what I'll find. I've feared the worst for so long that I don't dare hope lest the disappointment crush me."

Jason smiled. "Trust the King. What you find may not be easy to take." He looked over at Aurora, and Nestor followed his gaze. "But even in sorrow there can be joy."

Nestor smiled weakly. "Let's go."

Max Looked at Lachlaniel and Aurora. "Well future brother-in-law, we must get moving. I'd like to reach the main road before nightfall."

"If we hurry I think we can find an inn to sleep in. It may be late, but I'd like to sleep in a bed instead of on the ground. My body will thank me if there's something soft beneath me."

Max laughed and went to get the horses. Aurora touched Lachlaniel's face and stroked his hair but could find no words for her emotions. He kissed her. There would be time for words later.

Kesniel had allowed a less hurried pace for the first half of the day. They ate a peaceful and satisfying lunch, but as they mounted their horses there was a great rumbling that stopped them in their tracks. People ran screaming from the inns and shops. Some items fell from the shelves of merchants and the sound of breaking glass could be heard in every direction. But as quickly as the rumbling came it also went. People tried to get back to what they had been doing or else began cleaning up. To Kesniel, though, the rumbling struck his heart with both joy and fear. A sense of urgency swept over him.

"Forward men!"

The streets grew wider and less crowded in spite of a growing number of businesses. By the time they slowed to a walk the streets were all but deserted. Through the rest of the afternoon they encountered less than fifty people, and those few were scurrying from place to place like they were chased by Kieran himself.

They found it difficult to locate an open eatery. Businesses of all kinds were shuttered and locked. Even inns and liveries were closed and would not answer the knocks on their doors. It was night when they found a place to eat. Afterwards, they continued on. They did not stop again, and if they had, no inn would have opened to them.

It was late in the third watch when they arrived at the gates. The gatekeepers were reluctant to allow admittance, but Wilmot was expected and he persuaded them to open the gates and let Kesniel and his men in.

"Is all this the result of the rumbling earlier?" Theron asked.

"I don't know. It isn't usual. Something's gotten everyone frightened. The city's gates are never closed," Wilmot replied.

Kesniel looked around. "Do you think we can find lodging? The men must rest and the horses are weary." He glanced over at Ewald who was nodding in the saddle. "Even stout Ewald is ready to fall from the saddle."

"If there's no place to take us, there is a dome of meeting near here. It won't be comfortable but at least it's shelter and there will be friends."

The men spread out trying the nearby establishments as well as looking for liveries that would take the horses. After an hour, they met back. Rooms had been found at several larger inns which were almost vacant. Liveries too had less business and were looking for customers to keep their daily revenue up. Wilmot walked with Kesniel and Ewald to their inn from the nearby livery.

"It's eerie. I've never seen the city like this. It's like all the nonresidents have fled and the residents are bracing for some huge storm." Wilmot shook his head in disbelief.

"There is a storm coming, but not one of nature." Kesniel sniffed the air at the doorway before entering the inn. "I can almost smell the trouble coming."

Ewald studied his friend. "I hope it can wait until after breakfast and a good sleep," he quipped.

"I hope so too, my friend. I hope so too." He looked back at Wilmot as he stepped across the threshold.

Lachlaniel, Max and Aurora had been astounded at the response of the businesses where they stopped. Most of the inns simply didn't answer their doors. The few that did were only frightened voices within telling them to go away, that there were no rooms available. It was mid morning when they stopped at one that had a small image of the Bridge burned into its sign. The innkeeper opened to them readily and bade them welcome. The innkeeper's wife, however, had more reluctance in her voice.

"She's frightened." The innkeeper said.

"It seems everyone on this stretch of the road is," Lachlaniel replied.

The innkeeper looked from side to side as though there might be someone listening. "Somethin's happenin'. Your welcome, but me and me missus are packin' up. Tomorrow we're headin' inta the city."

"One night is fine with us."

"Come in then. "Course I don't know where we'll put 'im up." He motioned to Max. "None o' the beds will fit him, sure enough."

"Perhaps I can sleep on the floor of the great room."

"Righto. No other guests to disturb you down here anyway."

Max's stomach grumbled.

Lachlaniel took the cue. "Could we get something to eat? I'm starved."

The innkeeper looked at Max. "We'll do our best."

His wife mumbled as she went to the kitchen, "Just as well. Keep us from wasting the food we have to leave behind."

They had a midday dinner fit for a king, venison and beef, chicken and veal. The vegetables seemed to have no end in quantity or variety. The fruits were delectable. And it was topped off by a wine that had surely been aged for many years. Lachlaniel and Aurora could not sample even a small portion before they had their fill, but Max tasted everything and even had seconds of what he considered the best. The innkeeper and his wife and children also ate from the feast but at another table to give their guests some privacy. Once everyone was done, the wife and children cleaned up while the innkeeper showed his guests to their rooms.

The night was long and cold. Max slept by the fire and was warmer than anyone in the inn. Lachlaniel slept fitfully as a draft wriggled its icy fingers through cracks around the window pane, which had not yet been caulked and readied for the winter, to slide under the blankets prickling his exposed skin. Late in the night he got up and put on his clothes. Then he crawled back in bed hoping to get some sleep. The others were much the same.

As dawn came, there was a cry in the streets. A boy of ten was crying. His parents, brothers, and sisters had been killed. He was the only one in the house that had escaped. The innkeeper, his family and guests had been roused by the commotion and were finishing throwing on their clothes when the inn was rocked by an explosion. Lachlaniel, who was already dressed, rushed outside. Clouds of black smoke billowed into the air that was only dimly lit by the stones. The livery three doors down and across the street had been turned into rubble. Fires were beginning to take hold. A mutilated body lay in the street. The boy who had been crying lay still next to the wall of a building nearby. Lachlaniel rushed to him. He was alive but unconscious. Residents and guests poured into the streets. Men scurried about trying to fight the fires while women cared for the few survivors that were pulled from the debris.

A cry rang out and then another. Several men and women went down never to move again as arrows flew without sound to their targets. The rescue efforts stopped as people ran for shelter—any shelter. Lachlaniel stood up, the armor of the King shining. He was approaching the inn as Max and Aurora came out to help. They expected more arrows but none came. By the time they had carried the wounded to safety, the fire at the livery was out of control. Slowly, men came into the open and fought the fire, but it was hopeless.

By midmorning, all that could be done had been, and a caravan of refuges began forming and headed for the city gates. Max, Lachlaniel and Aurora led the way. There were few other servants of the King throughout the crowd. They positioned themselves on the periphery to protect the people as much as they could. Occasionally, an arrow would fly from some secretive spot only to be fended off by the shield of one of the King's servants. As the crowd moved forward, it grew until the Ebenchaim could no longer protect everyone and the arrows began hitting their marks. People grew nervous and panicky. Finally, like milling cattle before an approaching storm, all that remained was for that small sound of stone striking stone, a horse whinnying, or even windblown leaves striking the herd to start the stampede. It came. A baby began crying, and people started pushing and shoving in an effort to get away from *them*. People fell and were trampled to death, others were crushed in the press, children were separated from parents, and those who tried to help often fell victims themselves of the blind terror that had infected the crowd. The Ebenchaim tried to split them into smaller groups and move them down side streets to get them calmed down but to no avail. Mephistopheles smiled.

The eerie quiet of the night before continued into the afternoon. Ewald was roused by the clank of metal on stone outside his window. He looked down in the street. There was a stiff cold breeze blowing. A metal cup lay on its side in the street. He watched until a sudden gust blew the cup a few feet further down the street clanking as it went. He pulled his head back in.

It just isn't natural. If I didn't know better, I'd think I was the last man alive in the city. Maybe I am! No. No. Get a hold of yourself man.

He dressed and moved into the hall. The sound of snoring came from Kesniel's room and his muscles released some of their tension.

Fear! It's like fear is part of the cold wind blowing through the streets. The enemy's work no doubt. Don't give in to it. Breathe.

Wilmot's voice sounded from behind a door to the right. "Who's there?" His voice was filled with apprehension.

"Ewald. There's naught out here but me."

The door opened a crack. Wilmot scanned the hallway as best he could and then opened the door a little wider. "There's something strange going on."

"There's fear in the wind. You've got to fight it. One of the Halvoord taught me, 'When you're afraid, trust in the King'."

"Wise words. I wish my heart could accept them as easily as my mind."

Wilmot turned his head and looked down the hall. It was empty. He opened the door and, sword in hand, cautiously stepped out to join Ewald.

"Let's get the others up." Ewald looked up and down the hall. "This is no time to be sleeping."

The men moved out of the inn and into the street in twos and threes, shields up and swords drawn. They were expectant and nervous. All were seasoned warriors, but many had their stomachs tied in knots. More than one wretched from the cold nameless fear that clung to their spines, yet they moved forward. Ewald and Kesniel had persuaded Bercan that it was safer for him to go with them than to remain alone in the inn. Still, there were times they both had to grab him to keep him from fleeing to some imagined place of safety.

"Draw your sword Bercan me lad." Ewald's tone was light as though the foe was merely a grass snake, but his own heart was filled with foreboding as was every heart there. "A drawn sword helps allay fear."

Bercan drew his sword. The tip made circles in the air as his hands trembled.

"Your shield, boy. Take up your shield."

Ewald's voice was friendly and reassuring.

"That's the way, me lad. Now, stay with me and Kesniel."

If Kesniel had heard Ewald's soothing tones to Bercan, he gave no indication of it. "Form a circle! Now sing men!"

The men closed ranks around Ewald, Kesniel, and Bercan. They broke into a song of praise to the King. A warmth seemed to well up from the ground. A warmth the bitter wind could not penetrate. Bercan's hands were the first to steady. Each man could feel fear being replaced by joy. They marched toward the nearest dome of meeting singing as they went. Before and behind them, windows opened. Ebenchaim in the buildings joined the song. Soon, throngs filled the streets. The Ebenchaim were drawn by the song of the King. The rest followed to get away from the fear.

By the time they reached the top of the steps at the dome of meeting, there were more than a thousand people following them. The guards spread out and Kesniel stepped forward. The men continued to sing softly in the background as Kesniel addressed the crowd.

"People of Chara. The time has come to choose. This city is besieged by the Basaners and the legions of darkness. The choice is not between destruction and the life you've always known. The choice is between the light and the darkness. It's between serving the King or Kieran. There is no longer any middle ground. Look behind you!"

The crowd turned. Blackness crept over the city wall and oozed into the streets. Several women fainted. Men dropped to their knees.

Shouts came from the crowd, "What must we do?!" "We'll all be killed!"

"No! There is time. This is only a vision. Your eyes have been opened to see what will soon be. The Bridge is near. Now is the time to decide, but you must not delay. Serve the King and this city will live. Shun Him and you will perish."

"What of our homes? Our possessions?"

"They belong to a world that is fading and will soon be lost. Use what you have in the King's service and it will be replaced by greater things in His Kingdom beyond the Bridge."

People began to move. Many sought the men behind Kesniel who directed them to the Bridge. Others fled to their homes or looked for some imagined security close at hand. The Ebenchaim that had followed stood unmoving.

Kesniel became angry. "Why are you standing there! Do you think you can cling to the things of this life? If you belong to the King, then prove it! The people of this city—the King's Great City—will lose their lives because of your idleness and double mindedness. You think you're wealthy? You've chosen rags instead of the King's clothes. You think you have wealth? You're bankrupt. You have nothing! Are you blind to what is happening around you?"

People wept, others began assisting those who wanted to cross the Bridge, and some threw down their stones in disgust and walked away.

Ewald frowned. Kesniel looked at him and back to those walking away.

"Ebenasa."

Ewald looked at him. "What?"

"Ebenasa. You've seen them before. Before you crossed the Bridge. Gunnar, the stone carrier. That's what Ebenasa means: stone carrier."

"Ebenasa." Ewald said as though it was a bite of rotten food he couldn't spit out quickly enough. "What now? We know what's coming, but how do you prepare a city this size for assassins and saboteurs?"

"First things first. This was but a small group. We must spread out across the city. Speak at every dome of meeting. The residents must be warned. The Ebenchaim must be awakened from their slumber and sloth. The rest must be directed to the Bridge."

"And then?"

"Petitioning the King is our best defense. Then we'll have to take things as they come." Kesniel looked at the sky and shivered. The thought of what lay ahead, of the loss and destruction they would bring, were icier than the winds displaced by the warmth of the King's song. "We must hurry. Delay can mean death."

Kesniel walked back to the men and began giving orders. Ewald looked back to the crowd. "Yes, but death for whom?"

Chapter 25
Refugees

Lachlaniel held Aurora close. They looked down from a rooftop. The streets were once again deserted. The wounded, dead, and dying had been pulled from the avenues and by roads.

"You and Max must make sure the people get into the city."

Max looked down on his brave young friend. "What about you?"

"The King has another task for me."

Aurora clung to him. "No. Don't leave me. You were almost killed. I almost lost you."

He pulled her head to his chest. "Shh. Shh. I'll be alright, but I *must* go. You can't keep me by holding on to me. The King will take care of me. You must stay close to Him. Petition Him for me and for these folks. Let me go, and He'll keep me for you."

She looked up into his unseeing eyes and ran her fingers through his hair. "It's so hard. I don't want to lose you." She fought back tears. "I want the King's will, but my heart wants you."

"This time it's different. The things that happened were my fault, but He's taught me what I couldn't see before." He paused and smiled. "I was truly blind then. Blind to my own faults. Thinking I was more than I am. The things He has for me to do I can't do. Only He can. The power is His. The plan is His, and He guides my steps. So don't worry. He's with me, and He'll bring me back to you."

The golden glow that always surrounded her in his mind was even brighter now. He could perceive hot tears beginning to trickle down her cheeks and even the trembling of her lips. He brushed the tears away, took her head in his hands, and touched his lips softly to hers. She wrapped her arms around him and deepened the kiss. His hands slid down her back, and her hands held her firmly to him. Time seemed to stop until they heard Max behind them.

"Ruphmmm. Pardon the intrusion, but we must get moving. The afternoon is fading and these people must get into the city before night fall."

Lachlaniel looked up at Max and then back to Aurora's face. "Don't worry my friend. There's a way into the city close at hand."

"Where? How do you know?"

Lachlaniel smiled at Aurora. "Leofwine showed me. When we first came up here, He whispered to me."

Aurora pulled away, startled by the revelation. "I didn't hear Him."

"You were distracted. His still, small voice is overpowered many times. We have to be careful to watch and listen for it."

She beheld him with new eyes. "You've grown," she whispered.

"I've learned much. When this is over, we'll have time to talk. Until then, there is much to do." He kissed her hands. "I must go." He looked to Max. "Come with me. I'll show you the entrance while she talks to the King."

Nestor and Jason carried the litter with Nestor's son up the hill to the flat. Nestor looked at his son's face, at the scars that weren't there the last time he saw him. Tears came to his eyes, not only for his son but for the others he had seen.

Fire and blood and smoke. Thank You that we found him in the midst of that chaos. So many others fared worse at their hands. So many died. I understand Lachlaniel's rage. I'm sure I understand what he came to understand. It all seems so wrong. Yet I trust You. You know what you're doing.

He knew that Leofwine could hear his thoughts, but he didn't expect an answer. A smile came to his lips when he felt the Presence by his side and the scent of fruit blossoms touched his nose. He relished the peace he felt and the joy of finding his son until Jason's voice broke into his thoughts.

"It's not too far from here, but let's take a rest." Jason wiped his forehead. "The house has been used too often, but the Basaners should be in disarray for quite some time."

"Won't it take years to rebuild from the destruction?"

"Yes, but that won't stop them from looking for us. We may have a few days. Perhaps a week or two."

"I still don't understand what drives them so. I know they hate the light, but why not be content to dwell in the darkness?"

"That's difficult to say. The answers may be as many as the Basaners themselves. Fundamentally, they're rebels like Kieran. They don't want anyone to rule over them. They want to be "the master of my fate and the captain of my destiny" as one of their poets puts it."

"It's incomprehensible that anyone could be so foolish."

"Is it? Has it been so many years that you've forgotten your life before crossing the Bridge?"

Nestor fell silent thinking back on the early years of his life. His reverie ended and he looked squarely at Jason.

"It was so long ago. I was so foolish then. Yes, I wanted my own way and it cost me dearly. I had forgotten. 'I shall find my own place, and I shall be king!'"

"Few are the people who do not fall into that trap. I can remember those days too. May I never forget them lest I fall again into that error. Let's get moving."

The two men picked up the stretcher with its unconscious boy and moved down the road towards the trees. The two men were lost in their own thoughts until a cold wind struck them in the face.

Nestor's light clothing was no protection against the frigid breeze. "Brrrr. How much further?"

Icy fingers found an opening at the collar of Jason's shirt and slithered inside. He shivered. "About two hundred yards. Let's hurry. This cold won't help your boy."

The men took longer strides in an attempt to cover the distance without jostling Nestor's son.

"There on your left."

"I can't see it." Nestor said as the wind tore tears from his eyes and forced him to squint.

The wind had picked up and Jason was forced to yell. "I'll tell you when to turn!"

Jason too was forced to squint. He watched the ground at the edge of the road for the entrance.

"Turn now!" He looked up. Someone was standing in the barn door, but he couldn't see who through his tear-filled eyes. "Not far now!"

Whoever it was, he was bringing out a horse to help block the wind. He met them fifty yards from the house. The warmth of the animal brought some relief from the cold. In short order, they were inside. They transferred Nestor's son to the bed and Jason went to make a fire. The wood bin was very low but it was enough to get one started. The man from the barn had put away the horse and came in with a load of wood. It only half filled the bin. He retrieved a coat and went out for another load.

The wind howled at the door like a hungry wolf as Jason put more wood on the fire. Nestor entered the room and went immediately to the warmth emanating from the stove.

"It's freezing in here." He rubbed his hands and held them out to the fire. Are there any blankets?"

"I'll get them."

Jason went to the closet in the other bedroom, grabbed an armload, and headed to the bedroom where Nestor's son lay. The boy was still unconscious but shivered from the cold. Jason covered him with three blankets and brought the last one to Nestor.

Nestor took the blanket and looked at Jason. Aren't there any more? I'm not taking the last one."

Jason stood beside him and faced the fire. "There are more, but you're the one wearing summer clothes anyway."

Nestor took the blanket and wrapped it about his shoulders. "I didn't expect to be gone into winter. This is beyond unexpected. It's unnatural."

"Kieran's doing." He gave a sardonic laugh. "Or one of his minions."

"I could do without it. I think it's time for an audience with the King."

Jason turned his back to the fire. "Give me a minute to get the chill out of my bones and we'll go together."

Lachlaniel brought Max to the entrance into the city. Large bushes had overgrown the doorway.

"I never would have found it."

Lachlaniel smiled. "Perception does have advantages over sight at times. Thank the King, He has blessed me with it."

They took axes they had brought from their horses and began clearing the way to the door. Max's side was clear before Lachlaniel had downed the first bush.

He put his hand on Lachlaniel's shoulder. "You go get the others. I'll finish here."

Lachlaniel laid aside his axe and mounted. It was getting colder and it would be dark soon. Lachlaniel touched his heel to Aman's side, and the horse sprang to the gallop. In minutes, he was back at the inn where he had left Aurora.

As he opened the door, an angry gust tore it from his hands and it opened wide banging the wall. Aurora and a little man grabbed it and pushed it shut.

Lachlaniel kissed Aurora. "It's brutal out there. How's it going rounding up the refugees?"

"The Ebenchaim are hard at work. This place is filled as well as most of the surrounding buildings."

"Any more trouble from the Basaners?"

The little man handed Lachlaniel a hot mug. "In this weather? They're likely sheltering as we are."

"Good. Max will be back soon, and we can start ushering the people to the entrance. It would be best to get them all in before dusk but that's not likely to happen. Whatever the case, there must be no delay. No one is to stay outside the city tonight."

"I'm not leaving my inn."

"Do you wish to die at the hands of the Basaners while defending your inn?"

The man frowned. "No."

"Then you'd best go with everyone else. They won't leave anything alive, man or beast that remains outside the walls." He took Aurora's hands and kissed them. "I have to go."

"Not until you've gotten something warm inside you."

"She's right, sir. You won't get far in this weather without food and more clothes than you've got on."

"Alright, but if I'm going to be warm then Aman should have something too. Do you have a large blanket and some oats."

"That I do sir."

He whistled and two teenage boys came running from the kitchen. A quick conference, and they were off to gather the needed items. The man disappeared into the kitchen as well and moments later brought back a steaming platter of food. He set it down on the table.

"Please, sit and eat."

"I must tend to my horse."

"The boys will do all that. You make yourself comfortable. It's likely all the comfort you'll get till journey's end."

"There's more here than I can eat."

Aurora took his hand and sat in a chair beside him. "I'll keep you company."

He smiled and she smiled back. The light of the fire glowed in her sapphire blue eyes. The lantern above the table made her golden tresses shimmer with her every move. Sights he perceived but dimly. The hour passed pleasantly and all too quickly.

They were finishing the last bites when Max squeezed through the doorway. He stood up and his head brushed a rafter. The innkeeper gasped. He had seen Max outside earlier, but having a human mountain in his great room was a sight he hadn't been prepared for.

"What kept you?" Lachlaniel said with his head cocked to one side.

"I met with the Ebenchaim. Men are already taking the people to the entrance."

"Good. The quicker the better. Our innkeeper thinks the weather has the Basaners seeking refuge from the cold. I'm not so sure."

"Another two hours should see them all inside."

"Well done Max." He wiped his mouth and stood up. He took Aurora's hand and led her to the fire. "Be careful. Stick with Max and do what he says. I don't want to lose you now."

She kissed him and looked deep into his eyes. "That goes double for you. Seeing you die once, was more than my heart can bear." She sniffed and wiped a stray tear from her eye. "So you be safe. I'll see you in the city."

They kissed again and held each other close. Max tapped Lachlaniel on the shoulder.

"I hate to break this up, but we've all got work to do."

Aurora touched Lachlaniel's cheek. "He's right. Oh, how I wish he weren't, but he's right."

"The sooner I go the sooner we'll be together again." He pulled away from her and went to the door. "Take care of her Max!"

He grabbed the handle and braced himself for the cold and the wind. The wind was as strong as ever, but he managed to hold onto the door this time. Aman was around the corner of the building and out of the wind munching oats contentedly. Lachlaniel pulled the feed bag over his ears and stored it.

"Many miles to go, old fella." He mounted, and they moved through the back streets to the main road fighting the wind all the way. Once at the main road, they turned east, and Aman began to canter. The going was slow as the wind turned to the northeast and struck them in the face. Ice pellets began pelting them after midnight, but by the third watch they turned south. The wind and sleet let up about dawn as they turned toward the house where Jason waited.

Lachlaniel took Aman to the barn. He removed the saddle and began rubbing him down. He didn't hear when the barn door opened.

"You go inside and get warm."

Lachlaniel jumped. It was Jason.

"Sorry. I didn't mean to startle you. Go on I'll finish here. You best get some food…and sleep too. We don't have long."

Lachlaniel nodded. The trip had been an exhausting one and what lay ahead would not be an easy task.

Ewald woke with a start.
Where am I?

The room was unfamiliar. He had fallen into the bed bleary-eyed and bone tired the night before. He sat on the edge of the bed and put his head in his hands.

The Bridge. I've never seen so many people. More than that left the city though. Poor, ignorant people. They won't escape. Only darkness and torment await them. They may flee the Basaners, but the Basaners couldn't care less about them. It's the other terrors that will devour them. The Basaners are here for us.

He stood up and dressed. The last piece of armor in place, he opened the door, stepped into the hall and headed down stairs. The others were waiting.

"Well, our sleepy sergeant has deigned to grace us with his presence."

"Knock it off Asher. I'm not in the mood for your pitiful attempts at levity."

Kesniel slammed his fist on the table. "Enough! You men are behaving like the darklings. You're Ebenchaim. I know you're tired, but there's work to be done. The King's work."

Ewald looked at the floor.

Like picking up that stupid breastplate instead of the King's. Guess I still have a lot to learn.

"Sorry."

"It's not me you should apologize to. And you should apologize to Ewald, Asher."

In unison, they mumbled, "Sorry."

Kesniel wasn't going to let them off that lightly and his face showed it. "Pretty pathetic apology if you ask me." He waited a moment. "Well?"

"Sorry Asher."

"Me too."

"I should give you both punishment duty. Maybe I will later, but there are more important things right now. We must continue to try to get the inhabitants across the Bridge, but the resident Ebenchaim must bear the brunt of that work. Asher, that's for you. Get them moving. We have very little time before the enemy strikes.

"Ewald, you must see to the gates. The defenses have been neglected for years. The gates must be well guarded. We'll be stretched too thin if we use our troops for all the gates. Split the work, one of our men with one of theirs. I hope their guards haven't forgotten everything they knew.

"The rest of us must shore up the defenses as best we can. Theron, you'll come with me. We'll have to find the armory and hope there's still some usable weapons. And by all means petition the King for what you lack. Dismissed!"

The men scattered in different directions as they left the building. Ewald had tagged a number for gate duty. It was several minutes before he saw Bercan among the men following him.

"Halt! Bercan! Front and center!" The lanky teen reluctantly came forward. "What do you think you're doing?"

"I don't want to sit and do nothing."

"You're too young yet. What would Max say? Or your mother for that matter. She's already going to skin you alive for sneaking out."

The boy hung his head and kicked the ground with the toe of his boot. Ewald looked around. The nearby livery caught his eye.

Just the thing.

"If you want to be helpful, then there's the spot for you. Most of our horses are stabled there. You make sure they're taken care of and help with them any way you can."

A look of horror crossed Bercan's face.

"*The livery!* Like as not they'll have me cleaning stalls."

"Don't despise the day of small things. Patience. Your time will come."

"I know. I know."

"Of course, I could ask Max to find you something to do when he gets here."

Bercan's look changed to shock. "No, no, no. The livery will be fine."

"Good. Go get busy. I'll be checking those horses myself when I get done."

"Yes sir."

Bercan looked dejected but moved as though he carried an urgent message. Ewald smiled and turned towards the gate.

"Double time!"

The guards in formation began running.

Max, Aurora, and the refugees reached the exit. They had been walking all night, but even in the tunnels, the stones gave them an indication of the passing of time. There was a labyrinth outside the walls and it had taken hours and a great deal of effort before they found the main path into the city. Even then, the way was only half again as wide, which led to doubts as to whether they were on the right path. Max heaved a sigh of relief when he turned a corner and saw a door in front of them.

"This should be the way out."

He pulled the great ring that hung on the door, but it didn't budge. Grasping the ring with both hands, his muscles bulged. He could hear the splintering of wood and the screech of tearing metal but the door wasn't moving.

"Move back. Everyone move back. I don't want to land on top of someone."

No one ignored that warning. They backed past the last corner. Max gripped the ring again. He heaved and the door came off its hinges. Several of the adjacent stones fell to the ground. Max found himself lying on his back with the door on his chest.

Aurora looked down at him and giggled. "I'd say that door hadn't been used in a while."

Max pushed the door off and leaned it against the wall. He was about to get up when Ewald sprang through the opening his sword at the ready. His stance relaxed and he burst out laughing.

"I should've known."

He extended his hand and helped his friend to his feet.

"Where are we?" Max asked.

"Near the main gate. This door leads into a conference room next to the old barracks. We tried to get it open several times. All we really needed was you."

Max rubbed his arms. "I almost didn't get it open either."

Heads popped around the corner to see if it was safe to come out.

Aurora looked back and motioned to them as to a shy child. "It's okay. We're in the city now."

Ewald looked at her and whispered, "You're in the city, but I wouldn't say 'it's okay' just yet."

"They've been through a lot. They need some reassurance."

Max shoved the fallen stones out of the path with his foot. "She's right. Let's get out of here. I want to know how bad it is, but not where they can hear."

Ewald lead them into the conference room and through the barracks. A flood of men, women and children followed them and poured into the street. The cold winds howling through the city struck their faces. It was like being plunged beneath the frigid waters of a frozen stream.

Max shivered and motioned for Aurora to stay in the barracks. "I can see the weather hasn't changed. If anything it's gotten colder."

Ewald shivered. "I'll have one of the women bring your sister some winter clothes. In the meantime, we need every man that can bear arms on the walls."

Max's mind turned to the defense of the city. "What about the gates?"

"They're defended as well as we can afford. There just aren't enough men. This place is huge."

"Any sign of the enemy?"

Ewald shook his head. "Not other than the cold. It's eerie. What about the refugees? Are they Ebenchaim?"

"A few."

"We must try to get the rest to cross the Bridge."

Max grunted. "We didn't even have time to think about that. Until we got them in the tunnels, we were harassed by assassins."

"There's no more time to sit on the fence. They must choose now."

"We've got to get them some place safe first."

Ewald scratched his beard. A light came to his eyes.

"Follow me.

Chapter 26
Confronting Evil Men

Lachlaniel looked at Jason. "How's his son?"

Jason leaned back in his chair. "He'll mend."

"Is he well enough for you to leave him?"

Jason put his hands behind his head and rocked the chair back on two legs as he stared at the ceiling. "Yes. They could be on the road home now." He rocked the chair forward and rested his forearms on the table. "They'll need a cart."

Lachlaniel stood up and paced with his hands behind him. "Good. You and I must leave as soon as we can, no later than noon. Is there a shorter way to the city than the main road?"

Jason picked up his cup and took a sip. "Yes. It isn't well traveled. It's rocky and treacherous at night."

"How quickly can it get us to the city?"

"Half to three quarters of a day."

Lachlaniel gave a weary smile. "Excellent. We must get to the city before nightfall."

Jason looked at the man he had nursed from the doors of death four times. "I'll get everything ready. Nestor can help me. You need to rest."

"If I help we'll be ready all the sooner."

"If you help the trip will take twice as long."

Lachlaniel thought for a moment, and the weariness washed over him. "You're right."

"Go get some sleep. I'll call you when we're ready."

Lachlaniel swam out of the depths of sleep. "What?"

"It's time."

"What time?"

"Time to go."

"No. I mean what time is it."

"Not yet noon."

Lachlaniel sat up. "What about Nestor and his son?"

Jason grabbed his hand and hauled him to his feet. "They're on their way home. Your lunch is hung on your saddle. You want to chat some more or shall we be off?"

"Let's go." He threw his cloak over his shoulders. "Is it still cold?"

"Freezing."

He walked from the bedroom through the kitchen and passed his hand over the stove and the last of its fleeting warmth. Lachlaniel followed and paused by the stove. His mind went back to the march through the snow.

"It's the enemy." He turned and followed Jason out the back door. "The wind has died down a bit."

"Yes. I noticed when I brought the horses out."

The two men mounted, and Lachlaniel found a sandwich in a pouch hanging from his saddle horn.

"Which way?" Lachlaniel asked.

"Across the field behind the barn. We'll come to a stream, which is probably frozen by now, and we'll run into the trail about a hundred yards beyond."

"Lead on." The words were barely distinguishable through Lachlaniel's mouth full of food.

The men of Agapay had their hands full as they tried to stop the influx of foes that scaled the walls. The men of the city reinforced their efforts, but Chara was so huge that even with their help, they were too far apart to stop everyone that got to the top from getting into the city. It wasn't an all out attack. These were infiltrators sent to sow confusion.

Explosions could be heard in the city as the saboteurs began using the black powder they had hidden long before. Now was the day for its use, and use it they did. Buildings collapsed amid screams of terror followed by the moans of the injured and the dying. People ran from place to place seeking refuge, but no place was safe. The infiltrators acted with impunity.

Wyn and Bercan ran into the street when there was an explosion nearby. Smoke rose into the air down the street.

Wyn looked at the rubble that had been his home. "My dad!"

Bercan tried to grab him, but he tore away and ran.

"Wyn! Stop!" He ran after his new friend. "They may still be around just waiting for rescuers!"

Wyn refused to listen. He began throwing bricks and moving rubble. An arrow whizzed over his head. Bercan pulled his shield and stood to Wyn's back. He deflected three arrows before he could even say a word.

"They're shooting at us!"

Heedless, Wyn continued plowing into the rubble. Bercan heard the sound of running and looked down the street. A man with a hammer in one hand and holding a door over the top of his head with the other was running toward them.

Bercan pulled his sword. "Wyn! You've got to stop! He'll kill us!"

Wyn turned to look as he threw away a part of a window sill.

"It's dad!" he said as he stood up.

An arrow grazed his arm and he fell to his knees. Bercan tried to cover his fallen friend with his shield. Wyn's father, Abiezer, arrived in time to keep an arrow from hitting Bercan who had left part of his own body exposed to protect his friend.

Abiezer dropped his hammer. "Let's get him out of here."

Bercan and Abiezer grabbed Wyn under his arms and dragged him across the street and out of the line of fire. Wyn tried to get to his feet but his legs collapsed beneath him. Abiezer tore the shirt sleeve from the wounded arm. "That was a fool thing to do."

"He heard the explosion and ran down the street." Bercan's face was full of concern. "How bad?"

Abiezer looked at the oily, discolored blood oozing from the cut. "It's not a bad cut, but the arrow was poisoned." There was pain in his voice. "If we don't get help he'll die."

"I know someone who might help."

"Let's go!"

Bercan started to grab Wyn.

"No." The smithy stooped down and gathered his son in his arms. "You lead the way I've got him."

Bercan passed through the winding alley to a main street. He paused for a second to get his bearings before venturing out with his shield in front of him.

"Hurry boy! We don't know how quick the poison will work."

Bercan began to trot in the direction of the inn where Kesniel had been.

"Faster! I can keep up."

Bercan stowed his shield and ran. They weaved their way down one street and another, but no more arrows flew their direction. There were sounds of explosions to both their right and left as well as behind them. Cries of anguish surrounded them. People were dying. Friends and relatives dredged through the debris in search of their loved ones all the while wailing in their travail over their loss. They arrived at the inn breathing heavily. Bercan stumbled up the steps and opened the door. Kesniel turned toward him as he collapsed inside the doorway. Abiezer stepped inside. He dropped to one knee.

"My boy… Arrow… poison…"

Kesniel and Theron took the limp form from his father's arms.

"Help him…please." The man fell on his face and rolled to his back.

"Theron, get Asher! Aurora!" He paused and yelled again as he and Theron hefted the boy onto a table. "Aurora! Come quickly!"

Aurora and another woman came rushing in from the kitchen as Theron bolted out the front door.

"We need the King's help."

Aurora glanced at the body on the table and turned. "Come with me. We must see the King!"

The two women entered the closet together. Kesniel took his handkerchief and wiped the blood from around the cut. He sniffed it. The odor was faint but definite.

"Aiden's gall."

Abiezer raised his head off the floor. "Bad?"

"Bad enough. If the arrow had done more than scratch him, he'd be dead already."

Abiezer tried to get to his feet. He stopped with one knee on the floor and breathed deeply a couple of times.

"What can I do?" he asked, rising to his feet.

"Nothing." Kesniel pulled out his stone and let some water drip into the wound.

"What are you doing?" Abiezer's tone was anxious and unhappy.

Kesniel continued without looking up. "You're not an Ebenchaim are you?"

"No."

"Water from the King's stone will wash out the poison so no more gets in his system."

"Then he'll be alright?"

"No. This will keep him from getting worse. What we need now is an antidote to the poison. That's why I sent for Asher. He's well versed in such matters."

Abiezer clasped Wyn's hand. The boy's face was pale; his hand clammy. "Hold on, son!"

"Bercan, get up." Kesniel's tone was commanding and urgent.

"Yes sir."

"Get some blankets." He paused and added, "And be quick about it."

Before he returned, Theron and Asher burst in.

Kesniel looked at them. "Aiden's gall."

Asher felt the boy's forehead. "Theron, I need a bowl and something that will work as a pestle." He opened his pouch, and pulled out a green leafy herb.

Abiezer looked at Asher in his bright colored clothes and his feathered cap. "Will he be alright?"

"He should be, but we won't know for a while yet."

Theron and Bercan returned. Kesniel and Bercan covered Wyn with the blankets while Asher pounded the herbs in the bowl.

"We'll have to hope this is enough because it's all I have."

Abiezer looked at him. "Can't we get any more?"

Asher looked at the man and kept pounding. "There's no time."

Kesniel smiled. "It will be enough. Aurora and the innkeeper's wife are petitioning the King."

"Does that help?" Abiezer's face was apprehensive.

"The King's will is not always the same as ours. In this case, I think it will be." Kesniel patted him on the shoulder. "Don't worry."

"Don't worry? My boy may die!" He watched as Asher spooned the tiny amount of oil from the bruised leaves slowly between the pale lips.

"You're not an Ebenchaim. You haven't learned to trust the King." Kesniel's tone was fatherly.

"I know nothing of your king." He took his son's hand again.

"But your boy's been across the Bridge. He trusts the King."

"Foolish child. Why would you break your father's heart?" The man wept.

"Perhaps he saw something in the King."

"What? What could he see in someone who would take a child from his father? In someone who wants his own way?"

"Perhaps he saw something in the King that reminded him of his own father." Kesniel led the man like he would have led his own son, to a conclusion the man could not come to by himself. "Perhaps he saw his father's love for him."

"Love? You talk to me of love while my boy is dying?"

The man looked at Kesniel and missed his son's tongue licking his lips.

"Your king is letting my city die like my boy…"

The hand he still held tightened on his own, but he did not feel it. The two women emerged from the closet.

"…and you talk to me of love?!"

A weak voice broke into his tirade. "Father. Father."

Abiezer felt the hand squeezing his. He looked down. Wyn smiled.

"I'm right here, son."

"Father. You should cross the Bridge. The King loves you as he loves me. The other side is so beautiful. He has so much He wants to give you."

"I know. You've told me before. I just don't want to lose what's mine."

Wyn's free hand patted his father's hand that held his own. "What do you have? The enemy of the King is trying to take it all away from you."

Abiezer's hand grasped the three and made the clasp complete.

"The boy's right." Kesniel put his hand on the man's shoulder. "It's the enemy that wants to steal from you. Whatever you give up to serve the King, He will give back to you more and better."

Abiezer's clouded eyes looked into his son's eyes. "More? Better?"

Kesniel smiled. "Beyond your wildest dreams."

Wyn tried to say something but his father stopped him. "Sh... Shh... You must rest." He looked to Kesniel. "I would give up everything for my son."

"The King requires nothing less than everything, the boy too, but if you give Him everything, you'll be joining your son as part of the King's family."

He let go of his son's hands as the boy fell asleep. "What must I do?"

"Cross the Bridge."

The day was far spent. Night was coming. Andre looked at his men from atop a little hill half a mile from the main gate. Many had entered the city and were wreaking havoc. Many more had fallen. The defenders were too busy to shoot at the enemy behind their walls.

A voice with an evil hiss said, "Now is the time."

Andre nodded. "Yes, my lord."

He prodded his horse and moved down into the avenues leading to the gate. Men gathered to him as he rode. He stopped at the crossroads and turned to face his men.

"Now is the time. Place the powder we have reserved by the gate. Once it's breached, the city is ours."

A cheer went up as they scurried to retrieve the deadly barrels of destruction.

Lachlaniel and Jason reached the door to the tunnels.

"Someone's been here." Jason scratched his head and dismounted.

"Max and I cleared the doorway. He took the refugees inside. Do you know the way through the tunnels?"

Jason pushed the door open. "Yes. It's a maze with many outlets into the city."

There was a great cry to their left.

"The Basaners." Lachlaniel stood up in his stirrups. "They haven't breached the gates, but there's lots of activity near there."

Jason shook his head in amazement. "I wish I could 'see' like that. There's nothing but building upon building between here and there. Your perception is better than the sight of anyone whose eyes aren't blind."

Lachlaniel gave a silent chuckle. "Can the tunnel accommodate the horses?"

"No."

"Then leave yours here."

Jason cocked his head. "You aren't coming?"

"No. I'm needed there," he said pointing towards the gate. "Andre hasn't yet entered the city. I must stop him before he does. But you'll be needed within."

"As you say."

Jason entered the tunnels shutting the door behind him. Lachlaniel urged Aman forward cutting across the field, between two buildings, and onto the street. He was met by armed men, but they were no match for a mounted rider with Lachlaniel's experience.

Word spread ahead of him, and the resistance ebbed and disappeared. He rode unhindered for more than a mile. He rounded a corner onto the main thoroughfare, and there before him stood Andre, torch in hand.

"So. The fall didn't kill you. My men told me you weren't easy to kill."

Lachlaniel dismounted and drew sword and shield. He moved forward.

Andre stooped and put the torch to a line of black powder on the ground. "I think this time I'll do the job myself and make sure about its outcome."

Lachlaniel remained silent and continued to walk towards Andre. Andre pulled a small crossbow from his back and fired three bolts. Lachlaniel kept walking and raised his shield. The bolts bounced off making the shield ring like a gong. The powder hissed as the fire continued its trek to the gate. Lachlaniel continued forward. Andre reloaded and fired three more bolts. Lachlaniel angled his shield and the bolts along with three more fired from the shadows of a side street bounced off harmlessly. Lachlaniel strode with implacable determination. Andre only had time to try once more. He looked to his left where the fire was closing on its goal as he loaded the crossbow. He fired again.

Lachlaniel held his shield in front of him as his armor began glowing. Andre's bolts once again bounced off the shield but three more sets flew from darkness and were set on fire and burned to ash by the light that now surrounded Lachlaniel. There was no pause in his gait as he raised his sword. Andre pulled his and held it at the ready.

"Come on. Come on! COME ON!" he shouted.

Lachlaniel paid no heed. His sword came down on Andre's. Andre was driven back and stumbled. He fell on his back.

"You've caused a great deal of trouble and destruction." The point of Lachlaniel's sword rested on Andre's chest. Andre's face was a contorted mask of anguish.

"You deserve death, but I am not your judge." Lachlaniel lifted the sword tip.

Andre's face turned to one of rage. Lachlaniel turned his back and kneeled. Knowing what was coming, he held his shield in front of him gritted his teeth and braced himself. Andre grabbed his sword and rose to his feet in an instant. He swung his sword at Lachlaniel's exposed neck with a shout of triumph. Before the blow could land, a tremendous explosion rocked the landscape. The blast rolled over Lachlaniel like water over an immovable boulder, but Andre was blown into the wall of a building and fell limp as a rag. Lachlaniel got up and walked to the archway where the gates had been. The fighting everywhere paused. Andre got up and limped into the shadows. A horse whinnied and the sound of hooves on cobblestones echoed in the night.

His foe vanquished, the victor took his stand on a flat stone atop the rubble in the archway. He didn't have to wait long. Men came running out of the shadows to storm the open gate. The rubble blocked the passage and made them climb to the center where Lachlaniel stood. They came brandishing clubs and whips, throwing stones, and a few wielded a sword. Lachlaniel used his shield on many sending them to the bottom of the heap in unconsciousness, but on some he was forced to use his sword. They were clumsy, slow, and ill prepared to face a well-trained, heavily armed, soldier of the King. No more than three could attack at once, and he was in no real danger. He took his time trying not to kill, but simply to incapacitate. The numbers made this difficult and sometimes impossible. Those that fell and rolled to the bottom of the heap of rubble were often trampled to death by those climbing to the top. Soon the ones at the bottom had to pull the bodies away just to clear a path to the heap.

The attack on the wall waned as it became centered on the breach and Lachlaniel. The Basaners were no longer infiltrating the city. The explosions came less often. Men in the city were beginning to capture or kill the infiltrators. The Basaners and their allies changed tactics and fired arrows at those on the wall. They fired at Lachlaniel as well often downing their own men. Lachlaniel was heedless of the arrows. They were stopped several feet from him by a shield of light. Someone was petitioning the King.

Chapter 27
Battle for The Tower

Kesniel, Max, Theron, Asher, and Ewald had gone to defend the tower. They arrived in time to stop the fuse from being lit. The struggle with the ten men was short. They were no match for Max. After he dispatched the first three, the rest fled. Kesniel and the others removed the threat of the explosives and in minutes they were alone and safe. The tower was secure.

Aurora had followed them. She remained out of sight until the way was clear. She hurried from her place of seclusion to the doorway only to be stopped by Max.

He swept her off her feet as she made for the door. "What are you doing here?"

"I came to climb the tower. I must see the battle."

He carried her through the door brushing past Asher and Theron who were standing guard.

He closed the door behind him. "That was foolish! You could've been killed!"

"And you and the others are perfectly safe I suppose?"

Max looked at her sternly, but had no words to rebut her argument.

"How can I petition the King for the needs of the battle when I don't know what's going on?"

Max frowned. "Well you're here now. This is as secure a place as any with us guarding it."

The door swung open. Ewald was standing guard outside with Asher and Theron, and they let a man enter.

"Jason."

"I've come to help find the Great Stone and get it into its place in the turret."

At that moment, Kesniel came from somewhere in the depths beneath the tower.

"The King told me He was sending us someone."

"Lachlaniel brought me safely through the Basaners lines."

Aurora's face lit up. "Lachlaniel! Where is he?"

"He fights at the main gate."

Aurora moved towards the door, but Max stopped her.

"I must go to him."

"No you don't. You wanted to see the battle from the tower. This is where you need to be. Now up the stairs with you."

Max blocked the way to the door and moved her toward the stairs. Aurora looked at him dejectedly, and turned to the stairs. When she turned away, she smiled and ran up the stairs.

Kesniel watched her but quickly turned his attention back to the two men. "We must find the Reliquary. No doubt that's where the Stone is. We'll need help with it. Max, get Asher and Theron."

"Let's split up." Max suggested as he headed for the door.

Kesniel raised an eyebrow. "A prudent suggestion."

Jason interrupted. "I've been to the Reliquary, but I've never seen inside."

Max returned in time to hear the comment with Theron and Asher trailing him. "Where is it?"

"I don't remember exactly, but it's on the west side of the main passage."

Kesniel smiled. "The hallway will be larger than the others to accommodate the Stone. It shouldn't be hard to find."

The five men began searching the corridor for the right hallway. In moments, they were standing before the door of the Reliquary.

Theron looked at the solid oak door. "I hope it isn't locked."

Max looked at him and tried to open it. "Locked. I wish Diaphanous were here."

Kesniel pushed past Jason and Asher. "Out of the way big man."

Max stepped aside smiling at his friend's comment.

Kesniel produced a key. "It fits the door to our reliquary. It should fit here too."

He slid the key into the lock and a loud click filled the corridor as he turned the key. Kesniel opened the door and a warm golden glow filled the hallway. Their souls flooded with joy, and they began praising the King for many things in their lives, but most especially for Eleutherias and the

Bridge. They stepped into the room as if treading on hallowed ground. Gathering round the Stone they paused, drinking in its warmth and light.

Without a word, they set to work removing it from its mounting and roll it into the hallway. The hallway was too narrow to let all five men work. It would have to be the four men or Max alone.

Theron looked at the big man holding the stone upright by himself. "Shall we take it or shall we let Max?"

Kesniel waved his hand. "Max, would you do the honors?"

"My pleasure."

He rolled the stone down the corridor as boy would roll a hoop, but gently, his heart filling with more joy at each touch. He reached the main hallway with his friends right behind. As he neared the stairs, Kesniel moved ahead. He bent near the stairway.

"Here's the groove. Just like ours."

Max maneuvered the stone into the groove. They meshed with a click. The men smiled but not for long. There was a thunderous boom that echoed through the hallways.

Kesniel shouted as he ran for the door of the Tower. "Theron! Asher! Get that stone to the top of the tower. Max and Jason! Follow me!"

At the gates, Lachlaniel was tiring but held his ground. He suddenly found there were no enemies before him. His sword dropped until the tip rested on the ground. He dropped to one knee trying to catch his breath. Then he saw the reason the enemy had departed. A darkness was moving through the byways towards the gate. He hung his head.

"Leofwine help me." He breathed with a sigh.

Strong arms lifted him to his feet. He raised his sword and shield and stood at the ready, the light of his stone filling the gap where the gate had been. He watched amazed as a small black figure with fiery red eyes approached. The figure did not seem nearly so formidable as the fifty-foot evil at Agapay had been, but Lachlaniel was not fooled. He grit his teeth and his muscles tensed for action. The figure stepped gingerly as he moved up the pile of fallen stones and rubble. He faced Lachlaniel and smiled an evil grin. Before Lachlaniel could move, there was a tremendous explosion. He was hurled up the street and slammed into a wall. He raised his head and looked back at the gate. A huge section of wall lay in ruins and the figure walked brazenly and with impunity down the street followed by hundreds of men.

Lachlaniel could hold his head up no longer. "Basaners."

He looked at the sky as it filled with ominous low-hanging black clouds. His eyes closed and he saw no more.

Aurora reached the top of the tower and looked over the parapet toward the gate. Dark clouds were beginning to roll in but only what was left of the top of the gate could be seen beyond the buildings. Fires were everywhere and explosions could be heard in the distance. She stepped into her closet, crossed the majestic throne room, and knelt before the King.

"Lachlaniel fights before the gates, child."

"Help him Lord!"

"Leofwine is there. Is your only concern for him?"

Aurora dropped her head.

The explosions. The city.

"My lord the city is in peril! There are not enough men to fight. Who can aid us?"

"I have. The Ebenchaim are rising."

She looked at Him and blushed. "I'm sorry. I know You can, but the enemy is already destroying homes and businesses, even the domes are being destroyed."

"It will all be over soon. The Stone is on its way to the tower."

"The Stone? What good will it do?"

"You will see, my child. You will see. Have faith."

Aurora stepped out of her closet to a blackening sky and a tremendous explosion that reverberated through the tower and made a gust of warm air rush from the stairway opening. She looked below at a black man-like figure. He raised his hand and a sickly green-yellow orb formed. He threw it at the tower. There was another explosion and a gust from the stairwell. The tower glowed a brilliant gold around her. She looked across the city.

Half of it seemed to be on fire. Everywhere, domes of meeting lay in ruins, and from many others, fires rose into the skies. Overhead, the clouds grew thicker and blacker. There was another explosion and her attention was drawn back to the street below. The tower glowed a brighter gold than before as she saw Max, Kesniel, and Jason crash through the doors and join Ewald to confront the Evil.

At the sounds of the explosions at the tower, Ebenchaim peered through windows and cracked doors to see what was happening. What they saw brought tears to their eyes and many a howl of pain from their lips. Their beloved domes of meeting no longer stood framed against the sky. Instead, there was fire and smoke and ruin. Doors opened wide and the Ebenchaim began a trek to the domes. For many, it was a trek they hadn't made in years.

Velvet lips nuzzled Lachlaniel's face as Aman tried to awaken his master. Lachlaniel opened his eyes, and breathed in that sweet, familiar fruit blossom he knew so well. A strong arm gripped his forearm and he gripped back. He was hoisted to his feet as strength returned to his legs.

"There's work to be done," a Voice whispered.

A resounding boom came up the street. It overpowered the nearby explosions. A glint of gold caught Lachlaniel's perception. He turned toward the building. A golden lance leaned against it, ready for use.

"You're needed with this weapon at the tower."

Lachlaniel said not a word. His lips pursed in determination as he picked up the lance and mounted Aman.

"Go and prosper."

Aman reared and sped off at a gallop.

The four men at the tower moved toward the black figure. Tentacles formed at its feet and grew into green worms of enormous size. They opened their mouths and hissed through jagged, razor teeth. The first struck at Kesniel. It wrapped about his neck before he could move his sword and squeezed. His sword and shield dropped with a rattle to the ground and his hands went to his throat. Max rushed to his aid. Another worm wrapped around him. His right hand gripped the worm to no avail. His left was squeezed against his side. Crashing waves of pain rose in his crushed hand and side pounding him like surf on the shore. He dropped to his knees, unable to help his friend. The other two sprang forward to confront Ewald, and Jason. They were pushed back by the ferocity of the attack, powerless to help. Their hands were full defending themselves.

Another ball of green fire struck the tower with a resounding boom. Aurora let out a cry and entered her closet. People thronged to the domes. They dropped to their knees wailed, beat their breasts, and scooped up dust and soot and threw it into the air over their heads. Another boom came from the tower, and it brightened burnishing the domes a bright gold. Closets opened, many that had not been used in years, some that never had. Transparent walls rose around the domes. The Basaners, bringing explosives to destroy them, were stopped in their tracks as the walls flared a brilliant blue at their touch.

At the tower, a blue wall went up around the men, and the worms, cut off from their source, withered and died. It was just in time too. Kesniel was turning blue. He fell to the ground gasping for air. Max too fell to the ground. His body was still except for a tremble in his chest as broken ribs struggled to bring air into desperate lungs. Ewald and Jason rushed forward and began tending the two men who lay close to death.

The Evil called and hundreds of Basaners came scurrying with kegs of powder and torches. The Evil turned his attention to the wall around the men, and fireballs rained down on it in time to some ghastly dirge, but the constant explosions masked the sound of approaching hoof beats.

Aman flew at top speed through the streets, his hooves clattering on the cobblestones and the steel of his shoes raising a trail of sparks. Lachlaniel lowered his lance and leaned forward to absorb the shock of impact.

The lance struck through the Evil left side spinning him around as the balls of fire disappeared from his hands. The horse struck him as he past and the Evil almost fell. Lachlaniel pulled Aman to a halt and turned for another run. Green blood flowed from his foe's wound. He turned to face Lachlaniel. Lachlaniel charged again striking the Evil's right side. Lachlaniel went a little further this time before stopping Aman. The Evil's hand filled with a fireball. There was no time for Lachlaniel to turn or raise his shield.

A flood of Ebenchaim had reached the domes and tens of thousands of petitions reached the ears of the King.

Aurora stepped from her closet. "Look out Lachlaniel!"

The ball of fire failed to reach the champion; a wall of blue absorbed the blow, smothering the explosion. Lachlaniel turned. A brilliant sight met his eyes, filling him with awe and joy. The Great Stone Chara had reached the top.

The Stone's light shone through Aurora, and dawn rose over the city though night had fallen. The Basaners were dismayed by the brightness. They dropped their torches and covered their eyes. The smell of death—their death—filled their nostrils. The fuses remained unlit as the Basaners fled in terror. Aurora lit up like the first burst of sunshine, sunshine which the world hadn't seen in thousands of years. Lachlaniel's joy reached the heights of elation.

Light from Aurora burst upwards and the blackened clouds turned gray and then white. A hole opened and a shaft of light fell on Lachlaniel and Aman. The great horse reared and snorted. When he came down, he pawed the ground.

The shaft of light spread, enveloping the Evil who trembled. Lachlaniel urged his great horse forward. Aman's muscles strained with all their might. Lachlaniel's lance was pointed at the Evil's chest. It struck home and the saddle was ripped off Aman's back. Lachlaniel fell to the street with his feet still in the stirrups. He was unconscious. The lance protruded from both sides of the Evil. He clenched his fist and loosed an unearthly banshee cry as he dissolved in the light that surrounded him.

The Evil defeated, his master, Mephistopheles, looked on from afar. His plans had been disrupted. He turned. As he went, he looked over his shoulder. There were more important things to consider now than turning this defeat into a victory.

Aurora descended the tower nearly knocking down Asher and Theron as she ran between them. She flew through the doors past Ewald and Jason who were still tending the fallen Kesniel and Max.

Strong hands on his right and left, and two hands from behind, lifted Lachlaniel from the saddle. He opened his eyes. Eleutherias stood at his right, but there was seemingly no one on his left or behind him. The hands let him stand on his own. Eleutherias moved to face him.

"Kneel, Lachlaniel, knight errant."

Eleutherias drew Lachlaniel's sword. He touched one shoulder, then the other, and then the top of his head with the tip of the sword.

"Give me your right hand."

Lachlaniel held out his right hand but continued to look at the ground before him. He felt Eleutherias take his hand and slip a ring on his finger. He looked up.

"Why me? I am a most unworthy servant of the King."

"Who is to say whether you are worthy or unworthy? Is it not the King, and I, and Leofwine who make those decisions?"

"Yes, my Lord."

"Then rise Lachlaniel, the King's newest Einar and the last."

Lachlaniel stood to his feet. His raiment changed. The tattered, road stained cloak changed to a beautiful, clean, new cloak with a crown on the back. His armor was filled with shimmering blue light. He looked beyond Eleutherias to his beautiful, smiling Aurora, still lustrous with the residual light of that dazzling new dawn for the city. When he looked back, Eleutherias held a crown. He placed it on Lachlaniel's head.

"I pronounce thee Lachlaniel, Einar – King-steward of the Great City Chara."

Lachlaniel stood astonished.

When He had me kneel I expected promotion – promotion I didn't deserve, but Einar and now King-steward?

He shook his head.

"Eleutherias smiled at his thoughts. "You do deserve it, and you *are* worthy. There is one other thing."

Eleutherias touched his eyes. The blackness rolled away.

"I can see! I can SEE!!"

"Yes, you can see. You will also still perceive just as you have. Do not depend too much on your restored sight. You were given the ability to perceive for a reason."

Eleutherias disappeared both from sight and perception. Aurora rushed to his arms. They embraced and kissed and her glow encompassed him too.

At the tower, the color had returned to Kesniel's cheeks, and he was awake. Max had not fared so well. His ribs and arm were crushed and his breathing was labored. Asher and Theron had come from the tower to help. Asher produced a few leaves of Uset's breath and Jason had flown to get some hot water.

Ewald frowned. "We need to get them moved inside somewhere where they can rest."

Theron stood up. "We'll need a very large stretcher and it will take all of us just to get Max moved, but Kesniel shouldn't be left alone. I'll start getting what we need." He hurried off to scour the area for useful items.

Jason returned as Lachlaniel and Aurora arrived leading Aman. Asher crushed the leaves and sprinkled them in the steaming bowl of water. Jason took the bowl and placed it by Max's head, and almost instantly, the herbal laden steam took effect. His breathing slowed and though still shallow it was much deeper than it had been. The pallor that had been unnoticed slowly disappeared.

Everyone let out a collectively held breath. They looked up and saw the crown on Lachlaniel's head.

Ewald's jaw dropped. "When did *that* happen?"

Aurora smiled. "Just now. Eleutherias made my future husband an Einar and King-steward of this city." She beamed at Lachlaniel, but he just blushed.

"Well!" Ewald blew the word out in astonishment. "I guess I'll have to start calling you sir!"

Lachlaniel shook his head. "We've been through too much together for you to start doing that."

"At least in front of your subjects then."

Theron returned with a door for Kesniel, very long, sturdy poles, enough canvas to make several litters, and eight men.

"Think you got enough cloth?" Aurora said raising an eyebrow.

"He's a big man and I didn't want it to rip. We'll triple or quadruple it around the poles. However far it will go."

Ewald nodded. "Good thinking Theron."

Lachlaniel started to scratch his head but stopped when he touched the crown. "We can attach it to Aman."

"That's fine, but…" Jason paused. "…the ends can't drag. He mustn't be bounced."

Lachlaniel began issuing the first commands of his office. "Asher, you and Theron take Kesniel. Aurora can lead Aman and the rest of us will get on the poles. The only question left is where to?"

Jason screwed up his face in thought. "Back to the inn. It's still intact and it's as close as any place."

They set to work making litters and moving the patients, gingerly in the case of Max, which wasn't easy. Aurora led out with the others trailing behind Aman. An hour's work saw the litters made and the patients moved. Jason reheated the Uset's breath and placed it by Max's head once more. They settled in for the long night of watching and waiting, all except Lachlaniel. He had one more task to perform as the new King-steward.

Chapter 28
Projects for Kesniel

Lachlaniel took several of Agapay's men away from fighting the fires and sent them to gather the Ebenchaim of the city. He waited at a plaza near the tower. It wouldn't be nearly big enough for all the people but it would have to do.

The people started arriving almost immediately, but it was nearly an hour before the plaza and beyond was filled. The people waited eagerly to hear what the man with the crown would have to say. At last, he raised his hand for quiet and the murmuring died down.

"People of Chara, Eleutherias has appointed me King-steward of this city. As your new ruler, I am here to get our work organized. The men of Agapay are already busy fighting the fires and removing the dangerous powder, something they have some experience with, out of harm's way. Before we can rest, the fires must be out, a watch must be posted at the gates and at the sites of the fires, and some must be standing by to petition the King against any need. Men, that's for you. Women, the workers will need food, so you and the children must make a search to see what can be provided. It's unlikely that the Basaners will return anytime soon. The Evil that led them is finished, and they are leaderless. The light of the Great Stone has terrified them. It will be some time before they get a new master, and he will probably think twice before attacking while the Stone's light shines forth. The next weeks and months hold much work for us in restoring the city. Work hard tonight and then get some rest. Soon, I will disclose the vision the King has given me for our city."

The people dispersed telling those who couldn't hear the speech, what had been said, then they set to work. Lachlaniel was busy deep into the night, checking security at the gates, visiting the ruined domes to see how the work was progressing, checking with the women and making sure everyone was fed. When the last of the fires were out and the residents had bedded down for the night, he trudged back to the inn. He paused in the great room. Max's pallet lay on four sturdy chairs. Aurora had fallen asleep with her head leaning on Max's good arm. Lachlaniel smiled, headed upstairs, and fell fully clothed into his waiting bed.

The morning dawned clear. There was no sign of the clouds of the day before or the light that had filled the sky. A warm wind had come in the night, dispelling the cold. It was a fine late summer day with hints that autumn was near.

The people of the city, weary from their toils but filled with joy and hope, slept late as did Lachlaniel. Those who had guard duty had relieved their counter parts in the night and eagerly awaited their relief. In short order, they too were home in bed. Some good women of the city had arisen and begun preparations to provide the tens of thousands of meals that would be needed this day.

Aurora, still asleep in the great room beside Max, was roused by the innkeeper and his wife whispering. His wife hurried out the door, as Aurora got up and stretched.

'I'm sorry my dear. We didn't mean to disturb you."

"That's alright. I need to get busy."

She followed him into the kitchen with the bowl of herbs that had dried out overnight.

"Can I help you?"

"They're pretty much used up, but they're all we have for the moment. I need to get boiling water on them and see if they can do Max anymore good."

"You let me do that. I can see you're still drained from your brother's ordeal."

"Thank you."

The innkeeper busied himself with his tasks and soon the bowl was heating on the freshly stoked stove. Next he set about getting breakfast for his tenants which only consisted of the people from Agapay.

"I'm glad to have you, especially the new King-steward. That'll be a great feather in my cap, eh?"

Aurora looked up. "You mean my fiancée?"

"Oh? You two are going to be married?"

"Yes. It won't be soon. Eleutherias says we must wait. The major repairs to the city come before we can begin to think about wedding preparations.'

"Oh," the innkeeper said, a note of sadness coming into his voice. "I'm sorry to hear that."

"Don't be. The King does all things well. His timing is impeccable."

"What a good attitude. I shall be glad to see you two married. You'll make a wise and good wife. Breakfast will be ready soon. Why don't you get the others up."

Aurora went back into the great room. She whispered in Ewald's ear, "Breakfast is almost ready."

The sleeping man rolled over and opened one eye. "What a beautiful way to wake up. A lovely wisp of a girl whispering of imminent food."

He sat up.

"Shall I get Lachlaniel? He must have come in very late."

Ewald cocked his head. "Yes. He'll have to get used to the heft of his new duties sometime. Now's as good a time as any to start. Besides, it's not that early anymore in case you haven't noticed." He pointed toward the window.

People were coming and going on the street, hauling away debris, carrying tools and supplies; most were whistling. Aurora smiled. Ewald got up and started waking Theron, Asher, and Jason.

He turned his head. "I've got these roustabouts. You get your honey."

Aurora giggled. "Alright."

She bounded up the stair, singing as she went. She fell silent as she neared the door. She gave a soft knock. There was no answer. She opened it a crack and peered in. Lachlaniel lay on his stomach, still in his clothes, his head turned to one side. She slid into the room leaving the door open and pulled a chair near the bed. She put her hand on his back and began to rub but jerked back. She could feel the scars beneath his shirt crisscrossing and overlapping.

Tears formed in her eyes. "Oh my poor dear Lachlaniel. What you must have been through!"

"What?"

"My dearest one." She leaned forward and kissed his cheek.

A tear dropped into his ear. "Hey!"

He sat up and stuck a finger in his ear to wipe it out. He stopped when he saw her face and the tears streaming down. "It's not Max!"

"No. It's you. Those scars!"

He sat on the edge of the bed and drew her into his arms. "It's alright. It's what I get for being a puddin'-headed fool."

"Oh, don't say that."

"It's true. It's my own fault. Too stubborn for my own good."

He brushed her hair back over her shoulders. "Don't cry. It's all over now. Our new lives lie before us, remember?"

She brushed away the tears and went to the wash bin to wipe away the streaks. "Breakfast is almost ready."

Lachlaniel stood and straightened his hair. "I'll be meeting with the King first."

Aurora went to the door. "I'll see you downstairs."

"Hey. Not without a kiss."

He took her hands and stood looking at her. Her beautiful white dress, the pearl necklace he had given her, the added glow his perception could see; they all combined to stop him where he was.

"What is it?"

"Now that I can see again, I just can't get enough of looking at you."

Aurora smiled and touched her lips gently to his. He started to pull her closer, but she pulled away.

"No. You need some incentive to get you downstairs faster." She laughed playfully. "I'll be waiting at the foot of the stairs."

She stepped through the doorway and looked back with a smile.

Lachlaniel left his room refreshed and clad for a day of new duties. He paused at the top for an instant as he caught sight of her and then bounded down the steps taking two at a time. He took her in his arms and held her close. Their lips touched, and they held a long kiss drinking in the love for each other they had missed over the intervening weeks.

Asher and Theron were watching Max. As much used as the leaves of the Uset's breath were, they still had a good effect on Max's breathing.

The clatter of plates in the dining room caused Ewald to lift his head and look.

"About time. I'm starved!" Slight movement from the stairs caught his attention. "Hey you two! We've got a sick man here. He doesn't need that going on."

Lachlaniel looked up. "Max." He let go of Aurora and moved to the side of his friend. "How is he?"

Asher had a worried look. "The Uset leaves are still working, but we have no more."

The door opened in time for his statement to reach the innkeeper's wife's ears. "No more what?"

Three other ladies trailed in behind her carrying loads of soft cloth material.

"Uset's Breath."

The second women piped up. "Oh. Is that all? I've got some at home. I like to keep it on hand."

Ewald stood up. "Well don't just stand there woman! Go get it! This man's life depends on it!"

The woman dropped her bundle and hastened out the door without a word. Lachlaniel knelt and took Max's hand. Max gripped Lachlaniel's hand but it was an extremely light grip.

Lachlaniel's face took on a shocked look. "He's bad isn't he?"

Asher looked at him. His face said not here, but he remained silent.

They moved into the dining room.

"Where's Jason?"

Ewald smiled at his young friend. "He's upstairs tending Kesniel. Don't worry too much about Max. He has the constitution of a horse."

Asher looked at Ewald and frowned. "That may be but horses die too."

A gasp came from the stairs. They looked over in time to see a closet closing where Aurora had stood.

"Ewald took his finger and thunked Asher on the head. "Lunkhead. She heard you. Any word about her brother dying should never have reached her ears."

Asher rubbed his head. "Well…"

"Well what? You knit-witted addle pate."

"Well, can you think of a better place for her to go to get help?"

Lachlaniel smiled. "Atta boy Asher. You're not slow. It is the best place, and we should all use our closets before we get to breakfast."

Ewald smiled. "Our new King-steward is thinking. A very good idea."

They took turns with Asher going last.

Ewald looked at Max. "One of you stay here. I don't want to leave him alone. I'll take over when I'm done and you can eat."

Asher came out of his closet as the woman with the Uset's Breath came rushing through the door.

"Here you are sir!" she said handing the leaves to Asher.

"Take them to the innkeeper and get them in some boiling water." He looked at Lachlaniel. "You can go eat now. I've got this."

"Aurora hasn't come out yet. I'll wait for her, but I'm going to go see how Kesniel is doing. If she comes out, tell her I'll be right back."

Asher nodded and Lachlaniel headed upstairs. Jason was sitting and talking to Kesniel who was sitting up in bed.

Jason turned to see who the visitor was. "I was just checking to see if our patient is ready to go downstairs and take some food."

"And?"

"He's ready to start moving about. It'll do him good, but I think solid food should wait today. His throat took a real beating."

"My stomach does not thank you," Kesniel said in a hoarse whisper. He paused and rubbed his throat. "But I think my throat does."

Lachlaniel looked at Jason. "What are you waiting for? Breakfast is on the table."

"You two get out of my room so I can get dressed. Can't an old man have any privacy?"

The two men smiled at each other and rose to leave.

Jason slapped Lachlaniel on the back. "He'll be fine by tomorrow. How's Max doing?"

"Asher is worried. Everyone's been to their closets this morning. We did get fresh leaves."

"That's good to hear." They reached the top of the stairs and headed down. "We can take some broth from the old and mix it with Kesniel's breakfast, such as it is."

Asher looked up. "What's that? Leftover juice from the leaves in Kesniel's breakfast?"

"Yes. It will help his throat heal."

"Well I never!" Asher was always listening for new ways to use herbs. "Never too old to learn a thing or two."

Asher handed the bowl to Jason as the women came back with a fresh steaming bowl.

Jason bent down beside Max. "How's he doing?"

"He's still breathing easy but very light. He opens his eyes every once in a while, but he still can't speak. Just not enough breath yet. He tried to whisper but I couldn't understand."

"It's good he's trying. It shows he's fighting, but make him rest anyway. Maybe tomorrow he can make a sentence or two. It's going to be a long slow process."

Aurora emerged from her closet. She'd been crying for a long time. Her eyes were bloodshot and puffy, her nose was wet and red, she'd been using her handkerchief a lot. Lachlaniel got up and took her hand.

"He'll be ok."

"The King said so too."

"Then let's go to breakfast."

"Not like this! I'm going to wash my face first!"

"Ok. I'll wait."

She rushed up stairs but paused when she heard him say, "But don't be long! I'm starved."

She smiled and was gone in a trice. It was then that Lachlaniel noticed the four women busy in a corner of the great room. They were sewing something, something large.

"What are you ladies doing?"

"We can't leave that poor man on that thing," the innkeeper's wife said pointing at the pallet. "We're making a mattress big enough even for him."

Asher looked up. "Good thinking. This thing can't be too comfortable. That'll help him breathe easier."

A voice from the top of the stairs caught Lachlaniel's attention.

"Let's go to breakfast."

Lachlaniel wasted no time after breakfast, nor did the others. The inn keeper was busy in the shed out back where sawing and hammering could be heard. He was joined by Theron and Ewald. This wasn't the sort of woodwork Ewald was used to, but he knew enough to be able to lend a hand. Theron, on the other hand could only sit back, watch, and chew the fat. Asher would be going out after his breakfast to scour the countryside for medicinal herbs. Jason was watching Max. Aurora was helping to make the mattress. Kesniel watched Lachlaniel through the window. Then he slid out the door.

He was making his way to the Residence. He had to ask directions many times. Many did not know where it was, and many had never heard of it. It was nearing noon when he came to a corner where the thoroughfare broadened. To his left was an acre of grass and weeds, an overgrown entanglement of what had once been a beautifully kept lawn.

He turned left into another broad way until he came to the path, for the encroaching vegetation made it little more than a path, to the Residence. The heavy doors were ajar and the hallway was dark. The foyer was thirty feet across and scattered with leaves, debris, and fallen plaster. A light came from overhead. He looked up to the gaping hole in the roof. He shook his head as great sadness swept over him.

How did they let it come to this? It's going to take time to restore this to its former glory. More time than I have. Perhaps it will be enough to just make it livable.

He entered the great hall with its throne. Many holes adorned its lofty heights and the wreckage was strewn across the floor. The throne was devoid of cloth, only the ornate wood work remained though it too was weathered and old. A bird sat on the arm of the throne looking about for nesting material. There was none to be had, and he took flight at Kesniel's approach. He shook his head and leaned on his staff.

I feel so old.

After a moment of gathering his strength, he left the hall and turned his attention to the living quarters. The King-steward's quarters were quite spacious, more so than his own, but it would be a very long time before repairs would make them adequate to live in. The other quarters were much the same except for the attendant's quarters near the end of the hall. These were small compared to the others. Even so, the antechamber was larger than the great room at the inn. The drawing room was quite spacious. The bedroom was smaller than the other rooms would have indicated. They were all in disrepair but nothing that couldn't be taken care of in only a few days. Plaster had fallen from the ceiling but there were no holes, The window panes were broken but the sashes were intact. The chandelier and wall sconces had long ago fallen and sent shattered glass sprawling across the floor. Remnants of broken furniture lay everywhere, and the walls were lacking almost all of their plaster and had holes with broken wood pulled out.

Someone was looking for something. Looters.

He shook his head.

Men. Greed. That's what brought this city down. Pride and covetousness.

"This will do. It will take work but it will do."

It was an hour after noon when he emerged.

They'll be wondering where I am.

He hurried and was back at the inn in less than a quarter of an hour. Aurora heard the door open and stepped from the dining room where the dishes were being cleared.

"Where have you been?"

"A little sightseeing of the city." His voice was still hoarse, but no longer just a whisper.

"Sightseeing? What kind of sightseeing could get you this dirty?"

Kesniel looked down. "The city's quite a mess. I'll go clean up."

She shook her finger at him. "You do that, because you're not getting any lunch until you do."

Kesniel smiled. "Yes ma'am." He looked around the great room. "Where's Max?"

"Upstairs. It's a good thing they had a larger room. Apparently big men aren't infrequent here. The women made him a wonderful mattress, and the men made a frame, all to his size of course."

"Is he any better?"

"Breathing easier, and he's been awake a lot. He wants to talk but can't yet. We have someone sitting with him reading the King's words. I think that's Theron at the moment."

"Good. Go get my lunch. I'll be ready before you are."

Aurora looked him up and down. "I very much doubt that."

Chapter 29
The King-steward

Kesniel slipped out again after lunch, but Aurora and Theron watched him from an upstairs window.

"Follow him. He's up to something, and it's too early for him to do much."

"Count on me."

Theron left the inn and followed Kesniel at a discrete distance. It wasn't hard. Kesniel was going straight to wherever it was. Theron hardly even had to worry about hiding. Once Kesniel turned looking both directions as though uncertain about the way, but Theron was quickly in a doorway.

Kesniel continued on until he reached the corner where the residence was. He turned right instead of left and was out of sight for a minute. Theron ran to catch up and peered around the corner. Kesniel was still walking down the street but turned right into a side street. Once again, Theron rushed to catch up. He poked his head around the corner and was met eye to eye with Kesniel.

"Well?"

"I uh, I…uh, I…"

"Yes?"

"Aurora thought you needed someone to watch out for you."

"The feeble old man isn't capable of taking care of himself, eh."

"No. No. That's not it. You were almost killed. You need to rest and not over do."

"We need to work on your stalking." Kesniel paused. He pursed his lips and squinted. "This will work out fine. I know you're going to tell her about me, but you're also going to work for me now. I want you to get a hundred men – carpenters, builders, workmen – and meet me at the residence in an hour. I have a project that's urgent."

"What about you."

"Scouting. If I'm successful, there'll be another project. Now off with you. We must finish and be back to the inn before sundown."

Theron hurried off.

What does he have in mind? Obviously a building project, but what?

Kesniel moved among the streets from one empty domicile to another. None were what he was looking for and the time was running short. He turned left to head back to the Residence when he saw a promising place. It was only one story unlike the other houses on the street. Still, it seemed large enough for his purposes. He opened the door and was greeted by the musty smell of an old and long empty home. Dust particles held a merry dance in the light of his stone, and he suddenly had a great need to sneeze. He took out his handkerchief and wiped his nose and then covered it and his mouth to prevent further irritation.

He began his survey with the room to the right just off the living room. It had a large window and was quite spacious.

Perfect for a bedroom. She'll be able to keep a close eye on him.

The living room was large and airy.

Perfect for entertaining.

The dining room and kitchen beyond were somewhat smaller though.

First drawback. A challenge for dinner, but perhaps not too much of one.

A small hallway led to the only bedroom which was almost as large as the front room, and there was a room that had a bathtub.

Extraordinary! Such luxury! There are not more than 10 such rooms in all of Agapay! And the Residence has four of those. I never expected to find this. This makes it perfect.

He looked around once more. There was little repair work to be done, at least on the surface. Even the windows were intact. The stonework in the kitchen would need attention. The doors need to be rehung. The water tanks in both the kitchen and bath were coming off the walls, but all in all this would be an easy job.

Four or five men for a day or two at most. The kitchen and dining are small...but it will do nicely.

He closed the door behind him and headed for his meeting with Theron. He was pacing in the great hall when Theron finally arrived.

"What took so long?"

"I couldn't just pull them all from one place. I split it between five…no, six separate sites."

"Yes, well…"

Kesniel ascended the steps to the throne so he could be seen and heard.

"I've pulled you away from the domes you're working on for something equally important. Your new steward is thinking of you and not himself (typical of stewards), so we must think of his needs for him. As you can see, the residence is in a sad state of repair. The King-steward, Lachlaniel, needs quarters. The Great Hall needs repairs."

Just then there was a rustle of wings and feathers far above which drew the men's attention.

"Tomorrow work must begin here. We're not looking to make all the repairs this place needs. That might take years. What we do want is to restore this hall and make ready a living space from which Lachlaniel can conduct his duties."

The men nodded approval.

"I've also found a small house for his fiancée nearby. We'll need about five of you to work on that tomorrow. This is not to be some slipshod duty. You don't work for me or for the King-steward. You work for the King. I want your best. The King deserves nothing less. Let's make this place a credit to your city.

"Theron will oversee the projects and report to me. I'll be around from time to time to see how the work is progressing. Meet here early tomorrow, say an hour after dawn, for your assignments."

One of the men from the back shouted, "For King and Country!" and the others joined in.

Lachlaniel rubbed his eyes, stood, and stretched.

"It's been a long day. Spread the word for everyone to go home. They need a good night's sleep. I want everyone to assemble in front of the tower an hour after dawn, so tell them it will be an early morning for them."

Ewald cocked his head. "What's up?"

"We're doing good, but we're neglecting our neighbors. Many of them haven't even crossed the Bridge."

"You should get some rest too."

Lachlaniel sat back down and adjusted his boot. "I'm going to. First, I want to tend to Aman. I'll see you back at the inn. And don't be long. You need the rest as much as anyone."

Ewald threw the flap of the tent back and hurried off on his business. He stopped at the top of the steps. His shoulders drooped and he let out a sigh.

More than you know lad. More than you know.

Lachlaniel entered the inn. Aurora and Theron whispered in one corner. Kesniel was asleep in a comfortable chair. He closed the door behind him, and Aurora rushed over smiling. He kissed her forehead.

"I was expecting a bit more."

"Sorry." He took her in his arms and kissed her. "Better?"

"Much. I can see you're tired beyond thinking. Dinner's ready. I'll have it on the table in a minute."

"How's Max?"

"Better. He was awake for long stretches today. It's still hard for him to breath, and I think it will be a while before we hear his voice. All in all, he's doing quite well. Asher found plenty of Uset's breath outside the city as well as some other herbs that will help."

"Kesniel looks worn out."

"He's got something he's doing behind my back. I've got Theron watching him so he doesn't overdo."

They moved into the dining room. Kesniel gave a sly smile.

After dinner, Lachlaniel went upstairs and looked in on Max. Jason was sitting by him reading. Lachlaniel knelt down and took Max's hand. He gave a feeble smile and there was a twinkle in his eye.

"He seems to be doing better. His grip is a little stronger."

Jason looked up. "He's making progress, but it's slow."

"That's good to hear…about the progress I mean. Is he eating?"

"Broth today, tomorrow he may get soup."

Max smiled.

Lachlaniel squeezed his hand. "You rest. Many petitions are going before the King for you." Lachlaniel felt his grip firm up. He smiled at the big man. "I'm going to get some sleep. Tomorrow will be a long day, but you rest. Getting better is the only work you're allowed to do."

Max smiled as Lachlaniel stood up. The hallway was dimly lit by his stone. His room felt comfortable, a strangely familiar environment in which to sleep after only a couple of days. He laid down, but his mind was awhirl with things he wanted to say in the morning. Eventually, sleep came.

Lachlaniel ate early and arrived at the tower just after dawn. He climbed to the top and surveyed the city below.

I hope they can hear me well enough. Of course, we could hear the guards on the tower in Agapay quite well, so I don't see why they shouldn't.

Half an hour after dawn people began showing up below. The numbers grew slowly at first, but as the hour neared there was a mass of humanity stretching more than a mile from the tower in every direction.

Lachlaniel looked at his hands. They trembled.

Silly. I've been in quite a few fights, but I'm nervous about speaking to people?

He moved to the parapet. His blue armor shone brightly, and he was silhouetted by the light of the Great Stone.

"Citizens of Chara, servants of the King, the King has shown me a vision of what He wants this city to be. I will tell you of this in a moment, but first I want to give you a charge. We have made a good start in clearing away the debris and preparing to rebuild the domes, but we mustn't lose sight of those around us. Many are hurting and impoverished. Many of our neighbors are residents of the city but not citizens. We must be aware of what is going on around us. Stop what you're doing anytime you see someone who needs help and make sure they get it. If they aren't Ebenchaim, show them the way to the Bridge.

"This will be a long and great work. Our brothers beyond our walls have been given a hard task by the King. They are to bring the Basaners to the Bridge. They cannot kill them or use weapons to defeat them. Instead, they must lay down their very lives in order to bring those in darkness into the service of the King. We are to help them. The King wishes to make Chara the King's Arsenal. The greatest thing we can do is bring petitions to the King. You saw how when we entered our closets the King defended us and set the Basaners to flight. Now, we must use our closets to defend our brothers in the field. To that end, we need people who will go out to them and keep us informed of their needs.

"This city has great resources. Our brothers will be tortured, some will be killed, others will suffer deprivations and hunger. They will need food, medicine, clothing, and building materials and manpower to make secluded safe havens where they can meet without the Basaners finding them. We must make every effort to produce and provide whatever they need. This work calls for generosity and selflessness, so give your best. Let's make this city a crown jewel for the King!"

The crowd erupted into applause and shouts. Their words were indistinguishable, but he could see dancing and rejoicing to the farthest extent of the crowd.

They must've heard me.

He smiled. When he turned to go down, he found that Aurora had been standing behind him beside the Stone. She kissed him.

"I'm not much of a public speaker."

"It was perfect."

Kesniel who had not gone to the assembly was conferring with the innkeeper's wife.

"Now you've got it straight?"

"I'm to get some other women and decorate and furnish the house when the workmen are done." She paused with forefinger to her face. "We'll need to get started right away. There's a lot of preparations to make."

"Not a word of this to anyone."

"Yes sir. Mum's the word."

He went to the door. "Make sure about that."

"Yes sir."

He left to find Lachlaniel.

The next step is to impart as much as I have learned about being a steward to my young friend. We'll be spending quite a bit of time together. I hope it helps him.

The next weeks were filled with work, work and more work. The gates were rehung, except for the main gate to the city which had taken more damage than the rest, and the domes that had the least damage were repaired, though not as yet restored to their former beauty. Other domes were in various states of repair. Business had begun to open. The smiths, stone cutters, and wood workers were stretching to provide the needed materials. The needs of the people had been seen to, and every day more and more people crossed the Bridge.

Kesniel and Lachlaniel stepped out into the brisk morning air to begin another day of talking and overseeing the work. Kesniel looked up and took a deep breath of the autumn air.

"The time has come."

"Time?"

"We must be getting back to Agapay. If we delay, travel will become difficult before we get home."

Lachlaniel looked at the sky and the bare trees. "I hope I haven't delayed you too long already."

"No, my boy, but we must leave in the next couple of days." He rubbed his knuckles and they cracked loudly. "So I've arranged a little gathering. Tomorrow, you and Aurora must make yourselves extravagant as befits your new station."

"Is this what you've been doing? Aurora said you were doing something behind her back."

"Yes. Well. Give an old man a chance to do something for the young people who mean so much to him, will you?"

Lachlaniel smiled and patted the old man on the back. "We'll be ready. What time?"

"Twilight. You'll be picked up. Now, I must leave you. I have to see to the final preparations."

Max had improved over the weeks. He could sit up with help, talking no longer gave him a problem, though he was quiet when he did speak, and he didn't need as much sleep.

He listened intently as Lachlaniel and Aurora came in and went to their rooms to get dressed for the feast. Before he knew what was happening, he was surrounded by Theron, Asher, and six other men. They had him out the door and headed to the stairs before he could say anything. Behind them, six other men entered the room. He was whisked silently out the door and laid on a thick bed of straw in the back of a cart. Jason sat in a corner.

"What just happened?"

"We're taking you to the feast. Don't you want to go?"

"Of course."

"Then lay back and take it easy. The cobblestones might give you some trouble but your driver" – at this Asher looked back and smiled down at him – "has orders to be as gentle as possible."

"Asher? I'll be lucky if I survive the trip!"

Max raised his head. Theron led the men who had carried him out. Max laid back. He could hear another cart behind them.

"What's in the other cart?"

"We're moving you to new quarters. Something more permanent and homelike. When you've had enough of the festivities, we'll take you there."

The ride was not long, and though a little bumpy, the cushion of the straw was sufficient to keep him from having much pain.

Can't see where we're going.

The cart turned left and he raised his head. They had turned into a broad avenue.

"Lay back. We're almost there."

A right turn. Where are we going?

Jason answered as if he had read his mind. "The Residence."

They pulled to a stop, and he was gingerly and quickly removed from the cart and ushered inside. The entry hall was far larger than the one at

Agapay. There was no debris, everything had been swept and cleaned, but there had been no repairs here. They entered the Great Hall. Fires burned in braziers near the tables, of which there were many. Overhead, new lumber could be seen where holes had been repaired. The tables were covered in food, and cooks and attendants rushed here and there finishing the preparations for the guests. The smells made his stomach rumble. Jason talked to him as they made their way to the head table.

"How do you feel?"

"Fi… as well as can be expected."

"We've got you bound up tight. You should be able to sit in a chair for a while, but it won't be long before you're uncomfortable."

"I don't mind. I don't want to miss this."

"I'll be keeping an eye on you so you don't overdo. We're going to put the litter on four chairs until Lachlaniel and Aurora get here. Then we'll move you to a chair for dinner. When you've had enough, we'll move you back onto the litter and you can continue to enjoy yourself, but at some point we're going to take you home."

Max nodded.

"You rest. They should be here in half an hour. In the meantime, I'm sure you'll have lots of attention from your brothers-in-arms as they arrive."

Max put his good arm behind his head and stared at the ceiling.

Wish I could have a bite. The smells are driving me crazy.

Chapter 30
A Feast and Farewells

Lachlaniel slid on his suede gauntlets. All was set. He stepped into the hall and his jaw dropped. Aurora was ready too. He let out a long slow whistle. Her sapphire blue eyes had never been bluer. There was the ever-present golden glow from her hair. Her lips were as red as a ruby. Around her throat was his pearl glowing with iridescence on her milky white skin. Her white gown had puffs at the shoulders. She had on gloves that reached to her elbows. The gown tightened to her waist where pink roses had been woven into the fabric. From there, it flowed out wide to her ankles. Around the bottom were more pink roses. On her feet were shimmering shoes that caught the light and reflected it in a hundred hues.

"Close your mouth, silly."

Lachlaniel was taken aback. He gave her his arm, and they descended the stairs and went out the door. A black carriage was waiting. Kesniel sat facing backwards. He rose as Lachlaniel helped Aurora up. He took her hand, and she sat back on soft white leather. Lachlaniel climbed in as though it were a cart taking a load of his produce to market.

"No, no, no!" Kesniel scolded. "You're not a farmer or a general. You're a King-steward. You must act like one."

Lachlaniel frowned. "What more must I learn?"

He sat back beside Aurora and the carriage moved forward, the horse's hooves making a clip-clop sound on the cobblestones.

"You'll be entertaining dignitaries. You represent the King and His city. Act like it. Have fun. Give Him your best."

"I'm not cut out for this. Speeches, entertaining. I'm not ready."

"He obviously thinks you are. Humility is a good thing, but don't let it rob you of doing your best. There's a fine line between humility and self-deprecation."

Lachlaniel nodded.

Kesniel smiled and changed the subject. "You two look magnificent. It will be a perfect evening."

Aurora raised an eyebrow. "But where are we going?"

"To a feast. Didn't Lachlaniel tell you? This is my last night in the city. Tomorrow I and my men must leave for home."

"What about the wedding?"

"My dear, you two still have very much to do. But in the spring I'll return for the big event. The dispatchers are already sending messages again so you be sure to keep me informed as the time draws near."

She smiled and gripped Lachlaniel's hand as the carriage took a sudden turn to the left.

"Watch what you're doing!" Kesniel commanded.

"Sorry sir. I wasn't expecting it so soon."

"Well slow down. We're not in a hurry!"

The horse slowed to a walk, and they turned into the drive to the Residence.

"Oh, Lachlaniel!"

"Incredible! Surely this isn't where I'm expected to live?"

"It is. Tonight, everyone from Agapay and some from Chara are gathering in your honor."

"No. It's too much!"

"Not for the steward of the King. Remember what you told the people about the vision the King gave you for this city. The King's Arsenal will be a place of power and influence far and wide. You will reach people with the light who have never heard of the King, just as you hadn't before you left your farm."

The carriage pulled to a stop. Lachlaniel helped Aurora to her feet.

She kissed him on the cheek. "He's right you know."

Lachlaniel shrugged in submission. "Okay, I give up."

He stepped down and held Aurora's hand as she touched the pavement. Kesniel followed and then led the way to the doors. The carriage turned and went to the back to await the end of the night. Kesniel stepped into the antechamber of the great hall. It was clean and tidy but didn't have the polished look of the Residence at Agapay, but beyond the doors of the great hall things changed. In the light of the stones and the braziers, the floors sparkled with a polished shine that would almost make a mirror blush. The marble floors were beautiful. Down the center from the door to the dais where the throne sat ran a red granite walkway that also gleamed. Tables filled with food flanked the aisle. There was still much work to be done here, but the citizens had put in many hours to make this event a worthy return to the glory of the past.

A man in a green dress uniform, very ostentatious, stood by the door holding a brass staff. Kesniel entered and the man rapped his staff with a resounding clap that drew everyone's attention.

"Kesniel, King-steward of Agapay."

Kesniel entered the hall and Lachlaniel and Aurora moved forward. The brass staff came down again, and the sound rang through the hall.

"Lachlaniel, King-steward of Chara and Miss Aurora."

Everyone stood. Lachlaniel and Aurora followed Kesniel to the foot of the steps.

Kesniel took Aurora's arm and whispered to Lachlaniel. "Go up and sit on the throne. Say something appropriate but not too long."

Lachlaniel climbed the five steps and turned and sat on the throne.

"My friends. Uhm…I wish to thank you for this honor…and…and I wish also to thank the citizens of this city for their hard work and, uh, preparations. Mmm…uh… Let the feast begin."

Everyone clapped and laughed. Four men moved a table across the aisle and put it against the tables lining the aisle, others brought chairs. Ewald was waiting at the bottom of the steps for Lachlaniel.

"Best speech I ever heard."

Lachlaniel grinned from ear to ear. They took their seats with Lachlaniel in the center, Aurora to his right and Kesniel to his left. To Aurora's right sat Ewald decked out in dress uniform as was everyone. A large chair was brought in and placed at Kesniel's left. Eight men carried in Max and helped him into the chair. He groaned as he sat but smiled as the attendants brought platter after platter of food and set them before the guests.

The night was light-hearted. Pipers and lyres, trumpets and drums provided music during the dinner. Afterward, there were singers and dancers. Max had enough of sitting. He was moved to the litter which was supported by four chairs. The conversations were long and good. Tales of exploits and heroic deeds were recounted. As it grew late, Jason noticed that Max had fallen asleep. He called for the men who carried the weary guest from the hall.

A little later, Kesniel whispered to Lachlaniel, "Time for the night to end."

He stood and Lachlaniel and Aurora followed him to the door of the antechamber. The guests followed and shaking the hands of Lachlaniel and Aurora they filed out and headed home. When the last guest had left and the attendants were busy with the cleanup, Kesniel looked at the two young people.

"I have a couple of things to show you." He started walking.

They glanced at each other with puzzled looks and followed.

"You won't be returning to the inn tonight."

"Then where…" Lachlaniel's voice trailed off. "Here?"

"Yes, for you at least. The King-steward having taken the throne should begin living in the Residence. It's not your regular quarters, That will be some time. In fact, it's only the quarters for your personal attendant. You don't have one yet, but that will come too."

They walked down darkened corridors, the light of their stones showing the way. The hallways were clear of debris, but no repairs had yet been done. They passed massive doors. Though they were closed, Lachlaniel perceived they were his real quarters, and he shook his head in disbelief. There were many other doors along the hall, but Kesniel didn't even pause. At the end of the hallway, he took the handle and opened the door. He ushered them inside. The room was lit by many candles and a fire glowed warmly in the fireplace. There were two couches and four chairs. One sat near the fire. A beautiful rug adorned the floor. One wall was lined with bookshelves filled with books. Lachlaniel went to the window. It looked down on what should have been a gorgeous rose garden.

Kesniel came to his side and put his arm around him. "This place hasn't been used in over seventy years." He sighed. "Its beauty will be restored. In time. In time." He turned Lachlaniel to the left. "Take a look at the bedroom."

Lachlaniel stepped into a room with only a few candles. A wardrobe stood near the bed. There was a desk with a candelabra. Pen and ink stood ready for correspondence. The bed was large with canopy and curtains.

Kesniel looked at the blank expression on his young friend's face. "This is home. The cook and her husband are quartered near the kitchen. Pull that ringer or the one in the other room and they will appear shortly.

For the moment, they're the only ones living here besides you. Now for my other surprise."

He led them back through the corridors and hallways to the front of the Residence where the carriage was waiting. The ride was short and quick, though the driver did remember to take it slow. They pulled up to a house whose stone walls glistened in the light of the Great Stone.

Aurora stepped down from the carriage. "It's like it's covered in diamonds!"

"This is *your* new home."

"Mine?"

"Yours."

The steps and door had been widened. They opened the door and a golden glow of candlelight and firelight flooded the street.

"Enter quietly. Max will be asleep."

Jason sat in one of the chairs by the fire, the book he had been reading lay on the floor. The chairs were plush red velvet wingback chairs. There was a matching couch just beyond. The rug that covered the floor was white with a pink rose in each corner. In the center was an oval of a country scene. The bay window was adorned by lace curtains with a pink rose design. A table stood in front of the window with a vase full of red, white, and pink carnations, their fragrance filled the room.

"It's so wonderful."

Jason stirred. "Sorry. I didn't hear you come in." He rose. "Perhaps this would be better left till morning. Your brother is sleeping and shouldn't be disturbed."

"In there?" Aurora pointed at the wide door.

Kesniel nodded. "Yes. The workmen altered things to accommodate his size. And I think Jason is right. There'll be time to see things in the morning. I wanted Lachlaniel to know where you would be living. I have a feeling the streets from the Residence to here will be well traveled. Time to go home, son."

Lachlaniel kissed Aurora. "Good night dearest."

"Goodnight."

Jason followed them out but paused at the door. "If you need me, I'm across the street."

She went to the doorway and leaned against the jamb watching them go.

Lachlaniel looked at the note by his bed. Kesniel had made sure he would be at the gate early. He dressed by the light of his stone and headed to Aurora's. When he arrived, before he could knock, the door swung open.

"I've been watching for you."

"A note from Kesniel?"

"Yes. Breakfast is ready. Get Jason. He's eating with us. He'll watch Max."

Moments later, they were seated before steaming coffee, and bacon and eggs. Conversation was light and steered clear of the departure of their friends. Aurora finished first and began clearing her dishes.

"I'll get Max's breakfast before I leave," she said as she entered the kitchen.

Jason swallowed his coffee hurriedly and set down his cup. "No need for that. I want him to sleep as long as he can. I'll get his breakfast when he wakes up."

Aurora returned from the kitchen and sat back down. The two men were finishing their coffee.

"Thank you."

"Don't worry about the dishes either. You don't want to delay your friends."

Aurora reached over and took Lachlaniel's hand. He could perceive her sadness. It mirrored his own. He stood up, cup in hand, and drained the last drops.

Setting it down with a clank, he said, "Well then, let's be going."

Aurora grabbed a coat against the early morning chill and Lachlaniel threw his cape about him. They rode in silence, Lachlaniel on Aman and Aurora on Cinnamon which had been bought and brought to the city by Kesniel's orders. They could see from a distance the men lined up on their horses and the three wagons of supplies he had ordered all waiting for the order to leave. Kesniel, astride his horse waited in the lane with Ewald standing beside him.

"I thought you two might not make it." Kesniel took a bag that hung at his side and handed it to Lachlaniel. "I found these in the reliquary."

"What is it?"

"Enkratia seeds. Plant these after the trees begin to bud. In three years, perhaps two, the King's fruit will be hanging from their boughs."

Lachlaniel looked at the bag. "Thank you. Thank you. When they produce, we'll be sure to send you some."

"Good. And I'll send you some Ariete and Gnosis fruit. A good way to start commerce between our cities."

Aurora stared at Ewald with a puzzled look. "Why aren't you on a horse?"

"I'm not going."

Lachlaniel's brow furrowed. "Not going?"

Kesniel smiled a sly smile. "No. He's staying with you. You need a good sergeant major who only takes orders from you. He's the start of your guard and army."

Ewald's grin spread into a broad smile, then faded. "Unless you don't want me."

"Not want you? I might be attacked by another wolf."

"Bah!" Ewald laughed. "You'd have your sword drawn and his head cut off before I could grab my hilt."

Just then a stranger walked by headed for the gate.

Lachlaniel grabbed his sleeve. "Whoa there. Where do you think you're going?"

"The King has called me and sent me out there, just as you said."

"What's your name?"

"Rishown."

"Before you go out there, we must see that you carry a load from the city to our people out there. Stay here. When my friends leave, we'll get you a cart and all the provisions it can carry. Nor will we send you empty-handed. We'll talk to the King and see what we should give you for your trip as well."

Kesniel drew his sword. "Draw yours too, Lachlaniel. Kneel Rishown."

Lachlaniel did so and followed Kesniel's movements. They laid the blades on the top of Rishown's head.

"May the King bless thee and keep thee whithersoever He sends thee. May you prosper in your efforts and be an instrument that brings many across the Bridge. And be sure to send regular messages to your King-steward."

Rishown got up. "I will sir, and thank you sirs."

"Time for us to go. Walk beside me to the gate."

They dismounted and the four friends trod down the lane. The only sounds were the clip-clop of the hooves of their horses and the noise of his men falling in behind them. Kesniel turned aside at the gate, its empty broken arch a stark reminder of what they had been through. Kesniel took Aurora's hand and kissed it.

He mounted his horse and said, "Keep an eye on our young steward. He's going to need a lot of help from you."

She wiped away a tear with her free hand. "I will. Be safe."

"And you use your closet and your stone. You're going to need to stay in constant contact with the King now."

Lachlaniel smiled. "I will."

"Ewald. I expect you to see that no trouble develops here."

"Count on me."

"May the King give you the eye of a hawk. Well, my friends the time has come."

He turned his horse and rode through the gate. The three quickly ascended the stairs and waved and watched from the wall until they were out of sight.

The End
Of
Book Two

Visit my website at larryparisbooks.com

Maps

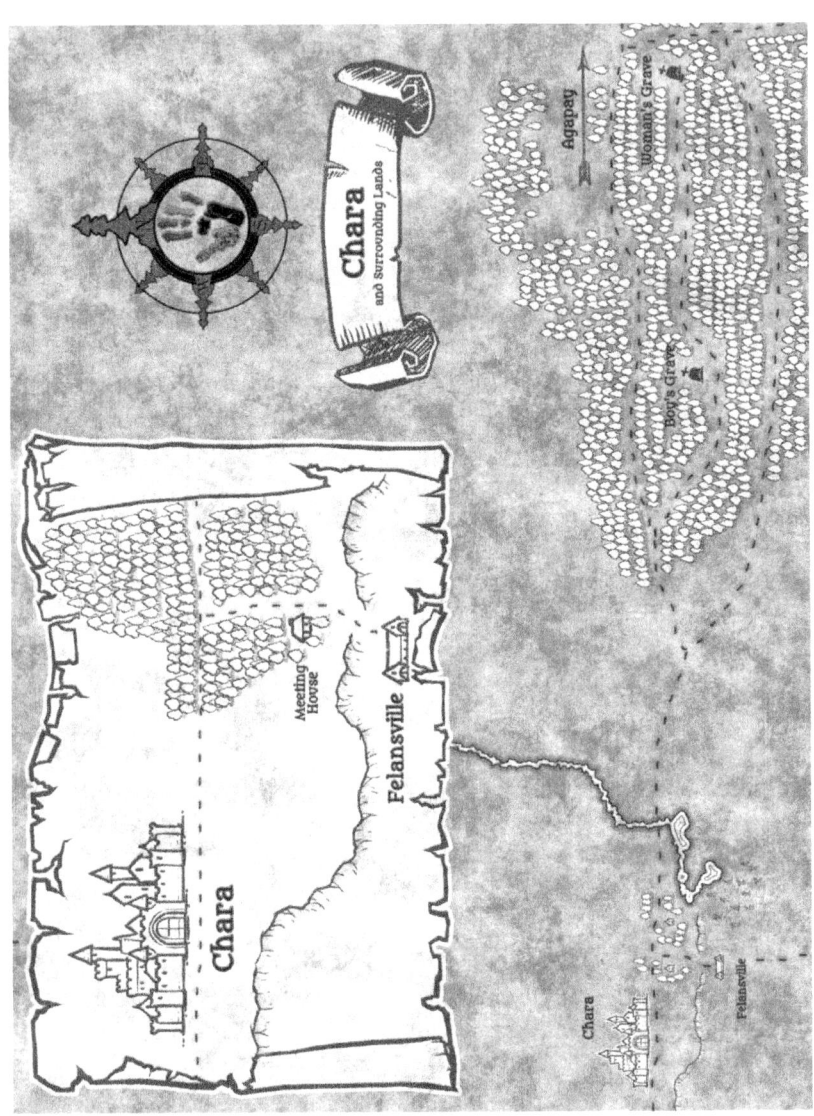

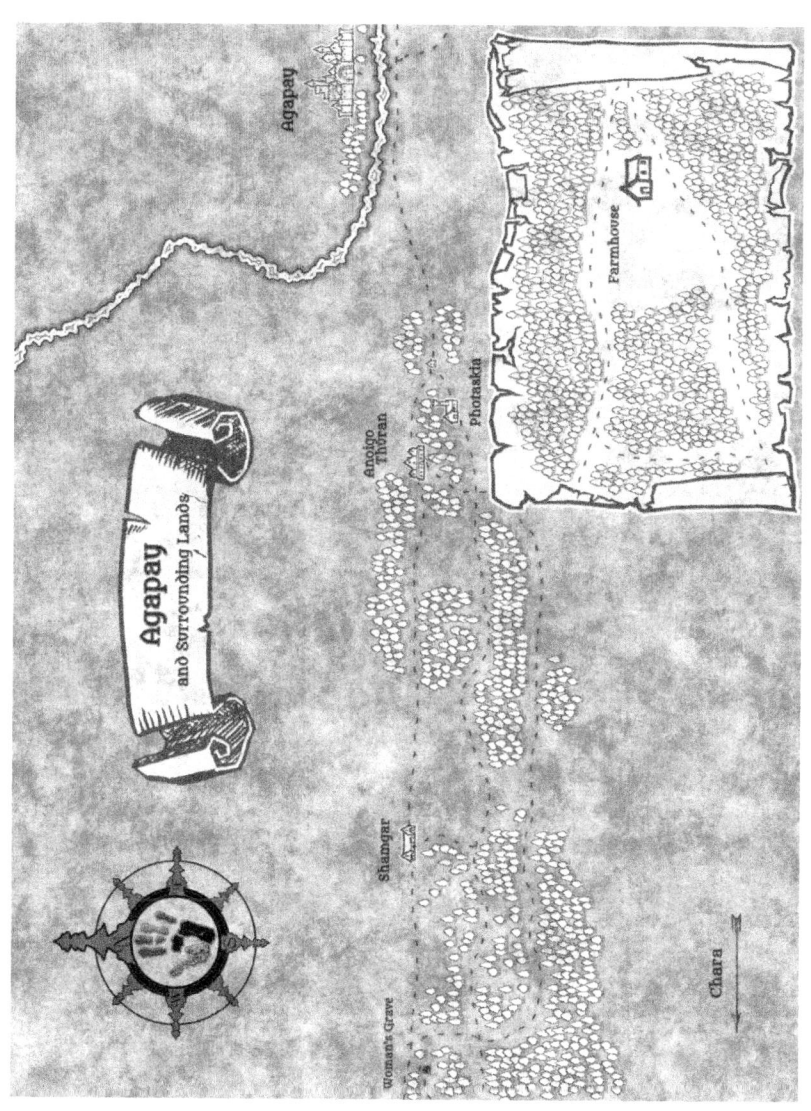

Names
Meanings and Pronunciations

Abiezer (Ab ee ay zer) – father of help (Hebrew)

Agapay (Ah ga pay) – love (Greek)

Aldhelm (Ald helm) – a veteran (old helmet) (Old English)

Aman (Ah man) – faithful (Hebrew)

Andre (Awn dray) – manly (Greek) of Felansville (Fell ans ville) – town of the young wolves (Irish)

Anoigo Thuran (An oy go Thur an) – open (Greek), door (Greek)

Arla (R la) – ingathering of the harvest (Keltic)

Arete (Ah re tay) – moral excellence, virtue (Greek)

Asher (Ash er) – happy, blessed (Hebrew), Kenspeckle (Ken speck ul) – conspicuous (Scottish)

Aurora (Or roar ah) – the dawn (Latin)

Basaners (Bass an ers) – from basanos, torment, torture (Greek)

Bercan (Bur kin) – little spear (Keltic)

Brigit (Bridge it) – strength (Keltic)

Capaleanan (Cap all e a non) – lover of horses (Irish)

Casamir (Cas a meer) – preacher of peace, also disturber of peace (Slavic)

Cashin (Cash in) – curly (Celtic)

Chara (Car ah) – joy (Greek)

Chuchoteur (shu sho tear) – whisperer (French)

Cinnamon (Sin a mon) – fire or brown (of unknown origin)

Cora short for

Cora Lee (Core ah Lee) – maiden, damsel, or virgin (Greek) and meadow (Teutonic)

Damon (Day mon) – one who subdues (Greek)

Dan – judging, perceiving truth (Hebrew)

Diaphanous (di af an us) – transparent (Greek)

Ebenasa (E ben ah sa) – stone carrier (Hebrew)

Ebenchaim (E ben kime) – living stones (from Eben - a stone [Hebrew] and Chaim – life [Hebrew])

Edom (E dum) – in this case an everyman reference though it means red (Hebrew)

Egkratia (Egg krash e ah) – self-control (Greek)

Einar (I nar) – enduring warrior (Teutonic)

Eleutherias (El u thear e ahs) – Liberator (Greek)

Elrad (El rad) – wise counsel (Teutonic)

Emmett (Em it) – industrious (Old English)

Ewald (E wald) – ever powerful (Teutonic)

Farrah (Fair ah) – joy (Arabic)

Felansville (Fell ans ville) – wolf town (Irish)

Fragel (Frag el) – the wielder of the cat o' nine tails or scourge (Greek)

Garth (Gar th) – a gardener (Teutonic)

Grady (Gr a dee) – illustrious, noble (Irish)

Halvord (Hal vord) – stone guard (Teutonic)

Hughes, Mrs. (Hews) – bright heart, mind, and spirit (English)

Ignatius (Ig nace e us) – Fiery (Latin)

Jason (J son) – healer (Greek)

Jocey (Jo see) short for

Jocelyn (Joss cell lin) – joyful (Latin)

Kerry (Carry) – dark (Celtic)

Kesniel (Kez knee el) – God is my strength (Hebrew)

Kieran (Ki ran) – black (Irish)   Formerly: Oriel (oar e el) – God is my light (Hebrew)

Lachlaniel (Lack lan e el) – champion of God (Celtic)

Leah (Lee ah) – weary (Hebrew)

Leofwine (Lee off wine) – dear friend (Anglo Saxon)

Max – greatest (Latin)

Meph or

Mephistopheles (Mef fis tof fell ease) or more properly

Mephosphilis (Mef ohs fill is) – not light loving or hater of light (Greek)

Nestor (Nes tur) – one who remembers (Greek)

Nosis (No sis) – from Gnosis knowledge (Greek)

Ophelia (O feel e ah) – help, service, benefit (Greek)

Photaskia (Fo tahs kia) – from photos – light (Greek) and skia – shadow (Greek)

Shamgar (Sham gar) – stranger (Hebrew)

Skotos (Sko toss) – darkness (Greek)

Solveig (Soul vig) – dark power (Teutonic)

Thelma (Thel ma) – nurse (Greek)

Theron (Th air on) – hunter (Greek)

Thoronis (Thor o nis) – bold, courageous (from Thoron [Teutonic] and Thoris [Gothic])

Tova (Tow va) – good (Hebrew)

Uset (U set) – Unseen (Danish)

Valisa (Va lis a) – Luminous, Bright (Finnish)

Velius (Vel e us) – concealed (Latin)   Also called: Dugal (do gall) – dark stranger (Celtic)

Viera (Vi era) – faith (Slavic)

Wilmot (Wil mot) – resolute courage (Teutonic)

Wyn (Win) – Joy, delight: also a friend (Old English)

Zenia (Zen e ah) – hospitality (Greek)

Flowers and Their Meanings
(In the order of their appearance)

Golden Hibiscus – friendship, found on her doorstep

Oak Leaved Geraniums – true friendship, at her door

Lilac – first emotions of love, on the doorstep

Asters – love and patience, doorstep

Yellow Iris – passion, at her place on the dining room table

Gardenia – secret love, on her favorite chair

Red Rose – love, on the window sill of her bedroom

Red Salvia – forever mine, by her head on her pillow

Tulip – declaration of love

Gladiolus – you pierce my heart on the table by her bed

Oleander – beware, on the barrel of black powder at Jocelyn's house

Tansy – malevolence, on the lid of a barrel of gun powder in the basement of the house where Aurora lives.

Lobelia – I declare war, between the bodies of Murphy and the horse

Black Rose – death, on the wall by the body of a guard.

Made in the USA
Middletown, DE
01 October 2021

KICKING THE HABIT
Quitting Pornography Under Grace

Joel Hughes, Ph.D.

Copyright ©2018 by New Paradigm Publishing

Kicking the Habit: Quitting Pornography Under Grace by Joel Hughes, Ph.D.

The views expressed in this book are those of the author.

Printed in the United States of America

Cover designer: Alex Herbers

Unless otherwise indicated, all Bible quotations are taken from the New International Version (NIV, 2011). Scriptures taken from the Holy Bible, New International Version®, NIV®. Copyright © 2011 by Biblica, Inc.™ Used by permission of Zondervan. All rights reserved worldwide. www.zondervan.com The "NIV" and "New International Version" are trademarks registered in the United States Patent and Trademark Office by Biblica, Inc.™ and all quotations meet the terms of use guidelines.

For information contact:

P.O. Box 1556 Stow, OH 44224

jhughes @ neoxenos.org (no spaces)

http://www.kickingthehabitbook.com

Table of Contents

Part I: Preliminary considerations

> In which I describe my rationale for this new approach to help Christian men stop using internet pornography and explain the smoking cessation metaphor on which it is based.

1. Do you want to quit pornography? — 5
2. Porn cessation is like smoking cessation — 15

Part II: Spiritual truth relevant to quitting pornography

> In which I outline some of what the Bible has to say on sexuality and topics that relate to using and quitting pornography, like the worship dimension to sexuality and your identity in Christ.

3. Pornography has a spiritual dimension — 31
4. Our identify in Christ defeats pornography — 37

Part III: Looking before you leap, or planning to quit

> In which you plan for a scheduled quit date, so that everything is ready and you maximize your chances for success.

5. Planning to quit part 1 — 49
6. Planning to quit part 2 — 61

Part IV: Breaking free, or quitting

> In which we learn that actively quitting involves both defensive and offensive strategies for coping with urges, breaking old habits, and establishing a healthier lifestyle incompatible with compulsive pornography use.

7. Quitting part 1: Defense — 71
8. Quitting part 2: Offense — 85

Part V: Your porn-free life, or staying quit

> In which we learn the risk factors for relapse, the difference between a lapse and a relapse, and make plans for getting back to quitting if anything goes wrong.

9.	Avoiding mishaps, lapses, and relapse	93
10.	What if I fail?	101
11.	Epilogue	107

Table 1: **Elements of Quitting**	19
Table 2: **Man's Part and God's Part in Quitting**	20
Table 3: **Spirituality and Porn**	31

Figure 1: **Phases of Quitting**	51

Appendix A: **Recommended Resources**	113
Appendix B: **References**	117
Acknowledgements	115
About the author	116

scientific literature, and there are some themes in the Christian books that may actually make stopping harder if they become a focus of "quit attempts" (a smoking cessation term). I'll have more to say about that later.

Furthermore, there is a spiritual dimension to stopping pornography that is simply not recognized by the scientific research literature. The spiritual dimension of pornography is only addressed by Christian sources. This is a major problem with the scientific literature. Although some problematic health behaviors—like not exercising enough—are just not that spiritual, there are other behaviors—like unprotected sex with same-sex partners—which are profoundly spiritual in nature. The medical and health psychology literature on unprotected sex would be mostly concerned with preventing the transmission of HIV and other diseases, whereas the Christian should be aware of the intensely spiritual nature of sexual sin and the varying levels of spiritual depravity that various sexual sins can reflect. Porn has a spiritual dimension, and in my view, the spiritual truths of the Bible must be integrated with the health behavior change literature for there to be any chance of success. Furthermore, some Christian sources have a more helpful theology of behavior change (*aka* sanctification, or letting go of sin) than others, so I will be very selective in the sources from which I draw when making spiritual recommendations.

What can this book accomplish?

With this book, I am offering you a new and different approach. If you already quit using porn, you probably don't need this book unless you are trying to help someone else who is struggling. If you are using porn and read this book along with completing all the homework and action items, you may greatly reduce or stop your use of pornography. I say "may" because I can't prove it. There has only been one randomized controlled trial of a behavioral intervention to stop pornography use among religious volunteers. They were Mormons, and it worked, but that was only one study. We'll take a closer look at that study later. The point is that this is "off label" prescribing. We know that escitalopram (Lexapro™) sort of works for depression, but will it work for bipolar disorder? There's no studies that prove that it works, but psychiatrists prescribe escitalopram for bipolar disorder all the time.

By the way, a *randomized controlled trial* is the gold standard of the medical literature, in which study subjects are randomly assigned to an intervention (e.g., a medication or some therapy) or a control group (e.g., a placebo, a waiting list, or no treatment). These groups are then compared to determine whether or not the treatment works using a controlled experiment. This research design is how we know that a new medication is safe and effective, and how we discovered that certain psychotherapies can eliminate panic attacks or reduce binging and purging in bulimia nervosa. But in the area of internet porn use, the scientific literature is just not there. Furthermore, none of the approaches offered in the Christian self-help books have been evaluated scientifically. How could they be? No one will fund an expensive research study of an experimental treatment for something that secular society is not convinced is even a problem. Therefore, I cannot cite any studies showing that this will work.

I am very confident that the elements I imported into the approach outlined here work for cigarette cessation, but will a similar approach work for porn cessation when combined with elements addressing the spiritual nature of porn use? I can't prove it, but it makes a lot of sense that it would. I think it's worth a try, for reasons that will become clear in the next chapter.

As an aside, anecdotes are not scientific evidence. Just because someone lost 50 pounds drinking grapefruit juice infused with ginger tea along with a daily fiber supplement does not mean that doing the same would help *you* lose weight. Anecdotes sell books and make very compelling stories, so people often believe them, but they are not valid scientific evidence. Therefore, there are no success stories in this book. Also, there are also no sordid autobiographical details about me. There is a long history in addiction counseling where some alcoholic, drug addict, or sex addict quits and becomes a guide to those who are struggling for freedom. Good for them; I have no problem with that. However, there is no evidence that former addicts make the best counselors. As an example, I was never a cigarette smoker, but I have helped a lot of people quit smoking.

Also, in the approach I will describe, I want to avoid social comparisons. If I write anecdotes about someone who struggled with porn to this or that degree, it invites a social comparison that we just don't need: unhelpful at best, and damaging to the quitting process at worst. You may feel better if you're not doing as badly as they were ("Wow, 6 hours a day, lost their job, started hiring prostitutes, got divorced…my problem isn't so bad, maybe I don't need help!"), and you may feel worse if you're doing worse than they are ("Oh no, they were racked with guilt from a thrice-weekly 15-minute habit…I've been buying masturbation toys and own stock in lube companies…I'm doomed!").

Additionally, I have encountered a number of men who have had essentially no trouble with internet porn at all. Don't compare yourself to them; you'll just feel jealous. Assume that, in our hypersexual, endlessly-connected, technology-drenched culture, nearly every adult male has been through the looking-glass (*and* that some have found a way back from "pornderland"). For example, over 35% of protestant clergy report that internet pornography is a current temptation.[2] These are the pastor types, who have a vested interest in minimizing their problems, meaning that it's probably an underestimate. So keep your focus on yourself. This is your problem, and there's no point in comparing yourself to anyone else to justify yourself or find more reasons for despair. The appropriate amount of porn use is *none*, so focus on making this about your path to porn cessation.

Why did I write this book?

I wrote this book because I need this book. I need a resource that is concrete, practical, and solution-focused for the men I work with. The men who ask me for help have already tried to stop on their own, and have read this or that book and installed this or that software, but it didn't work. Sure, we could debate whether they were sincere or trying hard enough, and perhaps they needed more intense help such as a group counseling program offered by a church somewhere. However, ultimately I'm writing this book to have it available for them: the men I know who need it. I want to make it available to all Christian men who would like to try one more approach—one that's a bit different.

I was also inspired by an epiphany that I had recently as I scoured the literature, read yet another Christian book on stopping pornography, and reflected on how I was trained in health psychology. Specifically, it occurred to me that there are a lot of commonalities between cigarette addiction and compulsive pornography use. When I was trained in smoking cessation, for which there is a massive scientific literature spanning over 50 years, I learned to do the things that worked. I was even certified as a trainer in a specific smoking cessation therapy. (The details are not important and I'm not advertising anyone's smoking cessation product.) The program I learned claims a 50% quit rate at 6-month follow-up, and we were able to achieve similar results in group treatment at a Veterans Affairs Medical Center where I interned. A 50% quit rate is about five times the quit rate for people who just try to stop on their own.

What if I simply imported the relevant approaches and techniques of smoking cessation into a book for stopping pornography use?

When I began to compare and contrast smoking cessation with the books on stopping pornography use, I became convinced that this could be a good and effective idea. Although they are often very helpful, some elements of the books on stopping porn are just barking up the wrong tree. We can discard that material and replace it with techniques known to work for one of the most vexing addictions to afflict mankind.

Furthermore, my background, which combines health researcher, clinical psychologist, and Christian minister, is probably somewhat rare. I thought, "What if I combine everything I know from these three domains into one approach?" From my research career I can draw on an academic approach to evaluating the literature and finding the hints and tidbits that might be helpful to apply to the problem. From my training as a clinical psychologist I can incorporate everything I know about how behavioral treatments work. And finally, from my work as an elder in my church, I can integrate this approach with my best understanding of the spiritual nature of sexual sin and how Christians grow spiritually and set aside the sins that ruthlessly cling to their lives. I became convinced that this was a good idea, so I began to write this book.

I will use the smoking cessation metaphor throughout this book, and I have designed an action plan that combines elements from smoking cessation with truths from the Bible. There's "man's part" and "God's part" to this plan. The techniques from smoking cessation are "man's part," or the things you can do to present yourself to God to be changed. The truths from the Bible describe "God's part," because ultimately you need to be set free from this fleshly compulsion, and no amount of self-help will accomplish that by itself; only Jesus Christ can rescue you from your flesh (Romans 7). So, I will try to combine the spiritual truths of how Jesus frees us from bondage to sin with the active role you play in submitting yourself to be rescued. In using the smoking cessation metaphor, I will even call trying to stop using internet pornography "porn cessation" and we will focus on achieving a successful "quit attempt," which are ideas directly lifted from the smoking cessation literature. The purpose of this terminology will become clear in the rest of the book.

Caution!

This book is not for everyone. This book is for Christian men who want to stop using internet pornography. First, if you are not a Christian, the spiritual dimension to pornography will be nonsense to you. You do not have access to the spiritual power of Jesus Christ and the Holy Spirit of God to help you. You do not believe in the existence of Satan or the reality of spiritual warfare as it may relate to pornography use. Second, this book is for Christian *men*. I understand that more women than ever are using internet pornography, but I have no idea whether they are using for the same reasons and therefore, I cannot make confident recommendations regarding what they should do to stop. Maybe the approach here would work for women, but at this point that's another topic for a different book.

Also, this book will not work if you are not willing to talk to anyone else about it. Recruiting social support is a mandatory part of porn cessation. This is not a *self*-help manual, because it will only work in the context of close Christian relationships. It can be completed by just you and one confidant, or in small groups, but the only context in which people achieve a successful quit attempt are relational. The reasons for this should be obvious. Why change if it's a secret no one knows about?

Also, if you are currently engaged in illicit or illegal sexual behavior, you need more intense help than this book can provide. Whereas there is little scientific research on behavioral treatments for porn cessation, there is a literature on sexual offenders, for example. So if you are a practicing sex offender or similar, please get professional help. "Self-help" is not responsible when professional help is a better option. Therefore, if you are using the internet to connect with other human beings to actually meet up and have sexual encounters, you need more intense help than this book can provide.

Third, if you don't think you have a problem or you don't want to stop, then you are not ready to implement an action plan. Smokers don't join smoking cessation programs if they are determined to keep smoking (or they just pretend, in order to get someone off their back). That is not successful, and neither is porn cessation for the coerced or noncommittal.

Over-engineered?

Some of you reading the later chapters will decide that the approach offered is overkill: too many steps, too complicated, too hard. Well, I agree that this approach is "over-engineered," which refers to the design of a product that is more durable or complex than absolutely necessary. I once bought an inexpensive "leather" recliner from a department store for less than $600. It looked great and was comfortable, until the reclining mechanism broke in less than a year. After another year, the leather wore through and I figured out that "bonded leather" means a wafer-thin coating of leather over fabric, which wears out instantaneously. I threw it away and went to buy a La-Z-Boy® recliner. I thought it would cost a lot more, but I found a fabric upholstered recliner on sale for less than $500.

Why La-Z-Boy®? It has a *lifetime warranty* on the reclining mechanism. That mechanism is over-engineered, so it is a robust smooth-operating recliner guaranteed to last. My point? Perhaps some of you can stop using porn by just using a couple or three tools or tips from the book. I don't recommend that. Sometimes it's worth the extra money or effort to get a top-quality product. For people who are quitting smoking, it's often literally a life-and-death battle. Some stop on their own, with a 10% chance of success each time they try. Some use nicotine replacement and/or medicine, which increases their chances. But those who work the full program were getting a 50% quit rate in the groups I ran. Applied to pornography, *if you're serious about quitting, it's worth it to take the time and implement as many of the recommendations as you can tolerate.* Even if it feels over engineered, it's designed to be that way, to maximize your chances of success.

Embrace the Pain

Finally, this is not going to be a painless process. Like quitting smoking, there will be a lot of discomfort involved in quitting porn. You are forcing your brain to re-wire itself, and you're asking God to perform open-soul surgery on you. Pain is to be expected during this process, and is completely normal. Peter once said "if you suffer, it should not be as a murderer or thief or any other kind of criminal, or even as a meddler" (1 Peter 4:15). Well, you've been suffering from feeding your flesh (Galatians 6:7-8), so putting it to death is going to hurt (Romans 8:14). There will be pain, and this is where some of the coping and accountability techniques we will discuss later may be helpful. One Marine I used to counsel said "pain is just weakness leaving my body." I don't know if that is a Marine Corps mantra or not, but I liked it. Any pain involved in cutting porn out of your habits is just weakness leaving your life.

Ready, Set, Go

If you are a Christian man ready to stop using pornography, if you have someone to talk to as you read this book, and if you can tolerate my smoking cessation metaphor, then keep reading and begin planning for a successful quit attempt. We'll start by fleshing out the smoking cessation metaphor, so that you can see the purpose of the various elements of this porn cessation program.

How to use this book

The first draft of this workbook consisted of six chapters and an epilogue. However, the feedback I received suggested that not everyone wants to read chapters that are 15 single-spaced pages long. Also, some people felt that four worksheets to complete at the end of some chapters was too many assignments to complete thoroughly in-between "recovery group" meetings. So, I divided some of the chapters and arranged them in sections. Of course, how you use this book is up to you. If you need to take 10 weeks to get free from porn, and want to have time to mull things over or discuss them in a group, that's fine. On the other hand, if you are working with an accountability partner and want to rocket through the book entire sections at a time, that would also be a good approach. If it were me, I'd consider reading the entire book over a weekend and then taking 2-4 weeks to re-read each section and do all the assignments with a trusted friend. Your pace doesn't particularly matter, although I do not recommend reading some of the book and then setting it down for long periods of time. Therefore, one assignment at the end of every chapter is to set a definite day and time that you will keep moving forward by reading the next chapter. Declaring your intention and scheduling an appointment with yourself increases the chances that you won't get distracted and neglect to do anything. Of course, what matters more than your schedule is your commitment to doing enough of the assignments and enacting enough strategies to kick the habit for good.

Chapter Summary and Assignments

- Quitting porn is like quitting any addictive health behavior, and smoking is a great example with a large scientific literature.
- Sexuality is also spiritual, so quitting porn requires both "man's part" and "God's part" for success.
- Combining insights from health behavior change and Biblical truth is a new approach that has a high probability of success.

Assignments

- Worksheet for this week: Are you ready?
- Head over to www.kickingthehabitbook.com to see if there's any free content created recently for you to download.
- What day and time will you read the next chapter? Make an appointment with yourself to keep up your momentum.

Worksheet 1: Are you ready?

Take some time to *privately* contemplate these questions:

- How much have you struggled with porn, really? How many years? How often? What types?
- Are you really ready to try to stop? Most people are "ambivalent" with conflicting motives. It's important to acknowledge mixed motives, so you're honest with yourself. Otherwise you may only try half-heartedly.
    - What makes you want to stop?
    - What makes you want to continue to use internet porn?
- Can you tolerate the smoking cessation metaphor? You don't have to like it that much, and maybe you've never been a cigarette smoker. But, can you appreciate that quitting cigarettes is incredibly hard for most people, so they have a lot better chance of success when they complete a bona-fide smoking cessation treatment?
- Are you willing to learn about the spiritual aspects of sexuality and pornography? Do you think God will help you quit porn?
- Can you suffer? What do you think will be the worst part of trying to stop porn?
- Who will work with you? Who can you trust? Who will read this book and talk with you as you do the work of quitting? You can't do this alone.
- Are you willing to spend a little money? You might want some of the books in **Appendix A.** You might need to install some software that costs money.

Kicking the Habit: Quitting Pornography Under Grace by Joel Hughes, Ph.D.
Copyright ©2018 by New Paradigm Publishing

Chapter 2

Porn cessation is like smoking cessation

Agenda for Chapter 2

To understand how the smoking cessation metaphor fits quitting pornography. For example, quitting cigarettes is *incredibly hard*, because nicotine is very addictive, especially in cigarette form. But smoking cigarettes has quantifiable negative effects—notably death—so there is a huge scientific literature on stopping smoking. There are fairly sophisticated smoking cessation programs that achieve a high rate of success compared to trying to stop without help. Internet pornography is a relatively recent phenomenon, but it has exploded in recent decades. There is almost no scientific literature on quitting pornography, but it is a highly compulsive behavior like cigarette smoking. It may not be physically addictive in the way that nicotine creates a physical dependence, but there are enough similarities that we can apply a lot of the smoking cessation techniques to quitting porn, if you're willing to accept that metaphor. This should provide guidance on what will work, and will therefore greatly increase your chances of success.

Cigarette smoking has a short history but a long future

Smoking cigarettes was rare before the Civil War. Then, a tobacco curing accident in North Carolina made cigarettes a lot better. Stephen was tending the curing fires in 1893, but fell asleep. He rushed to stoke the nearly extinguished fire, and the intense heat transformed the tobacco into a bright yellow color. Happy accident! Bright leaf tobacco was invented, and became very popular. During World War I, military personnel were issued cigarettes with their rations. By World War II, the best-selling *Lucky Strike* cigarettes were sponsoring the Jack Benny show. Most returning World War II veterans were addicted to cigarettes. However, awareness was dawning that cigarettes were responsible for the new epidemic of a rare cancer that physicians would previously have encountered only once or twice during their entire career: lung cancer. Since the Surgeon General's report in 1964, everyone knows that *cigarette smoking kills*. Half of all long-term smokers lose some years of life to cigarettes. Every year between 1 and 2 million Americans die of lung cancer, and lung diseases are now the third leading cause of death in America. Research on the dangers of smoking, smoking prevention, and smoking cessation has grown steadily. There is now a 60+ year history of scientific research on smoking. A search of the scientific and medical literature I conducted in July, 2017 found over 600 clinical trials of smoking cessation alone (i.e., experiments testing if a smoking cessation treatment works).

Smoking cessation is hard but possible

Why is there so much research on stopping smoking? Because it's necessary, and because it's *very hard*. Nicotine is incredibly addictive, and cigarettes are essentially a method of free-basing nicotine. Nicotine use causes physical dependence, so there are withdrawal symptoms and intense cravings when people try to quit. Some classic studies showed that the number of cigarettes smoked by heavy smokers was finely tuned to maintain a steady level of blood nicotine. When these smokers reported that they smoked more in social situations or when under stress, the lab results showed that social settings and stress levels actually changed the rate of nicotine metabolism, resulting in more smoking. They were maintaining a constant blood level of nicotine. The uncontrollable urges come from falling blood nicotine levels.

Cigarettes are also psychologically addictive. Smoking habits are deeply ingrained into people lives; so for example, a long term smoker may have lit up 100,000 times. Smokers may have made unconscious associations that trigger lighting a cigarette, like simply starting their car. Smokers have been known to say that they absent-mindedly lit another cigarette while one was still burning half-finished in the ashtray. Stopping these deep-seated habits is very difficult. Then there are the costs of stopping smoking. People gain weight when they quit. People often get depressed during the quitting process. People lose "friends" when they don't show up to huddle and chat outside the door during breaks. People are naturally reluctant to try to stop smoking, especially when they still feel fine.

Stopping smoking is so hard that the success rate is only about 10% when people attempt to stop smoking "cold turkey" on their own. That doubles or triples when you add nicotine replacement therapy or other pharmacological help. Also, the rate of smoking has gone down when society changes, in terms of higher tobacco taxes, growing negative attitudes, stricter smoking laws, or higher prices for a pack of cigarettes. Therefore, barriers to smoking coming from outside the person will reduce smoking. Although stopping smoking seems impossible, we know that fully half of the people who become regular cigarette smokers eventually quit.

Think about that. Half of smokers become non-smokers!

The obvious implication is that people who want to quit smoking should keep trying, because although the chances during any given quit attempt are probably only 10-30%, eventually many people get there. It's never too late to quit smoking. I remember one patient with severe chronic obstructive pulmonary disease who was smoking three packs each day when I met him. During our time working together, he gave up cigarettes for good. I'll never forget hearing him describe how delicious food started to taste after he quit. A baked potato is like candy for someone who hadn't been able to taste their food for 30 years.

Fortunately, we know a lot about how to quit smoking. There are some surprises, like the fact that teaching people the harms of smoking has little benefit when people are actively trying to quit. The time to give people information about the dangers of cigarette smoking is when they have no intention of stopping. People who are not even contemplating the possibility of changing their behavior can benefit from learning that one in three people who start smoking cigarettes will die of a smoking-related illness, for example. But once people have decided to quit, we've learned that the approach should change to bolstering positive motivation, and as we'll see later, this applies to stopping porn as well.

Smoking cessation groups spend a lot of time discussing the many benefits of quitting, which is the other side of the coin from the harms of smoking, but this is just the beginning of a successful quit attempt. Smokers know that stopping smoking also requires a complete overhaul of their environment, including getting rid of all smoking-related possessions. Stopping smoking also requires effective techniques for coping with urges and tolerating withdrawal. There's more to it than that, but the point for now is that there are more than a few analogs for the elements of a high-quality smoking cessation program that can be applied to porn cessation. Habitual pornography use is similar to cigarette smoking in many respects, such as the fact that it is a fairly recent phenomenon.

Internet pornography use has exploded in recent history

I remember when the internet didn't exist, or at least wasn't accessible. In college I heard rumors that my university was considering getting connected to the internet, instead of using giant servers to send local email from my login at the terminal in the computer lab to your login later at the same terminal. Back then, obtaining pornography in print or video form was a more sordid affair for most Christians. But, after the internet arrived, porn just comes to you free, easy, and in infinite varieties. Compulsive internet pornography viewing in 1990 was probably as rare as lung cancer in 1900, but has quickly overtaken the cigarette smoking rate in American men.

The literature on pornography has followed a similar path to that of cigarette smoking; the first step was to document the harms. Because secular society often considers pornography to be harmless or morally neutral, this literature is fairly small and has an uphill battle to fight. A lot of the literature concerns sex offenders and illegal activities, such as child porn or the relationship between porn and aggression toward women. Unlike smoking cessation, there are almost no clinical trials of programs to help people stop using pornography. A July, 2017 literature search found one case report of using medication to try to stop problematic porn use (Naltrexone)[3], one pilot study of a behavioral therapy for internet porn use[4], and only one randomized controlled trial of that behavioral therapy for reducing or quitting internet porn use.[5]

Therefore, we don't know much about how to quit porn from a scientific perspective. We know a lot more about how to quit smoking, as noted above. Some of the principles used in smoking cessation are very useful for porn cessation. For example, teaching people the harms of using pornography is probably not effective when people are actively trying to quit. That approach may actually backfire, because Christian men who want to quit already know about the harms and are ashamed and discouraged. The time to convince men that viewing pornography harms them is when they have no intention of stopping.

Once a man has really decided to quit, the approach should change to building positive motivation by listing the benefits of a porn-free lifestyle.

This is a simple but revolutionary idea, because books on quitting porn typically outline the dangers and harms of pornography use, which I am suggesting is not necessary and possibly even counterproductive.

Elements of the Quitting Pornography Program

Given how much we know about smoking cessation, I believe that it has great potential as an analogy for quitting porn. It should be possible to map the elements of smoking cessation onto porn cessation, with some modifications.

Table 1 lists select elements of a full-featured smoking cessation program, with their suggested counterpart for a pornography cessation program. This list is not exhaustive, as I just selected a set of elements that is comprehensive enough to be an effective smoking cessation program. I also grouped some specific techniques into categories such as "fences, defenses, and offense." These elements will comprise one of the two domains of the approach described in this book.

The first domain is all of the elements from the smoking cessation program, modified and applied to a porn cessation program. This is "man's part" in stopping porn, as you do the practical things that present you to God to cooperate with His work in your life in this area (Romans 6:13-14).

The second domain is the spiritual dimension that must be integrated with these elements imported from smoking cessation. This is learning about "God's part" in setting you free from bondage to pornography. The elements of porn cessation listed by "man's part" and "God's part" are presented in **Table 2**.

Table 1: Elements of Quitting

Smoking Cessation		Pornography Cessation
Self-monitoring & nicotine fading	→	**Self-monitoring & cutting back**
Social Support:	→	**Social Support:**
Support letters	→	Accountability software
Recruiting support	→	Accountability partner(s)
Fences:	→	**Fences:**
Getting rid (e.g., cigarettes)	→	Getting rid (e.g., porn stash)
Thorough cleaning	→	Installing the software blockade
No hidden triggers left	→	No hidden triggers left
Defenses:	→	**Defenses:**
Nicotine Replacement Therapy*	→	"Dopamine replacement therapy"
Coping with urges	→	Coping with urges
Getting through withdrawal	→	Being willing to suffer
Offense:	→	**Offense:**
Positive motivation	→	Positive motivation
Active coping	→	Active coping
Relaxation	→	Relaxation
Pleasant events	→	Pleasant Events

*And/or other pharmacological treatments not containing nicotine, like varenicline tartrate or bupropion hydrochloride.

Table 2: Man's Part and God's Part in Quitting

Man's part: Like Smoking Cessation	God's part: Spiritual Deliverance
1. Self-monitoring a. Cutting back	a. Word of God and prayer habits

2. Social Support
   a. Telling people your plan
   b. Snitch software
	a. Accountability
	b. Prayer: Romans 7

3. Fences
   a. Getting rid (Sweep and clear)
   b. Software blockade
   c. No hidden triggers left
	a. Search the heart for footholds
	b. Any "real" underlying problems?
	   (e.g., depression)

4. Defenses
   a. "Dopamine replacement therapy"
   b. Coping with urges
      i. Mindfulness
      ii. Acceptance and commitment
      iii. "Urge surfing"
      iv. Delay and decide
   c. Being willing to suffer
	a. Memorized meditation verses
	b. Grace
	   "there is no condemnation"[1]
	
	c. Suffering as a means of growth

5. Offense
   a. Motivation must be positive
      i. A firm commitment to quit
      ii. Rooted in core values
      iii. Benefits of quitting
   b. Active coping
   c. Relaxation
   d. Pleasant events
	a. Positive spirituality
	   i. Sanctification by grace: "know/consider/present."[2]
	   ii. Identity in Christ: "create in me a clean heart"[3]
	   iii. Spiritual benefits
	b. Ministry: fruitful is the new spiritual
	c. Fellowship

Kicking the Habit: Quitting Pornography Under Grace by Joel Hughes, Ph.D.
Copyright ©2018 by New Paradigm Publishing

---

[1] Romans 8:1
[2] Romans 5-7
[3] Psalm 51:10

Self-monitoring

The first element is self-monitoring. People who want to quit smoking should first start tracking the number of cigarettes they smoke each day. There are several reasons to track the frequency of smoking. Self-monitoring builds awareness of the extent of the problem and provides an objective baseline measure of how many cigarettes are actually being smoked. This becomes helpful in choosing the right amount of nicotine replacement therapy, for example.

Self-monitoring also results in cutting back. People who track the number of cigarettes they smoke will sort of automatically smoke less than if they weren't counting. This works for a lot of things; If you keep the beer bottle caps from each beer at the party in your pocket, you'll probably have fewer beers as you feel their number grow from 2 to 3 to 4 to "…maybe I better call it a night." Self-monitoring is also a basic building block of all behavioral therapies. If you have a behavior you want to change, any good therapist will make you do some self-monitoring. For the example of insomnia, how can anyone recommend changes to your sleep routine if you won't track your bedtime, get-up time, naps, and caffeine use?

The application to porn cessation is obvious. You will want to start tracking the number of times per day that you use. It will cause you to effortlessly cut back on the frequency, and you'll know where you're starting from in order to evaluate the success of your quit attempt.

Social Support

Smokers inform their immediate family and friends that they are stopping smoking. They mail or hand letters to their key support people to provide instructions on how to be helpful. This includes things like "don't let me bum a cig on break" and "don't leave your cigarettes on the coffee table" along with "please don't nag or yell at me if I screw up." Nearly anyone is willing to help a smoker by at least being nice and not handing them loosies when they look sad after dinner. The relevance to porn cessation is clear. Secret sins are more powerful when they're…secret. You can't stop unless you tell at least one trusted man in your life that you are going to make a heroic attempt to finally stop. If they look shocked and offended that you just admitted to using porn, glance at their right hand to see how much palm hair they grew from masturbating. (Kidding, that's a myth.) The point is that any man who can't even imagine having ever watched porn and is thusly dismayed by your weakness is either lying or not the right "accountability partner." In any area of addiction, openness is important. The first step is admitting you have a problem, right?

Fences

When smokers are preparing for a serious quit attempt, they put up fences. They get rid of their cigarettes, lighters, matches, ashtrays, and any other paraphernalia that makes it possible to smoke. They clean *everything*. They clean out their apartment or house, their car, and their desk at work. They don't want to stumble across a pack they forgot about. They want the smoke stench out of their clothes. They want the "smoke tinting" gone from their car windows. Sometimes they shampoo their car upholstery, so that smoking in the car again would ruin all their cleaning efforts.

Smokers also search for hidden triggers. Danger spots are the pockets of old jackets, the glovebox of the car, the drawer of a toolbox, and so on. They try to make sure there is nothing that they will accidentally discover three weeks into a quit attempt. In a moment of weakness, even the 4-year-old Marlboro 100's from the bottom drawer of the desk look tempting. Sometimes it's painful. Smokers may have to ditch a half carton of cigarettes, but they just remind themselves that they already wasted the money when they bought the cigarettes in the first place, so it's not really a waste now. The point of all the fences is that no cigarettes can sneak through. In the perfect scenario, in order to start smoking again, they would have to "borrow" one from someone who knows they're not supposed to smoke, or they would have to get in their nice clean car, drive to the corner store, and buy cigarettes and a lighter. The delay alone will give them more time to decide whether or not it's worth it and whether they really want to start this whole thing over again.

You can see a theme developing. Porn quitters throw away their entire stash. They scour every hard drive, portable hard drive, flash memory stick, and other storage place to eliminate any and all porn. Porn quitters clear out every browsing history from every desktop computer, laptop, tablet, and phone. They unsubscribe from listservs sending "news stories" with semi-pornographic click bait on the side of the screen. They scour all the possible hiding spots and triggers until nothing remains.

This is also when the software blockade goes up. There are a number of options that block sites relatively effectively (See **Appendix A**). They hand their phone to their primary support person, who enters a new password that locks the parental controls to block "adult sites." Hidden triggers must go. Perhaps it's time to take a break from the sleazy men's magazines. Perhaps they can't shop online at pantypalace.sales for their wife's Christmas presents anymore. It's more embarrassing to walk into a lingerie shop at the mall, if that's what your wife is into, but it's better than online shopping on a site that may become a "gateway drug" in a moment when conviction wavers. Some men may need to get their news from Huffpo or somewhere that isn't Reddit, at least for a while. The point, again, is to make it *really hard to use porn*. You would have to defeat the software, enter search terms, and consciously choose to dive in. That effort and delay makes it less appealing to open the can of worms again.

Defenses

Smokers need nicotine replacement therapy and sometimes other drugs like Chantix® (verinicline) or Zyban™ (bupropion) as well. It's just too physically addictive to quit smoking without a temporary replacement. Smokers also develop ways to cope with urges to smoke. These vary widely. Perhaps they drink 8 glasses of water each day, keep gum and snacks on their person at all times, chew on straws or tooth picks, or buy a new coffee pot for work. There has to be *something* to do when the urge hits and their hand automatically reaches into their pocket for a lighter. If they find a pack of gum there, spearmint can suffice for now, instead of menthol. Smokers also stay away from places where people smoke, and may avoid the places where they always smoked. If they always used to step out onto the balcony after dinner for a quick cigarette, maybe it's time to lock the sliding glass door and wedge it with a broom handle for a few weeks. The surprise of pulling back on the door only to find that it doesn't budge might be enough to remind a quitter that they are urging to smoke and have mindlessly walked to the "special smoking place."

Getting through the urges. This is also when a wide variety of techniques for getting through urges come into play. People listen to relaxation tapes, do self-hypnosis, run on the treadmill, meditate, or pray for relief. Smokers trying to quit invent ingenious distractions and delay strategies. Urges are inevitable when you're physically dependent on nicotine, and each person experiments with ways to "surf the urge" until the wave crests and subsides. With practice, they learn that urges are temporary and always go away if you wait a little bit.

The urges are caused by lack of nicotine combined with years of built-up habits. Nicotine withdrawal is a real pain in the butt, and recently-quit smokers find themselves irritable, angry, hungry, sad, anxious, restless, and generally not overjoyed with their new lifestyle. However, withdrawal is temporary, and when the suffering has been endured there will come a day when there are *no withdrawal symptoms*. The urges become less frequent. The person has essentially quit, and has become a non-smoker if they don't relapse.

Pornography is not a physical addiction. Porn cessation has some similarities with respect to defenses, but also important differences. Despite how strong the urges may feel; you are not physically dependent on web videos of naked women. There is no physical addiction like opiate addicts experience. The "addiction" is all brain chemistry[6] and habit, but not a true physical dependence. You will not experience hallucinations and seizures like the hard-core alcoholics going through delirium tremens. Still, defenses against porn use are extremely important. I believe that, with creativity, you can get what I call "dopamine replacement therapy." This is not a medication, but rather the other behaviors that give you the rush of dopamine that you are really craving when you open a new browser for an evening porn plunge. For an experienced user of porn, chasing images is like a compulsive gambler pulling the slot machine lever. There is a time-consuming repetitive behavior with an intermittent reinforcement schedule, as the user hunts for the "just right thing" that will fire those dopamine neurons in the prefrontal cortex of their brain. In a *Playboy* interview,[7] John Mayer described it this way: ""You're looking for the one photo out of 11 you swear is going to be the one you finish to, and you still don't finish."

So if porn is a hunt for a dopamine kick, like a rat pressing a lever that randomly injects their brain with cocaine about every 100 presses, how do you replace that? I'll say more later, but imagine doing things that would give you the "hunt" without the "smut." You could window shop on Amazon for the *perfect* stereo accessory, making sure you read all the reviews and checking a dozen different sites to compare prices. Hunting for a deal feels good, even if you don't buy anything yet. You could also scour iTunes for the song snippet that compels you to buy that tune right now for your running playlist. You could fire up your game console and start a new campaign on some first-person shooter game. You could also just eat a candy bar. Whether you go for matching the *hunt-chase-find* sensation or just pump dopamine into your brain with the brute force of hot glazed Krispy Kreme donuts®, there are alternatives to the rush of internet porn. Obviously some of these are not exactly *healthy*, but these fixes can be temporary, alternative solutions. The point is to replace the dopamine in a new and "harmless" way that is consuming enough of your attention so that porn is not tempting.

In addition to dopamine replacement therapy, there are many approaches to coping with urges that you can try. In the coming chapters I've selected a few including mindfulness, "acceptance and commitment," urge surfing, and the simple "delay and decide" approach, which can be devastatingly effective. The delay and decide approach is to set a timer for 10 minutes at the first tingling of a temptation to use again. Set the timer and tell yourself "not for 10 minutes." When the timer goes off, you might be busy with something else and not in the right mood anymore. You can also say "OK, now I can decide all over again; do some porn or set the timer for 10 more minutes?" Somehow telling yourself "later, if I decide to" is easier than a hard "no." Then when later comes, you probably will have come to your senses or be in a situation where you can't use. A meeting started. Someone called. People stopped by. You fell asleep. Crisis averted.

Finally, although there is no withdrawal from porn use, you will suffer through some temptation and urges. Because this is a book for Christian men, we will address this as "suffering as a means of growth." Even Jesus Christ learned obedience through suffering (Hebrews 5:8). We live in a completely fallen world, dripping with invasive sexuality that is trying to work you over and destroy you. There will be suffering. If you are using pornography compulsively or just casually, you have suffered real harm, and there will be pain as you let go and heal. However, this suffering can be transformed into powerful, long-lasting growth.

Offense

The best defense is a good offense. This old adage is attributed to George Washington,[8] who wrote a letter to John Trumbull in 1799 which said "…offensive operations, often times, is the surest, if not the only (in some cases) means of defence" (sic.). This is never truer than for smoking cessation, and by extension, porn cessation. It may be enough to build tall fences and solid defenses against the possibility of smoking (or porning). However, this puts people in the unenviable position of having a "just don't do it" mentality, which is a negative focus. A positive attack is more effective for behavior change. Therefore, there are four legs to the offense stool. They are (1) positive motivation, (2) active coping, (3) relaxation, and (4) pleasant events. These make for a sturdy, stable chair on which a person can sit confidently, knowing that they have turned the tables on the enemy.

Positive Motivation. Positive motivation is perhaps the most important offensive maneuver. Smokers who want to quit are not motivated by the horrors of death by cigarette. This runs the risk of inducing fear, guilt, and shame that motivate denial, avoidance of the issues, and despair. In contrast, positive motivation is powerful. Positive motivation starts with a *firm decision to quit.* Most people who try to half-heartedly quit smoking (or porn) have some ambivalence (mixed feelings and competing motives). People might want to stop because they fear lung cancer or are getting sinus infections too often, or they might be getting pressure to stop from their family. So they sort of want to stop, but they also don't want to miss out on the time they spend smoking on the balcony of their apartment after dinner. They want to significantly cut back, but they don't want to decline a cigarette if offered one (or if they bum one) when they're drinking out back on the deck with friends. Ambivalence is deadly. It allows an out, so when the cravings come or the person is in a situation that makes smoking seem like a pretty good plan, they have little reason to resist. A firm decision to quit is absolutely necessary, but not sufficient, to stop smoking. I think the same is true of porn cessation. If you are feeling guilty and want to cut back but keep a little "somethin' somethin'" for those lonely nights, you will not succeed. If people decide to mostly quit but haven't thought through the implications of quitting for the problems that eased their porn use (e.g., feeling hopeless about ever getting married, bored and lonely, under a lot of stress, bitter at their wife) then they probably won't succeed.

Making that firm decision to quit is essential, and can usually be found in a person's core values. The smoker knows that a deeper value than relaxing with a cigarette is their drive to live to see their grandchildren playing in the autumn leaves. They know that being able to practice football with their son or help their daughter train for cross country in high school is more important than smoking. The pleasure of the perfect cigarette on a crisp fall day is not as valued as being able to breathe when they wake up in the morning. Providing for their family by saving the couple thousand dollars a year they've been wasting on cigarettes is a core value. Values may be as simple as being able to sleeping through the night without having to sneak a cigarette in the middle of the night, and not having to blow the smoke up the fireplace in a failed attempt to avoid detection by their family. That would be a better fit for their core value of being a good husband and father. Good family men don't sneak around looking sheepish and smelling of smoke when they said they were quitting.

Applied to porn, Christians have an enormous advantage over the smoker. We have an identity in Christ. Understanding who we were made to be by God when we came into a relationship with Jesus Christ is a deep well for drawing out core values that don't fit with sneaking downstairs to find the iPad for a faux rendezvous with digital women in the middle of the night. In a later chapter we'll focus on our identity in Christ as a key part of the offensive war against porn.

Listing the positive benefits of stopping smoking is also a very powerful technique for building a solid motivation. There are many benefits of quitting, which smokers personalize to their own situation. One person may be eager to finally taste food again. Another may be excited about the extra hundred dollars a month they'll have from not buying cigarettes. Another may simply enjoy the feeling of confidence that comes from setting goals and attaining them. Applied to porn cessation, many people who try to quit are stuck in white-knuckle mode, trying to avoid the allure of porn without ever considering the considerable benefits of being the kind of man who does not use porn. After someone stops porn, they find that they can talk to women without seeing them through their "sex object colored glasses" all the time. They find that they become as virile as a 16-year-old boy, no longer worried about being able to get it up without a lot of visual assistance. Writing out a list of benefits of stopping is a very personal exercise. The benefits of quitting porn, like quitting smoking, vary from person to person. The power of keeping these benefits top of mind during the quit attempt is astonishing, and can lead to sustained determination.

Active Coping. The second part of a strong offense is active coping. This means proactively engaging in fulfilling and positive ways of fighting cigarettes or porn. Coping activities range widely, from putting on the nicotine patch every morning to reviewing the list of benefits that will start when the smoking is over. A lot of the coping techniques were also the defense that the quitter constructed. The point of *active* coping is that it is not *reactive.* Waiting for a problem is a great way to fail. During the throes of a nicotine fit, it is harder to resist if coping attempts are an afterthought. Planning in advance for coping techniques is far more effective, whether this means taking a walk every morning or planning a schedule for the week that avoids the old smoking haunts.

Applied to porn, Christians have another advantage. We have important things to do that are really incompatible with idle time spent masturbating to internet videos. Active coping can include ministry activities, like reconnecting with old friends, volunteering for service projects, and anything else that sounds like "eager for good works" (Titus 2:14). A lot of sensuality and carnal living grows in the fertile soil of sloth, so turning that around with an outward focus on serving God is a fantastic way to stay busy, distracted from the flesh, focused on the true, the noble the pure (Philippians 4:8), and ultimately marching toward the things of God (which is away from porn).

Relaxation. Relaxation is another part of the offense against smoking cessation, because cigarettes are little soothe-sticks. People who smoke inhale deeply hundreds of times each day, take frequent breaks from work and everything else, and generally enjoy the mild anti-depressant effect of nicotine. This absolutely has to be replaced with an active plan to relax. Relaxation can be breathing exercises, listening to recorded relaxation scripts, or meditation. It doesn't really matter so long as it's actually relaxing. Watching TV or playing video games doesn't count. If the heart rate slows and the muscles loosen, that is relaxation. Fire up the aromatherapy candles for a bubble bath if that floats your rubber ducky, but the point is that some form of relaxation and stress relief should be used to fight the tension and irritability that comes when nicotine withdrawal sets in, as well as replacing the relaxing function that cigarettes used to serve.

Applied to internet pornography, people may find that porn really served the function of breaking up the monotony, rewarding you after a hard day, or some other form of stress-management. This has to be replaced, not just resisted. A good offense includes a plan to relax on purpose, with a pre-chosen technique that works for you. The approach to relaxation doesn't matter—you can use the same techniques that smokers use.

Pleasant Events. Pleasant events are the final part of the offense. Putting down the cigarettes often unleashes the "black dog" of depression.[9] This is partly why many smokers are prescribed antidepressants like bupropion (Zyban™), although the benefits for smoking cessation may be independent of their antidepressant properties.[10] Depression and weight-gain are two greatly feared drawbacks to stopping smoking. Fortunately, stopping porn should trigger neither, unless your approach to dopamine replacement therapy involves too many hot fudge sundaes or was somehow keeping your melancholia at bay. Still, planning a number of positive, pleasant events for your life is a great way to transform the bleak iron-will approach to stopping into a fun enjoying-life approach.

The kind of events that count as pleasant and are therefore helpful for depression and other problems are those that are naturally reinforcing.

When you think about it, internet porn is pretend enjoyment in a fantasy world that lessens your engagement with the real world. Pleasant events should be concrete activities in the here-and-now. Again, Christian men are at a great advantage, because we believe in the importance of Christian fellowship. Choosing to combine stopping porn with a rededication to your local Christian fellowship is a fantastic way of grounding yourself in pleasant activities that bring a sense of true satisfaction and enjoyment. There's no harm in double-counting some of these offensive maneuvers, so it would be appropriate to sign up for a service project like a work day for Habitat for Humanity. Enlist your friends. Swing hammers together. That's social support, active coping, core values affirmation, and a pleasant event all in one.

Conclusion

If viewing internet pornography was a morally neutral bad habit that you wanted to stop, the smoking cessation approach would be all you need. However, Christian men understand that our sexuality is a profoundly spiritual aspect of our humanity as men created in the image of God. I have already started to hint at the ways in which this understanding can be incorporated into attempts to quit porn. Now it's time to consider in greater depth how sexuality reflects the image of God, how sex is really worship, and how it can go so horribly wrong in our fallen world.

Chapter Summary and Assignments

- There are hundreds of studies showing what works for quitting cigarette smoking. There are very few for quitting porn, so we adapted what we know about smoking cessation to stopping porn use.
- The basic approach for quitting starts with self-monitoring and cutting back, while you recruit social support in the form of at least one trusted man with whom you can read this book and complete the rest of the tasks. The other approaches are setting up fences and defenses, to keep the porn away or at least make it really hard to get. The final and most important approach is a strong offense, in which you actively cope with the difficulty of quitting and adopt a new porn-free lifestyle.
- None of this is enough, because sexuality has a spiritual dimension that traps you in your sin. God's part is absolutely mandatory for quitting porn, and that is the topic of Chapter 3.

Assignments

- Go over **Table 1** and **Table 2**. These form the outline for the activities described in the rest of the book. Is there anything you don't understand? Make a note of what you don't understand and keep a lookout for that topic when you get to the right chapter. Is anything left out? Does it seem like too much work? People who want to stop smoking are willing to do the work when they can't stop on their own, because they may be literally dying from smoking. Christian men who want to quit internet pornography should be willing to do a little work too.
- Do NOT freak out if you have not stopped porn yet. This may sound crazy, but I've had a lot of cigarette smokers get excited in the first group session and stop smoking *that day*. They always come back in a week having smoked just as much as ever, but this time they're discouraged, which drained away their motivation. You don't run a marathon with no training, and you won't stop porn on a whim, especially if it's become a compulsive behavior. You've been doing porn for years, so another week isn't going to kill you if you spend that week getting really, really ready to quit for good. I can't bring myself to say "*keep it up! You get one more week of porn!*" So quit if you can, but if you can only cut back by 50% and keep building your knowledge and motivation, that's good enough for now. Don't freak out.
- What day and time will you read the next chapter? Make an appointment with yourself to keep up your momentum.

Chapter 3

Pornography has a spiritual dimension

Agenda for Chapter 3

To understand that sex is worship, but when we pursue porn, we are asking fake sexuality to provide a false intimacy, a solitary unity, and an imaginary fulfillment rooted in self-worship.

Smoking is not an overtly spiritual problem. In contrast, pornography is sexual, and sexuality is directly connected to our spiritual nature. Therefore, key spiritual truths must be incorporated into a successful porn cessation program for Christian men. **Table 3** lists these elements, and they are covered in chapters 3 and 4.

Table 3: Spiritual truth relevant to quitting pornography

- **Sex is worship**
- **Spiritual warfare targets your sexuality**
- **Sanctification is by grace, not works**
- **Your identity in Christ defeats porn**
- **Fruitful is better than sinless**

Sex is worship[11]

Any serious student of the Bible is confronted by the fact that the Bible has a lot to say about sex. Sometimes this comes up in unexpected places. For example, sexual depravity is one result of rejecting God. In Romans 1, Paul constructs an argument that everyone knows that God exists and that ignoring this fact is an act of denial motivated by a desire to do wicked things. According to Paul, people have no excuse for not knowing that God exists, but people don't want to worship God, so their thinking becomes futile. Then they foolishly swap the worship of God for the worship of objects, like idols or nature or sex.

Although some atheists pretend to have intellectual reasons for denying the existence of God, these are often not really honest objections. True full-featured atheism is rare because it is unworkable as a lifestyle. Chinese sociologist Fengaang Yang documented the surprising truth that there are not really any atheist societies.[12] When China outlawed religion, people eventually turned to emperor worship. People have to worship something. C. S. Lewis said, "A man can no more diminish God's glory by refusing to worship Him than a lunatic can put out the sun by scribbling the word, 'darkness' on the walls of his cell." Timothy Keller once tweeted "No one simply denies the glory of God; we always exchange the glory of God for the glory of something else."[13]

What if you won't worship God?

One consequence of refusing to acknowledge and glorify God is sexual depravity. Paul wrote "Therefore God gave them over in the sinful desires of their hearts to sexual impurity for the degrading of their bodies with one another. They exchanged the truth about God for a lie and worshiped and served created things rather than the Creator—who is forever praised. Amen." (Romans 1: 24-25). Because humans *must* worship, they will find something to worship if they don't worship God. People alienated from God typically find their greatest source of meaning, purpose, and fulfillment to be the satisfaction of their carnal desires. In the 21st-century, this is accelerating, and people have defined their very identities by their sexual preferences.

If this sounds far-fetched, go read *Cheap Sex: The Transformation of Men, Marriage, and Monogamy* by Mark Regnerus.[14] He argues the provocative thesis that the invention of the birth control pill and the widespread availability of internet pornography have made sex "cheap," in the sense that men no longer have to work for it by developing a committed relationship (e.g., marriage). In turn, this leads to some changes in the sexual culture including increased diversity in sexual identity and orientation, as well as having the effect of driving people away from religion. Cheap sex secularizes. Cheap irreligious sex fertilizes the soil of sexual variety, and a lot of weeds grow in the garden like Paul said in Romans 1.

In the 1st century world in which Paul lived and wrote, sex was a big problem. They had temple prostitutes (i.e., sex trafficking of adolescent girls), child sexual abuse of male and female servants in the house, and rampant fornication and adultery. A wealthy man with a good position in society might have a wife for bearing children, a mistress for intellectual stimulation and sex, and a female servant for "daily use."[15]

Nothing has changed. Sexuality is getting weirder in America, even in the mainstream. The book "*Fifty Shades of Grey*"[16] sold over 125 million copies. Many people having sex are not remotely in a relationship, from alcohol-fueled hookup culture, to Tinder swipes, to the dreaded "situationship," in which two people are sexually together but she's not his girlfriend or even his "top side piece." Although they think they're just having fun, what they're really doing is worship. Sex is our search for worship. Sex is motivated by the desire to possess and be possessed by another. Every human being craves that oneness.

Some people say, "Girls give sex to get love; boys give love to get sex."[17] Women do provide sex for the promise and hope of a relationship, trying to connect with men emotionally and physically. Women also enjoy sex, so some have sex just for thrills. Men are notorious for feigning interest in a relationship to accelerate the development of enough "trust" to get some. However, these gender differences in motivation are only partly true, because what people truly seek is not just sex; they need worship. People want to worship and to be worshipped. People believe they can find a sense of total fulfillment, oneness, and even an identity in sex. In contemporary culture, people have replaced God with an attempt to get a transcendent spiritual experience in the "Big O." Total fulfillment is the goal of worship. However, the Bible is clear that only God can give that fulfillment, so only God should be worshipped. Only God can satisfy the deep sense of longing for complete identity and unity with another person. This is worship.

Sex expresses unity. We long to be united with God, in an intimate, loving relationship, fully possessed by the God who created us in his image. The highest description of a relationship we can have is found in Jesus words to his disciples "...you are in me, and I am in you." (John 14:20). Jesus spoke these words shortly before he died to end the separation between us and God. After Jesus paid for sin with his blood, the Bible says that our access to God became *direct* for those who believe in Jesus Christ. All the symbolism and ritual in the Old Testament seemed to have to do with *distance*. God would not relate to us directly—there was a separation between us and God, so we had to relate to God through priests, through sacrifices, and through formal structures and other symbols and ceremonies. Faith was very ritualized. This all signified the distance between us and God. Then in the New Testament, after Jesus atoned for sin, the rituals were amazingly reduced. The distance was eradicated completely—we were joined to Christ.[18]

In the same sense, there are aspects of a man and a woman's relationship that are supposed to be off-limits to them until their wedding night. Unmarried men and women are not supposed to relate directly and intimately as one flesh. When they marry, God removes the distance between them, and they become truly one flesh. Marriage, and sex in marriage, is a biblical symbol for relational unity that runs from Genesis to Revelation.

At the beginning of the Bible, we read that God created the earth and that God created man in his own image. Then God performed the first wedding. God's plan for humanity was to exalt us with a unique destiny among all creation, and marriage was instituted to symbolize part of that plan. We are designed to live in a loving relationship with God and to exercise authority over creation as we work with God to accomplish His aims. God has always existed in a unified, loving relationship; the Father, the Son, and the Holy Spirit are three and yet one.

God created us with a corresponding need to live in love relationships, and this is one way that we are like God. We need unity and diversity in relationships. The deepest human relationship we can have is marriage, which was invented by God to demonstrate this truth to us. So, one purpose of marriage was actually to reflect the character of God. Adam and Eve are diverse in that they are separate persons—yet they are a unity in that they can have a relationship in which they know and are known in a deeply intimate way. They discover their true humanness not in isolation ("alone"), but in community, and God demonstrated this to us by creating marriage between a man and a woman.[19] Jesus quoted Genesis when he was asked about marriage.

> "Haven't you read," he replied, "that at the beginning the Creator 'made them male and female,' and said, 'For this reason, a man will leave his father and mother and be united to his wife, and the two will become one flesh'? So they are no longer two, but one flesh. Therefore, what God has joined together, let no one separate." (Matthew 19:4-6)

In this passage, Jesus connected our complementary male and female human natures with God's provision of marriage to unite us as one. He also specifically emphasized that marriage is something that *God* does when he joins a man and a woman together. God uses the symbolism of marriage to communicate spiritual realities. In fact, marriage is also a symbol of the relationship between Jesus Christ and His church:

"For this reason, a man will leave his father and mother and be united to his wife, and the two will become one flesh." This is a profound mystery—but I am talking about Christ and the church." (Ephesians 5:31-32)

As Paul expands on this familiar concept from Genesis, we see something very deep: God created us with a need to live in love relationships. We need love relationships with each other, and we need a love relationship with God. So God designed our most sacred relationship in this life to be a picture of the relationship that he wants to have with us. As Michael Cusick so eloquently states in the title of his book, when we are surfing the internet for porn we are actually *"Surfing for God."*[20] This book is one of the resources listed in **Appendix A**—highly recommended for an expanded discussion of the spiritual dimension of pornography.

- *The point of all this is that when we pursue porn, we are asking fake sexuality to provide a false intimacy, a solitary unity, and an imaginary fulfillment rooted in self-worship.*

This does not work. Porn (and indulging the flesh in general) is not satisfying. Rather, the hunger only grows until it consumes you. I'm not saying that there's no pleasures in a season of sin (Hebrews 11:25), but rather that there is no ultimate fulfillment, no lasting satisfaction, and no true worship. Two implications of this fact are that real sex in marriage can be far, far better than anything pornography can provide. This should be our goal.

What if I'm single? For those who are single or who will never marry, the goal of marital sex may not be attainable right now, or perhaps ever. However, God has made other provisions for our fulfillment. Jesus never married. Jesus knows it's hard to be single, and even harder to never marry. He said "Not everyone can accept this word, but only those to whom it has been given. For there are eunuchs (i.e., *the unmarried and celibate)* who were born that way, and there are eunuchs who have been made eunuchs by others—and there are those who choose to live like eunuchs for the sake of the kingdom of heaven. The one who can accept this should accept it." (Matthew 19:11-12). If you are not married or will never marry, that can be a very difficult thing, but it is something you may choose to accept for the Kingdom of Heaven. Unfortunately, in our culture, we are taught to believe that we can only be fulfilled if we are sexually satisfied, which is to say that we are encouraged to exchange the truth about God for a lie and worship our own bodies rather than the God who created us. Who sold us this lie?

Chapter Summary and Assignments

- Sex involves worship. Porn is pointing your worship in the wrong direction.

Assignments

- Complete Worksheet 2: Porn and Spirituality
- What day and time will you read the next chapter? Make an appointment with yourself to keep up your momentum.

Worksheet 2: Porn and spirituality

Take an hour to privately contemplate or discuss these questions:

- Have you ever considered that sexuality is spiritual and not just physical?
- Are you trying to find "total fulfillment" in sexuality, including pornography?
- Are you married or single?
    - If you are married, is porn just "extra" or a substitute for your real relationship? Why?
    - If you are single, how is your porn use a way to avoid or substitute for a close personal relationship with God? Are you willing to switch directions on this and try to improve your relationship with God?

Kicking the Habit: The Christian Man's Guide to Quitting Porn like Quitting Smoking by Joel Hughes
Copyright ©2018 by Joel Hughes

Chapter 4

Our identity in Christ defeats pornography

Agenda for Chapter 4

Because sexuality is spiritual, our adversary the devil targets our sexuality by attacking us with temptation and accusation. The spiritual nature of sexual sin also means that quitting porn is "sanctification," which only happens by grace and not by self-effort alone. However, we have an identity in Christ that can help us defeat pornography, and ultimately we find that having a fruitful Christian life is better than a quest for sinless holiness

---

We all need to worship something. This side of heaven, God allows us to experience worship symbolically through physical intimacy in marriage. Sex, as God intended it, is a picture of the relationship God wants to have with us. This makes our sexuality a key target for Satan. When sex is going badly (e.g., pornography), we have difficulty seeing ourselves how God does, and we are distracted from accomplishing our purpose on earth.

Poisoning the well: Spiritual warfare targets our sexuality

From Genesis to Revelation the Bible is clear that we have an enemy.[21] For centuries, Satan has been very busy filling our heads with rubbish, spreading nonsense, and otherwise perverting our sexuality. That's what perversion means; to corrupt, distort, falsify, and generally alter something from its original form or purpose to destroy it. One of Satan's favorite tactics is what I call "poisoning the well." This is an ancient warfare strategy, which involves dumping poison into a water well, such as dead bodies. This ruins the drinking water, so the opposing army can't get a drink and will be weakened from dehydration.

God encourages us to "drink water from your own well" (Proverbs 5:15), encouraging us to be sexually satisfied in a faithful monogamous marriage. In contrast, a cursory glance at any culture will show that Satan has waged war against God's design for sexuality. When we succumb to pornography or another sexual sin, we drink poisoned water. Ultimately this has the effect of making us less satisfied with our lot in life, whether we're single or married.

It's not a coincidence that Satan went for the jugular on this one—perverting sexuality is both a consequence and a cause of rejecting God. Satan knows we need to worship, so if we reject God, we will inevitably try to worship sex. Conversely, people who worship sex aren't very interested in God. In 21st-century American culture wars, the sexual orientation and gender identity battles have been heating up for decades, and a common theme is the wholesale rejection of Jesus Christ on the basis of a prior commitment to drink from the poisoned well. People who believe that their identity as a human being is rooted in their sexual behavior are offended by any part of God's design or instruction that contradicts who they have decided they are based on their feelings.

For the Christian man trying to quit pornography, becoming aware of the spiritual warfare waging over the sex turf in our lives should lead to a more sophisticated appreciation for why porn is so hard to quit. There are real spiritual forces at work, opposing your efforts to stop.

Satan's tools. Satan opposes God's design for sexuality, and his tools are temptation, accusation, and so on. Temptation is easy to spot in America, it's everywhere. In every mall in America, there's a 10-foot tall poster hanging of a woman in lingerie staring at all the tweens with sultry bedroom eyes. Fantastic.

Throughout history, it hasn't ever been that much easier. Even Job had to take defensive measures: "I made a covenant with my eyes not to look lustfully at a young woman" (Job 31:1).

Accusation is also really easy for Satan to pull off against the unsuspecting Christian man involved in pornography. Masquerading as God (2 Corinthians 11:13-15) he shows up to be our "conscience" and suggests that we feel guilty. Typically, what we feel is shame and unproductive guilt instead of a healthy decision to change course (i.e., repentance). Satan is the accuser (Job 1, Revelation 12:10), but fortunately, Jesus Christ is always on our side (Hebrews 7:25). This spiritual attack is part of why this book focuses on a positive approach to quitting porn. Christian men would be better off resting in their faith, secure in their position in Jesus Christ, than succumbing to the accusation of the devil. If "there is now no condemnation for those who are in Christ Jesus" (Romans 8:1), then surely this extends even to men who masturbate to dirty videos.

Pray for deliverance. One critical implication of the fact that spiritual warfare targets our sexuality is that we need the power of Jesus Christ to defeat porn (as well as any other sexual problems). This is a spiritual war, not just a bad habit (Ephesians 6). Spiritual warfare must be waged spiritually, which includes a number of tactics such as faith, the word of God, and prayer. In particular, praying for deliverance from porn is a very good idea. In Michael Cusick's *Surfing for God*,"[22] he describes the need to ask Jesus Christ to rescue you from pornography. As we'll see below, Christ has already set you free even if you haven't broken free yet. Praying for deliverance recognizes that fact and acknowledges that there is a need for protection from spirit beings who attack your sexuality to keep you discouraged, focused on yourself, and feeling far from God.

Sanctification is by grace, not works

Because sexuality is spiritual, and quitting porn is also spiritual, I cannot emphasize enough the fact that success will not depend on your effort alone. Are there things you must do? Absolutely. Could you quit porn using your own wits, skills, and strength? Perhaps, especially temporarily. But ultimately, if the heart issues involved are not addressed (e.g., worship), you will not succeed. Who performs this "hidden heart surgery?" *Jesus Christ, not you*.

Sanctification is the process of spiritual growth that also involves moral change. Moral change is both positive and negative. Sanctification is what the Bible means when you read things like "clothe yourselves with compassion, kindness, humility, gentleness, and patience. Bear with each other and forgive one another if any of you has a grievance against someone. Forgive as the Lord forgave you. And over all these virtues put on love, which binds them all together in perfect unity." (Colossians 3:12-14). Sanctification is also what the Bible means when you read "get rid of all bitterness, rage and anger, brawling and slander, along with every form of malice" (Ephesians 4:31) and "put to death, therefore, whatever belongs to your earthly nature: sexual immorality, impurity, lust, evil desires and greed, which is idolatry" (Colossians 3:5). The positive side of sanctification is developing the patient, kind, humble, loving character that God wants. The negative side is getting rid of all the "Lie! Cheat! Steal!" and other things that are unbecoming of a Christian man. Where does porn fit? You got it; the negative aspect of moral change. Get rid of it, put it to death, lay it aside.

Every Christian in history starts this process by trying to "do better." This becomes an epic fail. Paul makes this clear in a famous passage in Romans. "I do not understand what I do. For what I want to do I do not do, but what I hate I do." (Romans 7:15). Yes, it's defeating. You try to act good and not bad, but eventually, you start to act bad and not good. You will fail every time. Are you doomed? It feels like it. Paul continues: "What a wretched man I am! Who will rescue me from this body that is subject to death? Thanks be to God, who delivers me through Jesus Christ our Lord!" (Romans 7:24-25). Ah! There's the answer—*you need to be rescued*. Your earnest campaign for holiness ends in death, but Jesus Christ can rescue you from your sins. Sanctification is spiritual growth, and cannot be accomplished by self-effort. The implications for pornography are clear; you must be rescued, and will not quit by trying to wage a heroic willpower battle.

Believe it or not, there has been debate on this point for centuries. Even in Paul's day, Christians were convinced that they could just "try harder." In my view, Paul slammed the door on this approach in another passage.

> "You foolish Galatians! Who has bewitched you? Before your very eyes, Jesus Christ was clearly portrayed as crucified. I would like to learn just one thing from you: Did you receive the Spirit by the works of the law, or by believing what you heard? Are you so foolish? After beginning by means of the Spirit, are you now trying to finish by means of the flesh?" (Galatians 3:1-3).

In other words, if salvation and receipt of the Holy Spirit is a free gift (*aka* grace) by faith in Jesus Christ, and not at all dependent on your trying hard enough to earn a ticket to heaven, why would spiritual growth be up to your self-effort? Are you going to finish what God started by trying really hard? Self-effort is what the Bible means by the law, works, and the flesh, when used in the context of trying harder to be good. It doesn't work. Again, the implications for porn cessation are obvious; it requires the free gift of spiritual change that only Jesus Christ can give. Even in the area of pornography, sanctification is by grace, not works.

As you might imagine, this is where things get confusing for many Christians. If sanctification is by grace and is a work of the Holy Spirit of God in my life, what is my role? I am not suggesting that you stop fighting the battle against pornography in your life. This is a workbook after all! Rather, it is critical to have the correct understanding of what is your part and what is God's part in this process. If you recall **Table 2: Elements of Quitting: Man's part and God's part**, there is a lot for you to do. There is so much to do that in the first chapter I cautioned you against objecting that the approach described in this book is too hard, overkill, and over-engineered. To make a long story short, your cooperation with God in this process comes down to three words: Know, Consider, Present.[23] These words were chosen by pastor and author Dennis McCallum, inspired by the writings of Chinese house church pioneer Watchman Nee, to describe the process of sanctification outlined by Paul in Romans 5-7.

Know. Sanctification starts with a firm grasp of your identity in Christ, which is a form of knowledge. Why? Because we are in Christ. If you are a Christian, this is a true fact, whether or not you believe it, whether or not you feel it, and whether or not you like it. To be a Christian is to be "in Christ." Is Christ addicted to porn? No. *Then neither are we.* In Romans 6:3 Paul states "...don't you know that all of us who were baptized into Christ Jesus were baptized into his death?" Baptized is a silly word that is just a phonetic rendering of the Greek word for "put into," so this has nothing to do with the ritual of baptism. Don't overcomplicate the idea; anyone who is a Christian has been "put into" Christ, which means that everything that happened to Christ happened to us. Christ died, so we died (metaphorically). He rose from the dead, so we rose from the dead (metaphorically).

In a similar passage, Paul states "I have been crucified with Christ, and I no longer live, but Christ lives in me. The life I now live in the body, I live by faith in the Son of God, who loved me and gave himself for me." (Galatians 2:20) Again, the idea is that Christ's death killed our sin and replaced it with the life of Christ, which does not include sin. This is not just the power of positive thinking, it is a metaphysical reality that we often forget, which is somewhat understandable because we are still sinning and continue to live in our flesh. That is, you're not a being of pure spirit and this ain't heaven, so until you physically die, you are stuck with the sin nature inherited from Adam (Romans 5:12). However, we can have a lot more victory if we keep the fact of our identity in Christ top-of-mind, with the effect this can have on our proclivity to sin.

Consider. Our identity in Christ makes sanctification possible, as we have been set free from slavery to sin. Romans 6:6-7 says this directly, "For we know that our old self was crucified with him so that the body ruled by sin might be done away with, that we should no longer be slaves to sin—because anyone who has died has been set free from sin." Although this is true, usually this fact is ignored in favor of more "important" realities like fantasy football rankings and the correct grill temperature for perfectly seared steaks. There's nothing wrong with regular life, but it can be pretty consuming and distract us from the knowledge of our new potential to behave like we want to. Therefore, in addition to having a basic knowledge of our identity in Christ, we need to reflect on that and adopt the attitude that it is true, especially when we don't feel like it's true. From Romans 6:11 "In the same way, count yourselves dead to sin but alive to God in Christ Jesus," we are to *count* (or consider) that we are in fact, dead to sin but alive to God. Paul is saying that knowledge is not enough, it has to be put into practice in our minds and in our behavior.

We need to adopt a mindset that our identity in Christ is true and that freedom from sin *and porn* is possible. Again, the mindset is not just the power of positive thinking. It's more like having the knowledge in mind so that you can act on it. If knowledge is a hot stock tip, then considering that knowledge means deciding the price point at which you will buy some shares. Finally, to "present" yourself would be logging into your trading account to complete the transaction. Without the knowledge, you don't realize that you could make money. Without the consider, you don't have a plan to buy any, so there is no profit taking. Without the considering, it's a missed opportunity.

To connect the dots with smoking cessation and quitting porn, let me emphasize how different this approach is from the humiliating shame approach of dwelling on all the damage porn causes and your compulsive, addiction-like quest for faux fun online. A mindset on your flaws is profoundly unhelpful because sanctification is by grace. It starts with *knowing* that you are in Christ and therefore dead to porn, followed by *considering* this fact to un-paralyze yourself and get ready for action. Paul is not an idiot. He knows you still leer at young women (if he were alive today he would not be surprised by your browser history). But he wouldn't judge. He would ask you to present yourself to God regardless of what you've done.

Present. Romans 6:12-14 is the action phase; presenting yourself to God. The key phrase is in verse 13 "Do not offer any part of yourself to sin…, but rather offer yourselves to God…". To present yourself is to show up for duty. You present yourself to work or school when you clock in and ask your boss "what am I doing today?" or take your seat and stare at the professor. To present yourself to God is to be available for His work. This means you cannot get free from internet pornography (or any sin) if you are not interested in serving God. Turns out, God has an agenda for your life. Exactly what that might be is beyond the scope of this book, but every Christian man should know that God did not create you and rescue you from death and the kingdom of Satan so you can do whatever the hell you want with the rest of your life. You've never had a boss that replied: "I dunno…maybe just masturbate all day" when you asked what to do for your work shift. It would be a worthy exercise to take stock of your life and figure out where and how you can serve God.

One reason that presenting yourself to God is so powerful for overcoming sin is that it is consistent with reality, whereas presenting yourself to porn is continuing to live in a fantasy world. If you were a prisoner, it would be crazy to keep sleeping in your prison cell after you were freed because the judge declared you innocent. You're not a felon anymore! Get out of the cell and go somewhere! Another reason that presenting yourself to God works is because it's hard to do incompatible behaviors simultaneously.

When I'm on a diet, I don't wash down bacon cheeseburgers with chocolate milkshakes. Eating the delicious diet food, like kale and tree bark (fiber!), provides motivation to avoid the fast food. So working away at studying the Bible and getting together with other Christian men for service projects can interfere with naughty screen time. Obviously, you can still do a lot of porn when you're serving God, like you can eat a lot of junk food in a prison cell when you're a free man on a diet, but it's inconsistent and uncomfortable. Yes, over 35% of Protestant ministers reported using porn, but that's probably a lot less than Christian men who are *not* ministers.[24] Serving God will crowd out a lot of sins, as your focus changes and you start walking in a new direction.

Applied to quitting porn, presenting yourself to Christ involves both serving God and setting up the fences and defenses described in later chapters. Arranging your life like a person who would be willing to obey God and is trying to quit porn will result in spiritual power for sanctification. After all, God doesn't often provide inspiration to those who aren't willing to listen. Combining these three concepts—Know, Consider, Present—is a turbocharged engine for sanctification running on spiritual petrol, and very different from the self-effort willpower approach. It's based on grace, the free gift of God instead of law, the self-earned "goodness." But it is not passive. Grace is not opposed to *effort*, it's opposed to *earning*.[25]

Your identity in Christ defeats porn

Having been put into Christ, and having been crucified with Christ, you are now free to live in the power of Christ. As Paul says, "...I no longer live, but Christ lives in me. The life I now live in the body, I live by faith in the Son of God...." (Galatians 2:20). This life based on your identity in Christ will defeat porn.

Many "origin stories" illustrate the power of identity. Luke thought he was just a water farmer on a desert planet with his stern overprotective aunt and uncle. Bored with drinking blue milk, he longed for an adventure that would take him to the bright lights and big cities he somehow knew were his destiny. Deep inside, he rebelled against the tedium of tinkering with robot farm hands when *BLAMMO!*—the trashcan-shaped robot squeezed out a hologram fragment of a beautiful princess declaring that Luke was "our only hope." Whisked off to worlds of awesomeness by a mysterious hippie monk from the wilderness, Luke comes to discover that he is awash in godlike power emanating from a microscopic virus or parasitic infection or something—you've seen the movies. The point is that his identity as Jedi knight and space-messiah gives purpose and focus to his otherwise mundane throwaway life. This the power of identity.[26]

False identity. Most people base their identity on nonsense, such as what other people think of us or how we define ourselves. These identities are culturally and psychologically constructed, and yet most people are trapped in the role they're assigned. In high school, you're typecast as "jock" or "nerd" or whatever stereotype would be in your generation's version of *The Breakfast Club*.[27] Then, as an adult, your occupation comes to define you. "I'm an exercise physiologist" or a "sanitation worker" or "phone monkey" or whatever pays the bills. People also assume identities based on race, ethnicity, country of origin, sexual orientation, personal characteristics, or interests. These are not real identities. Paul understood this when he said that he was an Israelite man circumcised on the eighth day, of the tribe of Benjamin, a zealous religious Pharisee, a gentleman, and a scholar. But all of these things from the "asset" column that formed his identity, he came to view as "just crap" compared to his identity in Jesus Christ (Philippians 3:8).

True identity. According to the Bible, your true identity is not what other people think or what you think of you, but what God thinks of you. If there's a God, then if God says you're something, that's what you are. God's identity for you is better than you think. God is the infinite, personal, absolute basis of all things in the universe. For those who are Christians, *aka* in Christ, that's the basis of our identity according to God. On the basis of our identity in Christ, we are as morally pure as Jesus Christ, seated at the right hand of God (Ephesians 1:20). God knows you still sin, but what he considers is your position in Christ and not your current condition. This true identity doesn't use internet pornography at all.

Living from our identity in Christ. When we come to terms with our identity in Christ, it becomes possible to live from this identity, which believe it or not, intersects with smoking cessation and applies directly to quitting internet porn. When people are trying to stop smoking, they work hard to adopt a non-smoking identity. They have become so accustomed to viewing themselves as a smoker that a lot of their behavior unconsciously flows from their smoker identity. They wander over to the cigarette aisle of the grocery store, and they walk into the gas station store after they fill their tank, seeking a new pack of cigarettes. They choose the smoking section of the restaurant and look for the smokers' lounge in airports. Therefore, smoking cessation programs spend time discussing the idea that once a person passes their quit date, they are a non-smoker. People are encouraged to flesh out the implications of adopting a non-smoker identity and envision how this applies to them. Obviously, this is a socially constructed (false) identity, but it still helps people stop smoking. For porn, it will be important to begin to adopt a non-porn user identity. However, this mindset is rooted in reality, because freedom from sin is a key feature of our (real) identity in Christ. This is the right mindset to have; when the quit date passes, you will live from your identity in Christ, free from sin—including pornography.

Fruitful is better than sinless

Shortly after I started attending a church in Columbus Ohio, my wife and I took some of the classes offered on Wednesday nights. In the second class, then called "Christian Principles 2," I had a life-changing experience. The instructor, Doug, boldly stated that the goal of Christianity is not to become sinless, but rather to become fruitful. He didn't say it that way, and it was embedded in a larger discussion of the theology of sanctification, but it was mind-blowing because my Conservative Baptist upbringing had instilled a lot of guilt over my moral failures and character defects. Perhaps it was the setting, as I thought a discussion of sanctification would be about learning to be less sinful. But Doug was firm; God wants us to be fruitful, and He knows we'll keep sinning until we die. A sin focus is a loser focus because it takes our eyes off the real target. This certainly accords with everything we've said about identity in Christ, a concept I had yet to grasp.

For me, this emphasis on being fruitful was revolutionary because I had spent so many years wondering when God was finally going to strike me dead, which had a dampening effect on my serving God. Right then and there

I determined to change my approach, and I never again avoided ministry from a sense that I was too messed-up and broken to be useful. To be honest, my sins did not evaporate away, but over the years I've becoming increasingly convinced that this is the right attitude. It certainly accords with scripture; "God's kindness is intended to lead you to repentance" (Romans 2:4). I never got less sinful by feeling bad that God was mad at me, but appreciating the goodness of God sure gave me a lot more peace and made me far more available for ministry than before.

This works really well for quitting porn. Stop worrying about your porn use and start figuring out where you can serve God.

- *As long as you're frustrated with your inability to stop porn, you have a negative sin-focus, you're living from your false identity, and you are stuck in a vicious cycle of self-effort and futility.*

This may seem strange for a book on how to quit internet porn, but it is consistent with smoking cessation and sanctification in general. Smokers spend a lot of energy contemplating the benefits of being tobacco-free, including all the things they'll do and all the things they'll buy with their savings. We'll get to the specifics later, but a positive approach is more effective than a negative approach, which is why I've taken the risky approach in this book of ignoring the harms of internet porn completely. Take it on faith if you have to. Fruitful is the new sinless. Try traveling that road for a while. That's the direction out.

Conclusion

Sexuality is spiritual, and closely related to the concept of worship, so quitting porn is a spiritual exercise. Therefore, it's not easily accomplished by self-effort. Sanctification is by grace through faith, and is the work of the Holy Spirit in our lives. We cooperate with this by knowing the things that God declares are true about us, considering these facts, and then presenting ourselves to God. One way we present ourselves to God is by being available for Christian ministry, like any good employee who shows up at work. As we focus on being fruitful instead of sinless, we will find quitting porn a lot easier. Now it's time to take a good look at where we're at with pornography and make a good plan for quitting, which is the topic of Chapter 4.

Chapter Summary and Assignments

- Quitting porn is "sanctification," or becoming more spiritual, which only happens by grace and not self-effort.
- Therefore, our identity in Christ defeats porn when we live from our new identity using the "know, consider, present" approach.
- Ultimately, a fruitful Christian life is better than being sinless. Fruitful is the new spiritual.

Assignments

- Complete Worksheet 3: My Identity in Christ
- What day and time will you read the next chapter? Make an appointment with yourself to keep up your momentum.

Worksheet 3: My identity in Christ

Collect some verses on your identity in Christ. A few are in the chapter, but you can add your own. Gather lots of verses. Don't hold back.

Reference	What it says about my identity in Christ
Galatians 2:20	
Philippians 3:8	
Ephesians 1:20	

Kicking the Habit: Quitting Pornography Under Grace by Joel Hughes, Ph.D.
Copyright ©2018 by New Paradigm Publishing

Chapter 5

Planning to quit part 1

Agenda for Chapter 5

To understand that quitting any compulsive behavior requires careful planning. There are many practical steps that you can take to get ready. These include setting a quit date, starting to meditate daily on carefully selected scriptures, recruiting social support, and self-monitoring.

My father taught me to fly fish on the blue-ribbon waters of the Deschutes river in Eastern Oregon. For dad, it was imperative to arrive before the sun rose, as there were limited fishing spots and intense competition. The gentleman code of fishermen dictated that you would not pull your car into a spot where other people had already staked their claim by parking in a prominent spot and standing spread out, effectively guarding the bank for 50 yards in both directions while they waited for the sun to rise. Given the urgency of arriving at O-dark-thirty, we would leave home at about 2 AM. Pulling in at 5 or so, we usually beat all comers to the "bathtub hole," the "mystery hole," or another such jackpot. We would then sometimes try to get a few moments of uncomfortable car sleep before the festivities began.

One year, we were especially eager to fish during the brief but intense stonefly hatch. Black and red flying bugs the size of grasshoppers swarmed the trees, air, and water for about a week once or twice a year. They would land on the river to lay eggs, and trout would rise with the trajectory of a Polaris missile launched from a nuclear submarine breaking the surface of the ocean. Loud splashes could be heard periodically, in any kind of water. Shallow, deep, fast, slow, it didn't matter once the fish realized that a feeding frenzy was underway. Determined to slay dozens of these little sliver-sided sharks (catch and release only, of course), we stormed off to the Deschutes one very hot day near the end of the hatch. We caught a lot of fish.

Then someone asked hesitantly, "did anyone bring any food?" In our haste and excitement, we had left home with nothing. A search of the car was fruitless, yielding not even an old package of crackers or mints from the glove box. We had nothing. We also had nothing to cook with, so unless we wanted to chew trout sushi like a bear during the salmon run, we couldn't eat the fish we were catching. By noon it was unbearable. So hungry. And hot. Of course, we also brought nothing to drink other than the coffee finished hours ago on the drive through the darkness to the river. So at about 1 PM, we tucked our tails back into the car and headed off to find food, surrendering a prime fishing spot to the people just finally showing up to fish.

Who forgets food and water? The day was not exactly ruined, but it would have gone a lot better and been a lot less painful if we had planned ahead. A lot of people don't plan ahead at all for major life decisions. That's bad. Apparently, the new 20-somethings are more likely than previous generations to move to new cities with no job, choosing a location before employment and assuming they'll figure it out when they get there. Unless they run out of money. A lot of people start businesses based on their passion, with no idea how to run a business. This is one reason a lot of startups fail. Just because you love organic grass-fed goat milk soap doesn't mean you know how to farm goats successfully. A lot of Christian men have a "just don't do it" mentality when it comes to porn. If it works for them, so be it. But many need more than good intentions. You really need to look before you leap, or failure is assured.

Look before you leap

The approach of planning for a specific day on which to quit pornography may seem unusual, as men are typically eager to get on with it once they've decided to make the change. But smoking cessation programs suggest that preparing to quit is important. Quitting an addictive or compulsive behavior will involve intense cravings, established behavior patterns, mixed motives, hidden triggers, and other barriers to success. It would be wise to scan the horizon for these barriers and make a plan for overcoming them before actually quitting. As I suggested at the end of chapter four, it's quite common for people to quit suddenly after the first meeting, but they also tend to blow carbon monoxide on their "did you smoke?" breathalyzer test at the next meeting. It's very discouraging to fail right as you're starting.

Now that we've covered all the "theory" in chapters one through four, it's time for action in chapters five through eight. The phases of quitting proceed as depicted in **Figure 1**. The first phase is getting ready to quit, or planning for the quit date. That is the topic of this chapter and the next chapter. The second phase is actually quitting, which starts on the quit date and lasts for perhaps 2-4 weeks. The final phase is staying quit, or relapse prevention. That phase lasts for years, as you settle into a new pornless happy-ever-after.

Figure 1: The Phases of Quitting Pornography

Set a quit date

The first step is setting a date on which you will quit pornography *for good*. Setting a quit date is easy. When people come to smoking cessation therapy, they set a quit date for about one week away. Just long enough to finish a short "to do" list, such as switching to a less-desired and lower-nicotine brand of cigarette (like regular to menthol), fading back on the number of cigarettes they smoke, gathering their circle of support, and contemplating their motivation to quit. If you've read this far, you're probably getting impatient to have an official quit date. Pick a day on the calendar a week or two away, and make sure you have plenty of time to get through the worksheets, checklists, and action items at the end of the chapter. I suggest picking a workday or school day, as opposed to a day off. The first few days are hard, so pick a day you'll be distracted and busy. In the days leading up to your quit date, plan on taking at least a half hour per day completing the worksheets and tasks on the checklists. You want to be completely set when it's time to quit. Write that day on the worksheets for this chapter. Keep that day in mind.

Yeah I know, you already quit. Fine. But you've quit a dozen times before, and you always started again. This time you're going to make that *firm decision to quit*, get ready with your fences, defenses, and offense, and pick a day that you will *actually quit*. This is not an excuse for one last 3-day bender until your hand is sore and your member bleeds, because there's no evidence that bingeing helps people stop. Rather, a firm quit date is an acknowledgment that a compulsive habit does not go away automatically without careful planning and a solid strategy. This is why I said not to freak out if you don't get to "zero" per day until your quit date—you're still getting ready.

Planning for the quit date

Planning for the quit date involves all of the elements of quitting listed in **Table 2**, but focuses first on the self-monitoring, social support, and fences. As the quit date approaches, plans are made for defenses, and the positive motivation aspect of the offensive game plan comes into focus. Given what was covered in Chapter three, it's critical to address both God's part and Man's part in planning to quit.

The Need for Self-monitoring

The first step is self-monitoring and cutting back on use of internet pornography. God's part in this step is to establish a daily habit of prayer and Bible reading. This is time for digging through scripture related to your identity in Christ, the power of Christ for sanctification, and other topics listed in the worksheet. Man's part is going to be recording the number of times per day that you use internet pornography, including the time of day, the device used (phone, laptop), and your mental state at the time. There are a number of reasons that this has to be done daily and recorded on the worksheet.

Self-monitoring is foundational to every behavior change intervention. First, every "real" behavioral therapy targeting adults (who can read and write) must include behavioral monitoring and worksheets. If your therapist just wants to talk about global warming and celebrity news, that's not therapy. They should be pushing paper across the desk that requires you to track your sleep, eating, exercise, or mood depending on what the problem is that you've come to them for help. The consensus of the scientific literature on behavior change is that self-monitoring is a key element of increasing or decreasing a behavior. People cannot accurately report what they're doing from memory, and they can't change what they don't notice, so a good therapist insists that you track the behavior. Tracking a behavior makes you aware of the behavior, allows you to start to see how it is operating in your life, short-circuits the tendency to mindlessly engage in the behavior without any awareness of why you're doing it, and actually changes the frequency of the behavior. For example, smokers who count the number of cigarettes they smoke will automatically smoke fewer cigarettes than those who don't. The power of self-monitoring for porn use would be worth it on that basis alone.

If you already quit, this is easy. Write "zero" on every day. Doesn't that feel good? However, *you must be honest*. If you actually use porn twice on Tuesday, you must enter "2" and fill out the rest of the worksheet. This is really important so that you can start to understand when and why you use.

By the way...Self-control ain't what you thought! Self-control is not a muscle that gets weak. There has been a recent scientific revolution in our understanding of self-control and willpower. A prominent (and longstanding) theory called "ego depletion" said that self-control is a limited resource that can get used up by "spending" it on something.[28] This self-control theory suggests the exerting self-control depletes the ego, which then leaves people with less self-control when a new challenge is encountered. This has been used to explain self-control for all kinds of things, like eating behavior, in which things like stress or effort in one area of life might deplete self-control to not eat the toxic food. However, recent evidence suggests that this is not the whole story.

The classic ego-depletion effect used freshly baked cookies and raw bitter radishes.[29] When participants forced themselves to eat radishes instead of cookies, they gave up faster on an unsolvable puzzle task. This was used to argue that self-control is a limited resource that can be used up. This study has been cited thousands of times and is considered a classic. This study makes intuitive sense, but I'm more interested in the reverse effect. When crunching through my unsolvable paperwork at my job, it feels like my resolve *not* to eat candy is depleted. When you're stressed out, will you lose resolve to *not* use porn? You don't have to be.

They were wrong. Other scientists started to question the ego-depletion studies. A recent meta-analysis ("mathematical summary") of the studies found that when certain factors are accounted for there is not much evidence for ego-depletion or the idea that self-control is a limited resource.[30] One of those factors is considering how many studies didn't work out and were thus never published. Finally, new studies started to cast serious doubt on how self-control was supposed to get used up and replenished. For example, a study related to food tested the ego-depletion effect using another one of the classic methods.[31] People were given a sugar-containing drink, which was supposed to preserve their self-control (guard against depletion) by raising blood glucose. This did not happen, which calls the whole ego-depletion effect into question. Turns out, the neuroscience was nonsense, as sugar water does not raise blood glucose quickly enough to replenish self-control as the early theorists thought.

The implications for stopping pornography are clear; is it the case that using self-control to resist can result in "using up" all the self-control you have? Apparently not. At least not in the way that ego-depletion theory has suggested. What does this have to do with filling out self-monitoring paperwork? We don't have time right now to explain how self-control actually works, but to cut to the punchline, *a major source of self-control is establishing habits*. Daily self-monitoring of any behavior is a powerful way to make or break habits, and since habits are a way to reinforce self-control, starting this habit immediately is important.

Self-monitoring

God's part. Why did Daniel pray three times a day (Daniel 6:10)? Daniel got down on his knees three times each day, even if he was threatened with death. Praying three times each day was not in the Law of Moses. To me, this suggests that Daniel built prayer into a habit that he could keep because the pressures of Babylon were just too much for someone that only prays when they feel like it. Apparently, Daniel already knew that self-control comes from established habits, not sheer force of will. Now many observant Jews pray three times a day, even though it is still not in the law, because they learned from what Daniel practiced. Daniel was the first to show the power of self-monitoring for establishing a prayer habit.

Get the **prayer and scripture** worksheet, and each day record the time you set aside for prayer and study of scripture. Include the place, the passage, and the basic content of the prayer. This must be done every day leading up to the quit attempt and every day during the "active quitting" phase, but you can stop after you have successfully quit for 30 days or so. Unless you love God, in which case you want to keep a prayer journal forever, right? Don't you love God? Kidding. Stay focused on quitting porn for this assignment. If you already have a prayer journal, it's perfectly fine to use that for this assignment, so long as you keep a daily record of prayer and scripture time.

Pray about anything, but it's a good idea to include the topics from Chapter 3. When we get to the active quitting phase, you should have started a daily prayer habit, and there'll be more specific suggestions on what to pray about.

Same for scripture. Read anything, but consider adding in suggested verses from any of the worksheets. I'll never forget something Christian Philosopher J. P. Moreland[32] said one day in chapel at Biola University when I was a college student. I can't quote him exactly (it was about 1990!), but it was something along the lines of how, in his experience, the only thing that he has seen consistently help men with their struggles with lust was memorization of scripture. He didn't explain how that works or why it would, but I never forgot his sincerity or force of his conviction that committing the word of God to memory was kryptonite for the lust that plagues Christian men. Howard Hendricks[33] also made a similar statement in a 2003 lecture in Columbus Ohio. "You know what I've discovered working with people (*struggling with porn or other addictions*) ... is that once I get a person on an intensive bible memory program, we begin to see supernatural changes in their life. It's a miracle, what God does."[34] Try it.

Man's part. Your part in self-monitoring is to record each day the number of times you use internet pornography using the worksheet or similar. As we've stated, this will automatically reduce the frequency of porn use. It will also allow you to start to see any patterns. Do you use when you're bored? Angry? Lonely? When do you use? Late at night? On a break at work or school? What's your poison; smartphone, laptop, or tablet? Getting some perspective on your moments of temptation will help you set up appropriate fences and defenses. I knew one man who stopped using the internet altogether to quit porn. That seemed extreme to me. How do you find the movie showing times? Is there still a phone number you can call at the theatre that will play a recording of the show times like they had in the 1980s?

If you chart your frequency for a week or two, it should start to drop off. Although we've committed to avoid comparisons with other people, I'm going to suggest that the most common answer people give for "when did you last use porn" is either today, yesterday, or within the last week. So, you may have a some zeros at first, especially if you already quit, but you still must just track it. Before the quit date and all the fences/defenses/offense go to work there is a chance you will have a "relapse" and have to put a number on the tracking worksheet. After the quit date, you can proudly put a "zero" in all the following days (but be honest). This provides a little positive reinforcement and keeps motivation strong. Seeing a string of zeros for a week or two is nice. When you get to 30 or 60 zeros in a row, you've quit porn! You can stop recording at that point.

Recruiting social support

God's part. When you're getting ready to quit is the time to recruit a support person. This can be the person who disciples you or some of the men in your men's bible study or small group. This can be a friend or relative, like your older brother. Just find a Christian man you can trust and tell them that you've decided to quit using internet pornography once and for all. You're leveraging the power of the Body of Christ and the bond that men of faith can have together. "As iron sharpens iron, so one person sharpens another" (Proverbs 27:17).

Ask your support person(s) to work with you on this project. If this seems awkward, remember that secrecy fuels our sins by keeping them hidden in the dark. Drag it out into the light, kicking and screaming if you have to. If you don't have a close friend, this is a great way to start building a real relationship with someone. If the person you choose seems shocked and dismayed, they're a hypocrite, or naïve, or they just don't understand human nature. We are all sinners in so many ways, so I am no longer surprised by much of what men tell me in confidence.

Brian Gardner's excellent *Porn Free: Renewal through Truth and Community*[35] has an expanded discussion of the importance of Christian community in men's campaign to address sexual sin and temptation in their lives (**see Appendix A**). It also has perhaps the best explanation of the doctrines of grace and identity in Christ of any of the Christian books on this topic, by the way. This is why I recommend having this book in your arsenal. The Planning to Quit phase would be a good time to check it out.

Tell your "accountability person" your quit date. Explain why there's a quit date if they look puzzled. Show them this workbook. Ask them to read it with you. Pray with them. Ask them to be one of the people whose email you enter into the accountability software you're installing on all your devices. Give them your cell phone and ask them to enter a password in the parental controls that only they will know. It is possible that you won't be able to go to some legitimate websites (e.g., breast cancer awareness month), but that's worth it. You can always find a desktop computer to do the research for your class paper on breast cancer. If they get "porn alerts" that you were on the National Cancer Society webpage, they know you weren't looking at boobies.

The point of being accountable is not to have someone else be the "sin police" in your life. Having "accountability partners" usually doesn't work because it just makes people want to be dishonest to look good, and it can set up a sin-focus in the relationship. There's no chance they can "hold you accountable." I see no evidence in scripture that other people can stop us from lusting. However, you do need spiritual support in the form of at least one person to walk with on this journey. The very best approach is to be in a close-knit Body of Christ *aka* church, with lots of solid relationships with other men. This is a major theme of the New Testament. It has been argued that the sin of porn is nothing compared to the sin of ignoring all of the commands about "one another."[36] Therefore, quitting porn is much easier if you enlist at least one trusted Christian man to help you.

Man's part. All smokers are supposed to tell their friends and family that they are going to quit. Sometimes they even write letters to hand out. The rationale is obvious; even a callous smoker will be less likely to hand a cigarette to a friend they know is trying to quit. In the case of porn, you don't need to tell everyone but you do need to tell someone as I've discussed above.

This is also when you install the snitch software on all your devices and fix your routers to filter out the porn. I won't get into the specifics, because technology changes all the time, but popular choices include the X3watch software (at http://x3watch.com/) by XXX Church (https://www.xxxchurch.com/) and the Accountable2You software (https://www.accountable2you.com/). Some of these are listed as resources in **Appendix A.** There is even a solution that combines hardware and software, the Circle® device with MyCircle™ software used by Disney.[37][38] It's cheap, easy to set up, and used at the Disney resorts so they have invested a lot of time and money in creating a technology that is hard to defeat. It requires the iOS or Android app to operate, and I suppose that one drawback is that it won't be much of a fence against porn if you are the network administrator for your home. Again, technology changes all the time so by talking with your friends it should be possible to find something that matches your situation.

For now, the point is that installing the snitch software, filters, and other blockades against pornography happens at the same time you recruit your social support. After all, what's the point of installing the software without anyone's email address to enter? If no one is notified when you surf for porn, the problem stays hidden and secret.

Chapter Summary and Assignments

- Quitting any compulsive behavior is more successful when people plan to quit and set a quit date.
- Use self-monitoring to establish good habits and track bad habits. Self-control is founded on habits, so modifying habits is a great way to increase self-control. Self-monitoring of porn use will also automatically reduce porn use.
- Recruiting social support gives you a better chance for success.

Assignments

- Complete Worksheet 4: Bible and Prayer Time Self-Monitoring
- Complete Worksheet 5: Porn Use Self-Monitoring
- What day and time will you read the next chapter? Make an appointment with yourself to keep up your momentum.

Worksheet 4: Bible and prayer times

Choose a quit date.

My quit date is: _____

Scripture and prayer record. (Make copies of this page and continue as necessary or use another prayer journal or your phone).

Date and time	Passage	Prayer topics
/ /		
/ /		
/ /		
/ /		
/ /		
/ /		
/ /		
/ /		
/ /		
/ /		
/ /		
/ /		
/ /		
/ /		
/ /		
/ /		

Kicking the Habit: Quitting Pornography Under Grace by Joel Hughes, Ph.D.
Copyright ©2018 by New Paradigm Publishing

Worksheet 5: Porn use self-monitoring

Choose a quit date.

My quit date is: _____

Self-monitor record. (Make copies of this page and continue as necessary or use another notebook or your phone; when you get to 30 or 60 zeros in a row, you can stop).

Date	# of times	Circumstances: time, location, device, how you felt, etc.
/ /		
/ /		
/ /		
/ /		
/ /		
/ /		
/ /		
/ /		
/ /		
/ /		
/ /		
/ /		
/ /		
/ /		
/ /		
/ /		
/ /		

Kicking the Habit: Quitting Pornography Under Grace by Joel Hughes, Ph.D.
Copyright ©2018 by New Paradigm Publishing

Chapter 6

Planning to quit part 2

Agenda for Chapter 6

Continuing to plan now involves altering your environment (e.g., porn blocking software) and considering the things that may make you vulnerable to porn. These include spiritual "footholds," which are deeper problems that have not been adequately addressed, and "triggers," which are reminders that make you want to use porn. Finally, appreciating the benefits of quitting is a more durable motivator than trying to resist temptation, because it is rooted in a commitment to core values.

As the quit date nears, you will need to reflect on your self-monitoring, and start to set up fences and defenses against being exposed to pornography. This includes some introspection (or group discussion) on what it is about you that makes you prone to compulsive porn use. Have you allowed the devil a foothold in your life? Are you constantly exposed to triggers? You'll want to renounce any footholds and eliminate or avoid triggers. Simultaneously, you'll start to mount a strong offense, which includes clarifying your core values in this area and elaborating the benefits you expect to gain by being porn-free.

Setting up fences

God's part. We're already on the topic of setting up "fences" against the coming porn invasion. It's important to have a defense that at least makes it harder to access pornography. However, you also need to search your heart for "footholds" and consider whether or not there are any serious underlying problems that are contributing to your problem.

In *Surfing for God,* (see **Appendix A**) Mike Cusick makes the excellent point that keeping a pornography habit opens us up to spiritual influence from our adversary. This works like bitterness, which the Bible says gives the devil a "foothold" in your life (Ephesians 4:27). If you have had a porn habit for very long, there is a good chance that your lust, guilt, shame, and so on has served to crack open the door of your mind to allow accusation, temptation, and so on from the Devil to climb in and stick around, causing trouble. Therefore, you probably need to do some soul-searching to think about whether or not you've unintentionally held on to something that keeps you vulnerable. In the case of anger and bitterness, the Bible suggests getting rid of it so that you don't give the devil a foothold in your life. *Until you are willing to put down your resentment toward someone, you will be vulnerable to spiritual attack.* How does this apply to porn? Until you are willing to put down your beef with the world or the people around you, you have left the Devil a foothold. As one example, you may have the attitude that you can keep "just a little" porn in your life, so you would stay vulnerable to continuing to use porn and all the spiritual attack that brings.

What are your footholds? The footholds are probably different for different people, but the point is to consider whether you're "holding back" some area of your life. This is like a resentful person who keeps their angry bitterness but pretends that they are on good terms with everyone. If you are holding back, like "I won't use porn unless everyone is gone for the weekend and I miss my girlfriend"—that's a foothold. You may also be unhappy that you don't have a girlfriend, which could make you vulnerable to the allure of cheap (fake) sex online.

Lust is also probably a foothold. You cannot escape sexual desire (nor should you!) but there is a difference between feeling your God-given interest in women and allowing yourself to wallow in sustained desire. If bitterness is an unrelenting anger that you won't dismiss, then lust is going beyond appreciating beauty into the place where you dwell on dark desires, nurturing temptation until it grows into a porn problem. If bitterness is described as a "root" that springs up like an ugly weed that destroys your relationships (Hebrews 12:15), then lust is a similarly mutated appreciation of sexual attractiveness that gives birth to sin and death (James 1:15). I don't want to press this comparison too far, as my only point is that the footholds you've allowed the devil are likely more than those the Bible mentions specifically (e.g., bitterness). The key to footholds is to drop them. Let it go. Don't hold on to anything that gives your adversary leverage to pull you back into bondage. There's no tug of war if you drop your end of the rope, right?

What are your footholds? Get rid of them.

Do you have underlying issues? It's also important to consider whether or not there are serious problems that contribute to your porn use. Everyone knows that people who were sexually molested or abused often act out in sexual ways. A trauma history is not at the root of every addiction or compulsive behavior, but unresolved trauma certainly makes it worse for a number of reasons. Sometimes a person has experiences in their past that desensitized them to inappropriate behavior. Sometimes people use substances (like drugs and alcohol) or experiences (like sex or porn) to feel better. Getting your love feelings from porn is pretty lame and empty, but a lot of people do it. Also, people who have mental health problems like depression or attention deficit hyperactivity disorder (ADHD) may have a hard time quitting smoking or porn. These things must be dealt with. It is conceivable that you have struggled to quit porn because you are depressed, have untreated ADHD, have bipolar disorder or schizophrenia, or have some other underlying problem that you've not dealt with? One *key feature* of many of these problems (anxiety, depression, trauma) is avoiding dealing with them. This leaves you vulnerable to "self-medicating" with alcohol, tobacco, drugs, or sex (e.g., porn). You really must take these vulnerabilities seriously and get help. Getting help is beyond the scope of this book, so you will want to talk to your social support and get some recommendations for a Christian counselor or therapist. You may need to see your physician, or even a psychiatrist in the case of severe mental illnesses like bipolar disorder.

One caution you should be aware of is that you must get consultation if you think you have underlying issues that make quitting pornography difficult. It is easy to deceive yourself with excuses like "but I'm depressed!" Your friends may see it differently (i.e., "you're not too depressed to stop using porn..."), so underlying issues must be dragged out into the light for your social support to see for themselves. Talking about it openly is also the first step toward facing the issue instead of continuing to avoid it.

Man's part. When it comes to setting up fences, your part is to get rid of everything, set up the software blockade, and eliminate hidden triggers. As I mentioned in Chapter 2, smokers search *everywhere* for any half-finished packs, loose cigarettes, or lighters. In the case of porn, you need to conduct a "sweep and clear" exercise to eliminate all pornography from your life. At the end of a chapter is a checklist that lists the likely spots, like the computer hard drive and portable media. Of course, there is a lot of variability here. A lot of men no longer hide magazines and VHS tapes under the bed, but whatever you possess must go. You should also clear all browser histories and basically any possible way to "accidentally" stumble across something from your (soon to be) past. Do your best to make it really hard to encounter any pornography that you put there, whether it's a downloaded file or a browser link.

In addition to getting rid of everything, this is when the "software blockade" goes up. Every device, from the work desktop to the phone, gets some version of porn-blocking software. Perhaps this can be accomplished at the router level, using OpenDNS[39]. I am not a computer expert, so I will refer you to a book in **Appendix A**, *How to Quit Porn*[40], which has a much more sophisticated description of porn-blocking that I am capable of. For your tablets and phone(s), I recommend setting the parental controls to block adult sites and handing the device to your trusted friend who then enters a passcode that only they will know. Yes, you will not be able to look up an interview with Mark Regnerus discussing his recent book *Cheap Sex: The Transformation of Men, Marriage, and Monogamy*[41] because the filter won't allow it, but you can always go back to your home desktop to access that content.

The basic point of content filtering is to make it really hard, or at least inconvenient, to access pornography when you're bored or itchy. Obviously, you may not have the authority to install blockers on every computer you could access, like the computers at work. For that you will have to exert some shred of self-control, and we'll get to those techniques later. However, blocking every device that you can will magically eliminate porn from just coming to you, for the most part.

Hidden triggers. Finally, it's time to search for "hidden triggers" in your life. Triggers are things that make you think of using pornography, and some are even unconscious associations. In the same sense that smokers find themselves wandering into the convenience store at the gas station to look at the wall of cigarette cartons, you may find yourself pulling out your phone when all the roommates leave the apartment for work. Locking down access on the phone will take care of that one, but what are your other triggers? If you have been leafing through the lingerie catalogs that end up in your mailbox, *and that leads to an internet surfing session*, then cancel that catalog or throw it away. If you read news articles online that have sexy clickbait advertisements, you may have to put up an ad blocker or use a different website for a while. If you like to drink a few with the boys on Friday night, *but then end up online after you get home*, you may have to stop drinking with the boys for a while. You should still go out, but get an ice water with lemon and eat some wings instead of drinking beer. Less carbs. The reason it is so important to identify and avoid these triggers is because, despite your best intentions, there are stimulus-response links that erode our resolve in the moment. Making sure you're not confronted with any triggers for a couple months is a really good idea.

Mounting an offense

Going on the offense against porn? Absolutely. You'll feel better if you come out on the attack, swinging with both fists instead of cowering in a corner wringing your hands and twitching with worried eyes darting back and forth to look for temptation. The fences and defenses will give you a chance, but now it's time to attack.

When Jesus said "...I will build my church, and the gates of Hades will not overcome it." (Matthew 16:18) he was saying that all of the fortifications the Devil throws up against the church will not stop the invasion. God is invading the earth, looking to rescue captives. He is not on the defense, just trying to keep Satan from causing too much damage. Paul said "The weapons we fight with are not the weapons of the world. On the contrary, they have divine power to demolish strongholds. We demolish arguments and every pretension that sets itself up against the knowledge of God, and we take captive every thought to make it obedient to Christ" (2 Corinthians 10:4-5). He was saying that we are attacking false ideologies with spiritual weapons, and taking captive every arrogant belief that opposes God to replace them with thoughts that honor Jesus Christ. In the war on porn, we have absolutely magnificent weapons.

God's part. In Chapter 3, we already learned that sanctification, which includes breaking free from porn, is by grace through faith. It is not something that we can do on our own power, but we have the power of the Spirit of God to transform us. Our job is "know, consider, present." Therefore, as you're getting ready to quit and during the quitting phase, keep reviewing the verses that relate to "knowing," such as Romans 6:3 and Galatians 2:20. Start to adopt the mindset that these statements are literally true, which is the "consider" part of the process. In addition, keep reviewing Romans 7:24-25, where Paul explains that we need to be delivered by Jesus Christ from our sins. Continue to pray for deliverance as the day of quitting draws near.

God's part in our offense against porn also includes reviewing the material on your identity in Christ. As discussed in Chapter 3, your identity in Christ will defeat porn. In your prayer journal or worksheet, start to include verses that focus on your identity in Christ, like the gloriously long complicated single sentence that is Ephesians 1:15-23. Paul was so excited that he jettisoned grammar entirely to get this on paper. These identity verses can be a big part of the "know" and "consider."

Finally, your offensive campaign against porn will include presenting yourself to God for good works (Titus 2:14). Start to reflect on the *spiritual benefits* of quitting pornography. In what ways has porn held you back from going "all in" to serve God? Have you been wrapped up in "everything that hinders and the sin that so easily entangles?" (Hebrews 12:1). How would it feel to "throw off" the porn? Would this help you "run with perseverance the race marked out for us?" (Hebrews 12:1) Could you run faster and longer if you lost 40 pounds? (OK, I can relate to this illustration but maybe you're a skinny dude.) Would you feel closer to Christ if pornography was not bothering your conscience? You would not actually be closer, as the identity verses are clear that you are *in Christ*, but when we're mired in the muck of porn we can feel distant and cold. That can all change. Start to list the *spiritual benefits* of a pornography-free life. This positive attack is important because conviction will waver in times of stress or boredom, and during those times the *benefits* will be more powerful motivators than the *harms* we think will come from just one more dip into the porn pool.

Man's part. Smokers set a quit date so they can get ready, and a key element of readiness is a *firm decision to quit.* Many people try to stop half-heartedly, because they don't like the health risks, but they love the nicotine. When it comes to porn, it's exactly the same. Most Christian men who try to quit make a reasonable effort, but either their approach is wrong (e.g., self-effort), or they haven't actually decided to quit. Quitting smoking or pornography or any other compulsive behavior requires an *absolute commitment to stop*. This is because we are always ambivalent, which means that we have mixed motives. There are harms and dangers of pornography, and there are also benefits. I'm not going to lie, sin is fun (for a season—Hebrews 11:25). If there was no attraction to dirty pictures and sexy videos, we would never have started to seek them out. Therefore, it's wise to be honest with ourselves and acknowledge that it's hard to make a firm decision to quit. The best approach is to root the decision in our long-term goals and core values, instead of our current feelings.

The only published clinical trials of a porn-cessation program I could find used an approach called "acceptance and commitment therapy."[42][43] In this approach, people are taught to *accept* the thoughts and feelings that war against their goals instead of denying them, trying to push them away, or trying to change them. In the case of depression, for example, people would be taught that "sadness happens" and instead of exerting monumental effort to never feel sad, it might be a better idea to allow the sadness to pass through your life without freaking out or fighting it so hard.

The flipside of accepting is *commitment,* which means that people are taught to take an inventory of their core values and long-term life goals, and then learn to live in ways that support their values regardless of how they feel. In the case of depression, people's core values might be family and fitness, for example. They would be taught to engage in those relationships and persist in their exercise routine, *even though* they feel sad and depressed. Living by core values is similar to living from your identity in Christ, which we already saw is a firmer foundation than living from your false identity or how you feel in any given moment. Applied to pornography, the (mostly Mormon) men in these studies were taught to accept the urges, feelings of temptation, boredom, or whatever they were feeling related to porn and then choose to live according to their core values instead. Did it work? The men in the acceptance and commitment group had a 90% reduction in the amount of porn they used, and over half quit completely. The reduction in porn use generally lasted when they asked again three months later. Wow. I'm sold.

When you're making that *firm decision to quit*, make sure that you're reflecting on your core values (and identity in Christ). When you're clear-headed and thinking rationally, you know that you don't want to use porn. That's not consistent with your identity or values. It's not important to erase every shred of reluctance to quit. Those we will *accept.* Sin has (brief) benefits like pleasure, so don't deny it. In the next chapter I will have more to say about accepting and dealing with the urges and surges of wanting to fall back into the old habit, but during the preparation phase it's really important to orient your thinking away from how you feel and toward your core values. This helps you make the firm decision to quit, this helps you see the spiritual benefits of quitting, and this helps you accept the pain that is coming.

Benefits of Quitting. Finally, once you made the decision to quit for good, you can think clearly about the good of quitting. This will be fun! People who quit smoking don't stop because of the dangers of smoking nearly as easily as they stop because of the benefits of quitting. Applied to porn, there are a number of benefits of being porn free. The worksheet at the end of this chapter lists a few areas in which you should see benefits: spiritual, mental, relational, physical, and occupational. There may be more, so go crazy with that worksheet. Write down as many benefits as you can imagine. The point is to have a mountain of evidence that life without porn will be great, and much *better* than life with porn.

Here's a preview:

Spiritual benefits. Feeling "light" and "free" because there is no guilt or shame from pornography. No longer weighed down by secret porn, resulting in more energy for Christian ministry.

Mental benefits. More mental energy and clarity, because there is no need to remember to cover my tracks. Like a liar who starts telling the truth, I don't have to remember what story I told each person. No fear when someone picks up my phone or uses my laptop to look something up. There is nothing to hide and they will not find anything. Mind is not preoccupied with sex all day every day, because I stopped wallowing in filth. Now I have energy to think about what I want to.

Relational benefits. Feel closer to my wife (or friends, if you're single). Just talking about this openly brings me closer to the Christian men in my life. They're giving me that "atta boy" look when they ask how it's been. When women walk by I don't look at them like a hungry wolf eyeing a delicious little lamb. Able to talk to women without thinking about sex.

Physical benefits. (For married men) Virility is at 16-year-old levels again. Getting hard from just seeing my wife's shadow on the sidewalk. No fear of the impotence porn can cause. More stamina in bed. (For single men) Testosterone levels are high, providing much energy to work out. Can masturbate in 30 seconds with explosive orgasms.[44]

Occupational benefits. All the time wasted on porn is reclaimed for work, study, or projects. No fear of detection by the system administrator. Feeling efficient and productive at everything because there's no anchor dragging me back down all the time.

There are so many benefits of quitting pornography, so have fun with this and make it really personal for you. Be so honest with yourself that you can't write down some of the benefits you envision. I know that I am close to the line of not-edifying in my examples, but that's intentional. Benefits need to be vivid, clear, realistic, personal, and memorable.

The reason that a rich description of the benefits of quitting is so important is because our commitment to core values is a much more powerful motivator than our attempts to resist temptation. You will absolutely eat the free chocolate donuts in the break room if your only strategy is resisting the temptation of their chocolatey goodness. You will not eat them if your strategy is a strong offense, as you consider the many benefits of your accelerating weight loss for example. The benefits of quitting will keep you going during the difficult times ahead. Try to make the benefits you list really personal. Core values should be "core" and not peripheral, and are most powerful when they touch on your identity. Vegetarians don't struggle with whether or not they should order the New York strip steak or the vegetable medley. They're a vegetarian. No willpower required.

Conclusion

Planning to quit may seem counter-intuitive, as most Christian men are eager to just quit immediately. However, there is serious work to do that you should not skip. When you have set a quit date, started self-monitoring your scripture reading, prayer, and porn use, recruited your social support, set up your fences and defenses, and made that firm decision to quit (complete with a list of the benefits), you're really ready. The quit date is coming, and that will be the day you start the next phase of quitting porn, which is the topic of Chapter 4.

Chapter Summary and Assignments

- Setting up fences like the snitch and blocking hardware and software gives you a great chance for success.
- Stopping pornography depends on a *firm decision to quit* that stems from commitment to core values, which are best illustrated by the benefits you expect to gain by quitting porn.

Assignments

- Complete Worksheet 6: Setting up Fences
- Complete Worksheet 7: Benefits of Quitting
- What day and time will you read the next chapter? Read the next three chapters (to the end of **Section III**) *before* you quit so that you are familiar with the new defenses and offensive strategies you'll need.

Worksheet 6: Setting up fences—Sweep and clear! Detect hidden triggers!

Get rid of it! All of it. Check these:

- ☐ Computer hard drive
- ☐ Portable storage media (micro USB memory cards, etc.)
- ☐ Browser histories, links, etc.
- ☐ Every Device!
    - o Desktop computer
    - o Laptop(s)
    - o Tablet(s)
    - o Phone

Software Blockade:

- ☐ Every Device!
    - o Desktop computer
    - o Laptop(s)
    - o Tablet(s)
    - o Phone (have someone enter a password and set the parental controls to block adult sites)

What are your hidden triggers? A trigger is anything that you find reduces your resolve not to go find pornography. Anything. Hanging out on websites with sexy click bait. Watching women's beach volleyball on TV. Watching TV shows that aren't porn but get you interested in finding porn. Anything. *How will you avoid these triggers for a while?*

Trigger	Avoidance Plan

Kicking the Habit: Quitting Pornography Under Grace by Joel Hughes, Ph.D.
Copyright ©2018 by New Paradigm Publishing

Worksheet 7: Benefits of quitting

List the benefits of quitting porn in all the areas that are important to you. Make them personal and positive.

Spiritual benefits: _____
_____
_____
_____

Mental benefits: _____
_____
_____
_____

Relational benefits: _____
_____
_____
_____

Physical benefits: _____
_____
_____
_____

Occupational benefits: _____
_____
_____
_____

Other areas? _____
_____
_____
_____

Kicking the Habit: Quitting Pornography Under Grace by Joel Hughes, Ph.D.
Copyright ©2018 by New Paradigm Publishing

Chapter 7

Breaking free, or quitting part 1: Defense

Agenda for Chapter 7

To describe the defensive strategies for the Quitting Phase. This phase is a *considerable amount of work*, and lasts 2-4 weeks until the urges fade and old h habits die. There are four worksheets to complete over these two chapters, and it is critically important to march through the process of completing as many quitting activities as you can tolerate. The "Preparing to Quit" phase built a platform from to launch your successful quit attempt, and now you must prepare an action plan to get through the urges, dismantle old habits, and transition to the attack. Chapter six is defense, and chapter seven will be offense. As always, rally your support to check in with you frequently during this critical period of kicking the habit.

In the second season of Netflix original series *Stranger Things*,[45][46] one of the boys finds a small but noisy slug monster in the trash can outside of his house. Inexplicably finding the creature cute, he adopts it as a pet and takes it inside. He starts to feed it candy bars, and it rapidly grows and becomes too big to handle. He has to move it to a secret place and carefully hide his special pet from his family and friends. Soon it becomes a very dangerous demonic dog monster intent on sucking out his life force or killing him in some terrifying way. Eventually, he can no longer conceal the monster and asks for help. All the boys agreed that he should kill it, but here the story becomes unrealistic. His particular dog monster ultimately leaves him alone, unlike the scores of other monsters it had joined to run in a murderous pack. He should have killed it.

Porn is your little slug monster. It started so small. It was so cute. So manageable, just a fun little diversion you would visit and feed from time to time. It was just a little secret pet you nurtured and fed. But the growth rate was scary, and pretty soon it became a dangerous force of destruction in your world that started to suck away your life force. Science fiction analogies aside, porn destroys men. I know I promised not to write about the harms of porn, but during the writing of this book in 2017 there has been a wave of accusations against powerful men ranging from sexual harassment to sexual assault and rape. The list of men resigning, being fired, and even facing prosecution for crimes from their past grows every day. Even supporters of a former President—Bill Clinton—have started to admit that he was a sexual predator and that the women who came forward to accuse him were mistreated.[47][48][49]

What is rarely reported in the media is the fact that use of pornography fuels misconduct toward women.

There is not a lot of research, but anecdotally some men who use porn heavily eventually cross a boundary from viewing to doing. For example, Larry Nasser, the physician who molested and sexually abused gymnasts as team doctor for U.S.A. Gymnastics was recently sentenced to 60 years in prison for possession of child pornography.[50] Infamous serial killer Ted Bundy was interviewed by Dr. James Dobson (who founded Focus on the Family®) on the day before he was executed for his many sexually sadistic murders, and I'll never forget how he linked pornography to his killings.[51] He said that he reached a point where merely viewing porn no longer satisfied him, and he wanted to *actually do* the things he was watching. Of course, he tried to get rid of the evidence since his activities with women were not consensual and were unspeakably violent and traumatizing.

Obviously, most men do not transition from watching to committing acts of extreme violence, but porn certainly has a bad influence on desires, motives, and boundaries. Many men in our culture do not view porn as a negative thing and are oblivious to the very real harms it is causing in their lives. However, Christian men are very aware that the once "harmless" little porn pet has grown into an unmanageable, destructive, demonic monster. You have to kill it.

When your quit date arrives—the date on which you will quit pornography *for good*— you will kill your porn monster, and kick the (compulsive) habit. I'm using the "kill" metaphor to emphasize that you cannot *manage* porn use; you cannot keep even a little bit in your life. Smokers who have even one cigarette after they half-heartedly try to stop are highly likely to soon return to their pack-a-day habit (or however many they were used to smoking). You made a *firm decision to quit*, and now it's time to make good on that commitment.

Quitting

You've worked hard to get here. You've been self-monitoring, you've recruited your social support, you've set up your fences and defenses, and you're transitioning to the offense. **Figure 1** shows the phases of quitting pornography, and we've reached the "quitting" phase, which starts on a chosen date and lasts for a few weeks. During this phase there is more work to do, but you are breaking free and entering an exciting, positive time. Let the adventures begin!

Figure 1: The Phases of Quitting Pornography

Keep it up!

The first action-item for quitting is to keep up the things you started when you were preparing for your quit date. You continue monitoring, but now you're entering a zero every day in the log. Keep monitoring until you're well into the "Staying Quit" phase—30 to 60 consecutive zeros. Continue to pray and review your Bible verses every day. Keep your support people close, meeting with them to discuss your progress. Mend your fences. Don't let the software blockade break down, and continue to work on any "footholds." For example, if you uncovered that your porn use was partly motivated by bitterness, depression, or some other deeper problems, you are probably not done working these through. It is critical to continue working on whatever underlying issues made you vulnerable in the first place. Now, in addition to that, in the "Quitting Phase" you transition to mounting a strong defense and launching a powerful offense. To these topics we now turn.

Defenses: God's Part

Memorized meditation verses. You already have some Bible verses chosen and ideally memorized. **Worksheet 8** lists a few key verses. Write them out by hand using your favorite translation and meditate on them.

In the Bible, meditation does not mean emptying your mind and relaxing. Rather; the opposite. Biblical meditation means to focus and sustain your attention on something. One Hebrew word translated "meditate" means something like muttering, or mumbling on and on about something. The literal word meaning illustrates how meditating on God's word (Psalm 1:2) or what God has done (Psalm 77:12) is like softly repeating these things under your breath as you go about your day. This is how you ponder, consider, reflect on, and otherwise "chew on" the Bible verses. Thus, meditating on your memorized anti-porn verses all day is a great defense against porn. Here are some examples of how this might look.

"I will not look with approval on anything that is vile. I hate what faithless people do; I will have no part in it." (Psalm 101:3)

- How would it feel to be the kind of person who does not approve of any sexually explicit images or videos? Does the original context of this verse (look it up!) support the application that porn can fit into the category of a "worthless thing" that the author will not bother to look at? Is there a connection between looking approvingly at "vile" things and being like the faithless person?

"I made a covenant with my eyes not to look lustfully at a young woman." (Job 31:1).

- In what ways is making a *firm decision to quit* like making a "covenant with your eyes?" Can you feel good about making a promise to yourself not to lust after pornography without becoming *self-righteous*? Do you think that quitting porn will help you treat women with more respect?

"I have the right to do anything," you say—but not everything is beneficial. "I have the right to do anything"—but I will not be mastered by anything (1 Corinthians 6:12).

- Under grace, you will not go to hell for looking at porn or doing any other thing that you have the "right" to do. But some things are just not beneficial. Do you feel that porn had mastered you at some point? Do you think that a firm commitment not to be mastered by porn, or alcohol, or food, or exercise, or anything at all is a good goal for a Christian man? The original context for this verse is a discussion of sexuality. Look up 1 Corinthians 6 and read the passage. This jewel of a phrase "I will not be mastered by anything" was written to counter the idea that things like visiting the local temple prostitutes aren't so bad under the grace of the gospel of Jesus Christ. Work through this passage, and constantly remind yourself: "I will not be mastered by anything."

As you can see, meditating on scripture is a fantastic defense against porn, and works perfectly alongside other concepts already discussed like using the power of your identity in Christ, praying for deliverance, and adopting a positive, grace-based approach to quitting porn use.

Grace: "there is no condemnation." In chapter 3, we made the point that sexuality is spiritual and therefore quitting porn is a spiritual activity. We also made the point that sanctification, or spiritual growth such as the moral change involved in quitting pornography, requires grace and not the law. This means that you cannot just try really hard, grit your teeth, and quit porn. Now that you have "put to death" (Colossians 3:5) your little porn monster, it's very important to continue in grace.

Grace means that, ultimately, it is Jesus Christ who will rescue you from pornography, and not your own efforts. This also means that we can stay positive during this difficult period, focusing on our identity in Christ and our position in Christ. For example, Paul writes that "Therefore, there is now no condemnation for those who are in Christ Jesus, because through Christ Jesus the law of the Spirit who gives life has set you free from the law of sin and death" (Romans 8:1-2).

During the quitting phase, do your best to stay positive and focused on the free gift of freedom from sin given to you by Jesus Christ. You are free from both the penalty of sin and slavery to sin. Your identity in Christ is the identity of a person who is free from pornography, and even if you slip up, you will not be punished by God.

It might be worth it to go back and review some of the worksheets from chapter 3. Keeping this positive focus on grace is how you can protect yourself from temptation and accusation. Many people fail because they hold himself to a standard of perfection, and then if they make a mistake, they beat themselves up and stop trying. But you have made a firm decision to quit, and your quit date has passed. So, no matter what happens, get back to quitting immediately with *no trace of guilt*. Suffering from guilt is a waste of time because God does not see you as guilty. Also, there will be plenty of suffering that you cannot escape!

Suffering as a means of growth. In chapter 1, I warned you that there would be some suffering involved in quitting porn. Some of the suffering you're experiencing is self-inflicted, as you discard a "comfort" you once used to entertain or soothe yourself. Now, without that avenue of false escape, you're confronted with your life and problems as they are. This is the same pain the drug or alcohol addict faces when they quit their "little helper" and are left with the underlying issues of anger, bitterness, boredom, or whatever else their drug of choice "helped" them ignore. However, the best attitude to have concerning this suffering is the long view, in which a little pain now will result in a lot of joy later. In fact, suffering can be very good for you.

In support of this idea, even Jesus Christ learned from suffering. According to Hebrews 5:8, Jesus learned obedience through the things that he suffered. It may seem strange to think that God can "learn," as He is omniscient, but the learning in view here is that of having a new experience. Jesus now knows what it feels like to endure incredible suffering and to obey anyway because it was the right thing to do.

In your case, quitting porn will bring some "suffering" which, if we look at it honestly, is laughable compared to what Jesus suffered and what many people suffer through no fault of their own. So, embrace the pain and do the right thing even though it's uncomfortable. You may learn something, as this process will definitely require you to rely more on God and less on yourself to get through each day. Also, quitting porn may reveal some other, deeper pains with which you should face head-on.

If your suffering unearths deeper pains as described here, there are many resources available to help Christians understand suffering,[52] as the full topic of suffering is beyond the scope of this book. For now, view any temporary discomfort from quitting your compulsive habit as a gain: an opportunity to learn, to grow, and to gain experience doing what's right even if it's not comfortable. Merely declaring your willingness to suffer will go a long way toward helping you get through the initial difficult weeks.

Defenses: Man's Part

Dopamine replacement therapy. One of the biggest dangers you face in the quitting phase is giving in to the urge to use porn. However, we know precisely how the porn was giving you pleasure; dopamine.

In your brain, the dopaminergic neurons fire when you search the web, hunt for the right picture or video, and enjoy the pleasure of viewing erotic images. The hunt itself involves a dopamine kick, like the nicotine that rewards smokers when they light up. You *crave* dopamine, especially after you've trained your brain to expect it regularly. Fortunately, there are a dozen ways to replace this dopamine that aren't porn.

The most effective dopamine replacement technique is also the most controversial: the instant you feel the urge to use porn, rub one out immediately without using any porn. Some of you consider this cheating and feel that masturbation is sinful in and of itself, whether or not porn is involved. However, the Bible recognizes a hierarchical ethic, and for example, there are examples of biblical characters being praised for breaking the 9th commandment. Rahab lied when she hid the spies in Joshua 2, but she is praised in Hebrews 11. There, she is said to have expressed her faith by lying to protect the spies. Therefore, whether or not masturbation is a great thing to do, it's not as harmful to your life as a compulsive porn habit. Also, your constant self-stimulating will wane with time as you learn to spend your time in more valuable pursuits.

The reason that this technique is so powerful is due to the magic of the refractory period. Porn sessions always end when you climax, because there is no ongoing need to "feed the beast" if nothing can happen. The refractory period flushes the urge to view porn quite effectively, so if you use this defense consistently, it may be a very effective weapon in your arsenal.

If you were so involved in smut that you have a hard time "making things happen" without visual stimulation, just relax. Trust the process. The human sexual response cycle is hard-wired into your body, and it works quite reliably if you don't gum it up or have health problems. You should be able to get things back in order after a few days of abstinence. I'm not going to get into the specifics of sexual dysfunction caused by porn and how to reboot the system because I want to stay positive and focused on quitting porn. However, most men should be able to restart their auto-manipulator motor with time and avoidance of images.

Of course, there are other ways to get dopamine. Essentially, anything that is engrossing and stimulating or pleasurable should do it. Eat a candy bar. Run on the treadmill. Play a video game. Some of these things are healthier than others, but when you're going cold-turkey, it's worth relying on a temporary alternative dopamine source. **Worksheet 9** has a place to write down some of the strategies you'll use for dopamine replacement therapy. Again, this only has to last for 30-60 days.

Being willing to suffer. If this sounds familiar, we have already covered suffering as a necessary and inevitable part of spiritual growth, but there is a "man's side" to suffering as well. Fortunately, you are not physically dependent on pornography like a smoker is dependent on nicotine, so you will not experience true withdrawal. Nonetheless, you must find a way to get through the quitting phase when you have frequent urges to indulge yourself with some dirty pictures and videos.

Getting through the urge to use pornography is not that different from the urge to do anything, like stay in bed instead of getting up for school or work, or the urge to play video games all day instead of finishing homework or exercising, and so on. Fortunately, God has given men an amazing ability to stuff their feelings down. This causes enormous problems in other areas of life, but the emotional ignorance of men is a topic for another book. For now, consider that suffering that comes with denying the urges to indulge the lazy, hedonistic child inside is just one more feeling that you can ignore. There is a reason that men can repress, deny, or be completely unaware of their feelings. Men can do incredible things when they push through like emotionless robots. Don't be a baby. It's not like you're being chased by angry barbarians from a rival clan, and you can make it through this. Remember, pain is just weakness leaving your body. Arm yourself with the attitude that suffering can be of great benefit and instruction (1 Peter 4:1). Let the pain come. You are undeterred. You are a man.

Coping with urges. In addition to replacing the reward that the porn led to, you also need to have proactive methods of coping with the urges themselves. You don't need all of the following strategies, so you can experiment with trying some of them until you find a mix that works for you.

Mindfulness. Mindfulness and mindfulness meditation has made it's way into the mainstream in the last 30 years,[53] although the origin of mindfulness is ancient history. Mindfulness is also strongly associated with Buddhism, and the definitions and approaches to mindfulness and meditation differ somewhat for the various false religions. I am not a fan of recommending mindfulness meditation to Christians, given the slippery slope to Eastern mysticism that this can entail. On the other hand, we ought not to let false religions "own" something God created, which is our mental capacity to pay attention without overreacting. In my view, you can separate mindfulness from meditation. I've already defined one appropriate form of meditation for Christians is to be thinking about Bible verses all the time as you go about your day. For Christians, mindfulness should just mean paying attention on purpose, and using that attention to keep from overreacting.

This is not too far from the definitions offered by famous proponents of mindfulness meditation. For example, Jon Kabat-Zinn of Mindfulness-Based Stress Reduction (MBSR) fame,[54] said:

> "Just so, it is clear what I mean when I use the word mindfulness, I am using it as a synonym for awareness...the operational definition that I offered...is that 'mindfulness is the awareness that arises from paying attention, on purpose, in the present moment, and nonjudgmentally.'"[55]

So mindfulness can just mean paying attention to what is happening right now, including noticing your urges to open up an incognito browser and loosen your belt.

Many Christians object to the "nonjudgmentally" part of the definition, which is completely understandable, because it sounds like we should not evaluate our thoughts. However, according to many experts, the nonjudgmental perspective is intended to be momentary. For example, Jon Kabat-Zinn also said:

> "Non-judgmentally does not mean that there will not be plenty of judging and evaluating going on—of course there will be. Non-judgmental means to be aware of how judgmental the mind can be, and as best we can, not getting caught in it or recognizing when we are and not compounding our suffering by judging the judging."[56]

In my view, we can simply agree not to overreact, which is to say we need not have an emotional or behavioral reaction to every thought that floats through our heads. I am not suggesting that you have no values or expectations about your urges to use internet porn. I certainly hope you condemn them as bad ideas and carnal feelings! However, it is probably impossible to eliminate every shred of lust from your mind, so urges to use porn will come.

What I am suggesting with my revised definition of mindfulness is that you use your mental capacity to pay attention to how you are thinking and feeling without overreacting immediately (or perhaps at all). Why shouldn't we overreact? The theory is that you should be able to pay attention what is happening in your head and heart so that you don't stay stuck in old patterns of responding without even having a conscious awareness of what you're doing.

How can you "practice mindfulness" in your quest to quit porn? I would not suggest adopting a mindfulness practice like some new spiritual discipline.

On this point, I disagree with most of the proponents of mindfulness, who believe that mindfulness training is required to pump up the mindfulness muscle.[57] In my view, mindfulness applied to urges would be the simple understanding that you will encounter urges, and that you will hold them at arm's length and examine them instead of mindlessly obeying them.

When you are heading into dangerous territory, such as when all the roommates leave for the evening and leave behind their iPad with no parental controls, you know that this is not safe for you. If this happens (or similar), you know that urges will come. But now, you will not reach for the iPad automatically like a caged rat pressing the cocaine-delivery lever. You have bigger frontal lobes than a rat, and you are forewarned that urges are coming, so you will pay attention and notice them. This approach is not intended to fan the flames of temptation, but rather to pump the brakes of self-control. Be alert and pay attention; don't react to every whim that enters your head. Paying attention at least gives you the chance to do something else instead of mindlessly following your feelings like an animal. That's what I mean by mindfulness in this context.

Acceptance and Commitment. How do you get the urges to use porn to go away? The simple answer is that *it doesn't matter if you have some urges.* Along with mindfulness-infused interventions, "acceptance strategies" are on the rise in contemporary psychology.[58] The best developed is Acceptance and Commitment Therapy, abbreviated "ACT."[59] This therapeutic approach has even been adapted into a "Christian" version.[60] ACT is way, way too complicated to describe fully in this workbook. Pertinent to this discussion, ACT was used to great effect in two published accounts of treating pornography use among young men.[61][62]

In the first study, six men whose religious beliefs were not specified received "off the shelf" ACT,[63] modified to address compulsive pornography use, for eight 90-minute sessions.[64] Their porn use was reduced by more than 80% for at least three months. After this promising proof-of-concept study, the next study was a randomized clinical trial comparing 12 hourly sessions of ACT to a wait-list control (i.e., no treatment for 12 weeks followed by the same ACT intervention everyone else got).[65] A total of 28 men (27 Mormon) were randomized to condition, and 25 men finished the study. Again, pornography use dropped over 90% with treatment (compared to 20% for those waiting in line), and at the three-month follow-up, porn use was still over 80% lower.[66]

These small, but promising, studies appreciated the paradox of internal urges and outward behavior, and this is the part of ACT that I want to borrow. That is, these men were viewing a lot of porn because of internal thoughts and feelings, but at another level, they did not want to be using porn. There is often a mismatch between the feelings that compel a problem behavior and a person's core values by which they judge the behavior as wrong. This mismatch cannot always be eliminated, such as when a smoker quits smoking for their health but still wants to smoke. Wanting a cigarette isn't the same as smoking one, and the former smoker may not be able to fully eliminate all desire for another cigarette (or at least not for a long time). Therefore, you can adopt the viewpoint that not all thoughts and feelings have to change for people to live meaningful lives consistent with their beliefs and values.

Some older therapies (like Cognitive Behavioral Therapy, or CBT), argued that dysfunctional thinking led to negative feelings. Therefore, fixing the thinking should reduce the symptoms of depression, anxiety, or whatever was vexing the therapy client. There is a lot of merit to this approach, and it certainly accords with portions of scripture (Romans 12:2, Colossians 3:2). However, there is no reason that people shouldn't be able to just accept some thoughts, feelings, and circumstances that are outside their control. This is the essence of the serenity prayer, written by Reinhold Niebuhr[67] [68] and made famous by Alcoholics Anonymous and other 12-step recovery programs:[69]

> God, grant me the serenity to accept the things I cannot change,
>
> Courage to change the things I can,
>
> And wisdom to know the difference.

Sound like acceptance and commitment? I think it does. So, what I am suggesting is that some level of lust and urges to use porn will have to be accepted and tolerated, without necessarily agreeing with them. Instead of trying to deny them, push them away, or transform them into something holy, it may be more effective to let them remind you of your commitment to stop. Your core value in this area of your life is to be the kind of man who is not mastered by smut-fueled lust, which is consistent with your identity in Christ. There are a lot of things you can do live consistently with this core value, whether or not the urges crash like waves against your rocks.

Urge surfing. If you can accept that urges happen and adopt a "mindful" attitude of paying attention to them without acting on them, you will be capable of "urge surfing," which is a fascinating experience if you have never appreciated that all urges are time-limited. If this seems too scary at first, try it first with a different drive like hunger.

Hunger operates on a 90-minute ultradian rhythm,[70] which means that it comes and goes at a frequency of about every 90 minutes. That means that although there are a lot of things that influence appetite and satiety, the hunger pains are rhythmic. If you're a well-fed plump American used to grass-fed beef, your hunger is not an emergency (unless you have hypoglycemia or some other medical condition). Thus, it is possible to feel hungry and push through, riding that wave until it subsides for a bit while you distract yourself with something else. If you legitimately need to eat and aren't just mindlessly stuck in stimulus-response because the lunch bell rang, the hunger will go away and eventually return later. The fascinating part is that you are fully capable of surfing that urge to eat something without actually opening the refrigerator.

Applied to lust urges, when one hits during your quitting phase, observe it and feel it, but don't give in. Perhaps this is safer to practice in a public setting. Just notice it, feel it, and watch it subside in a few minutes. You can't pay attention to anything indefinitely, and the porn urge is like anything else that clamors for your tiny attention span. If you can endure for 5 minutes, you may find that it's no longer a sex emergency and that you are just fine getting back to reading or watching TV or whatever you were trying to do.

Urge surfing may seem like playing with fire, but I am not suggesting you stoke the flames of lust. Don't let your mind wander all around like a drunken sailor. Rather, take a stance of stepping back and seeing it from a new perspective. The lust is not *you*, it is a *feeling* you are having or a stimulus-response cycle triggered by some event like the lingerie commercial you just saw on TV. The reason that this is an effective technique when used properly is because you will be confronted with dangerous times, when you have the urge and are alone with the motive, means, and opportunity. You can't just use pure avoidance to get away from all urges to use porn (although you should avoid as much as you can). Being able to steel your resolve for 10 minutes and then press forward with some alternative activity is a good skill to have in your arsenal.

Delay and decide. Speaking of 10 minutes, make sure you own a timer. Your phone has one. Set this timer for 10 minutes and keep it handy. At the first tingling of a temptation to start a "quick" porn session that you know will turn into a half hour or more, start the timer. Tell yourself "not for 10 minutes." This is probably best in the Preparing to Quit phase because, as you get stronger, you will no longer feel like telling yourself that you can do whatever you want after waiting 10 minutes. However, when the urges are overwhelming and intrusive in the early part of your journey, somehow it's easier to tell yourself "later" instead of "no."

After 10 minutes, when the timer goes off, there's a good chance that you have moved on to busy yourself with some incompatible activity and the mood is gone. Problem solved.

If the urge persists, you can tell yourself "OK, now I can decide all over again; do some porn right now or set the timer for ten more minutes?" Somehow "later" feels less depriving than "never," but when later comes you probably will have come to your senses. You may also be in a situation where you can't use. Maybe you're on the phone or people started texting. Maybe you're driving to work. Urges are gone or at least you can't use, and they will dissipate with time.

Again, this is best for the Preparing to Quit phase or early in the Quitting phase, when the urges frequently come, because as the days of abstinence stretch on you will quickly prefer to leave no provision for the flesh (Romans 13:14).

Now you're armed with several strategies for enduring the urges. **Worksheet 9** has a place to write down your choice(s) of which to use.

Chapter Summary and Assignments

After Planning to Quit, everything is set up for success. The quit date arrives, and you dive into the Quitting Phase. This phase is the most work, as you maintain some of the Preparing to Quit plans (e.g., daily prayer and scripture meditation). Building on the foundation of your firm decision to quit and your positive outlook anchored in sanctification by grace and your identity in Christ, you add plans to get through the urges, disrupt the old habitual responses, and launch your offense. First, the defense stopped your porn use, but now you must counter attack. The offense is ready and waiting in Chapter seven.

Assignments

- Complete Worksheet 8: Bible Verse Meditation
- Complete Worksheet 9: Dopamine replacement and coping strategies
- What day and time will you read the next chapter? There's only one chapter to go before your quit date!

Worksheet 9: Bible verse mMeditation

A powerful defense includes meditating on scripture. Here are some verses to get you started. Add some that you chose from Worksheet 4. Write out these verses using your favorite translation. Memorize them. Meditate on them. Some meditation questions are given as examples.

Meditating on scripture is also part of your offense, so add some verses about the blessings you have received in Christ.

Psalm 101:3 _____

Meditation Questions: How would it feel to be the kind of person who does not approve of any sexually explicit images or videos? Does the original context of this verse support the application that porn can fit into the category of a "worthless thing" that the author will not bother to look at? Is there a connection between looking approvingly at "vile" things and being like the faithless person?

Titus 1:6-9 _____

1 Corinthians 6:12-13 _____

Job 31:1 _____

Verse: _____

Verse: _____

Kicking the Habit: Quitting Pornography Under Grace by Joel Hughes, Ph.D.
Copyright ©2018 by New Paradigm Publishing

Worksheet 9: Dompamine replacement therapy and coping strategies

People who quit smoking temporarily replace the nicotine to dampen the cravings and ease the withdrawal. People who quit porn should have strategies to lessen and cope with the cravings while the habits associated with porn use fade. What will be your "dompamine replacement therapy?" How will you cope with urges? Several examples of replacement behaviors are given, but you can add more. Pick several. Examples of coping strategies are given. Form a strong intention to do these when a craving hits. These are called "implementation intentions"[71] which are a behavioral technique to break automatic associations and bad habits. They take the form of "when I (experience the first hint of a craving), I will (alternative coping behavior)."

Ideas for dopamine replacement

- ☐ Replace the "hunt-chase-find" dynamic by looking for things for my hobbies, interesting new recipes, new restaurants to try, the perfect movie to watch this weekend on Netflix, the perfect workout song, etc.
- ☐ Feed the epicurian inside; candy, carbs, the perfect sous vide steak, etc. Savor the flavor. Luxuriate in the aromas and the balance of tastes.
- ☐ Love letters: compose some email or snail mail expressing gratitude and encouragement to the people that are dear to me. Roomates, wife, coworkers, personal trainer, etc.
- ☐ Problem solving: become engrossed in constructing the perfect laptop stand over the treadmill, replacing bad light fixtures, finally unclogging the plumbing, rewiring the car stereo, etc.
- ☐ Workout warrior: running, lifting, treadmill, etc.
- ☐ Gaming campaign: fire up the videogame console for a quick melee, a new quest, or creating a new character.
- ☐ Other: _____
- ☐ Other: _____

Ideas for coping strategies:

- ☐ Mindfulness
- ☐ Urge Surfing
- ☐ Acceptance and commitment
- ☐ Delay and decide
- ☐ Other: _____

Key phrase: "When I (experience a craving), I will (coping strategy)!"

Kicking the Habit: Quitting Pornography Under Grace by Joel Hughes, Ph.D.
Copyright ©2018 by New Paradigm Publishing

Chapter 8

Breaking free, or quitting part 2: Offense

Agenda for Chapter 8

To continue the Quitting Phase, full steam ahead. You've been meditating on scripture and actively coping with urges. You've armed yourself to suffer and persevere like a man. Now it is time to fire up the offense and get positive about your new porn-free life.

Stopping porn with defensive maneuvers is not enough. The "rewards" you used to receive from online stimulation must now be replaced with *real* satisfaction in life. If you don't move out in a good direction, your motivation will wane as life gets boring and stressful, and you will want to slip back into temptation and sin.

Offense: God's Part

God's part in your offense consists of positive spiritual motivation, a grounding in sanctification by grace and truth about your identity in Christ, and a renewed commitment to ministry and Christian fellowship.[72]

Positive Spirituality. In sex-drenched first century Corinth, some of the Christians had decided that they could do whatever sexual things they wanted because it was just physical fun and had nothing to do with their spirituality. Sound familiar? Paul takes up the challenge of their false beliefs in Chapter 6, and the word he uses for "sexual immorality" in verses 13 and 18 is the Greek word "pornea[73]" from which we get "porn." Just saying.

Paul's approach is not to bury the readers in the Corinthian church in guilt and shame. Rather, he asks whether what they are doing is beneficial, which is to say, spiritually positive. He continues by suggesting that if it is not positive, then it is enslaving. He finishes his argument by explaining how sexuality *is spiritual* and showing how sexual immorality (pornea) is damaging, whereas their relationship with God is invaluable.

We should apply this logic to our own lives. Although we will not go to hell for looking at nude pictures or even engaging in sex outside of marriage (1 Corinthians 6: 14), these harmful behaviors are entirely incompatible with—

and detrimental to our experience of—the riches of God's love and grace that He generously showers on us. The down payment on our eternal inheritance is to be united with the Holy Spirit, which is an overwhelmingly positive thing.

To **Worksheet 8**, you should add some verses that don't deal directly with sexuality but which instead speak about the incredible blessings we receive in Christ. As you meditate on these truths, the worthlessness of self-indulgent internet fantasies should become obvious by comparison.

Sanctification by grace and Identity in Christ. These concepts were explained in Chapter 3, which you can review as necessary. When you were getting ready in Chapter 4, you already started to collect and learn some verses about grace and your identity in Christ. During the quitting phase, continue to work through these verses, as you meditate and memorize key phrases.

Although meditation on scripture is a key component of your *defense* against using porn, as you progress in the quitting phase you are switching to the *offense* because you are replacing an old dysfunctional behavior with a positive direction in your spiritual life. Offense and defense should all start to work together, as you set aside any guilt and shame by cultivating a positive spiritual mindset (Colossians 3:2). When your behavior matches your mindset, you're not *actually* more acceptable to God, but you will begin to *feel* like less of a hypocrite and loser. Carnality typically motivates avoidance of the things of God and, as you quit porn use, the impulse to avoid God should start to evaporate. You're also getting back all the time you used to waste on anticipating using, planning to use, using, and covering your tracks.

Spiritual benefits. Spiritual benefits were also explained in Chapter 3 and readied during the Planning phase described in Chapter 4, but now is the time for action! Complete **Worksheet 10,** in which you schedule ministry activities and plans for fellowship with other Christians. Ministry in this context just means serving other people, so many things qualify as ministry activities, but the key is to take *action* instead of procrastinating by passively planning. That is, embarking on a year-long quest to read through the entire Bible is not active ministry in the same way that committing to bring snacks to men's bible study or set up chairs for home church would be, and both of those examples are pretty minimal compared to making a bigger time commitment such as getting involved in a service ministry. Ministry activities typically involve active fellowship, as you commit to several planned encounters each week, such as attending weekend services, midweek events, and perhaps a scheduled breakfast or lunch meeting with a friend.

As an aside, this proactive approach to planning engagement in public spiritual activities is similar to a depression treatment called Behavioral Activation.[74][75] The rationale is simple; people who are depressed typically have stopped doing things that are positive and pleasant, because they have lost their motivation, and can't "feel the fun," and thus they start to avoid things that seem hard. The whole treatment boils down to scheduling pleasant activities and overcoming avoidance so that you *do the activities.* Not kidding—that is the whole treatment, in a nutshell. Even though it is very simple to grasp, Behavioral Activation is as effective as more complex therapies for depression.[76] There's just something about starting to *act* like someone who is not depressed that starts to actually alleviate the depression symptoms, which is consistent with the Biblical notion that feelings often follow behavior.[77]

Applied to quitting internet pornography, the rationale from BA would be that people who have been mired in solitary self-indulgence may have withdrawn from Christian fellowship and may lack enthusiasm in ministry. Their private behavior is at odds with being engaged publicly in spiritual activities. It is the case, though, that many men who are very busy with fellowship and ministry are also spending a lot of time using pornography, but that inconsistency is very uncomfortable. I've heard horror stories of people leaving full-time vocational ministry because they finally admitted that they were living a lie.

The goal of planning public expressions of spiritual activity such as ministry and fellowship is to get back to doing what is right, *regardless of how you feel,* so that you can start to reap the positive spiritual benefits of living as God designed you to live. If you feel like a fraud, that is just one of those feelings you'll have to ignore as you remind yourself that "there is no condemnation." You *will* feel better if you are helpful. Speaking about serving other people, Jesus said "Now that you know these things, you will be blessed if you do them" (John 13:17), so lace up your Nike's and JUST DO IT.™ Look! You're expressing faith by doing what is right in the expectation that God will come through for you!

Offense: Man's part

Motivation must be positive

By now, you've made a firm commitment to quit. When things get difficult, your conviction may start to wane as you rationalize all sorts of lies you'll tell yourself in an attempt to break your commitment. However, one of your positive motivations is the desire to keep your commitment to yourself. There's just no going back after the quit date, so let it go, give it up, and remind yourself that you are going to be a *man of your word*.

I've been repeating the need for a positive approach since the first chapter, so get **Worksheet 7** and review your personalized benefits of quitting. Read them every day, or commit them to memory. Think of more benefits as you encounter them. The reason it is so important to stay positive is not just because of "the power of positive thinking," or some other platitude, but because guilt, shame, and failure are triggers for bad behavior and motivate avoidance. Smokers who thoroughly elaborate the benefits they expect to reap by quitting are more motivated and better able to succeed. In a moment of weakness when your clicking finger is twitchy, remembering why you quit in terms of how it's going to benefit you is a great offense.

One of the benefits of quitting is that living a life free from pornography is consistent with your core values. There was no worksheet where you listed out your core values, like you would have had to do in formal Acceptance and Commitment Therapy (ACT). I left that out because this book is written for Christian men, so I'm reminding you that your core values are derived from your identity in Christ. Review **Worksheet 3**, where you found some relevant Bible references and wrote out what they say about your identity in Christ. If you want to elaborate on these truths with some more personal deeply held values, that's fine. The point is that a commitment to live in a manner consistent with your values is positive and active, turning the tables on the difficulty of resisting temptation. Instead of resisting, you're attacking. That's way more fun.

Active Coping, Relaxation, and Pleasant Events

The final step in actually quitting is planning your proactive approach to managing stress and your mood. Consider the fact that you have given up something that you used to enjoy, and which you may have used to manage stress or boost your mood. I'm not saying it was defensible, any more than I would advocate smoking or funneling liquor for stress relief. However, if your porn habit was used for stress-management, it has to be replaced with something that isn't dysfunctional or self-destructive.

Don't be fooled into thinking that you're fine without a plan for actively coping with stress, learning to relax, and having something fun to look forward to. On the one hand, you can double count your dopamine replacement therapy strategies from **Worksheet 9** and everything from **Worksheet 10;** they may also count as pleasant activities. On the other hand, that might not be enough. You will not be able to sustain the dopamine replacement therapy for very long (more on that in Chapter 9), and ministry activities can both relieve and cause stress. Therefore, **Worksheet 11** is designed to help you plan some active coping, relaxation, and pleasant events.

The key to relaxation and pleasant events is that they should be naturally enjoyable and relaxing or invigorating (for pleasant events). Screen time does not count: No TV, no movies, no video games. These things are mindless and passive, which do not achieve the desired goal of either 1) causing your heart rate to decline and your muscles to loosen (relaxation), or 2) engaging you in a positive experience that elevates your mood (pleasant events).

For relaxation, pick whatever suits your fancy but make sure that you like it, that you can schedule it regularly, and that you feel very relaxed when you finish. I've taught people breathing exercises and progressive muscle relaxation (PMR), while others prefer guided imagery or just listening to classical music with their eyes closed. In health psychology contexts, the "prescription" is often 20 minutes twice daily for two weeks, after which people are well acquainted with "the relaxation response."[78] However, I knew that people would probably only listen to their PMR tape once a day every other day for about a couple weeks. That's good enough. The goal is to know how to relax, to schedule it into your week, and to keep on top of stress instead of always playing catch up by reacting to the stress in your life. Being proactive about relaxation can replace bad stress management habits like smoking and porn that seem easier to grab when you "need" them.

For pleasant events, schedule some activities that are truly enjoyable for you. Go hiking, walk your dog, pet your cat, ride your unicycle, play your ukulele, or whatever puts a grin on your face. Life is better with natural fun sprinkled throughout. If the activity is meaningful, or consistent with your cherished values, or if it contributes to you meeting your goals for the year, that's even better. However, a relaxing activity can't be a torturous grind, so you may not want to start writing your novel (unless you're really into that sort of thing and it would *actually* be relaxing). Again, you must *schedule* these pleasant events and then actually do them. You are choosing to replace a compulsive habit with new alternative plans, and you are ensuring that your mood doesn't droop if life begins to feel boring and drab. Going on the offense is proactive, whereas defense is reactive. One element of man's part of the offense against internet pornography is to engage life with intentional plans for wholesome good times.

Chapter Summary and Assignments

The "Active Quitting Phase" is a lot of work. The offense includes positive spirituality, both in your mind (e.g., memorized verses) and your behavior (e.g., planned ministry events). "Man's part" in the offense includes reviewing your anticipated benefits of quitting and crafting a proactive schedule of stress-management and pleasant events.

Assignments

- Complete Worksheet 10: Ministry and Fellowship Schedule
- Complete Worksheet 11: Active Coping
- What day and time will you read the next chapter? Read the next chapter as you quit so that you are familiar with the three biggest risk factors for relapse.

Worksheet 10:   **Ministry and fellowship schedule**

Schedules ministry activities and plans for fellowship with other Christians should be planned, proactive, positive, and public. Private prayer and Bible study is not your ministry activity. Men's Monday prayer breakfast or studying the Bible with Billy on Tuesday are good ministry/fellowship activities. Recurring plans (e.g., a commitment to attend regular events like weekend services or home church) are a good way to make this into a lifelong habit.

Date/Day   Time   Ministry Activity or Fellowship Plans:

_____

_____

_____

_____

_____

_____

_____

_____

_____

_____

_____

_____

_____

_____

_____

Kicking the Habit: Quitting Pornography Under Grace by Joel Hughes, Ph.D.
Copyright ©2018 by New Paradigm Publishing

Worksheet 11: **Active coping**

Coping with stress, relaxing deeply, and enjoying pleasant activities works better with a proactive plan than a reactive after thought. Write down some ideas that work for you. No examples are given because they range so widely, from lighting the aroma therapy candles to a trip to the zoo. Some should be recurring, so schedule them on specific days of the week.

Stress-busting Strategies:

- ☐ _____
- ☐ _____
- ☐ _____

Relaxation Practice:

- ☐ _____
- ☐ _____
- ☐ _____

Mood boosting Activities:

- ☐ _____
- ☐ _____
- ☐ _____

Schedule:

Day	Time	Coping/Relaxation/Pleasant Event
Sunday		
Monday		
Tuesday		
Wednesday		
Thursday		
Friday		
Saturday		

Kicking the Habit: Quitting Pornography Under Grace by Joel Hughes, Ph.D.
Copyright ©2018 by New Paradigm Publishing

Chapter 9

Your porn-free life, or staying quit

Agenda for Chapter 9

To introduce key concepts for maintaining a porn-free life, such as "incubation of craving," the difference between a "lapse" and a "relapse," and three major risk factors for lapses and relapses. The length of time that the quitting phase should be followed varies for the different components, and some judgment is required. There are no new worksheets, closing summary, or action plans in this chapter, because all the plans have been enacted.

Apparently, rats like cocaine. They prefer food, but when cocaine is made available by pressing a lever, you can train rats to press the lever many, many times to get doses of cocaine. Spacing out the administration of cocaine so that they are required to press the lever more and more times to get the same cocaine provides a measure of just how motivated they are to get the cocaine. Then, you can take them off cocaine and make it impossible for them to get more no matter how many times the press the lever. After a while, they are no longer addicted to cocaine and stop pressing the lever.

Then, perhaps you move them to another new box where they live a happy cocaine-free life. However, when you put them back in the cage where they used to get cocaine, they will try the lever again, just to see if there might be more cocaine. The reminders in the cocaine cage prompted the rats to give it a shot, just for old time's sake.

This is where it gets really interesting. The *trying to start getting cocaine again after having quit* is a model of relapse in the rat, and the lever pressing is a measure of motivation: The more the rat presses the lever, the more it is seeking cocaine. What you may not have expected is that the rats' motivation to seek cocaine increases as the duration of abstinence increases. This is called *incubation of craving*.[79][80]

Incubation of craving means that the craving gets more intense as time passes without engaging in the compulsive behavior, but only when you are confronted with reminders of the compulsive behavior.

Incubation of craving has also been demonstrated in humans addicted to nicotine, drugs, or alcohol.[81] This may be part of why inpatient rehabilitation usually lasts 30 to 90 days. This concept also suggests that nicotine replacement therapy should last until all of the risk of relapse from "nicotine fits" has faded.

Applied to any other compulsive behavior, such as food, alcohol, drugs, or pornography, it is likely that the first day of the diet, or the first day without booze, or the first day without porn is not so bad. However, as time goes by, the danger of relapse increases. This is because, when you are confronted with a reminder of the old compulsive behavior that you have quit, the cravings are worse as more time goes by, up to a peak at maybe 30 to 60 days. We don't know how long incubation of craving lasts in humans, and incubation of craving has not been studied for compulsive pornography use. Obviously, we are not rats. However, there is every reason to expect, and anecdotal evidence shows, that craving to use pornography may grow in the first 30 to 60 days, especially if you are confronted with the reminders associated with your previous porn use.

What does this mean for quitting pornography? Simply put, it means that the first few days will be hard. It is very important to stay busy and avoid reminders and situations where you used porn. However, after a few weeks go by without any pornography, you are not out of the woods yet; There is a severe danger of a relapse when you are confronted with reminders, especially after a few weeks or even a month. Incubation of craving involves both time and reminders. To whatever extent possible, avoid reminders. The time we spent studying offenses and defenses should help, as well as awareness of "gateway drugs." The incubation of craving phenomenon also underscores why it is important to replace the function of porn in your life with other more positive activities, so that you are less vulnerable when the inevitable cravings come.

Figure 1: The Phases of Quitting Pornography

Lapse or Relapse?

The third phase of quitting pornography is Staying Quit, which many people would call *relapse prevention*. Staying Quit is a very important phase because quitting is easy for a day or two, or even a week, but staying quit for good is very hard. Fortunately, there are some strategies for this phase that you can employ to improve your chances of staying quit. Before we turn to that topic, I would like to point out that the decision to call this phase "staying quit" was very intentional. Likewise, in the smoking cessation literature, some people think that a more helpful way of thinking about having another cigarette after the quit date is a "lapse" and not a "relapse."

The rationale for these seemingly trivial semantics is because a relapse makes it sound like the person is doomed to continue smoking as much as they ever smoked. On the other hand, calling it a lapse recognizes the fact that it's very likely that a person trying to stop smoking will have another cigarette at some point, but that they should retain the new non-smoker identity that the person has worked to adopt. A person can have *lapses*, as opposed to a person becoming *relapsed*.

In the same sense, I cannot promise that you will never look at porn again after you have passed your quit date. There are no statistics kept on how many people try to quit and then start again. Anecdotally, given the phenomenon of incubation of craving, it is very likely that people will have a lapse and indulge the old habit at some point. I would suggest that, after your quit date has passed, you maintain a non-user identity indefinitely and that any lapses are immediately followed by a commitment to get "back on the wagon." You can also debrief the circumstances that led to your lapse. For example, did you find a site that your porn blocker or parental controls did not stop you from accessing? Perhaps it is time to enter that URL directly into your software to block it specifically.

The point is that, even if you make a mistake, relapse is not your destiny. Keep in mind that at least half of people who have ever smoked cigarettes are now former smokers! Lapses are not a relapse unless you stop trying to quit entirely and give up, which is a conscious choice. Choose not to give up. Get back to quitting, and you will get to a durable Staying Quit.

Three big risks for lapses

During 2015, the Food and Drug Administration (FDA) declared a daily-recommended value for sugar, which for me is nine teaspoons. Wow. Nine teaspoons is like, no sugar. None sugar. I can "eat" nine teaspoons of sugar in French vanilla creamer added to my daily-recommended allowance of coffee. Therefore, I announced that I would try "no sugar 2016." No *added* sugar that is. I resolved that I would not eat candy, cake, cookies, and other obviously sweetened things, but I didn't plan to read food labels to uncover clandestine sugars added to my food. For example, my favorite ketchup contains a teaspoon of sugar per tablespoon of ketchup—how do they fit it all in? I can eat ketchup by the pint if there are fries within arm's reach, so I cut down, but I did not switch to sugar-free ketchup.

In October 2015, I started planning and announced my plan at lunch with renowned health researcher Kate Lorig of Stanford Self-Management

Program fame.[82] She suggested a slight modification to my plan. She suggested that I allow myself sugar once a month or so, as this would tend to rip the rug out from under the "verboten!" effect. That is, the forbidden fruit is the sweetest fruit (no pun intended). One reason diets can fail is that they induce cravings for the off-limits—but highly desired—food. I thought she had a good point, so I indulged my sweet tooth once a month. That allowed me to look forward to Valentine's Day chocolate, Halloween candy, Thanksgiving pies, etc. In short, there were enough opportunities to celebrate and not feel like an outcast.

Late in the year, I was gearing up for the challenge and had already stopped eating sugar. However, I had a major lapse before 2016 even arrived.

Late in December I got some bad news and couldn't sleep. When it was clear that I wasn't going back to sleep, I ambled down the stairs at 6 AM and poured myself a big bowl of sugar-frosted fruit circles. I hadn't had a bowl of cereal in years, ever since my doctor told me that cereal was a bowl of Type II diabetes trying to happen. But this morning was different. I had bought a big bag of sugary cereal for the kids to eat over the holidays, and it called to me in my distress.

My mother-in-law Audrey seemed fine at Thanksgiving. We were looking at condos and planning for her eventual move from California to Ohio. We thought she had a few good years left, but at 85 it was clearly time for her to live closer to her relatives. During her visit, she had a couple of episodes where she was temporarily unable to communicate effectively for a minute or two, which I thought was a transient ischemic attack (TIA), or "temporary stroke." They greatly increase a person's risk of stroke in the next year, so we urged her to make a doctor appointment when she returned to California.

Her doctor said she was depressed and prescribed some antidepressants, but by Christmas, things were worse. She could no longer understand her bills and had trouble remembering names. She had to write down our phone number over and over and practiced calling us a couple of times to make sure she could dial phone numbers. My wife Kathryn and I were naturally alarmed.

Kathryn flew to California on December 27th. Audrey looked so bad that, as soon as Kathryn arrived, she rushed Audrey to the emergency room. After tests, they sat Kathryn down in a private consultation room at 2:30 in the morning and pointed to a screen showing a large mass in Audrey's brain. "I'm so sorry."

Kathryn called at about 3 AM. "It's a brain tumor," Kathryn wept into the phone. That was the end of my sleep for the night. Even though I was gearing up for "no sugar 2016" and no longer longed for treats, on the morning of December 28th life seemed brief and troubled, and I sought solace in cold milk and crunchy sugar.

This story illustrates two of the three biggest risks for lapses and relapse.

Reminders. The first is reminders, cues, and any "stimulus" that evokes a response. In my case, having cereal in the house made it possible to lapse into a sugar binge. Therefore, you should do what you can to avoid reminders and opportunities to lapse into porn use. Some of the fences stay up forever. You don't take down the software blockade, and you try not to run into any old materials you had neglected to discard. You were supposed to have made a clean sweep when you were getting ready to quit, but many smokers lapse when they find an old half-pack of stale cigs in the basement. Their best hope is to throw away the unearthed old pack of cigarettes immediately before their resolve fades. So when you run into a strong reminder of internet porn, solve it immediately: delete the pictures you accidentally found, install the blocking software on your new laptop immediately, etc. *Do not let reminders hang around.*

Negative events. The second big risk is negative life events. For me, the impending death of a family member trumped my desire to keep a sugar-free diet. You will inevitably have negative life events, and some may be severe enough that you care more about escaping the negative feelings, and being free from porn is the last thing on your mind. But now you're forewarned, so when your girlfriend breaks up with you to date your roommate or you fail a class, or similar, expect that staying quit from porn may seem like a low priority. These negative events need to be coped with, but you can choose healthy ways to cope instead of soothing yourself with sin. I did quit sugar shortly into 2016, and for the most part, it wasn't so bad, although I lost no weight (so I started eating sugar again, but mostly on special occasions). If you lapse into porn when something really bad happens, get back to quitting immediately.

Surging dopamine. The third big risk is the other side of the coin; when something really good happens. When you ride the dopamine roller coaster for any reason, there is a strong danger of going off the rails.

For example, when someone stops abusing drugs or alcohol and then suddenly "falls in love" with the girl behind the Chick-Fil-A® counter that he had never seen before, he may be headed for a relapse. The only words he has ever said to her was "uh…nuggets I guess," but now she's his whole world? This infatuation is an attempt to replace the now absent chemical high with a natural high, and although he may not realize that he bought a ticket for the dopamine express, he's already heading into the first turn.

The problem with big positive emotional events is that they incubate the craving for another big dopamine rush. Every addict knows a sure-fire way to get those neurons to fire.

In the case of internet porn, we already suggested some dopamine replacement therapy, but that should only last 30-60 days. After that, wolfing down another donut or playing another video game is not going to have the punch it once did. You should let that fade, and after that don't hunt for a new dopamine fix. A cigarette quitter doesn't keep wearing a nicotine patch forever; It's not as good as a cigarette, so eventually it gets boring, so they stop putting on the patch.

The problem is when the addict buys a winning lottery ticket, or starts dating someone new, or has some other life event that feels intoxicating. The rush rekindles the yearning to get high again and again.

The solution is that you are now forewarned. Most people know that reminders and unmanaged stress are warning signs for the danger zone, and they are. What you also need to know is that very positive events, which people sometimes fabricate just to get high on life, also point the way to a lapse. Just when everything is going great, and you feel like celebrating, disaster can strike. So, do not artificially create big spikes of dopamine in your life, and be wary when things seem "too good." This is when your guard is down but your desire for "another hit" is up.

How do you reconcile this advice not to get too happy with the scheduling of pleasant events and other proactive plans for pleasurable living? It's a matter of degree, which perhaps your support people can see better than you. You must complete **Worksheet 11**, and you should actually do the fun activities you scheduled. However, if your life events appear to be bringing you big hits of dopamine that seem out of place, that can be too much.

For example, perhaps you're suddenly shopping for a new motorcycle or convertible. You embark on a 1000-mile weekend road trip for no reason. On a whim, you build a deck in a home improvement frenzy. Or you decide to start chasing stock market tips or invest a bunch of money in the digital currency market. Now you're checking quotes all day in real time, like a gambling addict pulling the slot machine lever. To your supportive friends, these things looks like an attempt to catch a ride on the dopamine roller coaster, which is an unwise path to go down ("A faithful person will be richly blessed, but one eager to get rich will not go unpunished" Proverbs 28:20).

The most obvious tactic that thrill-hunters use is the "new relationship." Your friends are not trying to "harsh your vibe" when they ask why your Facebook relationship status suddenly changed after only one date which, coincidentally, was also when you were trying to stay quit from porn. To the people that care about you, this looks like you're just trying to replace the excitement of illicit fake sex with a new dating adventure. This newfound love may be a rebound relationship, and is not a good plan. Take it easy and slow down. If it's going to be a solid, lasting relationship, then there's no need to rush anyhow.

What you want to avoid is big intoxicating swings in your excitement level. The scheduled pleasant events, relaxation exercises, and active coping tactics bring a slow but steady mood boost, whereas chaotic adventures appear surprisingly like addict behavior, which is a gateway to the very reliable "fix" you can get from old habits like cigarettes or pornography. You can't always rig the game to pay out the reinforcement you're craving, but you can always light up a cigarette or fire up the laptop as a backup plan when the dice don't roll your way. Therefore, do your best to keep things relatively steady instead of histrionic, and listen to your friends when they seem concerned about your thrill-seeking. "Wounds from a friend can be trusted (Proverbs 27:6a)."

How long does this phase last?

When you're staying quit and trying to avoid a lapse or relapse, the question inevitably arises of how long you have to continue to "work the program." In the drug and alcohol addiction arena, the answer is that recovery lasts for the rest of your life. In contrast, in the smoking cessation literature, the suggestion is that quitting and adopting the non-smoking identity can be completed, after which people don't need patches or other smoking-cessation aids. For pornography cessation, I would suggest that the latter is more true, although sexual temptation is a lifelong battle all men face.[83][84]

Certainly, the self-monitoring can stop when you have 30-60 consecutive zeros. Continuing to self-monitor something that isn't happening could be counter-productive if that comes to serve as a reminder of what you used to like. In contrast, some fences stay up for the long term. There's no good reason to bring down the software blockade or disable the snitch software unless it costs a lot of money. Even then, switch to freeware after the yearly subscription expires. Why leave a hole in the fence? Plus, it could aid other around you—roommates, children, or those who come to visit.

Over time, some of your defensive strategies are no longer as necessary. The dopamine replacement activities should not be necessary after 30-60 days of zero porn use. There may not be many urges to cope with if you have avoided reminders for a few months.

Concerning the offensive tactics you set up, you may decide to quit the formal scheduling of events, relaxation practice, and other hassles. Many of the elements of your offense, however, have hopefully become your "new normal." Your firm decision to quit has been transformed into a firm non-using identity, and ideally, you have begun to realize the benefits of quitting that you had anticipated. If you made a habit of meditating on scripture and cultivated an appreciation of your identity in Christ, these things never really go away. Your ministry should be fruitful and growing, and sweet Christian fellowship became your preferred pastime as you increasingly understood how we are "members of one another" (Romans 12:5).[85]

Use your judgment for how long to stay active with your campaign to quit pornography (and consider the judgement of your social support). *Eventually, you have quit.*

One reason most diets fail to produce lasting weight loss is that they require effortful coping, and eventually motivation to follow the rules of the diet becomes less of a priority than some other requirement of life. If you recall, self-control does not "deplete" with effort, but rather appears to increase or decrease in response to shifting priorities. Therefore, self-control must be embedded in regular habits to be sustainable. Vegetarians don't struggle with how many hot dogs they should eat on the 4th of July. The answer is "none," because they don't eat meat, and vegetarian hot dogs are *gross*.

So when your identity and habits are that of someone who doesn't use pornography at all, you can be the judge of which of your new habits you'd like to keep and which you can jettison. The new knowledge and skills you gained along the way are not lost, and if you are surprised by a lapse after a long period of abstinence, you know how to pull the knowledge and skills back out of the box and get back to staying quit.

Assignments

- All the worksheets are finished!
- What day and time will you read the next chapter?

Chapter 10

What if I fail?

Agenda for Chapter 10

To discuss some common causes of "failure," along with suggestions for how to get back to quitting. When you have a "lapse," that should trigger some soul-searching to see if there is anything you could be doing to help or hamstring your efforts to stop.

As I wrote in the first chapter, no studies have evaluated whether or not this program will work. There probably never will be any studies. So, results may vary, and I want to address what I foresee to be common causes of "failure."

Anecdotally, when I discuss quitting porn with men who have been struggling, typically they have installed a filter or blocker and read a book or two, which "didn't work." I remind them how much less porn they are using than they used to, and I always quote the maxim that "half of the people who start smoking become former smokers if they keep trying to stop." So, if you don't reach zero porn use, you didn't really fail, and it will be detrimental to the progress you *have* made to consider yourself a failure or without hope. You can choose to keep experimenting with approaches to stop, and you have a good chance of getting there. That said, sometimes the first quit attempt uncovers self-sabotage or serious problems that will require more extensive solutions or simply something you didn't consider on the first try.

1. **Did you make the firm commitment to quit?**

One of the most common reasons people don't succeed at quitting smoking, porn, or any other compulsive behavior is because they have not decided to stop. People are usually ambivalent, having conflicting feelings about their bad habit. People's mixed motives may only tip the scales towards "kind of trying to quit" mindset, with more weight on the "not quite ready yet" side. When people are "just trying," and have not made a firm commitment to stop, this erodes motivation. People may often feel pressured to change by other people, so they may *superficially* agree to stop, but they may not *really* want to. We all know of alcoholics who cannot be convinced that they have a drinking problem. People may even agree, in principle, that stopping is the right thing to do. However, wanting to stop and committing to stop no matter what it takes are different choices. If you relapse badly and aren't able to make much progress, it's time for some soul-searching. Do you really want to stop? Are you able to make firm commitment? Or are you lying to yourself or rationalizing some sort of backup plan that allows you to keep your options open? To have the best chance of success, it would be best to make sure you are absolutely resolved that you will stop before you even start planning to quit.

2. **Did you do the things you were supposed to do?**

Another common reason that people don't get the results they expect from any behavior change program is because they didn't actually do the work. The worksheets may seem silly to you. You may not think you need to fill out paperwork and talk about the discussion questions with anyone else. Maybe you don't. If you quit with only a modicum of effort, congratulate yourself on having successfully quit! Many people stop smoking cold-turkey, and although their odds of staying quit aren't great, this is the most common method of smoking cessation. Some people may only need the blocking and accountability software and are then finished with porn forever. Good for them! God delivers people from various addictions all the time. Praise God! However, people often struggle to change. We already agreed that the approach this book describes is over-engineered. If you are at the end of the book and asking why you didn't stop using internet pornography, there's no shame in hitting reset on the process and starting over with the Planning to Quit phase. This time—do it all! Install the software, set a quit date, recruit some social support, memorize your verses, and go through all the steps you can tolerate. Just keep telling yourself that no one ever got ripped by reading Muscle & Fitness® magazine[86] while they drank protein shakes from the comfort of their recliner; You have to lift the weights.

3. **Do you just need to try again?**

As stated before, a lapse does not have to be a relapse. If you get back to quitting immediately, you can cycle through the process a few times. No big deal. Most people who try to change a deep-seated bad habit struggle to make a lasting change. For example, long-term weight loss is an elusive goal for nearly anyone who has ever tried to lose weight. Unfortunately, chronic dieting may make things worse, and the body fights to avoid a large weight loss and may adapt to repeated episodes of calorie restriction in ways that are not helpful (why won't the body resist a large weight gain? I wish it would.). In the case of internet pornography, your body is not working against you, and there's no harm in experimenting with different tactics until you find the one that works for you. Can you defeat the blocking software too easily? Get help from a computer expert to make your devices more porn-resistant. Do you have a really hard time with getting through the urges? Try different approaches until you hit on something that gives you the resolve to outlast them. The point is that as long as you're still working on quitting, you're probably using way less porn that you would be if you gave up and didn't try. Many people can get to a long-term quit if they just keep at it.

4. Do you need to intensify your treatment?

Many people try to stop smoking cold turkey and fail. Then they try the patch or the gum or something like varenicline tartrate or bupropion hydrochloride. If that fails, maybe they join a support group. For extreme cases, there have even been inpatient smoking cessation programs. For drugs and alcohol, inpatient rehab is recommended when outpatient treatment fails. Applying this reasoning to compulsive internet pornography use, this book is at the "less intense" end of the spectrum. Obviously, people try first on their own, then with help. Early in the book, I suggested that people with more severe sexual problems (e.g., involving encounters with real people) would need a more intense treatment, like counseling or therapy. If you cannot stop using internet pornography *and* you have made a commitment to stop, are still trying, and completed the steps and exercises in this book, then you may have uncovered a more serious problem that must be addressed by intensifying your treatment. You may need to seek professional help, and there is no shame in accepting that you require help. In the case of serious drug or alcohol abuse, treatment often has to be ramped-up when people keep using. We always try the least restrictive approach first, so if you need a stronger dose of treatment, please find professional help. Given the audience of this book, I suggest starting by talking to your social support about getting referred to a competent pastoral counselor or other mental health professional.

5. Do you have any healthy source of love feelings?

You've probably never heard of Dr. Ralph Ankenman; the missionary-turned-psychiatrist from London, Ohio. He developed, but never published, a Bible-based "Love Therapy" that describes how people seek counterfeit love if they are unable to live according to God's design for their emotional life. One of his insights was that much of our behavior is motivated by our deep need for the present feeling of being loved. Infants in orphanages will actually die if they are not loved, regardless of how adequately they are fed. They must be physically cuddled and emotionally nurtured, or they are doomed. Even Harry Harlow's infant monkeys preferred the foodless but comforting "cloth mother" to the "wire mother" with the bottle of formula attached.[87] Life involves more than physical needs.

Applied to compulsive porn use, or any other self-soothing addiction, people who have no source of love feelings will struggle to drop even wrong sources of emotional energy to get through life. This is not an excuse, but it may explain why people with a zero balance in their "love bank account" can seem trapped in self-destructive behavior that even they recognize as dysfunctional. The mature approach to love is what Dr. Ankenman calls "victorious love output," which means that the person has matured in Christ to become a source of love instead of a black hole of emotional neediness. If you are chronically empty of love feelings inside, quitting porn will be an even more difficult battle. It may be that fighting this battle will help you to learn new healthy ways of getting the love you need. If this describes you, I suggest you acknowledge that lacking significant love relationships is one of those deeper issues that must be addressed. It's going to be a long road, but porn use may be a symptom of a life that feels insignificant and without substance. The only way out is to build your relationships in the body of Christ (1 Corinthians 12:27), which will provide you with the opportunity to make real changes as you become knitted into the fabric of your fellowship.

6. Is quitting porn a high enough priority right now?

Although I'm a health psychologist, I have on occasion suggested that people not try to stop smoking…yet. Even though smoking can be a life-or-death struggle, in rare cases people have other more pressing problems that need immediate attention. I'm not going to give any examples because I don't want to condone smoking. My point is that behavior change requires motivation and some self-control, which represent value-based choices that reflect our priorities. These choices are then ground into our daily habits until they allow self-control when priorities change. If you have pressing priorities that prevent you from devoting the necessary time and attention to quitting porn use, then you are unlikely to succeed. For example, if you have no social support, *that is a problem*. Working with at least one other person is probably required, so having no one to talk to will undermine your efforts. So if things don't go well, it might be a good idea to pause at the Planning to Quit phase and do what it takes to develop some relationships. Waiting to quit is a tough decision because no one wants to admit that they aren't ready yet to make a change for the better. Unfortunately, if quitting porn isn't a high priority for you—or can't be—it isn't the right time.

7. Do you have a relationship with God?

Before you write me angry letters, I must point out that many people are religious but have no relationship with God. When my father told his parents that he had placed his trust in the person and work of Jesus Christ to cover his sins, making a personal relationship with God possible, they cried in anger. They were religious people, and they were from Montana. Everyone knows that the good people of Montana always go to heaven, so why did he have to insult them with this "receive Christ" nonsense? Throughout history, many people have given God lip service but didn't *know* God at all. This is one theme of the New Testament, and Jesus reserved his harshest criticism for self-righteous religious leaders. So, all I am saying is that people who do not have a relationship with God do not benefit from any of the material about their identity in Christ because they are not *in Christ*. If the spiritual parts of this book seem like crazy talk to you, or if you are not displaying any of the power of God working in your life, please consider whether or not you have taken advantage of the good news of a relationship with God on the basis of faith in Jesus Christ. Your relationship with God is far more important than quitting pornography. There is no shame if discovering that you are unable to escape slavery to sin is what it takes to make you willing to cry out to God for rescue.

> "For God so loved the world that he gave his one and only Son, that whoever believes in him shall not perish but have eternal life. For God did not send his Son into the world to condemn the world, but to save the world through him. Whoever believes in him is not condemned, but whoever does not believe stands condemned already because they have not believed in the name of God's one and only Son" (John 3:16-18).

Assignments

- If you have had a "lapse" or relapse, the best approach is "rinse and repeat." Go back to chapter 5 and see if you can figure out what else you could be doing to quit.
- Either way, make an appointment to read the Epilogue in the near future.
- If this book helped you, consider leaving a book review or telling your friends, and maybe send me a quick email with any feedback you have. If there is ever a second edition, I want to make this book as effective as possible.

Chapter 11

Epilogue

When I was about 12 years old, my dad told me that pretty soon I'd become fascinated with the shape of girls' butts and stuff like that. It was an awkward conversation, and I was confused, but I had already started to notice girls. I'm not confused anymore. Having studied biblical teaching on sexuality over the course of my ministry and specifically while writing this book, I've become convinced that sex embodies the gospel. Stated more carefully, *sexual intimacy between a man and a woman in marriage is a physical revelation of the offer of a close personal relationship with God on the basis of a free gift through trust in the person and work of God the son, Jesus Christ.*

I know that sounds weird, but sexpert Dr. Julie Slattery of Authentic Intimacy® (authenticintimacy.com) has offered essentially the same interpretation,[88] and she's not the first person to make this observation. Every young man reaches a point in his life when girls are no longer "icky," and their bodies suddenly look interesting, and God created this drive to push us out of the home we grew up in and toward other people so we would "be fruitful and multiply" (Genesis 1:28). Puberty coincides with the approximate age at which young men and women need to start to take their relationship with God seriously. Although I received Christ at a young age, I was 12 when I awakened to the need to get serious about God: right about the same time I became interested in girls.

God created us, and he created us male and female. God did not need us, because he always existed in a unified, loving community as Father, Son, and Holy Spirit. But God's love overflowed to the point that He created us to so that we could have a relationship with Him. He created the universe, and He even created space and time,[89][90] so that we could exist in a life-sustaining environment.[91] God created our sexuality and gave men a strong sex drive so that they would initiate a relationship with a woman like God initiates a relationship with us. God created women with a less strong sex drive so that they would fulfill the role of responding to men like we respond to the love of Jesus Christ. All of this is spelled out in Genesis, and much of it takes place before the Fall when sin and death entered the world to create a barrier between us and God.

If it weren't for our sex drive, humanity would have died out long ago. Ask the zoo-dwelling giant panda. They're struggling not to go extinct, which is partly due to the panda's relative indifference to reproduction in captivity. However, in humans there are deeper reasons for sex than procreation.

Do you want to know what it feels like for God to want a relationship with you? You already know because it's built into your desire for a relationship with a woman. Do you want to know what it feels like for God to have to ask us to respond to Him of our own free will, with no coercion, no manipulation, and no pressure? You already know, because sex only works the way God designed it to when women respond of their own free will with no manipulation or pressure. The implications of how our sexuality embodies the relationship between God and man, which was later revealed to be the relationship between Jesus Christ and the church (Ephesians 5:22-32), are broad and deep. These are worth pondering as you study the gospel as the central theme of scripture.

Unfortunately, our adversary the devil tells us that "Stolen water is sweet; food eaten in secret is delicious!" (Proverbs 9:17). We come to believe the lie that the best sex is stolen. So men learn to lie, feign interest, nurture misplaced trust, coerce, and even force sex. Just get her drunk, tell her it's your birthday, pretend you're going out of town and she needs to "sleep you goodbye," run out of gas on a deserted backwoods road, make her feel guilty, tell her she's fired if she refuses, maybe just hold her down until she stops screaming, and so on.

Forced or manipulated sex that you weren't supposed to get is allegedly the best kind in our twisted impatience and frustration. Just download it from the internet or buy a sex robot if you have to. Buy it, steal it, just get it in any way you can. Of course, you're going to have to keep it a secret: just a little secret that nobody knows. Never admit your tactics, and cover your trail. Hope that nothing bad happens and that, God forbid, no one steps forward to accuse you with a #MeToo scenario.[92]

Stolen sex is what porn becomes for many men. Nothing more than stolen water and secret food, which just leaves you thirstier and hungrier than ever. In contrast to Satan's lie, God said "drink water from your own cistern, running water from your own well" Proverbs 5:15. That's the only water that satisfies. If you're married, *your wife is your only sexual partner*. If you're single, either you're motivated to get married or you learn to follow the rare path of celibacy that Jesus walked (Matthew 19:11-12).

When we believe the lie that secret forbidden sex is fun, we forget the next verse that finishes the proverb: "But little do they know that the dead are there, that her guests are deep in the realm of the dead" (Proverbs 9:18). The entire carnival of destruction that sexuality has become throughout the centuries, and especially in first-century Rome and the 21st century is a denial of the reality that sex outside of God's design is a trip into the dead lands.

These things aren't taught in most churches. This omission is a *monumental failure* because sex was designed to teach the good news of a relationship with God for free through faith in Jesus Christ, which is the most important thing about being a human being. It's no surprise that God built the reason for our existence into our human nature as male and female.

It's time to let go of the false belief that stolen sex is good sex, which is what this book was written to help you do. When you're porn free, you can face this world with a clear head and a clean conscience. For example, when you're porn free and married, you have more courage to address these issues with your wife. No more manipulation, no more begging, no more sneaking around, no more covering your tracks. Everything is on the table. You can ask her for whatever you want, because she's your only partner for sexual activity. Do you want to dress up like pirates and reenact a ship boarding? What's wrong with you! That's sick! Seriously though, I'm not saying you're going to get whatever you want. I'm not saying that what you want is reasonable or honors God. If you've done a lot of porn, your sexual appetites have likely expanded and become distorted along the way. Your wife has her own issues to work through, so I'm not saying you'll get anything at all. But, you can talk about your sexual desires openly, secure in knowing that you're not taking some on the side from the world wide web. If she borrows your phone or tablet to look up something on the internet, she won't accidentally find something you didn't want her to see. The guilt and shame of cyber cheating won't hold you back from being open and honest.

Try this line: "Hey wife! Was Adam created for Eve or was Eve created for Adam? Who's the helpmate in this marriage? Yeah, I thought so."

Or maybe don't say that, ever. I assume no liability for what your wife does to you for that little quip. There will still be conflict in the bedroom, because we're only human. Becoming truly Christ-like, even in our sexuality, is a lifelong process that won't be complete until we are with Him. The point is that a man who is completely faithful to his wife can at least talk about how he wants intimacy to be expressed in his marriage with a clean conscience.

What if you're single or can't get what you want? Men are somewhat less likely than women to reproduce, in part because men are about three times as likely as women to have disabilities that make marriage unlikely (e.g., developmental disability, autism, traumatic brain injury). Jesus never got married. Surprisingly, he even recommended this lifestyle choice to those who could accept it (Matthew 19:12-13)! Most men would not willingly choose to stay single throughout their life, but because marriage is supposed to be a free will choice, not all men find someone who will say "yes." Also, marriage won't solve your problems with unfulfilled sexual desires. Sexual frustrations are rampant among the married, even in Christian homes.

If you are in the unfortunate position of not being able to have a satisfying sex life for any reason, then you will have to dive so deep into the ocean of God's love and grace that you can no longer hold your breath and you drown. Let me explain. Usually, we hold our breath and only enter the deep waters of God's loving kindness for as long as we can hold our breath. When our diaphragm starts to spasm from the effort of suppressing our self-will, we surface for air and get back to living the life that we control. In a way, a severe injustice like being unable to fully realize God's design for your sexuality can become a "severe mercy"[93] if that's what it takes for you to break and die. It will feel like drowning and dying, and it is; It is dying to the self, like Paul talks about in Romans 6:4-8.

However, being broken of self-reliance in every area of our life, including our sexuality, is consistent with our identity in Christ. As Paul says, "I have been crucified with Christ and I no longer live, but Christ lives in me. The life I now live in the body, I live by faith in the Son of God, who loved me and gave himself for me" (Galatians 2:20). Only in Christ can you find the secret to contentment that Paul describes in Philippians 4:10-13. Why was Paul content? What was the secret? He knew that his own power was nothing, but that God could strengthen him to do anything necessary (2 Corinthians 12:9). He also knew that the mind-blowing blessings God shared with him and prepared for him were far, far greater than any suffering he would endure in this life (2 Corinthians 4:17).

I know that the pain of not being able to find a relationship or express God's design for your sexuality is one of the deepest hurts that any man can endure.

August 6th, 2016 on a beautiful warm evening in the park, I taught part of the story of Samson to our church fellowship from Judges 13-15. Samson's great weakness was women. He lost his eyes, his freedom, and eventually his life because a woman talked him into revealing the secret of his great strength. He is still portrayed in the Bible as a man of great faith. Ultimately, his hair grew back, God renewed his strength, and he took his revenge on the Philistines. Women, or lack thereof, can be a path to great suffering in men's lives.

Before and after that teaching, I was speaking with a friend about his recent trip overseas. He showed me pictures of Ephesus, and we laughed as we wondered why there are so many stray cats in that city. He wore a permanent smile and looked like a white Jesus with his full dark beard and long hair. If you listen to the recording, near the end, you can even hear people laughing as I point out that my friend had followed Sampson's example in not cutting his hair, as he was sitting right up front. Later that evening he played board games with his friends deep into the night. The next day, a Sunday, alone in his apartment, he put a handgun to his head and ended his life.[94]

My friend showed no outward signs of depression or hopelessness. I'm a clinical psychologist, and I didn't have the slightest suspicion that he was suffering like that. I had been laughing with him just one day earlier. We spoke about his plans for the future. I was absolutely stunned by his taking his life, and everyone who knew him was devastated.

Later I learned that the focus of his pain was the fact that, as a single man in his late twenties, he had become convinced that he would never form a lasting relationship with a woman. He was athletic, adventurous, attractive, loyal, employed, and had many wonderful skills and abilities, but skill with women had eluded him. On that basis he killed himself. Although this frustration may not drive many men to suicide, in many ways the pain of unfulfilled yearning for love can be life-threatening and damaging in many other ways.

Samuel Stephens, the leader of India Gospel League,[95] encounters a lot of demonic spiritual activity in India. He recently told me that demonic activity in India is typically characterized by self-destructive behavior on the part of the affected person, including urges to harm or kill themselves. I believe that my friend was similarly influenced by a distinctly spiritual attack, in which what he believed to be a great weakness was exploited by the Devil to destroy him.

All men share this pain, to varying degrees. None of us escape the struggle over our inability to have an intimate sexual relationship with a woman in the way that we envision. Rare is the husband who is continually intoxicated by his wife's physical love (Proverbs 5:19). Whether single or married, we will suffer in our frustrated sexual and relational desires. Suicide is not the solution, and neither is pornography.

Again, the only solution is to dive so deep into the ocean of God's love and grace that you are absolutely unable to surface to breathe the air of self-willed struggle to get what you want. David also had women troubles, and in the 23rd Psalm, he wrote that the Lord "restores his soul" (Psalm 23:3). This phrase expresses the fact that Jesus Christ can put even the most shattered man back together again. David experienced triumphs and failings many orders of magnitude greater than anything we will ever face, and if David can fully trust the Lord to restore him, we can too.

The drowning metaphor is intentional because it is accurate. Our identity in Christ is that of a person who was buried with Christ, which we publicly declared when we were baptized with water. When we received salvation on basis of Jesus' death by crucifixion, we died in Christ. This includes the death of our selfish demand to express our sexuality on our own terms, which I recognize can be a very strong drive with terrifying consequences and savage hurts. However, you cannot rise from the dead unless you first die, and Jesus wants you to exchange the life you're trying to build on your own for spiritual life right now and eternal life forever. Jesus will give you this for free if you are willing to die in Him. One implication for this life is that dying to self includes the death of your sexual frustrations and attempts to soothe them. So go ahead and die to self, because when Jesus raised you from the dead, you rose to a whole new life.

Appendix A: Recommended Resources

Books:

- Anderson, Neil T. *A way of escape: Freedom from sexual strongholds.* Harvest House Publishers, 1997.

    ISBN: 978-1565078277

    This book by the popular author of *The Bondage Breaker®: Overcoming Negative Thoughts Irrational Feelings Habitual Sins.* Harvest House Publishers, 2006.

- Cusick, M. J. (2012). *Surfing for God: Discovering the divine desire beneath sexual struggle.* Harper Collins.

    ISBN: 978-0984033508

    This book has a good discussion of the counterfeit fulfillment men seek in pornography and other sexual sins.

- Gardner, B. (2011). *Porn Free: Finding Renewal through Truth and Community.* Costly Grace Media: Columbus, OH.

    Brian's book has the best explanation of grace, identity in Christ, and the value of Christian community.

Software + Hardware:

https://meetcircle.com/

Software:

https://www.accountable2you.com/

https://x3watch.com/

https://www.opendns.com/

https://everaccountable.com/

Acknowledgements

I had no aspirations to author any book, and I certainly did not intend to write this book. However, about five years ago I was overcome with an impulse to start reading all the Christian books I could get into my hands. Initially, my motive was to learn about church planting, so naturally, that led me to Peyton Jones' book *Church Zero: Raising 1st Century Churches Out of the Ashes of the 21st Century Church*.[96] That led to writing some articles for Peyton's eZine *Church Planter Magazine*[97] and reading some early drafts of his next books, including *Reaching the Unreached: Becoming Raiders of the Lost Art*.[98] These experiences gave me the confidence that maybe I could write. I started a manuscript that will hopefully be finished one day, but in July, 2017 I abruptly altered course and started writing this book. I was prompted by a situation with a friend, whose wife dragged him over to my house to get help with his compulsive porn habit. The core concept (smoking cessation) came to me at a church conference I was attending in July, so I stopped paying attention to the teaching (sorry) and started the outline, which became the basis for this book.

I would like to thank Peyton. I would like to thank the McCallum family, who were instrumental in founding my church homes Xenos and Neoxenos, and who have so profoundly influenced my ministry and theology (in alphabetical order): Connor, Darlene, Dennis, Keith, Kyle, Martha, and Sean. I would also like to thank my rag-tag band of brothers, the earnest warriors of NeoXenos,[99] who used early versions of this workbook in their recovery group, or who contributed to the book by helping with the cover, providing feedback, assisting with copy-editing, and so on. They must remain unnamed for obvious reasons, but their contributions are greatly appreciated.

Of course, I could not have written this without the unfailing support of my wife.

Most of all, I would like to thank my Lord and Savior Jesus Christ.

About the author

Dr. Joel Hughes is a professor, clinical psychologist, and church elder at Xenos Christian Fellowship of Northeast Ohio. He received his B.A.'s at Biola University in SoCal, an MA in Clinical Psychology at the University of Colorado at Colorado Springs and his Ph.D. in Clinical Psychology at The Ohio State University. Dr. Hughes is a professor at a public research university, and also a husband, father (of three), and very active in his local protestant evangelical fellowship (neoxenos.org). Dr. Hughes has been involved at Xenos Christian Fellowship since 1996 (Columbus Xenos from 1996-2000), except for a hiatus when he completed an internship and post-doctoral fellowship in Durham NC from 2000-2003. Dr. Hughes was raised in a Baptist church and became a Christian at a young age. At Xenos Christian Fellowship in Columbus (xenos.org) he became very involved in a home church and other ministries. After moving to take an academic position, he became involved with Xenos Christian Fellowship in Northeast Ohio. He was a deacon for several years and helped plant a home church when the college student home church split into two predominantly post-college young adult home churches. He eventually helped replant the college ministry. Now an elder at Xenos Christian Fellowship, he helps lead home churches and works with young leaders.

As a member of the faculty at a public research university, the views expressed herein are Dr. Hughes' alone and not intended to represent the views of any public or private institution, or any funding agency. Dr. Hughes' views expressed here are not intended to accurately or fully reflect all the doctrinal and theological positions of Xenos Christian Fellowship. As a workbook is not a substitute for formal treatment, no part of this book is intended to diagnose or treat any condition, mental or physical. Dr. Hughes' views in this book are not intended to discriminate against or defame any person, real or imagined, or any group whether categorized by race, ethnicity, age, gender, sex, sexual orientation, eye color, or favorite color.

Contact information:

You can contact me via email at jhughes @ neoxenos.org (the spaces defeat the autobots) or P.O. Box 1556 Stow, OH 44224.

If this book helped you, let me know. It would help if you indicate what parts of the book were helpful or not helpful so that future editions can be improved.

If this book helped you, please consider leaving a review on Amazon and recommending it to your friends.

References

[1] https://en.wikipedia.org/wiki/Evidence-based_practice

[2] Ahmad, Zeba S., John Thoburn, Kristen L. Perry, Meghan McBrearty, Sadie Olson, and Ginger Gunn. "Prevalence rates of online sexual addiction among Christian clergy." *Sexual Addiction & Compulsivity* 22, no. 4 (2015): 344-356.

[3] Capurso, Noah A. "Naltrexone for the treatment of comorbid tobacco and pornography addiction." *The American journal on addictions* 26, no. 2 (2017): 115-117.

[4] Twohig, Michael P., and Jesse M. Crosby. "Acceptance and commitment therapy as a treatment for problematic internet pornography viewing." *Behavior Therapy* 41, no. 3 (2010): 285-295.

[5] Twohig, Michael P., and Jesse M. Crosby. "Acceptance and commitment therapy as a treatment for problematic internet pornography viewing." *Behavior Therapy* 41, no. 3 (2010): 285-295.

[6] Any real neuroscientist would laugh at my description of how dopamine is involved in compulsive pornography use. All of our popular-press explanations of neurotransmitters are over simplified, but it works for this book on a practical level.

[7] http://www.billboard.com/articles/news/959433/john-mayers-sexually-racially-charged-playboy-interview-sparks-outrage

[8] https://founders.archives.gov/documents/Washington/06-04-02-0120

[9] Winston Churchill popularized this metaphor that has roots as old as Horace (65-8 BC)

[10] Hughes JR, Stead LF, Hartmann-Boyce J, Cahill K, Lancaster T. Antidepressants for smoking cessation. Cochrane Database of Systematic Reviews 2014, Issue 1. Art. No.: CD000031. DOI: 10.1002/14651858.CD000031.pub4.

[11] This is an overstatement because worship is only one aspect of the spiritual nature of human sexuality, but "sex as worship" fits the argument in Romans summarized here. The spiritual dimension of sexuality is deep, and this chapter only skims the surface toward the end of including elements relevant to quitting pornography.

[12] Yang, F. (2006). The red, black, and gray markets of religion in China. *The Sociological Quarterly*, 47(1), 93-122.

[13] Timothy Keller (@timkellernyc) 2/21/15, 12:00 PM. This tweet seems related to a quote from his later book: Keller, Timothy, and Kathy Keller. *God's Wisdom for Navigating Life: A Year of Daily Devotions in the Book of Proverbs*. Penguin, 2017.

[14] Regnerus, Mark. *Cheap Sex: The Transformation of Men, Marriage, and Monogamy*. Oxford University Press, 2017.

[15] Stuart, Ben. "Ephesians Part 8: Marriage." (Lecture)." Breakaway Ministries. Posted April 8, 2014.

[16][16] James, Erika Leonard. *Fifty shades of grey*. Vintage Books, 2012.

[17] Some of this section was inspired by the teaching of Ray Stedman at https://www.raystedman.org/ My major theological influences include Ray Stedman, Dennis McCallum, Keith McCallum, Gary Delashmutt, and my late father Howard G. Hughes. I have tried to cite them whenever I know that they are the

source of ideas presented here, but it's likely that I have not given them the credit they deserve.

[18] This section inspired in part by the teaching of Ray Stedman. http://raystedman.org

[19] This section influenced by the teaching of Dennis McCallum and Jim Leffel on this topic. http://xenos.org

[20] Cusick, Michael John. *Surfing for God: Discovering the divine desire beneath sexual struggle*. Harper Collins, 2012.

[21] McCallum, Dennis. Satan and His Kingdom: What the Bible Says and How It Matters to You. Bethany House, 2009.

[22] Cusick, Michael John. *Surfing for God: Discovering the divine desire beneath sexual struggle*. Harper Collins, 2012.

[23] McCallum, Dennis. *Walking in Victory*. NavPress, 1994.

[24] Ahmad, Zeba S., John Thoburn, Kristen L. Perry, Meghan McBrearty, Sadie Olson, and Ginger Gunn. "Prevalence rates of online sexual addiction among Christian clergy." *Sexual Addiction & Compulsivity* 22, no. 4 (2015): 344-356.

[25] Willard, Dallas. *The Great Omission: Reclaiming Jesus's essential teachings on discipleship*. Zondervan, 2006.

[26] Lucas, George. *Star Wars Episode IV: A New Hope.* Film. Directed George Lucas. America: Lucasfilm. 1977

[27] Hughes, John. *The Breakfast Club*. Film. Directed by John Hughes. Universal City, CA: Universal Pictures, 1985

[28] Baumeister, Roy F., Ellen Bratslavsky, Mark Muraven, and Dianne M. Tice. "Ego depletion: Is the active self a limited resource?." *Journal of personality and social psychology* 74, no. 5 (1998): 1252.

[29] Baumeister, R. F., Bratslavsky, E., Muraven, M., & Tice, D. M. (1998). Ego depletion: is the active self a limited resource? *Journal of personality and social psychology*, 74(5), 1252.

[30] Carter, E. C., Kofler, L. M., Forster, D. E., & McCullough, M. E. (2015). A series of meta-analytic tests of the depletion effect: Self-control does not seem to rely on a limited resource. *Journal of Experimental Psychology: General*, 144(4), 796.

[31] Lange, F., & Eggert, F. (2014). Sweet delusion. Glucose drinks fail to counteract ego depletion. *Appetite*, 75, 54-63.

[32] http://www.jpmoreland.com/

[33] Howard Henricks was a professor at Dallas Theological Seminary for over 50 years and the author of over a dozen books.

[34] Hendricks, Howard. "Building Character in the Life of Your Disciple." Plenary Session, Xenos Summer Institute, Columbus Ohio, July 17, 2003. https://www.xenos.org/teachings/?teaching=939

[35] Gardner, Brian. *Porn Free: Finding Renewal through Truth and Community*, Costly Grace Media, 2011.

[36] McCallum, Dennis. *Members of One Another: How to Build a Biblical Ethos Into Your Church*. New Paradigm, 2010.

[37] https://meetcircle.com/

[38] https://meetcircle.com/mycircle/

[39] https://www.opendns.com/

[40] Mckay, Brett S. *How to Quit Porn*. Semper Virilis Publishing: Jenks, OK. 2015.

[41] Regnerus, Mark. *Cheap Sex: The Transformation of Men, Marriage, and Monogamy*. Oxford University Press, 2017.

[42] Crosby, Jesse M., and Michael P. Twohig. "Acceptance and commitment therapy for problematic Internet pornography use: a randomized trial." *Behavior therapy* 47, no. 3 (2016): 355-366.

[43] Twohig, Michael P., and Jesse M. Crosby. "Acceptance and commitment therapy as a treatment for problematic internet pornography viewing." *Behavior Therapy* 41, no. 3 (2010): 285-295.

[44] I know this is controversial, and I'll address that later.

[45] *Stranger Things*. "Chapter Three: The Pollywog." 3. Directed by Matt Duffer and Ross Duffer as the Duffer Brothers. Written by Matt Duffer and Ross Duffer as the Duffer Brothers with additional writing credits to Jessie Nickson-Lopex (executive story editor), Paul Dichter, and Kate Trefry (staff writers). A Netflix original production, October, 2017.

[46] *Stranger Things*. "Chapter Nine: The Gate." 9. Directed by Matt Duffer and Ross Duffer as the Duffer Brothers. Written by Matt Duffer and Ross Duffer as the Duffer Brothers with additional writing credits to Jessie Nickson-Lopex (executive story editor), Paul Dichter, and Kate Trefry (staff writers). A Netflix original production, October, 2017.

[47] Goldberg, Michelle. "I Believe Juanita." *New York Times* (New York, NY), Nov. 13, 2017.

[48] Baker, Peter. "'What About Bill?' Sexual Misconduct Debate Revives Questions About Clinton." *New York Times* (New York, NY), Nov. 15, 2017.

[49] Steinhauer, Jennifer. "Bill Clinton Should Have Resigned Over Lewinsky Affair, Kirsten Gillibrand Says." *New York Times* (New York, NY), Nov. 16, 2017.

[50] Astodec, Maggie. "Gymnastics Doctor Who Abused Patients Gets 60 Years for Child Pornography." *New York Times* (New York, NY), Dec. 7, 2017.

[51] Bundy, Ted. "Ted Bundy's Last Interview." Interview by James Dobson. Florida State Prison, Starke, FL. January 23, 1989.

[52] Merker, Amy and Campbell, Lee. *Constructive Suffering Workbook: Building a Biblical Perspective for Your Pain*. New Paradigm Publishing, 2016.

[53] Crane, Rebecca Susan, Judson Brewer, C. Feldman, Jon Kabat-Zinn, S. Santorelli, J. Mark G. Williams, and W. Kuyken. "What defines mindfulness-based programs? The warp and the weft." *Psychological Medicine* 47, no. 6 (2017): 990-999.

[54] Kabat-Zinn, Jon. "An outpatient program in behavioral medicine for chronic pain patients based on the practice of mindfulness meditation: Theoretical considerations and preliminary results." *General hospital psychiatry* 4, no. 1 (1982): 33-47.

[55] Kabat-Zinn, Jon. "Mindfulness-based interventions in context: past, present, and future." *Clinical psychology: Science and practice* 10, no. 2 (2003): 144-156. Page 146

[56] Kabat-Zinn, Jon. "Too Early to Tell: The Potential Impact and Challenges—Ethical and Otherwise—Inherent in the Mainstreaming of Dharma in an Increasingly Dystopian World." *Mindfulness* 8, no. 5 (2017): 1125-1135.

[57] Lindsay, Emily K., and J. David Creswell. "Mechanisms of mindfulness training: Monitor and Acceptance Theory (MAT)." *Clinical psychology review* 51 (2017): 48-59.

[58] Kohl, Annika, Winfried Rief, and Julia Anna Glombiewski. "How effective are acceptance strategies? A meta-analytic review of experimental results." *Journal of behavior therapy and experimental psychiatry* 43, no. 4 (2012): 988-1001.

[59] Harris, Russ. *ACT made simple: An easy-to-read primer on acceptance and commitment therapy*. New Harbinger Publications, 2009.

[60] Ord, Ingrid. *ACT with Faith: Acceptance and Commitment Therapy for Christian Clients: a Practitioner's Guide*. Compass Publishing, 2014.

[61] Twohig, Michael P., and Jesse M. Crosby. "Acceptance and commitment therapy as a treatment for problematic internet pornography viewing." *Behavior Therapy* 41, no. 3 (2010): 285-295.

[62] Crosby, Jesse M., and Michael P. Twohig. "Acceptance and commitment therapy for problematic Internet pornography use: a randomized trial." *Behavior therapy* 47, no. 3 (2016): 355-366.

[63] Hayes, Steven C., Kirk D. Strosahl, and Kelly G. Wilson. *Acceptance and commitment therapy: An experiential approach to behavior change*. Guilford Press, 1999.

[64] Twohig, Michael P., and Jesse M. Crosby. "Acceptance and commitment therapy as a treatment for problematic internet pornography viewing." *Behavior Therapy* 41, no. 3 (2010): 285-295.

[65] Crosby, Jesse M., and Michael P. Twohig. "Acceptance and commitment therapy for problematic Internet pornography use: a randomized trial." *Behavior therapy* 47, no. 3 (2016): 355-366.

[66] Reading the fine print, it didn't look like 8 or 12 sessions of ACT were absolutely necessary. My suspicion is that when the men grasped the core concept and started acting on their convictions instead of obeying their feelings, the porn use started to wane precipitously.

[67] Zaleski, Philip, and Carol Zaleski. *Prayer: A history*. Houghton Mifflin Harcourt, 2006. P 127

[68] Shapiro, FR (2014, April 28). Who wrote the Serenity Prayer? The Chronicle Review. Retrieved from http://chronicle.com/article/Who-W rote-the-Serenity-Prayer-/146159/

[69] Shapiro, Fred R. "Who wrote the Serenity Prayer?." *Yale Alumni Magazine* 71 (2008): 6.

[70] Kalra, S. P., and P. S. Kalra. "NPY and cohorts in regulating appetite, obesity and metabolic syndrome: beneficial effects of gene therapy." *Neuropeptides* 38, no. 4 (2004): 201-211.

[71] Gollwitzer, Peter M. "Implementation intentions: Strong effects of simple plans." *American psychologist* 54, no. 7 (1999): 493.

[72] Gardner, Brian. *Porn Free: Finding Renewal through Truth and Community,* New Paradigm Publishing, 2011.

[73] Interlinear Bile from WORD*search*® Bible Software powered by LifeWay. Product 8380, Build 11.0.3.84 https://www.wordsearchbible.com/

[74] Martell, Christopher R., Sona Dimidjian, and Ruth Herman-Dunn. *Behavioral activation for depression: A clinician's guide*. Guilford Press, 2013.

[75] Hey…I just came up with the "four P's" of behavioral activation for spiritual benefits: Positive, Proactive, Planned, and Public.

[76] Cuijpers, Pim, Annemieke Van Straten, and Lisanne Warmerdam. "Behavioral activation treatments of depression: A meta-analysis." *Clinical psychology review* 27, no. 3 (2007): 318-326.

[77] McCallum, Dennis. *Walking in Victory*. NavPress, 1994.

[78] Herbert Benson, M. D., and Miriam Z. Klipper. *The relaxation response*. Harper Collins, New York, 1992.

[79] Neisewander, Janet L., David A. Baker, Rita A. Fuchs, Ly TL Tran-Nguyen, Art Palmer, and John F. Marshall. "Fos protein expression and cocaine-seeking behavior in rats after exposure to a cocaine self-administration environment." *Journal of Neuroscience* 20, no. 2 (2000): 798-805.

[80] Wolf, Marina E. "Synaptic mechanisms underlying persistent cocaine craving." *Nature Reviews Neuroscience* 17, no. 6 (2016): 351-365.

[81] Wolf, Marina E. "Synaptic mechanisms underlying persistent cocaine craving." *Nature Reviews Neuroscience* 17, no. 6 (2016): 351-365.

[82] https://www.selfmanagementresource.com/

[83] Arterburn, Stephen, Fred Stoeker, and Mike Yorkey. *Every man's battle: Winning the war on sexual temptation one victory at a time.* Waterbrook Press, 2009.

[84] Arterburn, Stephen, and Fred Stoeker. *Every Young Man's Battle: Stategies for Victory in the Real World of Sexual Temptation.* WaterBrook, 2004.

[85] McCallum, Dennis. *Members of One Another: How to build a biblical ethos into your church (2nd Ed).* New Paradigm Publishing, 2015.

[86] https://www.muscleandfitness.com/

[87] Harlow, Harry F. "The nature of love." *American psychologist* 13, no. 12 (1958): 673.

[88] Julie, Slattery, "Date Night: Let's Talk About it with Dr. Julie Slattery. Youtube video. 2:17:43. Uploaded July 20, 2017. https://www.youtube.com/watch?v=ZltSFT4JY6U

[89] d'Souza, Dinesh. *What's so great about Christianity.* Regnery Publishing, 2008.

[90] Dinesh, D'Souza, "How Do I Know God Exists," Youtube video, 42:47, Uploaded September 4, 2013, https://www.youtube.com/watch?v=1Ien2Ah3lEY&t=3s

[91] Behe, Michael J. *The edge of evolution: The search for the limits of Darwinism.* Simon and Schuster, 2008.

[92] The #MeToo twitter hashtag (https://twitter.com/hashtag/metoo) erupted in October, 2017, as many women started to denounce sexual harassment and assault after the accusations against Harvey Weinstein became public. This hashtag has been used millions of times, but by the time you read this the viral movement may have subsided. Here "#MeToo scenario" is used to being accused of having engaged in sexual harassment or assault.

[93] Vanauken, Sheldon, and Joy Mitchell. *A severe mercy.* Harper & Row, 1977.

[94] Many suicides could be prevented if guns were stored securely. Using a trigger lock and storing the gun and ammunition separately reduces the risk of suicide by gun to the same level as people who do not own guns. If you or anyone you know expresses the intent to commit suicide, please get help. The national suicide prevention phone number is 1-800-273-8255. http://www.suicidepreventionlifeline.org

[95] www.iglworld.org

[96] Jones, Peyton. *Church Zero: Raising 1st Century Churches Out of the Ashes of the 21st Century Church.* David C Cook, 2013.

[97] https://churchplantermagazine.com

[98] Jones, Peyton. *Reaching the Unreached: Becoming Raiders of the Lost Art.* Zondervan, 2017.

[99] Yes, I know I'm borrowing some of this phrasing from Brad Neely's *Wizard People, Dear Reader.* Illegal Art, 2004.